Praise for Tom Mendicino's debut novel,
PROBATION

"Thoughtful, textured, and poignant . . . [A]n exciting, impressive debut. Written in an honest voice that's both dully depressed and acutely, emotionally observant, the prose is compellingly painful yet frequently funny, as well. There are many moments of lyrical beauty, plus enough cinematic twists and turns to keep readers anxiously racing through the chapters (though they are best when savored)."
—*Time Out New York*

"A potent debut."
—*Publishers Weekly*

"Achingly honest."
—Vestal McIntyre, author of *Lake Overturn*

And praise for his follow-up,
THE BOYS FROM EIGHTH AND CARPENTER

"Tom Mendicino is a supremely gifted writer with an eye for the most telling of details."
—Lisa Scottoline, *New York Times* bestselling author

"At the heart of this capacious and suspenseful novel is the bond between two very different brothers, but its larger context is the Italian-American family: its values, loyalties and responsibilities. Tom Mendicino writes with honesty and compassion, and the reader can't help but root for his endearing characters."
—Christopher Castellani, author of *All This Talk of Love*

Books by Tom Mendicino

PROBATION

THE BOYS FROM EIGHTH AND CARPENTER

E-Novellas
KC, AT BAT
TRAVELIN' MAN
LONESOME TOWN

Published by Kensington Publishing Corporation

STEALING HOME

TOM MENDICINO

LYRICAL PRESS
Kensington Publishing Corp.
www.kensingtonbooks.com

Lyrical Press books are published by
Kensington Publishing Corp.
119 West 40th Street
New York, NY 10018

All Kensington titles, imprints, and distributed lines are available at special
quantity discounts for bulk purchases for sales promotion, premiums, fund-
raising, and educational or institutional use.

Special book excerpts or customized printings can also be created to fit
specific needs. For details, write or phone the office of the Kensington
Special Sales Manager:
Kensington Publishing Corp.
119 West 40th Street
New York, NY 10018
Attn. Special Sales Department. Phone: 1-800-221-2647.

LYRICAL PRESS Reg. U.S. Pat. & TM Off.
Lyrical Press and the L logo are trademarks of Kensington Publishing Corp.

First Electronic Edition:
eISBN-13: 978-1-5161-0494-9
eISBN-10: 1-5161-0494-3

First Print Edition:
ISBN-13: 978-1-5161-0495-6
ISBN-10: 1-5161-0495-1

Printed in the United States of America

CONTENTS

KC,
AT BAT

For Paul Mendicino

He sang his songs calm and steady, like he was in the middle of a storm, men hurling past him.

—Bob Dylan on Ricky Nelson, *Chronicles: Volume One*

BOOK ONE
Hello, Mary Lou

The first lesson he'd learned was that he would be spending the entire summer after graduating high school answering to the name Buddy. His birth certificate, Social Security card, driver's license, all the official documentation of his existence, still confirmed his identity as Charles Beresford. But no one on the crew wasted any time or effort trying to remember if he went by Charlie or Chuck or Chad. Or Bill or Mike or Dave, for that matter. He was beneath contempt, the lowest of the low, the worst possible brand of sausage, their name for the high school and college kids who swelled their ranks during the peak moving season for a restless nation in search of better opportunities and friendlier climates. Meat, that's all they were. Dead meat, if they slowed down the job or otherwise screwed up.

"Buddy, what the fuck am I supposed to do with you?" the dispatcher sputtered when Charlie appeared at his desk at precisely six in the morning the first Monday of June. An emergency phone call was placed to Mr. Ryan of Ryan Allied Van Lines, who immediately put to rest any doubts about young Mr. Beresford's suitability to spend the summer on the crew of one of his moving vans.

"I don't give a fuck if he wipes your ass and holds your dick while you take a piss, just find something for him to do," he shouted at his dispatcher, not knowing, or caring, that his bellowing voice could be heard by anyone in reasonable proximity to the dispatcher's speakerphone, including one Charlie Beresford.

"Wait till he gets the fucking bill for your worker's comp claim," the dispatcher grumbled, resigned to carrying out the boss's orders. "He'll be singing a different tune then."

"What worker's comp claim?" Charlie meekly inquired.

"The one you'll be filing after two hours on the fucking job."

The dispatcher's reluctance to assign Charlie to a crew was nothing compared to the open revolt by the drivers, who balked at any attempt to saddle them with a hundred-fifty-five-pound scarecrow constructed of toothpicks and rubber bands. They threatened an uprising, objecting to being forced to carry human deadweight, but the dispatcher quickly laid down the law, crushing the revolt by six forty-five a.m.

"The next one of you assholes who bitches about the kid gets the methadone clinic job in Arbor Hill. So do I got any volunteers who want him for your crew?"

Apparently even a day with Charlie Beresford was preferable to hauling filing cabinets out of dingy clinic offices, listening to verbal abuse from the clients, and needing to put a full-time guard on the truck to ensure that everything that couldn't be locked down wasn't pilfered. Four drivers swallowed their pride and offered Charlie a place on their crews. The dispatcher pulled him aside for one last word of advice before sending him on his way.

"I'm putting you with Bruno. He's a mean, dumb Polack, but he won't let you break your back your first day out. You'll put on some muscle by July if you live that long. Until then, stick to packing and cleaning the shit out of the basements and attics. Think you can handle that, buddy?" he asked, grinding a Marlboro Red between his teeth.

It had been nearly four months since the night Larry Coleman, Charlie's best friend since sophomore year, overcame his skittish nerves, his courage fortified by a half bottle of Boone's Farm Strawberry Hill, and asked Charlie if he would think he was some kind of freak if he admitted that he liked Charlie more than as just a friend. When Charlie didn't respond by punching him in the face, Larry confessed he thought Charlie was the handsomest boy he'd ever seen, as good looking as that dude from The Strokes, and that it was getting harder and harder to resist the urge to grab him by the shoulders and kiss him so hard their teeth would rattle, just like Heath Ledger and Jake Gyllenhaal in *Brokeback Mountain*.

Sweet, fruity wine and adolescent libidos being a deadly combination, Charlie had willingly succumbed to Larry's physical advances, though their frenzied, awkward gropes and grunts (Charlie actually caught the skin of his own scrotum in the teeth of his zipper) seemed more like the antics of the suburban nerds in *Superbad* than the epic legend of soul-crushing passion between a pair of exquisitely beautiful Wyoming cowboys. Still, it was reassuring for Charlie to discover there was at least one person who thought he was attractive, that, indeed, at least Larry Coleman found him worthy of being loved. And even if Larry, with his thirty-eight-inch waistband and benzoyl peroxide–resistant back acne, wasn't the type of boy that Charlie fantasized about when he reached for his pecker to wank himself to sleep, he was the only other upperclassman at the Augustinian Academy for Boys whose favorite new band was The National and who appreciated the unparalleled genius of Thurston Moore and Sonic Youth.

Larry Coleman, despite his physical shortcomings, happened to be a great kisser with a natural instinct for poking his tongue into the deepest recesses of Charlie's mouth. Larry was learning how to give a decent blow job, too, after gagging the first few times when Charlie, despite his best intentions, was unable to hold back until Larry could take it out of his mouth. Charlie was less enthusiastic about satisfying Larry's physical longings and would roll on his back and doze off the minute he climaxed, not even offering a helping hand as Larry beat off. Once he even yelled at Larry for coming on Charlie's belly instead of on the bedsheets. But Larry didn't seem bothered by the distance Charlie insisted on maintaining, assuming that whatever they had together was meant to last forever. He'd even MapQuested the shortest route between Syracuse University, where they'd both been accepted for early admission, and Hanover, New Hampshire, the site of Dartmouth College, which had recently notified Charlie he'd jumped from the wait list to the rolls of the incoming freshman class.

Charlie's good fortune meant Larry would need to find a new roommate at Syracuse come fall. But they still had all of June and July and a few weeks of August sharing a tent as counselors at Algonquin Peak Summer Camp, a rustic sanctuary costing the parents of the Upper East Side and Westchester County a hefty ten thousand dollars a season to provide their privileged sons and daughters opportunities to, according to the brochure, "strengthen athletic abilities, cultivate artistic talents, and learn important character-building lessons while building self-esteem." Larry, a gifted doubles tennis player despite his girth, had been on the staff since he was fifteen; he'd gotten Charlie a gig when the guitar instructor unexpectedly notified the owners he wouldn't be available to return this summer, the rumor being he'd been busted for selling pot to the underclassmen at his New England boarding school. But Larry's best-laid plans for their unforgettable passage to manhood were swiftly derailed after Charlie's mother finally consulted the family doctor when the lump she'd been ignoring under her right armpit finally left her unable to lift her arm above her head. She'd insisted the family sit down to pork chops and mashed potatoes that evening, that grace be said, and Charlie keep his elbows off the table. But even his precocious little sister, Madeline, sensed something was different, off-kilter, a pall settling over the table despite their mother's best efforts at business-as-usual.

"Madeline's asking you a question, Paul," Charlie's mother informed her distracted husband, her voice more snappish than she had intended.

The berry pie was store-bought, not homemade, final confirmation that all was not right in the Beresford household. Charlie's mother told her children to sit up and pay attention. She had something to tell them. She had to go into the hospital. Her sister had offered to come stay at the house, but she thought they could make do on their own for a couple of days. Charlie could look after Madeline; neither of them were babies, after all.

"Now I want both of you to listen to me," she announced as they pushed the blueberry filling around their plates. "Your father is a worrywart, but I promise you that everything is going to be fine."

The procedure was scheduled for the next morning, enough precious time already wasted. Charlie's assignment was to keep Madeline occupied during the seeming eternity until their mother was brought back from the operating room. He pacified her with Happy Meals and strawberry milk shakes, and they frittered away several hours at Toys "R" Us and Barnes & Noble until their father finally summoned them late in the afternoon, looking a decade older than he had that morning. He explained to Madeline that her mother had had a big operation and was going to be sick for a little bit, promising she'd be all better real soon, the same old Mommy she had always been. Later, driving to the hospital for evening visiting hours, he shared the horrific details of the radical mastectomy with his son. Charlie tried not to cringe as his father described how his mother no longer had a nipple, the very thought of her intimate anatomy being more than he could bear. She had a long, hard haul ahead of her, his dad explained, and he hoped Charlie understood how important it was for him to be there for her this summer, even if there was nothing he could actually do. Just knowing he was close by would be a big comfort, his father assured him.

"I'm really sorry about your mom," Larry had said, sounding dejected and demoralized after Charlie delivered the bad news. "Maybe you can still come up for the second half of the season if she's feeling better," he suggested, his mood brightening a tiny bit at even the slimmest prospect of salvaging a month of togetherness.

"We'll see," Charlie responded, remaining stubbornly noncommittal despite Larry's crestfallen face. "I'll call you every night," he promised, trying to cheer up Larry.

"The cell reception at camp sucks," Larry moaned. "It's the fucking mountains. Sometimes you can't even get a signal."

Charlie's spirits soared at this welcome news. He'd already tired of needing to return forty or fifty text messages a day, feigning interest in the minutest detail of Larry's every waking hour. He didn't really give a shit about the awesome song streaming over Pandora radio or the latest outrageous gay double entendre on *Family Guy* or the amazing picture of Johnny Depp in the surf at Saint-Tropez that Larry just found in the new issue of *Us Weekly*. Now, thanks to the Adirondack mountain range, Charlie wouldn't even need to feel guilty about not returning voice and text messages. All he needed to do was say he'd never received them.

Dartmouth seemed to be a cruel tease, a macabre joke. Charlie was certain he'd never live to pass through its ivy-covered gates. He'd mistakenly assumed his enormous sacrifice of foregoing two-plus months of squatting in latrines, taking group showers, and listening to Larry Coleman's lame-ass opinions about his favorite bands had earned him a reprieve from needing to join the ranks of wage slaves for the summer. He'd figured he would need to be available to drive his mother to and from chemotherapy and to keep an eye on Madeline, making sure she wasn't abducted by child molesters and fixing her the occasional peanut-butter-and-jelly sandwich. He'd be free to spend his time working on finishing his latest music project; he had almost a CD's worth of deeply lugubrious songs that he'd hoped to send to Thurston Moore if he could find someone who knew his address. He would pull all-nighters polishing the pieces of rock criticism he'd published in the high school paper for the portfolio he intended to show the editors of *The Dartmouth* daily when he arrived. He'd even called the local progressive rock station offering his services as an unpaid intern, completely unaware that his father's best friend since childhood, Oliver Ryan, the local franchisee of the nation's largest long-distance moving company, had offered to put him to work at a decent wage until he departed for Hanover, New Hampshire.

His crime was needing tuition money and the sentence was long days loading the contents of the split-levels and ranches of Schenectady and Albany for a one-way trip to the Sunbelt. The first week was a living hell, endless hours of physical torture and mental fatigue. Each night he crawled home to a tube of Bengay and was sound asleep by ten, still exhausted when his father pulled him out of bed before sunup and pushed him out the door, thermos in hand. He ached in places he'd never known existed, but he'd survived, if barely. He hadn't even been the first newbie to fall. That dubious distinction had been earned by an All-Conference tackle from Mohawk Valley High School, two hundred sixty-five pounds of solid muscle, strong as a bull, who worked himself into a state of dehydration on the unseasonably hot first Monday in June. He'd collapsed on the basement stairs of a four-bedroom, three-story job in Troy and tumbled down the steps, gone by two in the afternoon, never to return.

The monotony of Tuesday was broken up by a bloody fist-fight in the half-loaded van between Bruno and one of his regular crew, a scrawny inbred who looked like one of the crazies from *The Hills Have Eyes,* who ended up with a broken thumb for unwisely challenging the driver's intelligence. Even worse than the altercation was the boozy reconciliation between the two pugilists at a downscale titty bar where all the strippers were on a first-name basis with Bruno. Charlie, who had never been drunk on Jäger shots before, gratefully accepted a ride home with one of the dancers when he realized Bruno and his erstwhile antagonist had settled in until last call. She offered him a hand job in his parents' driveway at the bargain rate of twenty dollars, leaving him babbling incoherently, struggling to come up with some pathetic excuse why he had to decline.

On Wednesday, too hungover to object, he broke his cherry with his first "humping," the technical parlance for hauling heavy cartons on your back.

"Not bad for sausage. You're stronger than you look, buddy," Bruno complimented him at the end of the day. "You're gonna fill out real good before the summer's over."

Thursday's job was the type Bruno hated most—a house filled with heavy, awkward pieces of large furniture, priceless antiques, according to the wiry, dog-faced lady of the household, who followed them up and down the stairs, holding her breath as they negotiated sharp turns and angles, taking every opportunity to remind the man in charge of the large insurance claim she intended to file if there was any damage. She'd loudly objected to Bruno's practical suggestion that heavy moving pads would protect her precious cargo from the sudden deluge that began late in the morning.

Bruno called an early lunch break until the rain subsided, and the crew retreated to the safety of the van. The two Mexican day workers huddled together in the back, squatting on their haunches, jabbering in Spanish as they tore through the smelly lunches they'd packed in greasy paper bags. Charlie settled in a brighter corner with a protein bar and a well-thumbed but barely read copy of *Infinite Jest*. Bruno hunkered down with a liter bottle of Pepsi and his laptop. Charlie assumed he was downloading free amateur pornography, grainy videos of leathery sluts with a taste for beast-on-girl sex with slobbering pit bulls, only to discover Bruno was a huge fan of the Streisand/Kristofferson *A Star Is Born* and that he knew all the lyrics to "Evergreen."

The peaceful interlude ended abruptly when the mistress of the house came stomping up the van ramp, cell phone in hand, saying the dispatcher wanted to talk to Bruno, who was promptly ripped a new asshole because the bitch had called to complain that the crew was sleeping on the job. Bruno handed her the phone, saying nothing, and ordered everyone back to work before barricading himself in the master bathroom, telling Charlie he needed to take a shit.

"Lousy plumbing in these old houses," he announced when he finally emerged, a smug smile on his face, and told Charlie and the Mexicans to find another toilet if they needed to answer the call of nature. Twenty minutes later, they heard the door of the off-limits bathroom slam shut. The woman came charging down the stairs, waving a plunger, enraged, her threats peppered with curses. Bruno didn't need to say a single word; the piercing glare of his ice-blue eyes was sufficient warning of the folly of engaging him in a confrontation. At the end of the job, her treasured antiques safely loaded into the van, she even paid the crew a generous tip.

There was a phone message waiting when Charlie got home that night. The manager of McDonald's was impressed by the application Charlie had dropped off at the drive-through that morning. Sweating over deep fryers seemed like paradise compared to spending the summer in the back of a moving van. He decided to take the coward's way out and resign by voice mail message over the weekend. He could survive one last day of Bruno's living hell. Friday morning he was assigned to a load-and-deliver crosstown move. His last hurrah was going to be a twelve-hour day with the driver cracking the whip because it wasn't a job transfer and the client was paying out of his own pocket. The hell with it, he thought. Why prolong the agony when he was quitting anyway? He summoned his courage and tried to overcome the onset of dry mouth. He was minutes away from announcing his resignation when a hand clasped his shoulder and a sympathetic voice promised solidarity in misery.

"Looks like we pulled the shit end of the stick. Guess it's you and me today, buddy."

Charlie's knees went wobbly, his voice tight, when he found himself standing face-to-face with a genuine high school hero. The name on the young man's birth certificate was Kevin Conroy, but he'd been called KC since his first Little League season. His ability behind the plate and his prowess in the outfield were almost mythical; his batting average and number of errorless innings were legendary. The Augustinian Academy yearbook had entire pages dedicated to the exploits of the Mighty KC.

"You want one of these?" KC mumbled through a mouth full of Boston cream, offering the doughnut box.

"Naw," Charlie muttered, his voice barely audible. "They're too sweet and make me sick to the stomach," he blurted out nervously, instantly regretting his confession, certain that KC, who was licking the last of the custard from his long, elegant fingers, would think he was an incredible pussy.

It was going to be a long day, still unseasonably hot for early June, and Bruno's crew was small, just KC and Charlie. Charlie nudged close to Bruno when the three of them squeezed into the cab. Bruno hated air-conditioning, claiming it fucked up his sinuses, so the driver was particularly ripe that morning, his armpits already damp with sweat. But Charlie was determined to avoid even the slightest physical contact with KC, who was too preoccupied with trimming his nails to notice Charlie squirming.

"You ain't getting that shit all over my truck, are you, kid?" Bruno grunted.

"Relax, bro. It's cool," KC said, tossing the clippings out the window.

Cool was his birthright. Not cool as in "hip," like the assholes who told you they were into your favorite band before it became so passé that only the worst geeks were downloading its music. KC was cool as in Bond, James Bond, cool. Capable, confident, slightly distracted, as if he occupied an entirely different space from ordinary mortals and the rest of the world was only occasionally worthy of his attention.

The load-and-deliver was easier than expected, no Victorian armoires to maneuver, no king-size mattresses to grapple. Charlie did his fair share of humping. He hustled all day, unaffected by the heat, carrying weights he couldn't have lifted Monday morning, driven by the fear of being thought inadequate by KC. Not that KC seemed to care. KC knew only one work speed: slow. Bruno could only murmur snide remarks under his breath because KC, like Charlie, was off-limits, protected by higher forces that insisted he never be asked to lift any weight that could strain his arm and shoulder or cause him to injure his lower back or pull a hamstring.

"They're paying that little shit to stand around and look pretty," Bruno muttered to Charlie, confiding in him as if he were a peer or an equal. "Fucking Oliver Ryan sponsors the superstar's American Legion team."

Driving back to the depot in the hazy dusk, Bruno made a pointed comment to Charlie, the highest praise for sure, sincere but also meant to embarrass the member of his crew for whom such compliments would not be forthcoming.

"You know, buddy, keep working like that and you'll be a hell of a humper soon."

KC rolled his eyes as they hopped out of the truck and

waited for Bruno to park and unlock the front door so they could punch the time clock. KC helped himself to a pinch of chew and offered Charlie the bag. He waved it away, clueless about what to do with it.

"Smart guy," KC said. "I'm trying to quit."

The brown juice would have turned Charlie's stomach if it had been dripping from anyone else's chin.

"You went to Augustinian, didn't you?" KC asked.

"Yeah," Charlie mumbled, utterly dumbfounded to discover that the mighty KC Conroy, at one time, had taken notice of his miserable existence. He still had a vivid recollection of cowering in the locker room, self-conscious of his bony limbs, averting his gaze as KC emerged from the steamy mist of the showers, his thick black chest hair wet and slick, his long brown cock slapping against his thigh, laughing as he gracefully negotiated a gauntlet of buddies snapping heavy wet towels at his perfectly shaped buttocks.

"Me too," KC said, as if Charlie wouldn't know.

The day's heat lingered despite the late hour. Charlie felt weighed down by exhaustion; he fought the urge to close his eyes, struggling to keep from falling asleep on his feet until KC's casual question, completely unexpected, snapped him out of his stupor.

"So, you wanna hang out tonight?"

Charlie? Hanging with KC? Impossible. He couldn't play pool. The only card game he knew was hearts. He'd never done tequila shots and didn't like the taste of beer. He was damn sure KC didn't intend to get shit-faced on Boone's Farm Strawberry Hill. Charlie would pass out on the spot, exposed as a homo, if some girl pulled up her blouse and offered him a feel. He'd embarrass KC in front of his posse, forcing his new friend to humiliate him to save face.

"Sure," Charlie said, stuttering, knowing he'd regret it the rest of his life if he didn't say yes.

In the end Charlie was relieved, and more than a little disappointed, when KC's idea of a big Friday night was chugging liter bottles of warm Mountain Dew and watching *Field of Dreams*. KC's parents had a cabin on Lake George where they spent every summer weekend, so the boys had the house to themselves. KC had a Legion game in Schenectady Saturday at noon, then a night game in Newburgh at seven. He needed eight hours of shut-eye to be at the top of his form. There was still time for a couple hands of blackjack or a game of *Call of Duty* after the credits rolled. Charlie pulled Stratego from a stack of board games and challenged him to a match.

"No way, buddy. I always lose that fucking game. You have to think too much."

So they settled on *Call of Duty* and, of course, KC's quick reflexes and hand-eye coordination made short work of Charlie's offensive moves. It didn't help that Charlie was distracted by his host's hairy legs and barely concealed crotch.

"You gonna spend the night?" KC asked nonchalantly, as if the invitation had already been accepted.

When Charlie called home to say he was staying at Kevin Conroy's house overnight, "Yes, THE KC," his father asked no questions except to inquire if KC was interested in playing in his softball league.

"Cool," KC said when Charlie told him he'd gotten the green light. "Man, it's time for sleep." He tossed Charlie a pillow and blanket to make up a bed on the couch. Charlie slept like a baby, dead to the world. Hours later, in the middle of the pitch-black night, he felt a hand on his shoulder, gently shaking him.

"Hey, are you sleeping?"

"I don't think so," Charlie said, blinking his eyes and drawing himself up on an elbow, wondering if, in fact, he was still fast asleep and this was a dream. He was horrified to feel an erection poking through his briefs.

"Would you think I was weird if I slept down here with you?"

"No," Charlie said, pushing his back into the cushions to make room on the sofa,

"You won't tell anyone about this?" KC asked as they lay side by side.

Charlie was aware KC wasn't wearing underwear. His heart pounded and his breath was shallow as he lay perfectly still, not knowing what to do next.

"No."

"Promise?"

"Promise," he grunted as the Mighty KC in the flesh rolled on top of him, grinding and rubbing, skin on skin, panting in his ear.

"Shit, buddy, it feels so fucking good."

Charlie was skittish the rest of the weekend, unsure of the consequences of the strange and unexpected events of Friday night. KC had been polite enough Saturday morning, even offering him a bowl of Rice Krispies and a banana, though, pleading he was late for batting practice, he'd dropped Charlie at the bus stop rather than driving him home. He'd barely spoken in the car except to ask Charlie if he liked Ricky Nelson as he slipped a disc of his greatest hits into the dashboard player. The only Ricky Nelson song Charlie knew was "Hello, Mary Lou," an okay sort of Hollywood-Goes-Rockabilly tune to his indie-music-scene-snob ears, but he'd quickly assured KC that the singer was cool. *See you Monday,* he'd said as he stood on the curb, hoping KC might want to hang out again, but KC merely nodded, shifted gears, and pulled away.

He downloaded the entire collection of Ricky Nelson singles on Sunday afternoon, unable to decide if the music was really as good as it (surprisingly) sounded or if he was biased by his new infatuation with KC. That night he couldn't fall asleep, tossing and turning, twisting the sheets between his long thin legs, anticipating Monday morning. For the first time in his life, he awoke before the alarm rang and was dressed and ready to leave the house before the appointed hour. He fretted about the swollen red pimple that had appeared on his forehead overnight, round and hard as a jelly bean, not yet ripe enough to squeeze, too large to be camouflaged under a thick coat of acne cream.

He lingered in the dispatcher's office until the last stragglers drifted from the coffeepot and the vending machines to join their crews, waiting in vain for KC to saunter through the door.

"Let's go, buddy!" Bruno shouted. "Stop drag assin'. We got a long day ahead of us."

"Where's KC?" he blurted out, unable to think of a more subtle inquiry on the spur of the moment.

"It's Monday, buddy. That little pussy never works on Monday. He plays ball all weekend, and his fucking delicate body needs the rest. That little asshole must be blowing old man Ryan," he snorted.

Tuesday morning, after the longest twenty-four hours of Charlie's life, KC ambled into the dispatcher's office as the day's assignments were being given, barely acknowledging Charlie. Charlie, who, much to his mortification, had lit up like a Christmas tree when KC entered the room, somehow managed to refrain from making a beeline to the table where KC was hovering over the doughnut box, trying to make an informed decision between a glazed and a chocolate frosted. Charlie made a studied attempt at nonchalance, pretending to be completely absorbed in the screen of his cell phone as KC approached, only to yelp like a startled puppy when KC goosed him, pinching the cheek of his ass.

"Be cool, buddy," KC laughed, quickly scanning the room, satisfied that curious eyes hadn't seen, and didn't seem interested in, his little indiscretion.

"I almost called you yesterday," he said, offering Charlie a bite of his half-eaten chocolate frosted.

Charlie's heart flipped at this unexpected announcement.

"But I didn't have your number. You never gave it to me," KC mumbled as he shoveled the doughnut into his mouth.

Charlie fumbled with his phone, almost dropping it on the floor.

"Here, I'll send it to you now," he said eagerly.

"I'll get it later," KC said, swallowing the last of his breakfast in two huge bites. "Tell that fucking asshole Bruno I'm in the can when he's ready to leave," he said as he turned and headed for the lavatory the crew genteelly referred to as the shithouse.

Every Friday afternoon, KC asked the unnecessary question: "So, you wanna hang out tonight?" The only variation in their routine was ordering pizza or Chinese takeout. KC slouched in his father's recliner, dangling his bare legs and slugging Pepsi or Mountain Dew, absorbed in *Bull Durham* or *Bang the Drum Slowly* or *Major League.* The night would end with an encore of *Field of Dreams* or an hour of video games or Texas hold 'em while Ricky Nelson chirped be-bop-baby on the sound system. KC had a decent music collection, a lot of early grunge, Pearl Jam, and Soundgarden. Charlie could even forgive the Foo Fighters discs after discovering KC owned a Social Distortion CD, though KC admitted he'd bought it for a buck at the flea market because he liked the cover. But mostly KC played vinyl records that had belonged to his grandfather—Gene Pitney, the Everly Brothers, and especially Ricky Nelson, leaving Charlie soon wondering how many times in his eighteen years KC had listened to each of Ozzie and Harriet's kid's *Greatest Hits.* A hundred? A thousand? Ten thousand?

After KC called lights-out, they would wrestle on the sofa until their briefs were around their ankles and KC had pinned Charlie to the cushions. Charlie let KC put his dick in his mouth and his finger up his butt after KC promised Charlie could do the same to him. But whenever Charlie tried to kiss him, KC would turn his face, his jaw clenched tight, adamant there were certain intimacies he was unwilling to share. KC would head up to his bedroom after they finished, and Charlie would toss and turn, unable to sleep, frustrated, but too timid to complain, certain that even the slightest expression of dissatisfaction would end in permanent exile from the Conroys' paneled family room. Still, even though their relationship felt one-sided, that Charlie wanted to be with KC and KC only wanted someone to rub up against, Charlie was happier, less lonely, more content than he could ever remember being, certainly more than when Larry Coleman had his tongue down his throat.

Bruno had all but given up on him, resigned to the fact that he'd fallen under the pernicious influence of the indolent ballplayer. He took to calling them the Olsen twins, a high witticism for a man of his limited abilities. If KC wasn't traveling overnight to some corner of upstate New York for a Sunday morning game, he would ask Charlie to spend the entire weekend at the house. In late June, much to Charlie's surprise, KC even agreed to travel to New Paltz where Mike Watt, revered by generations of punk rockers, was headlining. Charlie was thrilled, sharing his idol with KC, and KC even claimed to appreciate the show though they had to leave before the encore because KC had to be at batting practice by noon.

Charlie grew bolder as the weeks passed and even dared to occasionally take the initiative, calling KC just to check in and say hello if he grew bored and restless. He didn't question why KC sometimes wouldn't answer his cell and didn't return messages or texts, assuming he was out with his teammates, drinking and carousing, ever vigilant that his different lives never intersected. Charlie became more and more comfortable, even allowing himself to believe that he and KC were actual friends, buddies, albeit strictly within the confines of boundaries that were never to be crossed.

He accepted that KC's games were strictly off-limits. One

weeknight he'd driven to a local game at an Albany ball field, expecting to be able to watch unnoticed among the crowd, a blurry, anonymous face in the horde of cheering fans. He'd arrived to find a small gaggle of parents and siblings and girlfriends huddled in the bleachers, the only spectators, and drove away quickly, hopeful that KC hadn't recognized his car. The only baseball he'd seen all summer were the televised Mets games he watched with his father, who assumed his son's new friendship had kindled, at long last, a healthy interest in sports. He'd only suffered through those to be prepared in case KC ever wanted to talk ball, which he never did, reserving his few words to discuss strategy for *Call of Duty* or to complain about the complete and total bullshit of Ryan Allied Van Lines, in general, and Bruno, in particular, who KC swore was a secret homo who wanted to get into Charlie's pants. Charlie had resigned himself to being excluded from the most important part of KC's life until a dead battery in KC's car on the morning of the Fourth of July proved stubbornly resistant to a charge from Charlie's cables.

"You're not going to embarrass me, are you?" KC asked, forced to accept Charlie's offer to drive him to the ballpark in time for the first pitch. "You don't have to stay. I'll get a ride back," he insisted as they pulled into the parking lot, clearly anxious that Charlie might pull out pom-poms and start cheering his name on the third base line.

KC slowly inhaled, becoming the Mighty KC at Bat as he sighted some of his teammates horsing around in the outfield. It was an early afternoon game, to be played under the glare of the midday sun. Most of the boys were milling around the backstop, slugging energy drinks, conserving their strength and staying hydrated. A few of them swatted fungoes while others threw long toss, a herd of graceful gazelles in long blue baseball socks, shouting cheerful insults and obscenities, getting loose before taking the field to challenge their opponents. KC grabbed his glove and cleats and, mumbling thanks, shuffled off to join them. Charlie's emotions raced between the sharp pain of rejection and a fierce rage, and he vowed never to speak to this fucking asshole again, when KC turned on his heels and jogged back to the car.

"I want you to stay," he said shyly. "Just tell everyone you're my cousin, okay?"

He played the game like an artist, gracefully and effortlessly, capable of feats no one else on the field would even attempt. He hit for the cycle that afternoon, impressing the Mets scout looking at prospects. His teammates idolized him; he was gracious and humble, cheering their more meager accomplishments, encouraging and consoling them after fielding errors and poor at bats. Once Charlie thought he saw KC look into the stands to make sure he'd seen the difficult outfield assist he'd accomplished with ease. He carried the team to a one-run victory and a lead in their division on his capable shoulders.

Charlie lingered by the car, excluded from the camaraderie of teammates, feeling awkward and conspicuous, waiting for KC to break away. He knew better than to approach him now, that an intrusion would invite questions, prompting him to spin some stupid story about being a cousin from upstate, hoping no alumnus of Augustinian was present to call him out. Players walking through the parking lot barely acknowledged him, completely uninterested in who he was or why he had come to watch them play. Still, he longed to be invisible, wishing he could hide under the car, unnoticed, until it was time to leave.

"You're Paul Beresford's boy, aren't you?"

The older man seemed to appear out of nowhere, taking Charlie by surprise.

"Hey, Mr. Torok," Charlie mumbled, wanting to slink away, mortified at being caught staring at KC by his coach, of all people.

Charlie's father was the business agent for the electrician's union, and Darrell Torok had been the president of a local chapter for as long as Charlie could remember. Once, five or six years ago when Charlie was just a kid, his dad and he had driven out to Darrell's farm to look at the puppies his hunting dog had recently whelped.

"You might as well take one," Darrell had insisted when Charlie's father hesitated, disappointed by the sickly condition of the litter. "Whatever's left at the end of the week I'm gonna drown in the creek."

Charlie was horrified, close to tears, and even his father had seemed unsettled as they drove home with two of the puppies.

"He's a strange guy," his dad had said. "Comes from living alone out there all these years."

Darrell Torok was a nice-looking man, responsible, with a good trade and a steady income, but, though he was still young at thirty-seven, no one tried fixing him up with their sisters or daughters. He was an odd duck, different, kept to himself. Set in his ways was the polite way to say it. It was understood he was eligible in name only. Darrell Torok was a confirmed bachelor, his free time devoted to maintaining his working farm and coaching American Legion baseball.

"I almost didn't recognize you. You were always such a skinny kid," Darrell commented. "Took after your mother. Looks like you're starting to fill out."

"I've been moving furniture this summer."

"That how you know KC?"

"Yeah," Charlie mumbled. Darrell Torok obviously knew he wasn't KC's cousin, but the answer still felt awkward. Charlie was uneasy that the older man was aware he'd come to the game because of KC, but Darrell asked no more questions, content to stand jiggling his keys in his pockets, staring at the boys gathering their equipment and changing their shoes. After an excruciating eternity, a few minutes feeling like four hours, KC came running toward them, a half-eaten Granny Smith in his hand. He eyed Charlie nervously, as if

Charlie couldn't be trusted, that he'd cracked and revealed all of KC's deepest secrets.

"Hey, superstar, the scout was so impressed he's going to ask the assistant GM to come see you play when you get back to Florida. What do you think of that, Charlie?" Darrell asked.

"That's cool," Charlie said, not understanding the nuances of professional scouting, but having a strong premonition there was still a long, uncertain future before KC would make it to the minor leagues.

"The guys are waiting to go for pizza. You riding with me, KC?" Darrell said.

"I can't go, Coach," KC protested, sounding almost defensive. "I need to go see my Pop-Pop. Charlie's gonna drive me."

Charlie nodded his head, knowing he could hardly deny him transportation to this sacred obligation. Darrell reached over and squeezed his right arm.

"How's your old man, Charlie?"

"He's okay."

"Well, tell him I said hello. Keep up the hard work. That's some pretty impressive muscle you got there. Hope you come out to see more of our games this summer," he said, his smile almost a smirk, as if he could read Charlie's thoughts. "You be on time, you hear me, superstar?" he said, turning his attention to KC.

"How do you know Coach Torok?" KC asked, sounding, to Charlie's ears, slightly paranoid as he settled into the passenger seat of Charlie's car and kicked off his cleats. The smell of his funky feet was overpowering and, to Charlie, oddly arousing.

Charlie told him about the doomed puppy litter, admitting that he'd been scared of Darrell Torok as a kid. KC insisted Charlie was dead wrong. Darrell was the coolest guy on the planet. He'd even flown to Tampa–St. Pete when KC's junior college team made it into the play-off rounds. Even KC's parents hadn't made the trip.

"Sorry, buddy," KC said sheepishly, taking a cursory sniff of his armpits. "I guess I better shower before we go see my Pop-Pop. I really stink."

His thick curls were matted with sweat. He hadn't shaved. His left shin was crusted with dried blood where he'd ripped his uniform sliding into third base, throwing caution to the wind to nail down the cycle. He was rank and dirty, an unholy mess, and Charlie was certain he would never again see anyone so beautiful, or love someone as much as he loved KC at that moment, not if he lived to be a hundred.

Everyone at the nursing home knew KC by name. Everyone, that is, except for his Pop-Pop. The older ladies on the staff, liberated by middle age, fussed over him, mussing his curls, telling him he needed a haircut. They complimented the color of his polo shirt and expressed concern over the brush burn on his shin, offering to swab it with antiseptic to fight off infection. The younger girls were bolder, blatantly flirting with him. One forward LPN, barely legal drinking age, invited him to join her at her parents' backyard picnic after her shift.

"He's in his room, KC, watching television," a matronly nurse said as they approached the unit desk. "Try to get him to eat something."

Charlie followed KC down the hallway of the nursing home, trying not to seem unnerved by the obvious futility of the care and maintenance lavished on the frail and elderly residents wobbling on canes and pushing walkers, all of them beyond any hope of full recovery or chance for independence. No one living under this roof was ever going home again.

"Hey, Pop-Pop! I'm here!" KC said, his voice full of cheer as he wrapped his grandfather in an affectionate hug, half lifting him from his wheelchair.

"Scooby-Doo," the old man grunted, pushing his grandson away, clearly irritated at the unwelcome distraction from the capers of the cartoon canine on his television screen.

"Scooby-Doo to you, too!" KC repeated, laughing merrily. "Pop-Pop, I want you to meet my buddy Charlie."

"Hello, Pop-Pop," Charlie said awkwardly.

The old man was dressed for a January blizzard despite the midsummer heat outside. His tiny skull peeked through the collar of a thick cable-knit sweater; his face was wasted away to its most prominent features—the Roman nose; the floppy, fleshy ears; a gaping toothless smile. Only his eyes—fierce, blazing black diamonds like his grandson's—still seemed alive as they followed the antics of Scooby-Doo.

KC pulled up a chair next to his grandfather and asked Charlie to hand him the plastic cup of applesauce on the bed table.

"There should be a spoon there, too. And give me that cup of ice water. Pop-Pop has to drink through a straw."

He patiently fed the old man the applesauce, one small spoonful at time, gently wiping his mouth every few bites, holding the cup of water under his grandfather's chin while he sucked on the straw. Pop-Pop giggled and snickered as he ate, preoccupied with Scooby-Doo while KC quietly recounted every at bat, each pitch thrown, every swing of his triumphant game. KC helped the old man into the bathroom after he finished eating. Charlie could hear the toilet flush and Pop-Pop struggling, trying to resist his grandson's efforts to wipe his bum and get him into fresh pajamas. "I love you, Pop-Pop," he said, kissing him on his bald scalp when it was time for them to leave. "I'll be back soon."

"He doesn't remember me most of the time," KC said as they drove back to his parents' house. "But some days I think he knows who I am," he insisted.

Charlie wanted to cheer him up and, saying the events of the day required a celebration, suggested they drive downtown to watch the fireworks show at Empire State Plaza.

"I got to play in Glens Falls tomorrow morning. The holiday tournament. Coach Torok is picking me up at eight and we're driving up tonight."

"Okay, sure," Charlie said, feeling stupid and angry with himself, thinking for the first time all day of his own family, remembering he had promised to stop for charcoal and lighter fluid after spending the night at KC's. His dad had planned a small cookout, just hot dogs and store-bought potato salad, the menfolk working the grill, a little vacation for his sister and recovering mother. It was six o'clock now and his father hadn't even bothered to call, resigned to Charlie's irresponsibility and his callow abdication of the few duties his family asked of him, accepting that his only son could not be depended upon.

"Pull the car back there, behind the garage," KC insisted, and Charlie did as instructed, only to be stunned when KC, untrimmed azalea bushes and towering evergreens providing cover from any curious eyes watching from neighboring windows, grabbed him by the cheeks and kissed him on the mouth.

"I never hit for the cycle before," he said, finally wresting his tongue from Charlie's throat. "I wish you could come to Glens Falls, buddy. I'll see you at work," he said, as he dashed into the house.

Charlie summoned the courage to call his father, who said that his mother had been nauseous and retreated to the icy sanctuary of her air-conditioned bedroom hours ago. Madeline had gone to the fireworks with Aunt Geri and her family. Could Charlie stop at the supermarket and pick up a frozen pizza?

He bought a sausage pie and a quart of chocolate milk and, on impulse, grabbed a shabby potted geranium, on sale for $2.99, to surprise his mother when she came down for breakfast in the morning.

Sometimes Charlie would admit to himself he was feeling a bit restless. Except for the one trip to New Paltz to see

Mike Watt, the routine never varied. Fridays and, now, most Saturday nights meant watching DVDs, playing video games, eating takeout, and drinking soda. KC's Legion schedule was demanding—games most weeknights with three, sometimes four, on the weekend. KC cherished the few hours left to relax and chill, leaving few opportunities for time away from the reclining chairs of the Conroy family room.

Charlie doubted KC's teammates led such a monastic life or were as obsessed with discipline as their top player. KC had insisted Charlie attend all of his local games after he'd hit for the cycle, ballplayers being superstitious creatures by nature. Sitting on the first base line for nine innings, Charlie had overhead plenty of loud, boisterous conversations among the players on the bench, tales of beer parties and eager pussy. Earlier in the summer, he'd assumed KC was at least an occasional participant in these blowouts, though lately he'd begun to realize the superstar of the team had a reputation as a loner, aloof and standoffish. Most of the boys admired him, treating him with respect and deference, but a vocal minority had begun to resent him, accusing him of being a snob who thought he was too good to party with them.

He'd rather hang out with that little queer, he'd overheard the shortstop, an ugly little pockmarked Latino kid, say last week.

He can't help it if his cousin's a faggot, a right-handed flame-throwing KC defender protested. *He didn't get to pick his fucking relatives.*

Charlie knew better than to share that nasty little exchange with KC. The season would soon be over and KC would be back at junior college, the names and faces of the roster of his American Legion team in Albany quickly forgotten. But he finally summoned the courage to dare to ask KC why he never partied with his teammates, never attended their keggers, even avoided joining them for postgame celebrations at Pizza Hut whenever possible.

"Because they're all assholes," KC said bitterly.

Which is why Charlie never expected to find Jay Del-duco, the catcher on the Legion team, in the backseat of KC's car as they headed south to New Jersey to see Pearl Jam play at the Meadowlands.

"Because Delduco's the one who scored the tickets when the show sold out in twenty minutes," KC explained when Charlie grumbled at the prospect of spending four hours in close quarters with KC's most obnoxious teammate. "I put it all on the line so we could go to this concert," KC said, de-claring Eddie Vedder to be totally hot, the first really gay thing Charlie had ever heard him say.

KC and Coach Torok had gotten into a loud argument with KC threatening to quit unless he and Delduco were given dispensation to miss a pair of games as the team was on the verge of making the championship tournament. KC was adamant and had gotten his way, but only after Darrell Torok had extracted his solemn promise to not indulge in any of the illegal substances commonly smoked or swal-lowed by idiot kids at rock concerts.

"What's that shit you're playing?" Delduco complained from the backseat two songs into the Teenage Idol's *Greatest Hits.* "Who's that fag singing?"

"Ricky Nelson, a-hole, and he got more in pussy in a week than you'll see in a lifetime," KC said, trying not to sound irritated as he tossed the CD case over his shoulder.

"I don't know, man. This dude looks pretty gay to me," Delduco concluded after a quick study of the cover photo.

KC hit the eject button and loaded a bootleg Pearl Jam. Delduco was too busy trying to match Eddie Vedder note for note to notice that KC's knuckles were white from gripping the steering wheel and that he was grinding a plug of chew between his molars. KC didn't relax until they were sitting in traffic on the Garden State Parkway, Delduco snoring and farting in his sleep. Charlie muttered under his breath as he reluctantly answered his ringing phone.

"Hi," he said, trying hard not to sound irritated. It was completely embarrassing that his father was calling to make sure they'd arrived safely. "I'm okay. I'll text you when we get there."

His old man hadn't trusted the judgment of a seventeen-year-old kid who'd never spent a weekend alone a hundred and fifty miles from home, only reluctantly agreeing to the trip after his more practical wife reminded him that in a few weeks Charlie would be out of the house and perfectly free to make his own decisions about his comings and goings.

"Jesus, my father is so lame," he said after hanging up.

"Hey, he let you come, didn't he? And it was very cool of him to let us use his gas card. Just relax."

Delduco flopped onto his stomach in the backseat, cutting a gruesome fart that smelled like roadkill.

"Sorry about that shitbag, buddy," KC apologized as he slipped the Ricky Nelson disc back into the player. Subject acknowledged and just as quickly closed, he turned up the volume and hit the repeat button, playing "Lonesome Town" four times in a row.

They found a Travelodge in the industrial wasteland outside Elizabeth, New Jersey, which only charged sixty bucks a night, a cool twenty dollars each. Delduco took one look at the pair of double beds and announced he didn't care where his companions slept as long as it wasn't in his bed since he wasn't going queer tonight. Charlie said he'd take the floor. The rough carpet and the rumbling traffic speeding down Highway 1 kept him awake. He spent most of the night pounding his thin pillow and rolling from side to side, jacked up from too many Mountain Dews, too restless to sleep.

"Hey, buddy, you all right down there?" KC whispered.

"Yeah."

"You wanna change places?"

"I'm okay," Charlie said, suddenly content, knowing KC was awake, too, unable to sleep.

He finally dozed off, only to be awakened hours later by

the crackling lightning and booming thunder of a violent summer storm crossing northern New Jersey. Delduco never stirred, but KC's bedsprings creaked as he tossed on the mattress, talking in his sleep, *I don't want chocolate cake, I want ice cream,* his bare foot jutting through the sheets, kicking at some phantom intruder.

Saturday afternoon, Delduco insisted they meet up with his cousins before leaving for the stadium. They were sisters, and the younger one, Elise, looked like Kelly Clarkson, pretty, but regrettably pudgy. The older girl, Alison, was tough-looking beyond her years, hardened, with an ugly winged creature, a bird or dragon, tattooed across her shoulder and down one arm. The sisters passed a cigarette between them, flashing the chipped black polish on their nails. They insisted they were starving, though Elise looked like she never missed a meal or snack and Alison like she had refused food for a week. They piled into a booth at Burger King, the five of them squeezed tightly together, KC wedged between the sisters.

Elise latched onto KC, asking him stupid, flirty questions, teasing him and giggling when he caught her sneaking one of his fries. Alison was less forward, cooler, picking at the edges of a cheeseburger, tearing the bun into little pieces that she scattered on the paper wrapping. Delduco was ramped up, charged with energy, too wired to notice how uncomfortable KC was when Alison grabbed one of his hands, claiming she could read his fortune in his palm.

"What's it say?" Elise gushed.

"I can't tell you," her sister said, thinking her husky voice sounded sexy and mysterious.

"Yes, you can! Come on!" the younger girl protested,

"I'll tell KC, but not you guys," Alison said, coyly, leaning forward and whispering something in his ear.

"I don't know," he mumbled, blushing. "Maybe. We'll see."

She laughed as she slouched on the seat, sucking the dregs of her Coke from the cup.

Delduco and his cousins passed a joint in the Meadow-lands parking lot, arguing about the vintage and potency of the weed. Charlie reluctantly refused to take even a single hit, an act of solidarity with KC. The day had been overcast and the air oppressively humid, but the sun finally emerged an hour before the opening act took the stage. Alison grabbed KC by the arm when the headliners began their set, jumping up and down with the music and shoving her tits in his face. She tried forcing her tongue past his clenched teeth during "Jeremy," but he pushed her away, high-fiving Charlie when Eddie introduced "Alive," the two of them swept up in the euphoria of a chorus of thirty thousand hoarse and unmusi-cal voices sing-shouting the familiar words of the song. There was a house party in Teaneck after the concert; Alison promised KC a wild time and, yeah, his weirdo friend could come, too. Delduco thought KC had lost his mind when he begged off, saying he wanted to go back to the motel. *Suit yourself,* he said, *just make sure you don't leave before I get back in the morning.*

"That girl wanted to fuck you," Charlie said, thankful when the Delducos drove off with a pimply little freak with a pierced eyebrow and the two of them were alone at last.

"You know what? Let's find some beer," KC said as they walked to the car.

Charlie couldn't have gotten served by a blind bartender in the darkest, crummiest dive in New Jersey, and KC was carded the first place he tried. But the kid at the liquor outlet store didn't hesitate to take a twenty for two sixes of cheap beer.

"Buddy, we're gonna get drunk tonight," KC promised as they pulled up to the Travelodge.

Sixty bucks a night only gets you broadcast networks and

basic cable so after the recap on *Baseball Tonight* the only
thing on television was a rerun of *Porky's* with no tits and
asses, the dirty words bleeped, and a ten-minute commercial
break every six minutes. The high school sluts in the movie
reminded Charlie of Delduco's cousins. Half loaded and liberated from any inhibitions, Charlie turned to KC and, emboldened, asked him a question.

"Have you ever fucked a girl?"

Charlie wasn't the only one in that motel room feeling the
effects of alcohol. KC fell back on the bed and sighed at the
ceiling.

"If you tell anyone I'll have to kill you," he said.

"I won't."

He propped himself on his elbow and, staring Charlie in
the eye, solicited a solemn promise.

"You swear?"

"I swear."

He flopped back on the mattress and looked away.

"I tried it once. It didn't work. I guess I wasn't very interested."

Charlie had nothing to say. He'd never even tried it, never
had the opportunity. But the embarrassed confession was
deeply satisfying, the first time the two were on a level playing field, equals, the Mighty KC at Bat without the advantage.

"There was this girl from Mount Mercy. Ashley Brooks,"
KC confided. "She was supposed to be my girlfriend. At
least that's what everyone called her. She's a real nice girl.
Smart. She wants to be a veterinarian. We're still friends. I
talk to her every week."

Charlie felt the cruel stiletto of jealousy piercing his
heart. He hated this fucking Ashley Brooks beyond reason,
certain that convention and expectations would eventually
reunite the young couple.

"She's getting married this Christmas to some guy she

met before he shipped out to Afghanistan. I hope he doesn't get killed."

Charlie, who had discovered atheism while still under the custody of the Augustinian order, made himself a sincere if selfish promise to pray for the young recruit's safe return from the battlefield.

"Is she the girl you almost fucked?" Charlie asked, unsure if he wanted to know the answer.

"Naw, she's real religious. She wanted to wait until she was married. That's what she said when we were going out together. But she's doing it with the soldier now. She says she'd feel bad if he died and they'd never done it."

"Did you have another girlfriend?"

"No. Just Ashley. I didn't really know the girl I tried to do it with. She's from Schenectady. She was somebody's sister or cousin. I don't remember anything about her except she had pimples on her back. How about you? You ever have a girlfriend?"

"No. No girls."

"You ever do stuff with other guys?"

"Did you?" Charlie asked, defiantly.

"No, never," KC protested. "Just you," he insisted, sounding defensive, as if he expected Charlie to challenge him. "Tell me the truth," he said, abruptly changing the subject. "Do you only like Ricky Nelson because I do?"

"No, man. I really like him."

"Good," he said, smiling. "I get real sad when I think of him going down in that airplane. He must have been really scared when he knew they were gonna crash. Hey, did I ever show you something?"

He pulled a frayed and badly faded baseball card from his wallet. It was older than either of them, Topps 1961 issue, Mickey Mantle, No. 475, personally autographed, *Best Wishes, the Mick.*

"My Pop-Pop gave it to me when I hit my first Little

League home run. He'd been saving it for me since before I was born."

He finished his six-pack and started working on Charlie's. Charlie was dizzy and the only way to stop his head from spinning was to close his eyes.

"Hey, buddy, you're not crashing on me?" KC asked as he locked the dead bolt and fastened the security chain, wedging a chair under the door handle as an additional precaution in the unlikely event Delduco found his way back to the motel before checkout time in the morning. He lifted the sheet and crawled into bed beside Charlie, naked, with his equipment fully working. But instead of grinding against Charlie, he pulled him close, sliding his hand between his legs and slipping his tongue into his mouth. Charlie figured KC must have been really drunk to admit what he told him next.

"Man, it's almost the end of July. I wish the summer wasn't going to be over so soon. I'm really gonna miss you when I go back to Florida, Charlie."

"Coach Torok wants you to come, too. You don't have to if you don't want to. I'll tell him you have to go somewhere else, with your mom and dad. It'll be okay."

KC seemed irritated, even angry, when Charlie accepted the invitation after deciding that spending a couple of hours with Darrell Torok was better than sitting alone in his room trying to write record reviews, too distracted by thoughts of where KC was and what he was doing to be able to commit a complete sentence to paper.

"I'll be cool, KC. I won't do anything to embarrass you."

"I know that, buddy," KC said, sounding resigned. "That's not it. Never mind. It's no big deal. Come on, Charlie. He's waiting for us in his truck."

Charlie had never seen KC rush for anyone before, but

now they were running across the parking lot, clearly in a hurry.

"You douche bags better wipe your feet before you get into the truck if you don't want me to smack you upside your heads," Darrell barked as they approached, watching the boys like a hawk, making sure that they didn't track mud onto his new floor mats. "You guys hungry?" he asked, sounding cheerful, as if his threats of physical violence had been a joke.

"I guess so," KC mumbled, sounding surprisingly unenthusiastic at the prospect of a charred rib eye and Bloomin Onions at Outback Steakhouse.

"You ought to be, my man. You had a good game today, KC," Darrell said.

"It was okay." KC shrugged.

He'd been on base three times—two hits ("knocks," as Charlie had learned to call them) and a walk—as he came to the plate with two outs and no men on, bottom of the ninth, his team behind four to one. He ran the count to three and two, patiently waiting for *his* pitch, and sent a fastball middle-in over the outfield wall, his efforts ending in a four-to-two loss. Charlie had been to enough of KC's games by now to know KC was ruminating over the day's failures, settling into a dark mood that could last for hours, sometimes until morning. But the coach had insisted on celebrating clinching a play-off berth in KC's last year of eligibility for Legion baseball earlier in the week. A few generous tips of his hip flask into their Cokes helped get everyone in good spirits.

"You boys must really be thirsty," the waitress exclaimed when they kept calling for the bottomless refills.

"How come you don't play ball, Charlie?" Darrell asked, making sure Charlie felt included in the party.

"Because I suck," he blurted out bluntly, starting to feel lightheaded from the rum.

"Is that true? Does he suck, KC?" Darrell asked, making KC squirm in his seat, his eyes pleading to be let off the hook.

"Yeah, it's true. I suck big time, don't I, KC?" Charlie laughed, playing along, assuming the double entendre would sail over the clueless coach's head.

"Chill out, Charlie," KC insisted. "Don't pay any attention to Darrell. He's just yanking your chain."

Darrell winked at Charlie, co-conspirators against the dour and humorless young man. Sated with red meat and deep-fried onions, KC finally started to relax, growing more and more animated with each glass of spiked soda, becoming talkative, not his usual taciturn self. He even broke into uncontrollable giggles, laughing at some private joke between him and the coach.

"What? What are you laughing at?" Charlie asked, indignant, realizing he must be getting drunk as his elbow slipped off the table.

"Darrell thinks you look like Malcolm in the Middle," KC snickered.

"No fucking way," Charlie protested, his voice too loud, drawing reproachful stares from the young father protecting his family at the next table. He blushed, embarrassed. He did resemble the young actor a bit, unfortunately. His mother had been wrong when she promised his face would someday grow into his rather large ears.

"Be cool there, hoss." Darrell smiled. "You trying to get me into trouble?"

Dessert was ordered and Darrell called for the check. Charlie assumed the evening would soon be over and they could go back to KC's house, watch *Field of Dreams*, play *Call of Duty*, but Darrell was in no mood to call it a night.

"Anyone up for the hot tub?" Darrell asked as he slapped down cash for the check.

"Hell, yeah!" KC shouted in his outdoor voice. "How about it, buddy?"

Charlie had no choice but to agree. He was well on his way to being shit-faced, but KC seemed even drunker, cranking up the volume on the truck radio when the DJ played one of his favorite Tom Petty songs.

"Sing harmony with us, buddy," KC pleaded, smiling at Charlie, his pitch-black eyes looking bright and cheerful. Darrell provided croaking, tuneless backup vocals to "I Won't Back Down."

Darrell Torok's house was less sinister than the gloomy Bates homestead of Charlie's unreliable memory. It was an unremarkable farmhouse, renovated several times over the decades, the kitchen outfitted with the latest Sears Kenmore appliances, no different from the home Charlie had grown up in.

"Run out back and pull the cover off the hot tub, KC," Darrell ordered. "I'll be out in a minute."

KC seemed familiar with the layout, even knowing where to find a glass when Charlie asked for a drink of water. He led Charlie through several rooms to a back door and into the backyard.

"Look at that, buddy," KC said, pointing at the bright full moon in the star-studded sky.

Charlie squinted into the man in the moon's scowling face. It was quiet out in the country, peaceful, even a bit eerie, no streetlamps or brightly lit windows to illuminate the black shadows. A tractor was parked at the open door of the barn. Tomato plants were staked to poles in the large vegetable garden, tied with strips of white rags. Rows of field corn in the distant field rustled in the warm night breezes. The water bubbled in the hot tub and the strong scent of chemicals lingered in the humid air. KC and Charlie were both stricken by a sudden onset of modesty, undressing slowly, looking away from each other. Charlie carefully folded his pants, and KC fiddled with the shoelaces of his sneakers. They slipped into the water quickly, keeping their underwear on, submerging their bodies to their shoulders, hiding be-

neath the bubbling surface. KC quickly drew in his leg when
their toes casually brushed in the cramped pool.

"Hands where I can see them," Darrell Torok barked,
laughing at his stupid crude joke. He was wearing baggy
swim trunks, holding a bottle and three plastic glasses in his
hand. He slid into the water between Charlie and KC, his
bulky frame a barrier between them.

"A toast," he said, waving the bottle over his head.

"To what?" KC asked.

"To buddies. Friendship," he said, filling the glasses with
a golden liquid.

"What is it?" Charlie asked.

"Slivovitz. Plum wine," he laughed. "Made it myself. The
fruit is from the trees in the orchard out back."

Sweet as Mountain Dew but powerful enough to take out
an ox, the first shot went down easily. Darrell poured a second round, then a third.

"T.M.C.," Darrell announced, kicking off his trunks and
tossing his bathing suit out of the pool.

"What?" Charlie asked, feeling lightheaded, dizzy.

"T.M.C. Too many clothes," KC explained as he threw his
briefs out onto the lawn.

The overpowering smell of chlorine brought Charlie close
to retching. His knees buckled when he stood. He stumbled,
tripping over Darrell's ankles, nearly falling face forward,
but he steadied himself by grabbing the ladder.

"Don't even think about puking in my pool, kid," Darrell
warned, his voice hinting at dire consequences.

Charlie somehow scrambled out of the hot tub and ran toward the back door.

"The bathroom's the third door on the left," Darrell
shouted.

They were laughing at Charlie as the screen door
slammed behind him. He found the toilet and dropped to his
knees, dry-heaving into the bowl. The rum and slivovitz still
sloshed in his stomach, but he felt better, if not sober, as he

staggered to his feet. He stared at his bare shoulders and chest in the mirror, feeling exposed, though no one was looking. He lingered, locked in the bathroom, until he heard knuckles tapping on the door and KC asking if he was all right.

"I'm okay."

"Hurry up then, buddy. I got to piss real bad, and Darrell will kick my ass if I pee in his hot tub. You okay?" KC smiled, his hair a tangled mess of wet curls, as Charlie opened the door.

"Yeah, of course," Charlie lied, wishing they were back in KC's den, watching television, drinking Pepsi, and eating chips.

"Darrell's great, isn't he?" KC asked, not waiting for an answer as he slipped by Charlie and straddled the toilet for a long piss.

Charlie slowly shuffled down the hallway, stopping to peer into what had probably been the dining room, the table and chairs and sideboard now replaced with a magnificent vintage Bally Fireball pinball machine. The flaming alien painted on the back glass, armed with a blazing sphere, dared him to accept the challenge. He paused to study the playfield, then yanked the plunger and launched the ball into play, quickly running up the score with eleven ramp shots in a row. He slapped the flippers, racking up points, the feeling of invincibility swelling as he pulled off a perfect death save.

"Impressive," Darrell Torok murmured over Charlie's shoulder, shattering his concentration long enough for the ball to slip past the flippers and roll down the drain. "Let me show you a few tricks," he said, sounding almost ominous.

Charlie stepped aside, staring at Darrell's broad back as the older man, a beach towel wrapped around his waist, nudged the cabinet with his hips. Darrell Torok was master of the playfield, in complete command of the machine, his quick reflexes controlling the movement of the ball. He skillfully juggled the flippers, smacking his targets, his score racing ahead of Charlie's. Fireball must have leaped off the back glass and possessed him!

"Not bad for an old man," Darrell said, laughing, after he finally tilted, the exhausted machine locking down for a well-deserved rest.

"Damn, you're good," Charlie conceded, his voice barely audible.

"Come on, KC," Darrell urged. "Let's see what you can do."

KC was unsteady on his feet and gripped the machine with his hands, laughing as he confessed he'd never played pinball bare-assed before.

"Don't get your dick caught in the flippers," Darrell warned, mocking him.

"Just watch this shit," KC boasted, arching his back and rising on the balls of his feet, tensing his muscles, his shoulder blades rippling in his taut back as he worked the flippers. He flexed his glutes and tossed his head, laughing as he racked up his score.

"You okay there, big guy?" Darrell asked as Charlie swayed on his feet, the room beginning to spin around him.

"Yeah," Charlie mumbled.

"I think you need to take a break," Darrell said, laying a solicitous hand on the younger man's shoulder. "Come on, it's time to put you to bed."

Charlie tried shrugging his hand away, but finally yielded to Darrell's firm but gentle guidance, allowing himself to be led up the staircase and down the hall. As they approached the open door of a darkened bedroom, he heard the unmistakable monosyllables of pornography, a woman grunting and groaning, begging to be fucked. In the dim, flickering light of the television screen, he saw a bottle of lubricant, a box of tissues, and a flesh-colored dildo shaped like a cock on the nightstand beside the bed. He pushed Darrell aside and ran down the hall, passing KC on the staircase, nearly tearing the screen door off its hinges as he flew out of the house and into the yard. His stomach heaved again and he fell to his knees, vomiting on the lawn. He grabbed a pool towel to wipe his mouth and crawled onto a chaise lounge, pulling his knees to his chest, passing out on the chair.

The sun was up when he finally awoke, KC shaking him by the shoulder, shoving his pants and shoes into his hands. KC was already dressed. He seemed agitated, nervous, and told Charlie to hurry, that Darrell was waiting for them in the truck. There was no singing as he drove the boys back to Charlie's car, no Tom Petty on the radio. Darrell didn't speak to Charlie, wouldn't even look at him, and drove off without saying good-bye when he dropped them in the parking lot. The day was already hot and the air in the car was stifling. Charlie's head was throbbing and his throat was parched. KC looked hungover, too; his pupils were bloodshot and he had dark circles under his eyes. Charlie wanted to know where KC had slept, why he hadn't come looking for him after he'd escaped from Darrell's bedroom, but he was wary of asking. He sensed this was one of those occasions when he needed to let KC be the first to speak, and KC was quiet, alone with his thoughts, saying nothing until Charlie pulled into KC's driveway.

"What are you doing today?" KC asked as they sat in the parked car.

"It's my little sister's birthday. My parents are having a party. Not really a party. Cake and ice cream."

"Can I come?"

Charlie was startled by the unexpected question.

"It's just the four of us and a couple of Madeline's friends. You'd be really bored."

"Okay," KC said, opening the car door, trying, unsuccessfully, to hide his disappointment.

"My mom made lasagna for dinner. Her lasagna's the best," Charlie said, extending an invitation.

"Cool."

"I'll come pick you up around three."

"Okay."

"Do you want me to come in with you?" Charlie asked shyly.

"No, naw," KC said, mumbling, embarrassed, suddenly seeming as if he couldn't wait to get away. "I'm kind of a mess right now. I'll see you later."

"How do you spell Madeline?"

KC looked like a television star when he cleaned up and made himself presentable. Charlie was wearing his beat-up, punk-rock Converse All Stars and jeans with the knees artfully ripped, but KC had dressed for the occasion. He'd put on a clean red polo, a genuine Lacoste; his Levi's were pressed, and his Sperrys were new, not yet scuffed and creased by sweat. He'd shaved and beat his unruly mop into submission, training it with styling gel. When he got into the car, Charlie had thought he could smell cologne.

KC had insisted they stop at 7-Eleven where he carefully read the inscription in every birthday card in the greeting card rack before choosing the most suitable one for a ten-year-old girl. Then he asked the Pakistani woman at the register to swap a crumpled bill from his wallet for the cleanest, crispest twenty in her drawer.

"That's too much money," Charlie protested, shamed that his own gift had only set him back fifteen bucks—two Amelia Bedelia paperbacks that Madeline rejected disdainfully as books for little kids, instructing him to exchange them at Barnes & Noble for the adventures of Clarice Bean, reading material more suitable for a sophisticated young woman of her advanced years.

"No way, buddy," KC insisted. "I just wish I had a little sister of my own," he explained, a comment that made no sense to Charlie, who knew there were three younger Conroys, the youngest of whom was a five-year-old girl.

"You do," he said, puzzled.

"It's not the same," KC said, wanting to change the subject. "Never mind."

Madeline didn't seem impressed by or interested in the unexpected guest until she opened the card and discovered an unexpected treasure in the envelope. She embraced KC with a big hug and, avaricious little soul that she was, asked him why he was friends with her stupid, clueless brother who thought she was still seven years old.

The men retreated to the television room after singing "Happy Birthday," leaving Charlie's mother to supervise five rambunctious girls supercharged on sugar. The Mets were playing an afternoon game in Los Angeles, and Charlie's father was intent on impressing KC with his knowledge of the game. He compared KC favorably to David Wright, the old man's favorite player, for some reason believing KC, who was a speedy center fielder, played an infield position. KC was polite and respectful, agreeing with every insight shared by Mr. Beresford ("Call me Paul. No need to be so formal"), scrunching his face in goofy asides to Charlie when the old man wasn't looking. Charlie cringed at his father's racially tinged comments on the work ethic of the Latino players, but KC merely shrugged, saying playing a hundred-sixty-two-game season could wear a guy out. Truth be told, baseball still bored Charlie to tears if KC wasn't playing, and he wandered out into the kitchen where his sister, the party over and her guests sent home, sat at the table watching a YouTube video of singing kittens on her iPad.

"Is your friend staying for dinner?" his mother asked as she looked up from stacking glasses in the dishwasher.

She'd prepared her kids for the worst, warning them of the debilitating effects of chemotherapy, though she'd been fortunate and hadn't lost her hair. But her skin was an ashen gray and her gaunt, skeletal face seemed haunted, defeated.

She'd taken to wearing her husband's dress shirts, buttoned at the neck and hanging to her knees, trying to hide her frightening weight loss. She was irritable most of her waking hours, nauseous from the treatments, her movements still restricted by the painful incisions of her surgery that hadn't yet completely healed. Charlie's father had tried to persuade her to agree to a family outing, a movie and cheeseburgers at Applebee's, to celebrate their little girl's birthday, but she'd insisted on the party and preparing Madeline's favorite meal for her special day. Charlie appreciated her efforts, his stomach growling at the smell of the lasagna baking in the oven.

"Well, I hope he's hungry," his mother said. "The little one's already stuffed herself with cake and ice cream."

"He's always hungry."

She steadied herself on the kitchen counter, resting on one arm. She stared at Charlie and opened her mouth to say something, but then looked at her daughter at the table and decided to let it pass.

"Tell them we're sitting down at the table in fifteen minutes."

"I will."

"Oh, Charlie. Larry Coleman called here last night. He said you haven't returned his phone calls."

"Never got 'em," Charlie said quickly. "The cell reception in the mountains really sucks."

"You said suck," Madeline said, laughing, looking up from the iPad.

"Well, he was coming through loud and clear last night," his mother said wearily, slicing a tomato to add to the salad.

Charlie's father admired KC's impressive appetite almost as much as his athletic abilities, which, at long last, seemed likely to reward Oliver Ryan's once pathetic Legion team with a long overdue championship.

"You don't even know how many thousands of bucks Ollie's spent sponsoring that damn team over the years. He told me he's building a display case in the office to show off the trophy."

KC accepted another serving of lasagna, complimenting the culinary skills of his hostess. Charlie, who had had seventeen years to learn to read the expressions on his mother's face, was thankful that she was able to restrain herself from chastising their guest for eating with his elbows on the table, a pet peeve and, in her judgmental mind, the sure sign of a lack of parental discipline.

"How come you stopped playing Legion ball in high school?" Charlie's father asked.

KC, conscious that his table manners were under observation, was careful to chew and swallow his food before opening his mouth to speak.

"Coach Torok had a plan for me," he said, pausing to take a sip from his milk glass. "He wanted me to play travel ball after my sophomore year. Better competition. I'm just playing for Mr. Ryan this summer to stay loose until off-season practice starts in September."

"You have a girlfriend, KC?" Charlie's father asked.

"Sure," he answered, not skipping a beat.

Charlie nearly choked on a mouthful of lasagna at this unexpected revelation. KC had told him his old girlfriend Ashley Brooks was going to marry someone else, a soldier.

"We'd like to meet her sometime. Maybe she has a friend who Charlie can ask out."

"Okay," KC said casually, as Charlie's mother offered him a third generous helping. "But she doesn't get to Albany very often. She lives in Rhode Island."

"What's her name?" Charlie's father asked.

"Mary Lou," he said.

"That's an unusual name for a young girl of your generation," Charlie's skeptical mother observed. "Don't you have a brother who was in Madeline's class last year? I think I've met your mother."

Charlie began shoveling the food off his plate, trying to finish quickly before the inquisition could begin.

"Maybe," KC said.

Both Charlie and his mother suspected KC wasn't entirely certain where his little brother went to school or what grade he was in.

"A little carrot-headed boy," his mother said, pressing the issue.

"Peter," KC conceded.

"Right, Peter."

"Peter Conroy," Madeline confirmed. "He's a jerk. You're nicer, KC."

KC laughed and graciously thanked her.

"Charlie says your parents are gone every weekend," his mother said, pursuing the interrogation.

"They have a cabin at Lake George. I have to play ball so I can't go."

"I wanted to buy a place up there a few years ago," Charlie's father interrupted. "But the prices were out of my league."

"Who feeds you all weekend?" his mother asked, clearly disturbed that a woman would leave a growing boy, even one who was eighteen going on nineteen and been away to junior college, to fend for himself.

"We always have plenty of food here," Charlie's father offered. "Charlie, you ought to bring KC home for supper more often."

Caught up in a moment of generosity, Charlie's father seemed to have forgotten that dinner in the Beresford household was a haphazard affair while his mother was in treatment, mostly takeout and frozen entrees, Madeline existing on chicken fingers, Charlie and his father on pizza and wings. His mother shot her husband an exasperated look, clearly irritated by his idea of opening a neighborhood soup kitchen.

"Ollie wants us to come see the play-offs," Charlie's father announced. "We're really looking forward to it, right, Connie?"

"We'll see how I feel," she said as she stood to clear the plates, her husband objecting, saying the boys would clean up after they finished eating.

Charlie and KC took Madeline to the movies after dinner. Charlie wasn't as enamored of Pixar rodents as his companions and his mind wandered, his guilty conscience unsettled. He'd received sixty-two messages from Larry in the past three weeks, returning none. He excused himself and retreated to the bathroom, intending to make the long overdue call. He rehearsed his excuses, hoping he could fake enough enthusiasm to convincingly lie. At some point in the conversation, he'd have to tell Larry he missed him. He dialed the dreaded number, but much to his relief, the call rolled into voice mail.

Larry had recorded a new greeting with "Girlfriend in a Coma" as a lugubrious background so that every caller would know he was suffering through a summer of misery in the Adirondacks. Charlie returned to his seat in a much better mood than he'd left it. Madeline was completely absorbed in the animated antics on the screen as Charlie plopped down beside KC and, without thinking, purely on instinct, picked up his hand. KC bolted upright, his head on a swivel, searching the dark auditorium for curious eyes, finally slumping back in his seat when he was satisfied no one was watching, squeezing Charlie's hand in his lap.

The movie ended just before nine, and Madeline insisted on a side trip to Dairy Queen, her every wish their command for the three hours remaining of her birthday. In the short course of an afternoon and evening, she'd fallen under KC's spell, vying for his attention, beaming whenever he smiled at her.

"Are you in love?" she asked abruptly, between spoonfuls of Chocolate Xtreme Blizzard.

"Maybe," KC said, teasing her.

"I know you're in love," she said boldly.

"Oh, yeah?" He laughed. "What makes you so smart?"

"I saw you holding hands with Charlie."

Charlie's face blazed bright red. He aggressively challenged his little sister, threatening she could get in really big trouble for making things up.

"My hands were cold and Charlie was warming them up," KC said, interrupting Charlie's tirade, his voice calm and unflustered.

"It's summertime. No one's cold in the summertime," she countered, sucking the dregs of her Blizzard through her straw. "I think you and Charlie are in love."

Even the most precocious ten-year-old has a short attention span, and Madeline was easily distracted by the chocolate Labrador puppy running between the outdoor tables. It had been a long day and she quickly dozed off in the car as Charlie drove KC home. Every window of the house was brightly lit, and a Nissan Pathfinder was parked in the driveway, evidence the Conroys had returned from Lake George and were immersed in their Sunday night routines. KC seemed reluctant to get out of the car; he put a pinch of chew in his cheek, grinding the tobacco between his teeth.

"Can I stay at your place tonight?" he asked, spitting a stream of brown juice out the window.

He dashed into the house, returning a few minutes later with clean clothes and a toothbrush in a paper bag.

"Play this, okay?" he asked, handing Charlie a CD of *Ricky Nelson's Greatest Hits* and for one brief, fleeting moment Charlie thought KC was going to kiss him right there and then, in the Conroys' driveway with Madeline gently snoring in the backseat.

Charlie had slept in his small bedroom for seventeen years and never before been so conscious of his parents lying in bed on the other side of the wall. He knew his father could sleep through a natural disaster; some nights he could hear him snoring through the drywall. But his mother had always been a light sleeper. Since the surgery, she was up and down all night, making restless trips to the bathroom or kitchen or, sometimes, to the back patio where he suspected she was sneaking a forbidden cigarette.

He'd put *Ricky Nelson's Greatest Hits* in his old compact disc player. (Charlie was far more advanced than KC in transitioning to a digital music library. He liked the convenience and the instant gratification, though he knew as a music snob he was supposed to prefer vinyl.) He kept the volume low, playing "Teenage Idol" and "Travelin' Man" just loud enough to, hopefully, camouflage the sounds of his creaking bedsprings. He was reluctant at first, resisting KC's advances, afraid they would be caught in the act, but KC was insistent, covering Charlie's mouth when he tried to protest. Charlie pushed his hand away and hissed at KC through clenched teeth.

"Who the fuck is Mary Lou?"

"What was I supposed to say? I didn't want your dad to think I was some kind of loser who couldn't get a girlfriend."

KC flopped to his side, turning his back on Charlie. Charlie regretted his outburst, fearing the bond between him and KC was tenuous and could be easily severed by a few careless words, a harsh remark.

"Hey, you still want to mess around?" he whispered in KC's ear, daring to put his hand on KC's leg.

"No," KC mumbled, his face half buried in his pillow. "I don't want to just mess around tonight," he said, turning and gently rolling Charlie onto his back. He threw a leg over Charlie's waist, straddling him, and, with one quick, graceful move, lowered himself onto Charlie's erect cock, squinting and grimacing slightly as Charlie penetrated him. He slowly rolled his hips as he found his rhythm, moaning softly, closing his eyes, his mouth slightly agape, smiling. Charlie's shoulders sank back into the mattress; he was at a loss, not knowing what, if anything, he was expected to do. KC leaned forward, bending at the waist, shaking his head no, when Charlie thrust his hips forward, trying to drive himself deeper into KC's rectum.

"Just lie back, Mary Lou," KC whispered. "Let me do the work. Let's see how long we can go."

Charlie closed his eyes, concentrating on a black screen, the thought of his parents lying on the other side of the wall distracting him just enough to help him hold back as long as possible, determined not to disappoint.

"I'm real close," KC grunted, careful to keep his voice low.

KC arched his back and squeezed his sphincter. Charlie gasped, as if a crackling electric shock were racing through his body, far more intense than any orgasm that he'd ever pumped with his fist or that Larry Coleman had coaxed with his sloppy mouth. He opened his eyes and saw KC staring down at him, almost shyly, as if they had just awkwardly stumbled upon each other. After a long moment, they fell apart, lying side by side, breathing heavily, almost afraid to speak. Charlie touched his belly, tapping his fingertip in the sticky mess KC had spilled on his skin. His thoughts drifted back to health class and the lectures he'd been forced to listen to about AIDS, syphilis, and gonorrhea, grim tales of punishing scourges intended to coerce the young men of Augustinian into enforced chastity.

"You think we should use a rubber when we do that again?" he asked almost casually, not expecting KC's blistering, wounded response.

"I'm not a fag! There's nothing wrong with me! Maybe you're the one with AIDS and you're gonna give it to me!"

Charlie was too hurt to protest. He didn't dare challenge KC with questions about Darrell Torok and his creepy house, about how many times KC had been there, what had happened when Darrell and KC were alone. Maybe someday they would talk about it. But not now. He trusted KC. KC would never lie to him, not about something important like not having some disease. Ricky Nelson was singing about a garden party. The music seemed to soothe KC; he tapped his fingers on his chest, keeping time with the beat.

"How come you like Ricky Nelson so much?" Charlie asked, his voice surprisingly hoarse.

"You promise you won't think I'm really stupid?"

"I promise."

"Me and my mom lived with my Pop-Pop Nelson when I was a little kid. The three of us in his crappy old house. My mom and I had to sleep in the same bedroom because there weren't enough rooms. Me and Pop-Pop were real close. He made my supper and put me to bed because she tended bar at night. He got me up and gave me breakfast because she slept until noon. He had a lot of records that he played all the time, really old stuff, and I thought Ricky Nelson was my father because we had the same name."

KC rolled on his side and stared into Charlie's face.

"She married Ed when I was seven. He was real nice to me at first; he even adopted me right after the wedding. Then they had my brothers and sister. He says they're real Conroys because they all have orange hair, just like him. When he's drunk he calls me a nigger because my hair's black and curly and my eyes are really dark and I never get sunburned. He says my mother must have fucked Barry Bonds, that's why I'm a good ballplayer. He says she was a whore when he met her, that she doesn't even know who my father is."

"Did you ever ask her?"

"I don't want to know. I'd rather pretend."

Charlie's Aunt Geri had gone to Portland for her annual visit to see her grandkids, leaving his mother without her usual ride to the cancer center Friday morning. Charlie was recruited to drive over her objection that she wasn't an invalid and could manage a twenty-two-mile round-trip alone.

Ollie Ryan himself gave Charlie special dispensation for a day off so the dispatcher couldn't refuse despite being short-staffed, the ranks of summer sausages already decimated by early returns to campus and scheduled family vacations and more than a few fuck-this-shit-I-quits.

Charlie sat in the waiting room, ignoring his unopened copy of *Infinite Jest* (he hadn't gotten beyond page 89) and flipping through the pages of *Us Weekly*, stopping to study the paparazzi shots of Ryan Gosling lying on a chaise lounge by a Las Vegas hotel pool. He'd put his phone on silent and scrambled to retrieve it when it vibrated in his pocket.

wat r u doing

He snickered, knowing KC had probably disappeared ten minutes after the van arrived at the morning load and was checking box scores and texting on his phone.

nothing.

b suks.

. . . meaning Bruno had likely stalked his missing prey and was delivering some meaningless threat if KC didn't get his ass down into the cellar and start packing the contents of the basement into moving cartons.

*c u at 6,*Charlie wrote back, the scheduled departure time for the drive to Binghamton where KC had an early game scheduled in the morning.

He was staring at Ryan Gosling's muscular legs in the magazine when his phone began vibrating again. KC must have escaped the stupid Polack, he thought, pulling out his cell to find an unexpected, unwelcome text from Larry Coleman.

call me later

can't going to Binghamton tonite.

why

family stuff

Larry unleashed a flurry of text characters, more questions, the tone demanding.

at hospital.have to turn off cell, Charlie responded.

His mother finally emerged from the treatment area. He'd been relieved when she'd told him to wait in reception, having expected he'd be asked to sit beside her, keep her company, comfort her, as they stuck her with long needles and pumped toxic chemicals into her veins. She seemed a bit feeble, tired, and didn't resist when he offered to take her arm, taking slow and deliberate baby steps as they walked to the car. He started the engine and she reached into her pocketbook for a cigarette and a lighter.

"Don't say anything. And don't tell your father. I know I've got a ten-year-old daughter to raise and I'm going to quit, believe me. But it helps settle my stomach. I can stand just about anything but the nausea," she said as she blew a thick stream of smoke out the window.

Charlie had learned many lessons that summer, none so difficult as discovering that illness didn't always ennoble its victims, that some people became more difficult, growing ornery and contentious, when confronting adversity. His mother's bitterness over vague injustices and the many disappointments she'd suffered in her life had been unleashed by the cancer diagnosis and the gruesome aftermath. Madeline escaped her mother's critical tongue, but Charlie and his father had suffered through her blackest moods.

"You haven't been much help this summer. I told your father to let you go work at that camp, but he wanted you to stay home."

The remark stung Charlie; it was mean and undeserved.

"I could have driven you to your appointments every day. I didn't want to take that fucking moving job. Dad made me do it!"

"Watch your language," she said, tossing one butt out the window and lighting another. "Settle down. I'm not blaming you. I don't know what your father expected a seventeen-year-old kid was going to do under the circumstances. He's taking this very hard. I'm sure it's because he's terrified at the prospect of being left on his own to bring up your sister if I drop dead," she laughed.

"Maybe he loves you," Charlie protested, surprised to find himself defending his father.

"Charlie," she sighed, the tone of her voice announcing the importance of the message. "Your dad's going through a lot right now. I don't think he can handle any more bad news just yet."

Her words were vague, though their meaning was explicit. Charlie pretended to not understand.

"Maybe you shouldn't bring that boy around the house anymore. Even your father will figure it out soon enough, dense as he is."

Madeline must have betrayed him—innocently, or maybe not so innocently, telling tales of hand-holding in a dark movie theater, confiding that her brother and KC were in love.

"He was suspicious about your friend Larry, so he was real happy when you took up with this ballplayer. The day's going to come when you're going to have to tell your father everything, but this isn't the time."

He tried to protest, to insist she was mistaken, about KC, about Larry, about him, but the words never found the way to his tongue. She knew him too well, always had; he could never lie to her. He'd tried, many times, but his efforts had always failed.

"He's a nice boy, Charlie. I like him. And when I'm feeling better I'll work on bringing your father around. But I have too much going on to deal with this right now."

Her words seemed to mock him for believing his private thoughts and desires were safely hidden, unknown to anyone. He wasn't the ten-year-old boy who had poured out his soul to her over a glass of milk and a plate of Toll House cookies fresh out of the oven, seeking reassurance that someday he'd be at the top of the world, looking down at all the bullies who teased and tormented him. Once upon a time there was nothing, no secret, he wouldn't share with her. But his feelings for KC were his alone, something he didn't fully understand, their depth almost frightening to him. He resented her, wishing he had a mother like KC's who didn't care where he was or what he did or who he did it with. He tried to think of something harsh and mean to say to her, something that would hurt as much as her unfair criticism that he'd failed to provide the support and comfort she'd deserved and expected. He would tell her she didn't know anything, that she wasn't as smart as she thought, that he couldn't wait to leave for Dartmouth so she couldn't try to tell him what to do anymore.

But when he turned to confront her, the urge to be cruel was crushed by regret. She was right, as always. She'd been sick and hurting all summer, some days too weak to stand, not once complaining that her firstborn child never asked how she was feeling, if there was anything he could do for her. He'd spent the day of her surgery negotiating with God, making lists of many things he would do—and the few things he would give up doing—if only He would let his mother live. But his best intentions and sincere promises were quickly forgotten once the crisis had passed and life in the Beresford household had settled into the grim and tedious routine of her slow recovery. The few hours he spent apart from KC were consumed by thoughts of the two of them lying together on the sofa in the Conroy family room or riding home from a Legion game listening to Ricky Nelson sing the sad chorus of "Lonesome Town." He was going to stop being so selfish and inconsiderate. He was going to be the good son she deserved. He'd take her somewhere tonight, to the movies or out to dinner. They could sit together on the sofa and watch television if she was too tired to leave the house. No. He couldn't do it tonight. He was going to Binghamton with KC tonight. He'd start today. Right now.

"Hey, Ma, look! There's a Friendly's up there. You wanna

get some clam strips for lunch?" he asked, knowing they were her guilty pleasure.

She stared at him as if he hadn't heard a word she'd said, which, obviously he hadn't if he thought she'd be thrilled at the opportunity to fill her tender stomach with greasy deep-fried mollusks. She took a drag from her cigarette and, shaking her head gently, smiled.

"No, but you must be starved by now. I can have a ginger ale while you eat."

Charlie flopped onto his belly, trying to concentrate on the course catalog. The registration deadline expired in twenty-four hours. He'd tuned out any distractions—no music, no television, cell phone turned off. He was restricted to the house, recruited for babysitting duty, his father having persuaded his mother to agree to a "date night" to celebrate their twentieth wedding anniversary. The old man had been as giddy as a kid all day, asking Charlie a half-dozen times if he thought his mother was going to be surprised by the one-carat diamond he'd bought to replace the cheap engagement ring he'd given her two decades ago. She'd complained for three days about being forced to leave the house, but, in the end, she'd conceded, wearing a dress and putting on makeup for the first time since the surgery.

Madeline was downstairs, absorbed in *The Twilight Saga: New Moon,* a movie her mother would have forbidden her to watch only a few short months ago, before postoperative therapies had radically altered priorities, and protecting impressionable young minds from PG-13 romantic yearnings no longer seemed to be a matter of pressing urgency. Discipline had become so lax in the Beresford household that his mother merely shrugged her shoulders when she'd discovered her daughter deeply engrossed in the far racier antics of the *True Blood* vampires.

"Charlie!"

The scream was bloodcurdling. He jumped off his bed, running down the hallway in nothing but his Jockey briefs. Madeline was standing at the bottom of the stairs, clearly irritated at being distracted from the television, impatient to return to the soulful gazes of Bella Swan and Edward Cullen.

"Larry Coleman is at the front door. He wants to talk to you."

He grabbed his jeans and poked his feet through the legs, scrambling to find his sneakers. If only he'd listened to the twenty voice mails Larry had left in the past few days instead of instantly deleting them, he wouldn't have been caught off guard. Camp didn't end until mid-August, another week away, and if Charlie had known Larry was back in Albany early he could have agreed to meet him on neutral territory, like the food court at the mall. Instead Larry was standing on the front porch, likely to cause a scene, a problem that needed to be resolved quickly, before his parents came home from dinner.

"Don't let him in the house," he shouted as he tied his shoelaces.

"How stupid do you think I am?" she said haughtily, and Charlie, not for the first time, understood what a demanding little bitch his baby sister would soon grow up to be.

Larry looked like he'd had a few unfortunate encounters of his own with bloodthirsty vampires. Wan and pale, in need of a haircut, unhealthily thin, he'd dropped thirty, maybe forty, pounds, looking more punk rock than Charlie, who'd filled out over the summer, adding muscle to his wiry frame. Charlie stood in the doorway, not inviting Larry into the house, letting him bounce nervously on the balls of his feet.

"I'm kind of busy right now, Larry," he said, dispensing with polite formalities like *Hello* and *How have you been?*

"You want to go for a ride, Charlie? I got weed. Good stuff."

"I have to register for classes. Maybe later."

"You want me to come back in an hour?"

"I can't. I'm watching Madeline."

If his father were home, he'd be shouting at him to come in or go out, that he wasn't paying to air-condition the front lawn. Charlie was growing impatient, wanting Larry to take the hint, get in his car, and drive away.

"I've been trying to call you, Charlie. Animal Collective is on tour in Syracuse in September. I want to get us tickets now before they sell out."

"I'm gonna be at Dartmouth."

"It's not that far, Charlie," Larry pleaded, ignoring the reality of nearly three hundred miles' distance. "I'll come get you. I'll drive you back."

"I gotta go, Larry," he said, retreating into the house.

Larry grabbed him by the wrist, desperate, suffering the unbearable anguish of watching his first great love slipping away, crushed by the knowledge, suspected for too long, now irrefutably confirmed, that he had already kissed Charlie Beresford for the last time, that he would never see him naked again. He shoved a balled-up cotton T-shirt into Charlie's hand.

"I found this on eBay. I was going to give it to you for your birthday."

It was a vintage Sonic Youth 2000 Goo Tour T-shirt, in mint condition, a nice snug fit that would flatter the chest and biceps he'd developed this summer.

"Do you like it?" Larry asked.

"Yeah. Sure. Of course," he mumbled, embarrassed by the extravagant emotions suggested by such a gift, carefully and deliberately chosen, difficult to find, expensive or at least not cheap. "Thanks."

They stared at each other awkwardly, Charlie trying to think of some gracious way to say good-bye, Larry hoping that the shirt had earned him a reprieve.

"I thought camp didn't end for another week," Charlie finally asked, breaking the silence.

"I left early," Larry said. "I got fired. My father was going to sue them, and I had to tell him they caught me blowing another counselor in the shower. At least he knows for sure I'm queer now. I guess I'm glad it happened."

At first Charlie thought he was dreaming. The ring tone sounded distant, underwater. He rolled onto his back and opened his eyes, flinging his arm across his face. The phone went silent, and he flopped onto his side, drifting back into sleep, when it started ringing again, insistent. This was no dream. It was three in the morning and someone was calling him. He jumped out of bed, scrambling for the phone. He heard the squeaky bedsprings and creaking floorboard on the other side of the bedroom wall. That fucking Larry Coleman had woken his mother. The fat fuck—well, he wasn't fat anymore, but he was still a stupid fuck—must have over-indulged in his excellent stash and now, high as a kite, his eyes bloodshot, he was sitting on the edge of his bed in his underwear, stuffing his face with Pringles and pork rinds, deciding the middle of the night was a convenient time to call and cry about the breakup, not giving a rat's ass who he dragged out of bed. But the garbled, panicked voice on the line wasn't the one Charlie expected.

"Slow down, KC. I can't understand you. What happened? Why are you crying?"

Charlie tried to stay calm, hoping his steady demeanor would settle KC down. He was frightened by the power of KC's emotions, shaken and unsettled by the sudden fragility of the mighty KC at Bat.

"I . . . I think he's dead."

KC struggled with those few words, lapsing back into tears.

"Who?" Charlie asked, doubtful that the death of KC's stepfather or one of the orange-haired half brothers would arouse such deep feelings of grief. It was his grandfather, of course, the beloved Pop-Pop, who must have finally answered the Call Home, leaving KC behind, alone and unloved. Charlie was close to tears himself, the phone call irrefutable proof that his feelings for KC were reciprocated, that he was the person KC would turn to for compassion and affection in his time of crisis.

"Can I come over?" KC asked. "Please."

The question was a punch in the gut, forcing Charlie, for the first time in his life, to choose between conflicting obligations, between his romantic duty to KC and a filial promise to his mother. He would have to compromise, try to satisfy everyone, and likely end up pleasing no one.

"Where are you?" he asked.

Between wet, rattling sniffles, KC said he was parked behind the 7-Eleven.

"I'll be there in five minutes," Charlie promised, grabbing his pants and a shirt off his bedroom floor, running barefoot out of the house when he couldn't find his sneakers. The glowing orange tip of a burning cigarette meant his mother was smoking on the patio, but she either didn't see him or more likely ignored him, already knowing where, or at least to whom, he was running in the middle of the night. He took a few hits of the weed he'd found tucked into the sleeve of the shirt Larry had given him earlier that night, just enough to calm his nerves. He'd never come to anyone's rescue before; it all seemed almost unbearably romantic. He and KC would drive somewhere secluded—he was sure he could persuade KC to overcome his aversion to marijuana on this special occasion, for medicinal use—and afterwards he'd hold KC in his arms while he cried, grieving for the Pop-Pop who had thrown him his first ball.

But he arrived to find KC's car deserted in the parking lot, unlocked, windows down. He opened the driver's door, looking for the keys, and banged his head against the roof, startled, when he realized there was blood on the steering wheel and the door handle, a handprint smeared on the windshield. He panicked, thinking KC had been ambushed by junkies looking for money for a quick fix; he must have tried to fight them off and been beaten to a pulp, his wallet stolen and his broken body dumped in some secret hiding place. Maybe they were coming back to steal the car, and, finding Charlie, they'd batter him with the same clubs they'd used on KC. He ran back to his own car and locked the doors, furiously punching 911 into his cell when he heard KC shouting his name.

KC was stumbling across the lot, shirtless, missing one shoe. His face was bloodied, and his right eye was swollen nearly shut, barely visible through a narrow slit in the puffy bruise. His hands dangled from his forearms as if they were damaged, and he limped, dragging a stockinged foot behind him.

"Get in the car! Hurry up!" Charlie shouted. "We're going to the hospital!"

KC slumped in the seat. When Charlie turned the key in the ignition, he told him to turn off the engine. He dropped his head into his hands and started sobbing. The steering wheel and bucket seats made a comforting embrace awkward and difficult, but, with a few twists and contortions, Charlie was able to take KC in his arms, letting him cry into his shoulder, holding him until his neck was stiff and his back ached. At first, he assumed he was mistaken, that the words KC mumbled into his chest couldn't have been what he'd thought he'd heard. But when KC looked up to see his reaction, his face almost hideously contorted by anguish, he repeated the shocking statement, a confession Charlie wasn't sure he wanted to hear.

"I think I killed him, Charlie. I think he's dead."

"Who? Who died, KC? Your Pop-Pop?" Charlie asked, unable to believe KC had committed a dark and terrible crime.

"No. No. Not Pop-Pop. Darrell Torok," he admitted. "I'm gonna go to Canada. Tonight. Before someone finds him. Come with me, Charlie. Please!"

Charlie could barely recognize the confident, swaggering

boy he'd first seen strutting across the wet floor of the high school locker room, his bare feet slapping the puddles of shower water, proudly letting his long dick flop against his thighs. That boy had been everyone's hero, admired and envied by all. Tonight KC was just a frightened and confused kid, a sweet and wounded soul, who, lost and alone, had reached out to Charlie, needing his help. Charlie was bound to save him, do anything in his power to rescue him.

"I'm not going to Canada, KC."

KC sat up in his seat and smiled, knowing, as always, he was on his own.

"Neither are you," Charlie insisted. "You're gonna play in the big leagues someday."

"I fucking killed him, Charlie. You don't understand."

"I don't get it, KC. Why would you kill him?"

Charlie lit a small bowl and offered it to KC, who, under the circumstances, didn't protest or decline.

"It's too fucking weird," KC said, exhaling. "I don't want you to think I'm some kind of freak."

Charlie knew he was expected to reassure KC that nothing KC could say to him would ever cause Charlie to accuse him of being odd, strange, some kind of pariah.

"Tell me," was all he could manage.

He braced himself for the confession. Several times since the night in Darrell's hot tub he'd wanted to confront KC about what had happened after he'd passed out on the lawn, but he could never summon the courage to ask, never finding the right moment to bring up the dreaded subject. Now that he was on the verge of hearing all the dirty and disgusting details, he suddenly didn't want to know.

"He told me I was going to be somebody someday. A New York Met, maybe a Yankee. An All-Star. A millionaire. I've known him since junior Legion ball, when I was fourteen. He asked me if I wanted to make fifty bucks a day, helping him at his farm. Sometimes I'd stay the whole weekend when Ed and my mother were at Lake George. Ed was

glad to be rid of me, and it made it easier for my mom if I
wasn't around. Darrell was real good to me, paid for equipment, spikes, sneakers. He was the one who drove me all
over New York and Pennsylvania and New England when I
was playing travel ball, not my mother or her fucking husband. Darrell helped me get into junior college when I didn't
get drafted out of high school. He gave me plane tickets to
Florida and sent me money when I didn't have anything
to eat."

"Did he do stuff to you, KC? Weird stuff?"

"Can someone make you a homo, Charlie?" KC asked,
avoiding the question. "I wasn't like this before I met him,
not back then. I mean, I knew I didn't like girls. But I wasn't
queer. When did you know you were a homo, Charlie?"

Charlie exhaled, remembering how, even at the age of six,
his pulse would race and his cheeks would flush whenever
rough-and-tumble Tommy Cochran, the seven-year-old who
lived next door, would wrestle him to the ground. Tommy
would wiggle and writhe on top of him, refusing to release
him until he surrendered, frustrated that Charlie, a skinny,
weak kid, would never cry uncle. Charlie had always known.
Always. From the moment he first opened his eyes.

"I don't know," he said. "I can't remember."

"I knew about you. Everyone at Augustinian knew about
you. You and that fat kid."

Charlie was indignant, insulted, but mostly he was ashamed.
He'd been a fool, deluding himself that his secret had been
well hidden, that he'd been a master of disguise.

"Once I almost talked to you," KC admitted. "You were
sitting at the cafeteria table, alone. I sat down with my lunch.
I figured I'd just kick the shit out of my teammates if they
gave me crap about talking to a fag. But that fat sissy came
and sat down with you, so I left."

Charlie remembered the day well, how nervous he was
when KC dropped his tray on his table. His leg was shaking,
and he pretended to be too absorbed in *Raise High the Roof*

Beam, Carpenters to notice an uninvited intruder, hoping that KC wouldn't see his eyes drifting over the top of his book. KC's memory was inaccurate. He *had* spoken, asking Charlie if he was reading the book for English class, looking astonished when Charlie answered no. KC had crushed his milk carton in his fist and stood up to leave when Larry Coleman arrived and plopped his fat ass at the table.

"Darrell says fags are disgusting, like Elton John and Doogie Howser," KC said, taking another hit off the bowl before breaking down into tears again. "I don't think you're disgusting, Charlie. Do you think I am?"

Charlie put his arm around his shoulder, embarrassed and ashamed to discover he was aroused, that more than anything in the world, he wanted to lie on top of KC naked and kiss him on the mouth.

"I thought he was my friend," KC sobbed, trying to catch his breath. "One night we got a little drunk and he asked me if I ever thought about doing it with another guy. I told him no, and he said, yeah, that would be weird. He asked me if I wanted to lie on his bed and watch porn. After that first time, we'd drink some sliv or beer, get relaxed, and when I got a buzz, he'd tell me to take off my clothes and lie on the bed and play with myself. Most of the time he never even took his dick out. He said he'd do it later. I didn't want him to use his camera, but he promised me he'd never show anyone those fucking movies."

Lights. Fucking camera. Action. The fucker was video-taping KC jacking off, homemade porn, just like his sweet, nasty, homemade wine. "A fucking pervert!" Charlie shouted, unable to control his anger.

"He called me tonight. I hadn't been out to the house since, you know, that weird night you came out to the farm. I've been staying away since you and I started hanging out. But he sounded really sad, like he was crying. He said if I came over tonight he'd never ask me again. He was drunk when I got there. He was real nice and friendly at first, said he wanted to give me money for Florida. He tried to kiss me, put his hands down my pants, but I told him I didn't want to do that kind of stuff with him anymore, that we could still be friends but that was all. He said I was an ungrateful little cunt, a fucking faggot. He said he'd saved the videos of me playing with myself, talking dirty, using a fucking dildo; he'd burned them all on discs and was going to send them to any team that ever scouted me, to everyone.

"I fucking hit him. He hit me back. I wanted to kill him, smash his face into the wall. So I did. I hit him hard, with my fists. He went crazy, punching me, kicking me in the gut. He was like some animal, so I threw him against the wall. He hit his head against the table when he fell. There was blood everywhere. He was lying on the floor, didn't get up. He's fucking dead. I know it."

Despite the weed he'd smoked, or maybe because of it, Charlie's head was clear, his thoughts rational, logical, precise. The plan was simple: no complications, no possibility for error.

"Where's your phone, KC?"

KC pulled it out of the pocket of his jeans and looked up at Charlie, the perfect soldier, waiting for orders.

"Call him."

KC did as instructed, asking no questions.

"Now hand it to me."

Just as Charlie suspected, the sight of a little blood had inflamed KC's imagination. Darrell Torok answered the phone after three rings, his voice thick with booze and phlegm.

"I'm gonna break your neck, you little motherfucker," the coach spat, coughing into the receiver.

Charlie took a deep breath and prepared to speak, more confident and assured than he had ever been. He barely recognized himself as he took command.

"It's Charles Beresford, Mr. Torok."

"What the fuck do you want, you little faggot?"

The insult merely boosted his confidence.

"You know my dad. His brother is the chief of the vice division of the Albany police. I'm gonna call him and report you."

"For what?"

Darrell's unsteady voice betrayed him.

"KC was fifteen when you started making those videos."

"You fucking little fairy. Don't you fucking threaten me."

"They're gonna get a search warrant. Go through your fucking house, your computer, everything you own, you piece of shit. They're gonna arrest you, throw you in jail, you fucking pervert."

The line went dead. Charlie handed KC the phone and kissed him on the mouth.

"That asshole is running through the house grabbing every video he ever made. He's gonna have a nice little bonfire tonight," Charlie said, laughing. "Don't worry, buddy. You're safe."

"You're not gonna call your uncle, are you?" KC asked, one threat to his reputation headed for the flames while another was about to surface.

"Don't be stupid," Charlie said. "My uncle drives a beer truck. I don't know any cops."

KC stared at Charlie, his eyes brimming with wonder and respect. Then he blushed, looking abashed by the one last confession he still needed to make.

"That night you came out to the farm, Charlie," he said, looking away. "He wanted you and me to, you know, let him watch. He wanted to make a video of us. He said it would be fun, that you'd like it. He wanted me to ask you."

Charlie stared at him, not comprehending, unwilling to believe that KC had been so ready to betray him.

"But you got sick, so I never had to tell him no. He got real pissed, blamed me for letting you get so drunk. He called me your girlfriend, your little sissy bitch. He said we were just a pair of faggots."

KC's phone was ringing and Charlie picked it up to answer.

"Don't. It's him," KC said. "He knows he acted stupid. He wants to apologize. I don't want to talk to him."

Charlie started to protest, but simply turned off the phone, understanding that later in the day or tomorrow or next week or next month, the phone would ring again and KC would answer. He'd resolved nothing, rescued no one, hadn't saved KC from Darrell Torok. All he'd done was let his friend know he wasn't alone, with no one to call in the middle of the night.

Hours later, they were awakened by a tap on the car window. A Pakistani boy wearing a red cashier's smock was staring at them, obviously surprised to discover a pair of shirtless young men asleep in each other's arms in the backseat.

"Guys, wake up!" he said nervously. "If my parents find you out here, they'll call the cops."

Charlie knew there would be hell to pay for blowing off work, both he and KC no-call, no-shows. He was prepared for the consequences, half hoping to be fired when he punched in the following day. The dispatcher gave him a cursory, halfhearted chewing out, then handed him his assignment, saying he hoped whatever Charlie had been doing the night before last was worth missing a day's pay. He expected KC's punishment to be equally benign and was only slightly surprised, no red flags raised, when the dispatcher stopped KC as he strolled through the door, telling him Ollie Ryan wanted to see him in his office right away. Charlie lingered over the doughnut box, waiting for KC to return, picking through the rock-hard cake donuts, searching for something edible to put in his mouth.

"Let's get a move on, buddy," Bruno shouted, beckoning Charlie toward the front door.

"I'm waiting for KC," he protested.

"Don't worry about KC," Bruno said, and Charlie noticed the look shared between the driver and the dispatcher, finally sensing that something was amiss as KC came storming down the hallway, his face red and twisted with rage. He snatched his time card and punched the clock, then reconsidered, tearing it into pieces that he threw at the dispatcher's face.

"Keep your fucking money, asshole!" KC shouted as he slammed the door behind him.

Charlie threw his doughnut on the floor and went running after him, chasing him across the lot. He pounded on the window of KC's car as he tried to drive away, pleading with him to tell him what had happened, what had gone wrong.

"That fucker fired me. That fucking dirty piece of shit."

"I don't fucking believe it. They didn't do anything to me. He hardly said anything at all. How come they fired you?"

"Because I quit his stupid team. All he cares about is winning some cheap trophy to put in his fucking office and I fucking quit. Darrell called last night to tell me the schedule for the final round next week, and I told him to go fuck himself."

Charlie announced he was resigning on the spot in solidarity. He was done hauling their goddamned furniture, finished, kaput.

"Naw, don't get into trouble because of me," KC said, his anger quickly passing at the prospect of an entire day ahead of him with nothing to do. "I'm going back to Florida soon anyway. Call me later tonight. We'll hang out."

Oliver Ryan got his trophy for his custom-built display case. All it cost him was a manila envelope stuffed with two thousand dollars in crisp new fifties to persuade KC to change his mind. Right up to the moment of the final pitch, a long fly ball landing safely in KC's glove, Charlie was certain that KC had a secret agenda to throw the game, either by purposefully swinging at balls outside the strike zone or failing to chase down easy outs or attempting boneheaded plays on the base paths. But KC played like a house on fire, batting over .500 in the semifinal and championship games, driving in more runs with his bat than the entire rosters of the teams he almost single-handedly defeated. No one but Charlie seemed to be aware of the tension between the coach and his star. Only Charlie saw KC turn his back and walk away each time Darrell Torok approached him. No one connected the dots between the contusions on their faces. Darrell mumbled some excuse about spraining his wrist repairing a piece of machinery, when Charlie's father, who'd come with his wife to witness Oliver Ryan's moment of triumph, commented on the ACE bandage on his right hand.

The celebration on the field was blissful chaos, a jumble of exuberant boys tossing their bodies onto a dog pile. Only KC stood apart, limp as a rag doll as his teammates embraced him. He seemed lost, almost friendless, as he stood in the infield, searching for someone or something on the sidelines, smiling only when he sighted Charlie standing with his parents, waiting to offer their congratulations. Charlie's father pumped KC's arm, lavishly praising his efforts on the field.

"I don't see your mother here," Charlie's mother commented. "Did your parents leave before the end of the game?"

"They're away," KC explained. "They couldn't make it."

Oliver Ryan's bellowing voice summoned KC back to the field for the team photograph with the treasured trophy. He announced there would be a victory dinner that night at the Cheesecake Factory. Later, Charlie assumed, there would be unsanctioned and unsupervised celebrations involving kegs of beer and Captain Morgan rum.

"I guess I got to go. Thank you for coming," KC said quietly, looking down at his shoes.

Charlie's mother, ever vigilant, sensed some untold story, some shameful secret behind the young man's bruises.

"We're having spaghetti and meatballs for supper," she said. "There's plenty for everyone."

"Awesome," he said, his face brightening. "I'll be back in three minutes. Don't leave without me," he shouted as he ran off to preserve his moment of triumph for posterity.

They had one last weekend together before KC flew to Tampa–St. Pete. KC insisted they do something special, out of the ordinary, something different from hanging around the family room watching *Field of Dreams*. Charlie suggested they go to New York, find some really cheap hotel, go to a few music clubs, get tickets to a Yankees or Mets game if KC wanted to see some baseball. KC visibly squirmed at the prospect of wandering the streets of Manhattan. Charlie suspected it might have even scared him. KC said he had a better idea. Ed and his mother and the kids were in the western part of the state, attending Ed's brother's daughter's wedding in Elmira. The weather at Lake George promised to be spectacular, no rain in the forecast, the night sky so clear they could count the stars in the sky. They would have the cabin to themselves. KC would take Charlie fishing and they would fry up the catch for dinner. Charlie, less than thrilled, agreed, trying not to sound reluctant, squeamish at the prospect of being forced to gut cold, dead animals.

The cabin wasn't a building at all, but a double-wide trailer parked on a foundation of cinder blocks, hardly the idyllic, rustic, split-log sanctuary Charlie had imagined. The furniture was cast-offs from the Albany house, frayed and musty, the cushions damp from the humidity, and the water from the spigots was suspect, with a flat, metallic aftertaste. The cupboards were stocked with canned peaches and SpaghettiOs, instant coffee, and powdered creamer. KC said they should use the public latrine and that the shower hadn't worked for years. He'd barely locked the front door behind him when he threw Charlie on the bed Ed shared with his mother, stripping off his clothes, some demon inside him unleashed, insisting Charlie fuck his tight ass. He took it from behind, then flipped on his back, rolling on all fours again, finally shooting his load into the pillow Charlie assumed must be Ed's. After they'd finished, they lay naked on the bed, not talking, listening to the sounds outside the open window—birds and insects, a boy calling out to his dog, the lake water slapping the dock where the Conroys kept their boat.

"I wish we could stay here forever. Just you and me," KC said, his voice sounding almost regretful. "Promise me you'll never tell anyone about Darrell Torok. Promise."

Charlie swore he would never say a word, ever, even if it meant lying under oath. He knew KC was nervous about going back to Florida, though he wouldn't admit it. He'd gotten a call from his junior college coach, good news: KC was one of the lucky few invited to work out with the players on the Mets Instructional League roster, a showcase for scouts rating prospects for next summer's draft. But Charlie sensed KC dreaded being alone again, having gotten used to having Charlie around, someone to talk to, or more often not talk to, when he was feeling down.

"I'll come visit you in Florida. On break," Charlie promised.

"No. You won't," KC said, sounding experienced and worldly-wise.

There was an ancient sound system in the trailer, a receiver and tape deck and turntable, all too obsolete for the main residence in Albany. The radio reception was weak during daylight, but stronger at night. After midnight, KC sound asleep beside him, Charlie lay in bed, listening to a station he'd found on the FM band, a broadcast from a small local college, the DJ playing tracks he might have chosen himself, new bands like The Drums and Real Estate, old-school classics by Luna. His mind raced ahead to the future looming only a few weeks away; all the uncertainties, the challenges, of his new life suddenly overwhelmed him, frightening him, and, like KC, he wanted only to be able to stay here forever, safe and secure. He burrowed his smaller body into the warm crevices of KC's larger, stronger one, waking KC, who squeezed his hand and grunted something into his ear, something that sounded like *I love you,* before falling back into a deep sleep.

On Saturday, they took the boat out on the lake, stripping down to their shorts. The sun was hot, the glare from the surface of the water unforgiving, and when the heat became unbearable they tossed away their underwear and dove into the cool water of the lake. Too far from any other boats to be seen, they jerked each other off underwater, their feet paddling furiously to keep them from sinking. KC laughed hysterically, almost drowning, when Charlie screamed like a little girl, startled by an aggressive smallmouth bass that leaped from the depths of the lake, a shot out of still waters, its gaping mouth swallowing the little puddle of his semen floating on the surface.

Charlie's worries about cleaning his kill proved completely unfounded. They didn't catch a single fish; KC barely got a bite, and Charlie never dipped his line in the water. Dinner was hot dogs bought on a run to the local Price Chopper and dessert was an Entenmann's crumb cake. KC said his stepfather would never miss what they took from the cases of cheap beer, Bud Lite and Genesee, stockpiled in the trailer. Charlie smoked a bowl of pot, and later a second, though KC declined, fearful of facing random drug tests when he returned to play ball in Florida. They built a campfire and lay on their backs, listening to it sputter and crackle as they tried to identify the constellations overhead. They agreed on the Big and Little Dippers, but nothing else, so they made up their own names, competing to see who could come up with the grossest, stupidest things to call the ridiculous patterns in the sky. *Sagging Titties. Dick Dripping Cum. Turd-filled Asshole.*

They were drunk and happy when they stumbled into the trailer, KC falling into bed. The radio reception was terrible that night, and Charlie couldn't find the college station again. He flipped through a stack of KC's mom's old vinyl albums, looking for something soft and romantic for their last night together. He pulled out an ancient James Taylor record, the one where the smiling troubadour is wearing suspenders on the cover. He remembered how much he'd loved it when his mother had played it for him as a child, and dropped it onto the turntable. Crawling into bed, he pulled the sheets up to their shoulders as he and KC lay quietly, listening to the gentle, soothing music.

"That song's really pretty. Play it again," KC asked, and Charlie jumped out of bed and placed the needle at the beginning of the track.

"That's not easy," Charlie said as he crawled back under the sheets. "It took me forever to learn how to play the last part," he admitted, remembering the difficulty of mastering the intricate coda of "You Can Close Your Eyes."

KC sat up in bed, a look of shocked amazement illuminating his face.

"You can play guitar?"

"Sure," Charlie said shyly, realizing how little KC actually knew about him and all the things Charlie needed to say to him before he boarded a plane for Florida.

"How come you never told me?"

"I don't know. I thought I did," he mumbled, knowing that he hadn't.

"I wish we had a guitar here so you could play for me."

"I'll bring it the next time I see you," Charlie promised, reaching over and taking KC's face into his hands as they listened to Sweet Baby James sing his farewell lullaby, *you can sing this song when I'm gone.* Maybe someday, sooner than he could ever have expected at that moment, he and KC would drift apart. The time might come when it seemed important that KC had never read a book, that he watched the same movies over and over, that he could embrace only the familiar, the routine, a life of practices and drills and games, and dreaded change of any type. But at least for those last few hours, if Charlie could have had one wish, it would have been to have the power to stop the sun from rising in the morning so he and KC could lie together forever in the dark, not needing to speak, not wanting to move, not needing anyone else in the world.

Charlie still had a week left on his sentence at Ryan Allied Van Lines after KC boarded a flight for Tampa–St. Pete. His days and nights were consumed with regrets—plans they'd never made, things they hadn't done, conversations they'd never had—and his heart was heavy with the nagging fear that they would never have another opportunity to share the hundred, thousand, million things Charlie wanted to share. He tried to convince himself otherwise but was stricken by an almost paralyzing fear that the last chapter of their story had already been written. He wished he'd been nicer to Larry Coleman, understanding now how badly a broken heart felt. He'd even called Ticketmaster for tickets to Sunday's Bon Iver show in Utica, planning to invite Larry to make amends for his bad behavior, only to be told the concert had sold out weeks ago.

He retreated to the basement of his parents' house in the evenings, smoking endless bowls as he struggled to figure out the chords to all of Ricky Nelson's greatest hits, planning to record instrumental versions of the songs with his acoustic guitar for a disc he would mail to KC once he knew his address. He called and texted KC, getting no response. His stomach was twisted into a tortured knot, unable to tolerate more than coffee and American Spirits and small bites of cold pizza slices. He felt incurably sick each time he heard "Lonesome Town," the horrible pain in his gut making him almost regret ever meeting KC. By Thursday morning he was so distracted he lost his footing humping cartons of books down a steep staircase, almost causing Bruno to go into cardiac arrest when he found Charlie sprawled on the floor, certain he had broken his neck.

"One more day, buddy," the dumb Polack sighed in relief when Charlie pulled himself to his feet, shaken but unharmed. "Try not to kill yourself before tomorrow afternoon."

At precisely six forty-seven p.m. on August twenty-sixth, Charlie was released from prison, a free man at last. He punched his time card, intending to go home and pack while he listened to pathetic emo and tried to resist calling KC's voice mail, just wanting to hear his voice.

"Get in the fucking truck, buddy!" Bruno shouted, his words harsh but his tone surprisingly affectionate. "You don't think you're blowing off my fucking party, do you, you fucking little sausage. Not after I carried your scrawny ass all summer long."

It was Bruno's last day, too, the end of an era. Three decades of hauling furniture—thirty years of broken bones and sprained muscles, torn ligaments, and crushed fingers and toes—had taken their toll. Bruno was moving to El Paso where his daughter and her family were stationed, a warm, dry climate that might provide some relief from his constant aches and pains. He'd booked a private room at the Rendezvous Hideaway, a "gentleman's club" a few rungs up the ladder from the last establishment Charlie had frequented with Bruno. The bouncers were a fierce-looking crew, bursting at the seams from steroids. But they were friends of Bruno's and were willing to admit Charlie on Bruno's sworn oath that he had taken the kid's car keys and would deliver him safely home at the end of the night. Bruno gave the bartender his credit card, with instructions to keep running the tab until it maxed out at a thousand bucks. *After that these clowns can pay for their own drinks.* The dispatcher appeared at his side and tossed five hundred in cash on the bar to add to the tab, a gift from Ollie Ryan himself, in appreciation for the physical sacrifices Bruno had made for Ryan Allied Van Lines.

The bon voyage was rowdy and loud, occasionally necessitating the intervention of the humorless security staff. Bruno's old nemesis, the *Hills Have Eyes* mutant, was the first to be bounced. Bruno kept a cautious eye on Charlie throughout the night, but there were ample opportunities for the heartsick romantic to toss back shots while the man of the hour was distracted by more-provocative-than-usual farewell lap dances. The more Charlie drank, the sadder he felt, KC never far from his thoughts. The tequila loosened his inhibitions, making him want to unburden himself on Bruno, who, fortunately, could barely understand the slurred syllables rolling off his tongue.

"You're a good kid, buddy," Bruno assured him. "Now you're gonna let me take care of that little problem of yours," he said, whispering into the ear of one of the dancers, negotiating the terms of a transaction. The girl pulled on a T-shirt and sweatpants and, taking Charlie by the hand, walked him to a dirty old Chevy Malibu in the parking lot. She laughed as he swayed at the knees as she moved a child's car seat out of the backseat. She gently pushed him into the car, onto his back, and undid his zipper, pulling his pants to his ankles.

"Someone's excited," she giggled as she squatted on top of him, guiding his hard penis inside her, placing his hands on her soft little titties as she went to work.

He woke around noon on Saturday, the pain in his skull far more intense than a mere headache, with only the vaguest of memories of being rolled into his own bed. He was certain he was dying or maybe already dead. He had barely enough strength to crawl to the bathroom, and his vision was blurry when he tried to read the messages on the screen of his phone. KC had texted six times after midnight and left a voice message when Charlie never responded. *Hey, buddy, where are you? I miss you, man. Call me back,* which Charlie did immediately, getting only a recorded message, the one Charlie knew by heart. *Yo. I'm busy right now. Call ya back.*

He'd recovered enough by late afternoon to look presentable for the family celebration before his imminent departure for Dartmouth. His father had made reservations at a pricey steak house, no jeans or collarless shirts permitted. Madeline was moody, claiming she couldn't wait for Charlie to leave so she could inherit his flat-screen television, but her eyes started to water at every mention of Dartmouth. Before dessert, his father proposed a toast, telling Charlie how proud he was to have a real Ivy Leaguer as his son.

"Did you have a nice summer?" his dad asked as he sipped his whiskey and ginger ale.

"It was okay," Charlie mumbled, regretting that his eyes were brimming with tears, thankful, as always, for the thoughtful kindness of his wise, omniscient mother, who rescued him from embarrassing himself by threatening to drive to New Hampshire and throttle him if he didn't call home at least once a week.

The first thing Charlie did after arriving at Dartmouth was sign up to volunteer at the college radio station, offering free labor for the promise of an hour or two of airtime if one of the graveyard shift DJs got sick or, more likely, too high to spin a disc. His schoolwork was easier than he'd expected, and he thanked the Augustinian order for preparing him to keep pace with the alumni of New England boarding schools. The school paper accepted several of his record and concert reviews, only a few paragraphs in print to be sure, but a start nonetheless. More important, it was his introduction to the Dartmouth underground scene, such as it was, aspiring musicians and poets and graphic artists whose parents were paying exorbitant tuition for their self-absorbed kids to lie in bed until noon and spend their days drawing comic strips and recording DIY demos instead of going to class.

His new acquaintances were determined to impress, trumping each other's claims to-have-been-the-first-to-see-the-band-of-the-moment-in-some-obscure-hole-in-the-wall-club-back-in-high-school, though Charlie doubted their stories. He suspected that doormen in Hammond, Indiana, and Missoula, Montana, and even the cities of Boston and Philly and New York, were no more lenient about admitting baby-faced teenagers with crude fake IDs than they had been in Albany. He worked hard to cultivate friendships, eager to belong, to be accepted, to have his opinion solicited and respected. He dreaded appearing hopelessly clueless, no better than a frat boy or Young Republican who considered Coldplay to be the pinnacle of musical achievement.

"Dude, what the fuck are you listening to?"

Samuel Chatwick Lowell was a tall, lanky blond with sloping aristocratic cheekbones, almost comically large hands and feet, and an imperious manner that made him seem like he was in total and complete control of his world. More important, he'd already published a poem in the school literary journal and was the last person in the world Charlie wanted to catch him sitting on his bed with his guitar, trying to pick out the chords of a track of a Black Keys recording.

"Ah, man, my friend Larry at Syracuse has to review this shit, and he asked me to read his draft before he submits it. I think he fucked up a chord progression," Charlie explained, a convincing enough lie for one concocted on the spur of the moment.

"My little brother at Milton loves these dudes," Sam said,

dismissively. "I guess it could be worse. His roommate is so lame he thinks Nickelback are genius."

He laughed and plopped himself on Charlie's bed, reaching for the Yuck album jacket lying on the dustcover of the turntable.

"Dude, I fucking love this band! I knew there was a reason I liked you. You wanna get high?"

Whenever he was stoned, which was often, Sam would brag about his exotic sexual adventures at St. Paul's, on weekend escapes to Boston, and, of course, whenever he was home in New York, where his father was a financial asset manager for important clients in the arts. He was always casually dropping names that meant nothing to Charlie, dinner party guests at his parents' Upper East Side home, like the leading tenor at the Met and the neo-Expressionist painter whose retrospective had broken attendance records at MOMA. Sam claimed to be pansexual, a sexual "amoeba," whatever the fuck that meant, and he seemed knowledgeable about fetishes and orgy etiquette, but Charlie suspected his experiences were secondhand, something he read in a book, and that Sam was, in fact, a virgin, timid when it came to the actual physical act. Charlie understood he would have to make the first move. He realized he'd come a long way in a very few months as he confidently unbuckled Sam's belt, undid his zipper, and yanked his pants over his size-fourteen feet.

Six weeks after arriving in Hanover, Charlie had staked a claim to a small piece of uncharted territory. The future was still murky, but Albany was in the rearview mirror, starting to recede into the past. He was working in the library one rainy Tuesday night, struggling to discover some original approach to *Gilgamesh* for the paper he was writing for his Western Civilization survey course, when his ring tone announced an incoming text message.

Happy birthday buddy thinking of you

KC was off by one day, remembering Charlie's birthday

as Halloween when he was actually born on the thirtieth of October. But he'd done much better than Charlie, who'd forgotten KC's own birthday two weeks earlier, allowing it to pass unacknowledged.

Hey thanks. U 2

What r u doing

Writing a paper

About what

Charlie couldn't grapple with trying to explain *Gilgamesh* to KC in a dozen or so text characters.

Just stuff, he responded.

Call me sometime

Okay

C u

U 2

He called KC's house when he was back in Albany for Thanksgiving break, but his mother said he was in Puerto Rico playing in a holiday invitational tournament. They exchanged a few texts on Christmas Eve, and Charlie invited him to the house on Christmas night, even getting a bit excited at the thought of him and KC sleeping in his boyhood bed again. KC said he couldn't get away, but he still had another week before he went back to Florida. Charlie, however, was taking a train to New York first thing on the morning of the twenty-sixth, as Sam would have his parents' apartment all to himself after his family left to spend the rest of the holiday in Snowmass. That was the last Charlie heard from KC until he was awakened by an early morning phone call, six a.m., on a bitterly cold Saturday morning in February. KC was back in Albany: Maybe he could drive over to Hanover and spend a couple of days? Sure, that would be cool, Charlie said, knowing his roommate was skiing in Killington until Tuesday and he had the room to himself.

"Who was that?" Sam asked as Charlie slipped back under the mountain of blankets, his skin almost blue and his teeth chattering from the cold.

"A friend from high school. He's driving up to see me later today."

"Is he cute?"

"Not really," Charlie lied. "I guess he's okay," he conceded, wishing he'd been quicker on the draw, able to come up with some excuse why KC shouldn't visit.

"Hey, buddy," KC said shyly when Charlie met him outside the dorm. He was unprepared for the New Hampshire winter, shivering in his nylon official Clearwater Thrashers windbreaker. "So this is where you live?" he asked, waiting for an invitation to come in out of the cold.

KC was starving after the long drive, and they walked to a pizza joint, where he attacked a large pepperoni. Casual conversation could wait. He looked different to Charlie, older, more like a man, no longer a boy. He hadn't shaved for a few days; the stubble was rough, masculine looking. More shocking was his buzzed scalp; his head seemed larger without his crown of wild, unruly curls. He looked like the pictures of soldiers being sent off to the Middle East, their big, dark eyes glowing like headlights, staring into uncertain futures. Charlie realized a stranger was sitting across the booth, one he couldn't ever imagine having loved. A friend of Sam's from St. Paul's wandered into the restaurant, and Charlie buried his face in the menu, avoiding eye contact, not wanting to introduce KC, embarrassed by his white sneakers and warm-up jacket and the lingering scent of department store cologne KC always wore when he cleaned himself up.

"What do you want to do tonight?" he asked KC after they finished the last slice.

A new band from Montreal with a lot of buzz was playing at a local club. Everyone Charlie knew would be there, all the more reason to go to a movie at the metroplex off-campus where they'd be unlikely to encounter any of Charlie's friends. One look at KC and Charlie would be exposed

as a fraud, a geeky hick from a shitty part of Albany where
no one had a passport and a vegetarian lifestyle was considered an eating disorder.

"Whatever. I don't really care. It's just good to see you,"
KC said, smiling. He spoke in a low, confidential voice,
barely audible, making sure he couldn't be overheard, as if
they were still sitting in McDonald's back home and expressions of affection needed to be whispered. "You look really
handsome with that beard, Charlie."

His shy sincerity made Charlie feel like a perfect shit, a
frigging asshole, no better than the Dartmouth snobs he pro-
fessed to loathe but ached to impress. It was good to see KC,
too; he'd forgotten how black his eyes were, the way they
seemed to light up whenever he smiled. His new haircut took
some getting used to, but now that he was over the shock,
Charlie wondered how it would feel to run his palm across
the stubble on his scalp.

"Let's go hear this band from Montreal. They kind of
sound like Beirut," Charlie said, drawing a blank stare. "You'll
like them," he assured KC. "And the club is pretty cool."

KC didn't say a lot at the concert, always quiet by nature,
more so whenever he felt self-conscious. His team jacket
glowed like bright red neon among the thrift shop overcoats
favored by the Dartmouth underground.

"You wanna check our coats?" Charlie asked, hopefully.

"Naw, I'm okay, buddy."

Ordinarily, Charlie would try to work his way as close to
the stage as possible, but tonight he and KC lingered in the
back of the club, by the bar, on the sidelines. Most of his
friends simply ignored KC; none of them asked his name.
Sam was polite, shaking KC's hand when introduced, then
turned his back, inflaming Charlie's jealousy by engaging in
a heated discussion with a handsome junior about the merits
of the band's set. When KC went to the bathroom, a girl
Charlie knew from the poetry slam said his friend was cute,
but she couldn't get past the haircut. The program director at

the station mocked KC, calling him a bobblehead doll. The consensus was KC was classic rock and could never appreciate the band's virtuosity with feedback. He knew he should defend KC, but had to concede they were right. Charlie regretted his impulsive change of heart; it was a mistake bringing KC here, thinking he could fit in. They should have gone to the movies, some stupid slasher flick, and KC could have squeezed his hand in the dark like he had last summer, back before everything changed.

"Do you still listen to Ricky?" KC shouted over the noise.

Charlie kept nodding his head to the music, ignoring the question, pretending he hadn't heard.

After the concert, Charlie shrugged off an invitation to a house party, saying KC was beat after the long drive. Back in the dorm room, KC, sensing he'd disappointed Charlie, undressed and crawled into the roommate's bed and turned his face to the wall. Charlie lay on his back, torn between divided loyalties, his old life and the new, finally asking KC if he wanted to share a bed.

"Hell, yes!" he answered, rolling over and tossing off his covers.

KC didn't protest when Charlie reached for the condoms he kept by his bed. For the next few hours it was still last summer and nothing had changed. KC's body felt right with Charlie's; they still fit together perfectly, much more so than he and Sam ever could. There was genuine affection and an insatiable hunger in KC's kisses that Charlie had missed. KC thrashed on the bed like a wild man when Charlie penetrated him, his fingernails drawing blood on Charlie's back. They spent the night on that tiny mattress, KC sleeping in his arms. But in the morning, Charlie was relieved when KC said he had to leave early, before breakfast, that he'd just remembered he had something he had to do, somewhere else he had to be.

"You coming back to Albany this summer?" KC asked as he stood by his car.

"Yeah, probably," Charlie said, knowing he'd already made plans to intern in Boston.

For three and a half weeks, Boston was everything Charlie had hoped it would be. Sam Lowell's sister, a Harvard fine arts graduate student, was spending the summer as a studio assistant to a famous sculptor in Rome and offered to sublet her apartment near the Tufts campus to her little brother and Charlie at a reasonable rent. Charlie's internship at the weekly alternative newspaper was unpaid, forcing him to take a job selling cheap, overpriced clothes to fake hipsters at Urban Outfitters so he could pay his share of the expenses. The days were long and the work depressing—running the copy machine and updating advertiser contacts from nine to five, then enduring the haughty condescension of spoiled coeds from six until ten. Sam, of course, never woke up until one or two in the afternoon, when he'd gather his laptop and trudge to the local coffee shop to work on his novel in progress, a self-described Dennis-Cooper-meets-Haruki-Murakami-but-it's-totally-original-and-not-like-anything-you've-ever-read. After three weeks, he announced he was flying to Rome to chill with his sister until fall semester began. No worries, he assured Charlie, agreeing to live up to his promise to pay half the rent on the sublet through the month of August.

Somehow Charlie managed to survive the rest of the summer alone, subsisting on ramen noodles and six-packs of cheap beer. He slept around a lot, sometimes having more than one partner a night, even agreeing to an occasional threesome, preferring to arrange his assignations on Craigslist so he wouldn't need to spend his tiny discretionary income on the steep admission the flashy gay dance clubs charged for all-ages nights. In August, he started dating an Irish guy from Dorchester who was studying law enforcement at Suffolk. Brian O'Mallory wasn't very hip to the indie music scene and didn't know Mike Watt from Thurston Moore, but he loved the *Ricky Nelson's Greatest Hits* disc he'd found in the jumble of old CDs on the backseat floor of Charlie's car. He was low-key and easy and Charlie could relax and be himself with him, not always trying to be hip and intellectual. He spent the last weeks of the summer drinking with Brian in cheap dive bars that never carded, playing darts and the jukebox, making plans to spend next summer together in Provincetown bussing tables and doing menial restaurant work.

Charlie finally returned to Albany for his "vacation" a week before the fall semester started at Dartmouth, his only agenda to sleep until noon every day and stuff himself with his mother's cooking until he burst at the seams. But he arrived home only to discover the menus in the Beresford household hadn't improved from the haphazard mealtimes during his mother's recovery, though for far happier reasons. Charlie's mother, never one to do anything halfheartedly, was consumed by her new passions, yoga and cancer survivor support groups. Her afternoons and most evenings were fully booked with classes and gatherings and lectures. His father seemed to be a bit of a lost soul, clearly wistful for the old days when it was their children, not esoteric outside interests, that distracted his wife from showering him with loving attention. Her mornings were always free, however, and she insisted Charlie eat a big, hearty breakfast while he was home. Charlie couldn't refuse the stacks of blueberry pancakes and scrambled eggs, bacon and sausage (links and patties), scratch biscuits and gravy, steel-cut oatmeal, fresh baked scones, all of it washed down with buckets of orange juice and bottomless cups of premium coffee.

"You should call KC to see how he's doing," she announced unexpectedly on Wednesday morning while cutting him a generous serving of apple crumb cake after he'd polished off a huge bowl of fresh fruit and yogurt and homemade granola.

"I think he's in Florida," he mumbled, stuffing his face. "Or Puerto Rico maybe. I'm pretty sure he's not in Albany anymore," he insisted, turning his attention to his *The Walking Dead* comic book, a new obsession recommended by Brian O'Mallory.

"His father was killed yesterday afternoon. It was on the eleven o'clock news."

Charlie swallowed hard, shocked to be sure, but hardly saddened. He'd never even met the man and what he knew of him was awful.

"That's not his father," he explained. "It's his stepfather."

"Well, it doesn't matter now. He's dead. A terrible accident."

Drunk behind the wheel, Charlie assumed, probably drove his car through a guardrail, a head-on collision with a utility pole. KC's stepfather was an alcoholic, a mean and bitter asshole who berated and belittled his stepson whenever he had too much to drink.

"He was working construction at a building site downtown. The scaffolding collapsed. Three fellows were killed. I expect they all had families."

"KC didn't even like him. He'd call KC all kinds of terrible shit when he was drunk. KC's probably glad that he's dead."

"It wouldn't hurt for you to call him, Charlie," she said, her voice heavy with disappointment that her once sweet and thoughtful son had grown up to be such a selfish and callous young man.

After breakfast, Charlie went online, searching for the gory details of the accident, finding nothing but the bare-bones reportage. He tried calling and texting KC several times, the last time just before midnight, getting no response.

"I'm sure he's busy with his family. His mother must be a wreck," Charlie's mother suggested when he reported his futile efforts at breakfast, assuming she would consider his obligations as supportive friend had been fulfilled. "It would be nice if you stopped by the viewing tonight," she said, handing him the funeral arrangements she'd clipped from the obituary announcement in the morning paper.

She offered to drop him off on her way to yoga class, but he said he'd take his own car, causing her to arch a skeptical eyebrow. He spun around the block three times, tempted to just drive away, but, in the end, he feared his mother's uncanny ability to detect even the tiniest white lie even more than the possibility of a cold, maybe blatantly hostile, reception by KC at the funeral home. He took a last long drag on his cigarette and straightened his tie, rehearsing in his mind the words of sympathy he would offer his friend.

A pair of rambunctious orange-haired boys were chasing each other around the parking lot, their loose shirttails flailing behind them as they shouted obscenities that were mildly shocking in the mouths of children Madeline's age. They were undoubtedly the stepbrothers, real Conroys in their father's eyes. The little girl screaming to get their attention was clearly their sister. Two rough-looking young men with shaved heads and pierced ears, smoking their cigarettes down to the filters, shouted at the kids to settle down or they'd be sent back inside. No one seemed overwhelmed by grief.

The funeral parlor was an old Queen Anne in a residential neighborhood, with large windows that flooded the house with light and heat, challenging the overworked generator of the air conditioner. It was hard to breathe in the stuffy viewing room; the sickly sweet scent of floral tributes was overpowering. Charlie didn't know whether to blame the temperature or his nerves for the sweat dripping from his armpits. Overdressed women wearing too much makeup and potbellied men in shirtsleeves milled about, consoling one another, everyone a witness to the deceased's high moral character and the goodness of his heart.

There was an eight-and-a-half-by-eleven framed photograph displayed on the lid of the closed casket, a family portrait of Ed Conroy, his wife, and their three biological children standing on the dock at Lake George. There was no mistaking the woman greeting the mourners who lined up to offer a few kind words of condolence. KC's mother was tall and thin, still attractive after years of the wear and tear of a difficult life, her face cut with dark angles and creased by thousands of cigarettes, too many Percocets, and a nightly habit of indulging in cheap wine. Her hair was too long, too dark for a woman her age, but her eyes were compelling, fierce black orbs, like those of her firstborn son. Charlie shuffled his feet as he waited his turn to speak, trying to think how to introduce himself, finally settling on being a high school friend of KC's.

"I know you," KC's mother said as soon as he told her his name. "We've never met, but I know who you are. KC took you to the cabin once."

"Yes, ma'am," Charlie said, blushing at the memory of KC intentionally defiling her late husband's pillow.

"KC talked about you all the time last summer. About how smart you were. He was real proud that a boy like you wanted to be friends with him."

Charlie was speechless, dumbfounded. KC had rarely if ever spoken about his family, and Charlie had assumed he lived among them as if they were strangers, saying little, certainly not sharing intimate feelings and thoughts. Even more shocking was the revelation that KC had been impressed, even intimidated, by his intelligence, the only proof of which Charlie had ever given him was carrying around an unread copy of *Infinite Jest* the entire summer.

"I haven't seen him yet. There's a lot of people around," he said, trying to change the subject.

"He's not here," she said, her voice heavy with sadness, but also defiant, as if she expected to need to mount a defense to explain his suspicious absence.

"Oh, okay," Charlie said, not daring to question where he was or what he was doing.

"We'd heard he was drafted by the Mets this summer. Ed

was following him on the *Baseball America* page on the Internet. KC's in Tennessee, playing in the rookie league. Kingsport. I think that's the name of the town. He won't return my calls. I left him messages, asking him to come home for the funeral. I haven't heard a word from him."

"I tried to call him, too, but he wouldn't answer," Charlie said.

"He'll come back soon to see my father. He loves that crazy old man."

He felt awkward, standing by the casket, waiting to be dismissed, but she seemed reluctant to let him walk away, picking up his hand, pulling him ever so slightly toward her. A couple approached to pay their respects and she turned to speak to them, thank them for their words of comfort. She tightened her grip on Charlie's wrist, making it impossible for him to escape.

"Ed tried hard, kept trying for years, but KC always resented him," she said, turning her attention back to Charlie. Charlie looked around the room, hoping some other mourners would rescue him.

"I don't know," he finally said. "We never talked about stuff like that."

"What did KC tell you about the last time he was home, after his Pop-Pop had a stroke?"

"Nothing . . . I don't know. I haven't talked to him in a while."

"Ed, well, Ed found this stuff on KC's computer, terrible stuff. We had two young boys at home he had to think about. I think KC went to see you at your college when Ed told him he had to leave."

He felt himself flinch, ever so slightly, before freezing his features into an implacable mask. Charlie saw her trying to read the expression on his face, undecided if he was one of *them,* too; he sensed she was wavering, not knowing if she should challenge him or recruit him as an ally. He suspected that Ed had left her in dire straits, with three kids to raise, and that KC's signature on a professional contract was a powerful incentive for a loving reconciliation.

"He's a good boy. He really is. I'm sure that you are, too. You tell him to call his mother when you speak to him," she said, releasing her grip. "His brothers and sister need him now."

Afterwards, Charlie sat in his car, fumbling with a cigarette, his hands shaking too badly to light it. He dialed KC's number, knowing he wouldn't answer, intending to leave a long message, apologize for being such a thoughtless asshole last winter when he'd let KC walk away without ever asking why he had sought him out. He would plead with KC to return his call, swear that he had KC's back, forever and always. He would promise to never, ever betray KC to his mother, disclosing his whereabouts. KC could stay with him whenever he wanted, for as long as he needed. He'd prove he could be trusted. All he needed was another chance.

But KC had taken a preemptive strike, discontinuing his phone service, putting an end once and for all to unwelcome and painful intrusions from the life he'd left behind. *You can't get away so easy. You're not that smart. I'll call the nursing home. They'll know how to reach you,* Charlie swore. He rifled through the CDs scattered on the floor, unable to find the one he wanted, then remembered giving *Ricky Nelson's Greatest Hits* to Brian O'Mallory. So instead he drove the familiar streets of Albany with classic rock on the radio, songs his father still listened to, Boston and Foreigner, music his Dartmouth friends would laugh at as ridiculously lame but that Charlie secretly loved.

When the gas tank was nearly empty, it was time to go home. His mother was back from yoga, her car parked in the driveway. He knew his parents would be sitting in the family room, laughing at the stupid jokes on *Two and a Half Men* while Madeline complained she didn't understand what was so funny. He'd join them in a minute, sit in his favorite chair eating a bowl of chocolate ice cream, his nightly ritual back in high school, when it felt like nothing in the world would ever change, that everything would always be the same. But first he tried calling KC one last time, hoping his service had been miraculously restored. An automated voice assured him the number was still no longer working. He took a drag off his cigarette, then tossed the butt onto the lawn, fighting back tears, regretting his stupid mistake, having only himself to blame. He would be nineteen in a few months, older and more worldly than the boy he'd been only a year ago, but still young enough to believe that nothing again would ever hurt as much as knowing he'd let his friend slip beyond his grasp, the Mighty KC at Bat lost forever, only a name he might read in the sports pages someday, a face on a trading card, an elusive hero playing in the network Game of the Week, wearing a Mets uniform, poised, waiting for the fastball down the middle, taking the perfect swing, hitting a walk-off home run.

TRAVELIN'
MAN

Gratitude to Mitchell Waters who suggested I check in with KC again, and to John Scognamiglio who agreed.

Except a man be born again, he cannot
see the kingdom of God.
—John 3:3

Travelin' Man

"Come on, honey. You gonna make me get down off this stage and drag your pretty little ass up here?"

Even after three Jack and Cokes, he knows this isn't a good idea. He shouldn't even be here. He ought to be home, in bed, sound asleep. He's gonna wake up in the morning, just like the last time, and the time before that, and swear he'll never do it again, that he's done with *all that*. It's always easier to keep to the straight and narrow when the team is on the road, when he's without his wheels, and he's stuck bunking with three or four teammates in a crummy Days Inn where the rooms are so small they can't escape the stink of each other's craps. They pass the time playing Texas Hold 'em and sharing a few buckets of KFC and a couple of sixes of cheap local beer. It gets monotonous, living out of a duffel bag, but at least there aren't any opportunities to get into trouble.

But back here in Spokane, in the cramped, two-bedroom monthly lease he shares with two roommates, he gets antsy, bored with television and *Call of Duty*. Tecchio, the older of the two, has been kicking around the minor leagues for years and is at the end of the line; he's practically shacked up with the dental hygienist he's thinking of settling down with after the season. And Rodriquez is only eighteen, a few months out of high school, and homesick. He travels eighty miles to spend the night at his mama's house whenever he can. KC doesn't really like Tecchio's company. But he's happy enough to hang out with Rodriquez, watching idiots eat earthworms on stupid reality shows and ordering pizza. KC's afraid to be on his own, with too much time on his hands and the freedom to disappear for hours on end with no one to question his comings and goings. He'd tried running with the wilder boys on the team, prowling the local titty bars, getting soaking drunk, and ending the night at Asian massage parlors. But he'd ended up paying the girl a hundred bucks for her silence, knowing he'd never live it down if his teammates knew he couldn't get hard. So he stays at the apartment, alone most nights, with the lights turned off, watching the Mariners play on cable and listening to his Pop-Pop's old vinyl records on his turntable.

He calls California every night to check in with Coach Freeman. They talk about the day's game and Coach gives him an inspirational pep talk and a few Bible verses, then leads him in a prayer. KC listens quietly and promises to avoid temptation, to have faith in the Lord, Our Father, and to call if he's feeling sad and troubled, no matter the hour of the day or night. He tries falling asleep, reciting the words to the prayers the Freemans have taught him. But it's hard to concentrate. His mind is on other things, things a true Christian man would never think about. Sometimes, he'll try jacking off in the bathroom which only makes him hornier, so he'll reach for his iPhone, exchanging messages with strangers on Scruff and Grindr. Or if he's too impatient to wait for the slow drivel of essential information—WHERE R U, HOW BIG, C OR UC—he'll grab his jeans and his boots and run off seeking heat and noise, music and people, dancing and drinking, somewhere to lose himself in a crush of sweating bodies, everyone drunk and high and happy.

"Are you bashful, handsome?"

The voice is mocking, playing to an appreciative crowd that loves nothing better than watching a strapping looker like KC, a young man attainable only in their boldest fantasies, being taunted, nudged just to the brink of humiliation, by a scrawny, raspy-voiced transsexual named Darlene Duncan wearing a garish dress and stiletto heels. KC's up for the challenge and, tossing back a fourth Jack and Coke, climbs up onto the stage. He ignores the nagging voice in the back of his head warning him tomorrow morning is only a few hours away. He'll wake up with a throbbing headache and sunlight will feel like a hot iron pressed against his eyes. Somehow he'll manage. He'll make to it the ballpark and after he laces up his cleats, he'll be the Mighty KC again, shrugging off last night's excesses as easily as swatting away a mosquito.

"Cat got your tongue? Come on stud, stand up straight and let everyone take a good look at you."

Darlene struts across the stage, coyly brushing her body against KC's, letting her manicured talons settle on his crotch, giving his cock a gentle squeeze.

"Oh my!" she sneers. "Maybe you're not so shy after all! What's your name, big boy?"

KC leans forward and squints into the stage lights, searching for any familiar faces in the rowdy room. It's cool. No one he knows in Spokane has paid a ten-dollar cover to see this show. None of his teammates on the Chiefs would be caught dead in this place. He mumbles into the mike.

"Speak up, baby. Ricky, he tells me," she informs the audience. "This pretty little thing's name is Ricky."

All eyes are on him. One squat drunk troll rips open his shirt and bares his man boobs, wagging his tongue lasciviously.

"Come on, Little Ricky, don't keep your adoring public waiting," she urges him, apparently needing to pick up the pace of the contest.

It's fun, basking in the cheers. It's not all that different from the frenzy whenever he makes solid contact with a ninety-three mile an hour fastball or slides feet-first into home plate. He pulls his brand new red polo, its bright color still unfaded by detergent and the heat of the dryer, over his head. He feels their eyes roving his smooth, taut belly, following the faint wisp of black hair that snakes around his navel. Someone hands him a beer and he tips it into his mouth, chugging it in a single swallow. He takes a deep breath when he finishes. He feels light-headed, truly, deeply drunk. He thrusts his arms in the air, Rocky-style, and bends at the waist, drawing appreciative catcalls as he flexes his biceps. His pecs and abdomen are truly a wonder to admire. He's too swept up in waves of appreciation to notice that Darlene is annoyed by losing control of her audience, irritated at being upstaged by an amateur.

"Settle down, cowboy," she snarls. "Those go, too," she insists, pointing at KC's feet.

Darlene seems disappointed he doesn't take a drunken tumble, but KC is forever graceful, even in a state of advanced intoxication. He reaches down and pulls off his boots and his socks, balancing himself on a single foot without effort.

"Take your pants off now," Darlene says, barely concealing her contempt, eager to move on to the next, presumably more malleable, contestant in the Club Odyssey Wet Briefs competition. But tonight KC is a showman, flirting with his fans, showily unbuckling his belt, teasing them as he plays with his zipper, making them beg for more as he slowly reveals the hard muscles of his legs.

"Looks like we're blessed with a professional Chippendale tonight," Darlene says into the microphone, her voice dripping with sarcasm as she pushes KC towards a small plastic wading pool at the center of the stage. "Go on. Get in there. You're not going to melt."

KC slaps his bare feet in the shallow water. He knows the

entire room is staring at his crotch. His fans are getting restless. A few of them shout for him to take it off, begging for
at least a peek. He hooks his thumb under the elastic waistband and slowly pulls his briefs away from his skin, teasing
them with the promise of a glimpse of the fat dick cradled in
his underpants. Darlene slaps his hand hard, the cruel edge
of her voice making it clear she's not fucking around.

"Don't even think about it, asshole. I don't need the fucking cops in here threatening my license."

The crowd turns on her, booing and hissing her surprising
Puritanical streak.

"Fuck you all," she bellows, her voice full of fake cheer,
trying to salvage the situation. "I have a better way to show
you what Little Ricky's packing."

Darlene grabs a huge plastic Super Soaker and strikes a
commando pose, taking aim at KC's Jockeys. The water is
shockingly frigid, as if she were punishing KC for stealing
the show. The wet cotton clings to his skin and he feels his
penis shrinking, retreating into the safety of his body. The
cold water trickles down his thighs, sending goose bumps up
and down his legs.

"Turn around now Cowboy. It's time for us to all get a
good look at that tight little butt."

His impressively toned glutes and the well-defined crack
of his ass are a big hit with his appreciative audience.

"Thank you Little Ricky. You can step out of the pool and
let us all get a good look at our next contestant."

Darlene flashes him a look of pure malevolence. He's having
fun and doesn't understand why she won't play along. Impulsively, he grabs her by the hips and starts dry humping, pan-
tomiming a good butt fucking. The crowd roars, nearly tearing
off the roof. The sharp point of her elbow finds its target. The
pain in his groin is excruciating, worse than a kick in the
balls. She spins on her heels and smashes his nose with the
microphone, then grabs him around the neck and throws her
legs around his waist, sinking her teeth into KC's cheek. It

drops him to his knees. Enraged, a fierce, primal sound coming from his throat, his hands find her throat and he squeezes the breath from her puny body, slamming her head against the stage, sending her blonde wig sailing into the audience. She struggles, her long nails seeking his eyes, trying to blind him.

It's all a fucking blur from that point forward. He feels the firm grip of hands on his shoulders and the strength of three, maybe four, men prying him off the screaming drag queen. A fierce-looking dyke dives at Darlene, restraining her in a headlock. Someone is screaming *find his fucking clothes, get him the fuck out of here.* He hears a distant siren and more loud voices shouting. A few drunks are still laughing, urging KC to kill her, *kill that fucking cunt.* The cops arrive, seeming almost bored at being called to break up another catfight between a couple of fucking fairies. The younger officer, a boy with smooth, hairless cheeks, says he thinks KC's nose is broken and he needs to go to the emergency room. An older cop, clearly in charge, asks if anyone is pressing charges. KC shakes his head no, but Darlene is screaming like a banshee, insisting *that motherfucking faggot tried to kill me. I'm pressing charges.*

"Okay ladies, let's go," the older cop says, telling his partner to cuff the two of them and toss them into the patrol car. "Tell them to be nice to each other. To kiss and make up," he says sarcastically. A bitch match in a queer bar is lower on his priorities than even a domestic disturbance. The other cop, blonde and baby-faced, is polite to KC, almost gently leading him to the patrol car. Their eyes make contact and KC realizes he's been recognized. The young officer feels bad for the tall, broad-shouldered, handsome All-American Boy. He can't return KC's fake ID with a date of birth that would make him twenty-three, but assures him he'll see it gets "lost" before his belligerent older partner discovers it. He tells KC, who is quietly crying, not to worry, that he doubts he'll actually get booked. The nasty little drag queen, unfazed by her circumstances, is assessing the state of her makeup in her reflection in the window, muttering obscenities under her breath because the fucking cops won't let her smoke.

"I seen worse. No point in getting an x-ray. I seen enough broken noses to know you got one. They ain't gonna try to set that whopper 'til the swelling's gone down. It's gonna be two weeks before they'll touch it."

The Spokane Chiefs are vital contributors to the local economy and a source of municipal pride. Generations of drunken minor league ball players have been hauled to the police station in the back of a patrol car. Discreet calls are made and a club official drags his ass out of bed in the middle of the night to take custody of the latest bad boy to run afoul of the law. None of them ever get booked. Rumor has it that last year's National League MVP once struck a young man on a bicycle while driving under the influence in Spokane during his minor league career. The team paid off the family and the story never made the newspaper. Alan Chandler, the team's athletic trainer, has spent his entire adult life working in the low levels of professional ball and he thought he'd seen it all until tonight. None of his boys has ever been picked up in a queer bar.

The baby-faced cop offers KC a can of Coke. Mr. Chandler asks if the officer can bring him towels—paper will do if he can't find cloth ones. Just make sure they're clean. And bring ice. Plenty of ice. At least five or six paper cups filled with ice.

"You're a real bleeder son," Mr. Chandler says. His voice is gentler now, almost paternal. "This is gonna hurt like hell."

"I know."

"It's the only way to stop the bleedin'. Don't start squirming," the older man says as he places his fingertips on KC's nose and pinches.

KC nearly passes out from the pain and he's sure he's gonna vomit, but he manages to keep from spewing a belly full of beer and Jack Daniel's all over the station floor.

"You gotta breathe through your mouth, KC," Mr. Chandler cautions when, after what feels like an eternity to KC, he finally stops the flow of blood from the boy's nostrils. "Don't blow into your hankie, and, whatever you do, don't stick your finger up there when it starts to itch. Keep this ice pressed up against your nose as long as you can. Don't worry. I think you're gonna be even prettier than you was before," he teases. "Now stand up real slow now. You're gonna feel real lightheaded when you get up."

Mr. Chandler thanks the young officer for his help. KC turns away when the cop tries to shake his hand as they leave, unable to look him in the eye.

"KC, this young man is being polite to you. He's treated you better than you deserve and this is how you thank him?"

KC, abashed and almost paralyzed by shame, offers his hand and expresses his gratitude.

"That must hurt like a motherfucker," the cop says. "Stay out of trouble, my friend."

Mr. Chandler's car is a rusty old Buick. He warns KC to be careful; the springs are poking through the upholstery of the passenger seat. KC shakes his head no when Mr. Chandler asks if he's hungry *(Stop that boy, you hold that head still)*, but they pull into the parking lot of Denny's anyway. Mr. Chandler says they need to stop and get more ice.

"Try not scare the waitress with that face of yours," Mr. Chandler laughs as he opens the door of the restaurant for KC.

The after-hours drunks have cleared out and the early risers whose shifts begin before sunrise haven't begun to arrive. The waitresses gossiping at the register look annoyed at this unwelcome intrusion on the short respite between waves of demanding customers. An old lady at the counter, likely homeless, is peering into the pages of a paperback, a small heap of torn, empty sugar packs beside her coffee cup. The pain grows more intense as KC sits quietly, barely moving or speaking, trying to avoid Mr. Chandler's gaze.

"I'm gonna let you have three of these," the old man says, pulling a prescription bottle from the pocket of his jacket. "Go ahead. Swallow one now. Save the other two for when it hurts so bad you can't stand it anymore. Don't you go telling anyone I gave them to you."

KC stares at the pills in his hand.

"What are they?"

"Just Percocet. Go on. Two or three ain't gonna hurt you."

"These ain't gonna show up on a drug test, are they?"

Mr. Chandler shifts in his seat, clearly uncomfortable. He hesitates before speaking, carefully choosing his words to deliver the message with as much kindness as possible. It's impossible to soften the blow. There is no easy way to tell KC he's been cut from the team.

"You got a disease son," the old man says, one that, in his opinion, requires KC's swift expulsion from the roster. Not that he had any say in the matter mind you, Mr. Chandler reminds KC.

"I hope the other fellow's looking worse," the waitress says as she hands KC an improvised compress of ice wrapped in a dishtowel.

Mr. Chandler waves away the plastic menus she offers and orders a Coke for KC, then changes his mind, telling her to bring the kid a chocolate milkshake as he needs something heavier in his stomach. He orders a decaf for himself and again reconsiders, asking for a regular cup of coffee as he won't be going back to sleep at this hour. She can bring him a slice of lemon meringue pie too.

"Sorry, KC, but Keller says you got to go and he owns the team. He said he don't want to see your face again when I called him to tell him you'd been in a fight in a queer bar and the police were holding you until someone came to pick you up. He says the Spokane Chiefs ain't having any fruitcakes on the roster. Only the name he called you wasn't as nice a fruitcake," he chuckles.

"I got a contract!" KC protests, knowing that a stupid piece of paper means nothing to an owner determined to purge a clubhouse cancer.

"Look, you call your agent about that in the morning. Nothing you and me can do about it right now. I feel for you, young man. I really do. Someday you're gonna have to face the Lord and account for your sins. *Do not lie with a man as one lies with a woman, that is detestable.*"

"Leviticus 18:22."

The old man is surprised by KC's familiarity with the moral lessons of the Good Book.

"See. You already know."

The Percocet is beginning to take effect. The pain is dulled and each surge of panic and anxiety is milder, followed by long moments of peace, almost serenity. Soon enough, KC is swelling with confidence, knowing exactly the words Mr. Chandler wants to hear, a reason for the old man to go back to Keller and ask him to reconsider.

"I'm saved, Mr. Chandler. I accepted Jesus Christ as my Lord and Savior. Last year. Just call Coach Freeman. He'll tell you. Just ask Tecchio and Rodriquez," he pleads, citing his roommates as character witnesses. "They make fun of me for studying the Bible every night."

Mr. Chandler winces as he leans across the table, asking KC to turn his face so he can get a better look at his cheek.

"I was so busy worryin' about your nose I didn't even see that. What happened to you KC? Looks like something bit you. You're gonna need a tetanus shot."

The old man is shocked by the tale of a man in a woman's dress sinking his teeth into KC's flesh. He waves his hand, not wanting to hear the gory details. It's unsettling to him, the thought of young people acting like savages, their demons unleashed by liquor and drugs. He looks at KC as if he's toxic.

"That thing that bit you probably got AIDS," he says solemnly.

KC's stomach heaves when he realizes he could be infected. He bolts from the table, knocking over his milkshake, barely making it to the toilet before he throws up the entire contents of his belly. He's broken and despondent, knowing he's lost everything tonight. Mr. Chandler finds him on the floor, hugging the porcelain bowl.

"Come on, boy, pull yourself together," Mr. Chandler says, as KC struggles to his feet, blood dripping from his nose again. "If you're truly saved, you know the Son of God will forgive you if you come to Him with a clean heart."

KC stares at his image in the mirror above the sink. His bloated face looks like a lumpy pillow. There are two black slits where he once had eyes. Mr. Chandler, standing next to him, looks almost sympathetic. The old trainer was once a ball player too, a lifetime ago. Mr. Chandler accepted Jesus Christ as his Savior after a life of whiskey and whoring had driven his wife and kids away and cost him his chance of reaching the major leagues. KC straightens his spine and, lifting his chin, picks up Mr. Chandler's hand and asks if he'll pray with him. The old man reacts as if KC had just slapped a red-hot poker in his palm. He plunges his hands in nearly scalding water from the spigot, pumping half a dispenser of pink liquid soap into his palms, scrubbing away any lingering trace of KC on his skin.

"Keller said to let you have a week of per diems. That ought to get you where you need to go," he says, coldly.

"My car's still in the parking lot. Can you give me lift?"

Mr. Chandler agrees, reluctantly, knowing it wouldn't be very Christian of him to abandon the kid in a Denny's rest room. Mr. Chandler cranks up the volume of the car radio, tuned to the gospel music station. KC and the old man only speak so that KC can give him directions. Club Odyssey, the scene of his downfall, was once a K-Mart, the anchor of a strip mall that's fallen on hard times. The only other tenants are bail bond shops and nail salons, a Chinese take-out and a laundromat. At this hour, there's a single vehicle in the lot. KC's heart sinks when they're close enough to see the damage some vandal has done to his Blue Pearl Honda Civic. All four tires are slashed and the headlights and taillights have been smashed by a blunt instrument. The word FAG is spray-painted on the windshield.

"Can you take me home Mr. Chandler?" he asks, his voice weak and defeated.

"I can't have someone like you in my house," the old man says unapologetically.

"No. I mean my apartment."

"Keller don't want you back there around those other boys."

"Fuck him!" KC shouts, immediately regretting using such offensive language to a Christian man like Mr. Chandler. "I mean I paid for it. Two hundred fifty dollars this month."

Mr. Chandler considers KC's argument. They drive until they find an ATM and he asks KC to wait in the car. When he returns, he reaches to press a stack of fresh bills in KC's hand, then reconsiders, setting them on the dashboard.

"That's two hundred fifty dollars. Go ahead and count it. I'm gonna take you over to the Travel Lodge. Put you up for three nights. Paid in advance on my credit card. I'm gonna make sure you get your per diem in cash and someone will bring you your clothes. I'm gonna be praying for you KC. Praying that you find your way."

The banging on the door forces him from his bed. KC's still half-asleep, groggy from the second Percocet he'd swallowed after the pain jolted him awake when he'd rolled on his face. He doesn't remember where he is, why he's awakened in this strange room. Then it all comes crashing over him. The broken nose. The cops. Being cut from the team. Having nowhere to go and no way to get there. The pounding is louder now, more insistent, as he stumbles towards the door.

"Who is it?"

The simple act of speaking causes his face to ache. *Breathe through your mouth,* he remembers Mr. Chandler telling him.

"Housekeeping. You want your room cleaned today?"

"No," he answers, then remembers every towel in the room is either soaking wet from melted ice or damp with blood.

He opens the door, thinking it's early morning, and is surprised by the streaks of fading violet in the twilight sky. He calls after the cleaning lady, who is pushing her trolley down the concrete deck, "Wait!"

The housekeeper turns and stares at him, indifferent to both his battered face and the fact he's wearing nothing but his underwear. "Make up your mind. My shift's over in fifteen minutes."

"Can I have clean towels, please," he asks sheepishly, suddenly stricken by an attack of modesty. He crosses his legs and covers his crotch with his left hand.

"You need toilet paper?" she asks as she hands him a stack of towels.

He thanks her and closes the door to his room. He's overwhelmed by his circumstances, then panics, fearing that, sometime last night, he'd lost his cell phone. He finds it in the pocket of his jeans, but the battery's dead and he has no way to recharge it. His spirits soar when the phone in his room rings. It must be Mr. Chandler or someone else from the Chiefs, telling him to come to back to the ballpark, that he's being penciled into the lineup card, that all is forgiven and forgotten. He makes a quick bargain with God before picking up the receiver, promising to do whatever He asks if only things will go back to the way they were before last night.

"It is the registration desk calling," a heavily accented voice announces. "There is a man here for you. He says you must sign."

He dresses quickly and races to the office. He'd hoped the team would send a familiar face, a sympathetic ear willing to carry back his promise it will never happen again. But it's a stranger in a FedEx uniform who asks him to sign the receipt for the sealed envelope and the duffel bag with the Spokane Chiefs insignia. The courier scowls when he realizes he isn't getting a tip.

"Open the bag please," the dark-skinned man at the registration desk insists when they are alone. It's a command, not a request, polite but firm. The man speaks with authority. He's formal and dignified despite his short-sleeved sport shirt and sandals.

"It's just my stuff," KC explains, not wanting to dump his dirty laundry on the floor.

"Open the bag, please. I must be sure you are not having drugs delivered to my place of business."

KC is relieved that his phone charger is the first thing he finds when he unzips his bag. The man at the registration desk seems satisfied, saying he has seen enough, when KC pulls the Holy Bible from the duffel.

"How many more nights do I have?" he asks, uncertain how long he's been asleep, how many days since Mr. Chandler rented the room.

"Two nights. Your friend paid for three nights. Last night. Tonight. Tomorrow. Then you pay eighty-nine dollars a night to stay longer. In advance."

KC plugs in his phone as soon as he returns to his room. There are eight missed calls and three voice mails. All from Sacramento, from Coach Freeman's phone.

KC, it's John Freeman. I just got a strange call from the Chief's general manager. What's going on up there? Are you all right? It sounds like there's been some kind of big mistake. Call me as soon as you get this.

KC, I thought I would hear back from you. I called your g.m. again and he said I need to talk to you and your agent. That the Chief's lawyers told him not to discuss this with me. I don't understand why they are doing this to you. We're getting worried because you haven't called us back. Here, Miriam wants to say something to you.

Mrs. Freeman sounds more anxious than her husband.

Please call and let us help you, KC. John will get this fixed. I promise. Don't forget that we love you.

And, finally, one last message left in mid-afternoon.

KC, we've been calling every emergency room in Spokane. Where are you? Call me as soon as you pick this up.

No one from the Chiefs has called. Not Mr. Chandler. Not the business manager. None of his teammates. There's exactly two hundred and ten dollars in the envelope, seven days of per diems and a copy of the letter from the law firm representing the Chiefs to KC's agent formally informing him his client's contract has been terminated for breach of the morals clause. There's also a sheet of notepaper tucked under the cover of the Bible. Citations to Bible verses are printed in Mr. Chandler's handwriting.

Genesis 18:22-23.

The men turned away and went toward Sodom, but Abraham remained standing before the Lord. Then Abraham approached Him and said: "Will you sweep away the righteous with the wicked?"

And.

1 Corinthians 6:18-20.

Flee from sexual immorality. All other sins a man commits are outside his body, but he who sins sexually sins against his own body. Do you not know your body is a temple of the Holy Spirit who is in you, whom you have received from God? You are not your own; you were bought at a price. Therefore, honor God with your body.

And, finally.

Acts 3:19.

Repent then, and turn to God, so that your sins may be wiped out, that times of refreshing may come from the Lord.

He rips the paper into pieces that he flushes down the toilet. He's got more than four hundred dollars between the per diems and the cash from the sanctimonious reformed drunk. The money isn't enough to salvage his car. It won't pay for new tires, let alone replace the head- and taillights and remove the paint from the windshield. But he's got almost a thousand in his checking account. Fourteen hundred bucks should cover the repairs if he settles for retreads. He grabs his wallet, locks the door to his room, and goes in search of an ATM. The desk clerk says there's a machine at the convenience store across the street that charges a fee and a Wells Fargo branch two blocks away. He receives the same ominous message at both of them, TRANSACTION UNAUTHORIZED. It's only eight o'clock. Not too late to reach Frank Stapleton, his financial advisor, on his cell. And it's an emergency. He desperately needs his wheels back.

"KC, it's eleven o'clock at night," Mr. Stapleton's sleepy voice reminds him when he answers the phone. KC'd forgotten about the three-hour time difference between Spokane and Tampa.

"I'm sorry, Mr. Stapleton. But I need to talk to you."

"I've been expecting your call, KC. John said I would hear from you."

Mr. Stapleton and John Freeman have known each other since they came up together in the Pirates farm system. Their bond runs deep, strengthened by worshipping together at the New Covenant Christian Fellowship Church during the years Mr. Freeman coached junior college baseball in Tampa.

"The ATM won't take my card."

"I know KC. John told me to deactivate it."

"Mr. Stapleton, please. I really need money."

"Are you in trouble KC?"

Mr. Stapleton's voice is sonorous, like God speaking to

Moses on the mountaintop. It invites a confession and a plea for mercy.

"No. I just need money."

Mr. Stapleton reminds him his money's in a trust, with Coach Freeman as the trustee. He gets a small allowance to supplement his paycheck and, even then, he has to give a strict accounting of how he spends it. KC had agreed to the arrangement, even thought it was a good idea at the time, to ensure his future against his own bad, impulsive decisions and to put his assets beyond the grasp of his mother back in Albany.

"You know I can't send you money without John's permission. You call him, KC. Call him now. He wants to hear from you."

"I will," KC promises, a blatant lie.

"Will you pray with me now, KC?"

"No," he answers decisively as he ends the call.

Ten minutes later Coach Freeman is calling his cell. KC assumes the Coach has just heard from his friend in Tampa. He doesn't answer, letting the call roll into voice mail.

KC, call me and tell me where I can wire money for you to get back to Sacramento. I told Frank not to release any funds to you until we get this all straightened out. I talked to Jerry Breakstone at your agency and he says Bill Keller is crazy and a hothead. Jerry is calling the assistant g.m. of the Rangers about sending you to Hickory or Myrtle Beach. We know you didn't do anything wrong and that the things they are saying aren't true. The Lord is testing us, KC. We will be fine. Call me back.

Coach Freeman will know by KC's skittish response, his shaky voice, that he's lying when he denies the story the Chiefs are telling to justify their decision. The Coach will never believe KC's tall tale that he was jumped by two black guys coming out of the laundromat, that the cops got it all messed up, thinking he'd gotten into a fight with a drunk

coming out of the queer bar next door. His story sounds preposterous, even to KC. So he chooses the safer course of responding by text.

I AM OK I WILL CALL U SOON AS I CAN

Sacramento's out of the question, at least until he can
come up with a more believable explanation for being cuffed
and hauled off to the police station. He needs to get the fuck
out of Spokane, but can't even think about where to go until
he has his car back. He knows a gypsy repair shop run by
some scary Mexicans who will give him a good deal on a set
of retreads. They'll sell him used parts they've scavenged
from the salvage yard and might throw in scraping the paint
off the windshield for free. He's gonna need to pay for gas
and oil and eventually he's going to have to eat.

There's one man in Spokane who'll be willing to help.
Mr. McGwire has always been kind and generous to KC.
He's always telling KC that they're friends, good friends, despite the forty years' difference in their ages. Mr. McGwire
says it doesn't matter how they met—KC responding to a
post on craigslist by *a GEN dad seeking younger, fit son for
good times.*

Call me Red, he'd insisted, a nickname he'd been given many
years ago before his still thick hair turned silver. Mr. McGwire's
a rich dude, with a big house outside the city. Every few weeks,
KC gets a text or a call inviting him for steaks on the grill and
carrot cake. Red's made him promise more than once to
never be too shy to ask if he ever needs anything.

"Hi Red. It's Kevin," he says when Mr. McGwire answers
his phone. He's a little anxious since the unbroken protocol
has been that the older man contacts the younger to suggest
they get together. Mr. McGwire seems angry, or at least irritated, to be receiving a call from his young friend.

"I'm really, really sorry to call you," KC apologizes, regretting his impulsive decision. "But I wanted to let you
know I'm leaving Spokane."

Red's attitude changes and he even sounds concerned, asking if everything is okay. No problems or emergencies he hopes.

"No, no," KC lies. "I got promoted. I'm gonna manage a Radio Shack in Tacoma."

Mr. McGwire may be his friend, but he can't be trusted with KC's true identity. The guy Red knows is named Kevin Conroy, a shift supervisor at the electronics franchise in a mall on the other side of town.

"When are you leaving?"

"Tomorrow. I didn't know when you'd call and I wanted to say goodbye."

"We need to celebrate, Kevin! Why don't you come over around eleven? I'm at a banquet right now. I've got to give a testimonial after dinner. One of my best salesmen is retiring."

Mr. McGwire's dealership moves more Hyundais than any lot in the entire Pacific Northwest. He's got more money than he needs, but he's lonely. He's a widower and his daughter lives in California. Pictures of his grandkids are in every room of the house. They visit often, but Red is always down when they leave. His young friends are a distraction and he's willing to compensate them for their trouble and time. KC's his current favorite and always leaves with a hundred fifty bucks in spending money for doing nothing but letting Red watch him jack off.

"Remember not to leave your car out front. Park behind the garage out back."

The cab ride is twenty-five bucks, but you got to spend money to make money. Not that KC's looking for a handout or even a loan. He's gonna shoot for the moon and ask Mr. McGwire to lease him a car, maybe even an SUV, without a down payment. Red knows he's a stand-up guy, responsible, with a good job, and won't miss any payments. Maybe they can even drive to the dealership and sign the papers tonight. It's Mr. McGwire's business. He can do whatever he wants.

"Jesus Christ, what happened to you?" Mr. McGwire asks when he greets KC at the back door. He seems wary, debating whether to let him in. KC knows it must look bad. He understands why Red is cautious when a kid he barely knows, someone with whom he's spent less than six hours total, turns up at his door with a freshly broken nose and an ugly bite on his cheek.

"I fell on my face on the basketball court. They have to wait for the swelling to go down before they can set it."

It sounds reasonable to Mr. McGwire, who, thank God, doesn't ask him to explain the mysterious bite mark. He lets KC into the kitchen where his stupid little Shih Tzu is making a racket.

"Misty, you behave! You remember our friend Kevin. Now be nice!"

KC's given up trying to befriend the dog. She snaps at him if he tries to pet her and growls if he so much as says her name.

"Where's your car Kevin?" Mr. McGwire asks, looking out the window to make sure the Civic is parked behind the garage. "You didn't leave it out front, did you? I told you to never leave it in the driveway."

"No sir. It got stolen. Three days ago."

"How did you get out here?"

"In a cab."

"I hope you have insurance."

"I think so. I'm pretty sure. My mom takes care of all that stuff," he says, regretting a stupid lie that makes him sound too irresponsible to trust leasing a car.

Mr. McGwire changes the subject, asking KC if he wants to fire up the grill even though it's late. KC understands the subject of the stolen car is closed, for now at least. Red must have some kind of sixth sense and already suspects the true reason for his young friend's unexpected call.

"No. No thank you, Mr. McGwire."

"Red."

"Red."

"How about a beer then? Or a Coke?"

"Do you have any Dew?"

"Of course I *do*," Red teases and KC forces himself to laugh at the stupid joke.

Red says they should sit out by the pool and enjoy the cool breezes. It's a quiet, peaceful night. The water filter is humming and angry sounding crickets are chirping in the grass.

"In the mood for a swim?"

"I don't think so. Not with this," KC says, pointing at his damaged nose.

"Right. Probably not a good idea to get that wet."

Mr. McGwire puffs on his cigar and sips from his tumbler of scotch on the rocks. KC can see he's growing impatient; he's checking his watch every few minutes.

"Bugs are terrible out here tonight, Kevin. Let's go inside."

KC follows him into the house and up the stairs to the bedroom. Everything's set up as usual. There's a sheet draped over the upholstered easy chair beside the bed and a bottle of lubricant on the end table.

"Do you want me to take off all my clothes or just pull down my pants?" KC asks.

"I don't know when I'll see you again so let's make tonight special," the older man says as he sits on the edge of the bed.

Mr. McGwire is definitely a weirdo, but he's a polite one. He never touches KC, never takes off his own clothes, doesn't even pull his cock out of his fly. All he wants to do is watch KC jack off, then slips him the money and sends him on his way. KC feels a little uneasy about their arrangement. But Mr. McGwire's harmless, nothing like Darrell Torok, and KC is a grown man now, twenty years old, capable of making his own decisions. He's not the scared fifteen-year-old boy masturbating on camera because he was afraid Darrell would be angry if he refused. And the extra buck and a half is appreciated since he's expected to live on the lousy money the Chiefs pay and the meager allowance Mr. Stapleton deposits in his checking account.

KC sits on the chair and starts pulling on his pole. He used to feel self-conscious doing this. The first time he couldn't even get hard, but now he just closes his eyes and thinks about boys he's had sex with until he shoots his load on the sheet.

"So, are we going do something special tonight, Kevin?" his host asks, unbuttoning his shirt to bare his chest.

"Sure," KC reluctantly agrees. He ought to at least let Mr. McGwire jack him off, maybe even blow him, if he's gonna ask to lease a car without a down payment and no responsible adult to cosign. But he can't see beyond the older man's loose, flabby flesh and his chubby little man boobs and gently, but firmly, pushes aside Red's roaming hands.

"I got to go, Mr. McGwire," he says as he grabs his clothes and shoes, fleeing down the stairs and out the door. The taxi dispatcher says it will be forty-five minutes before she can send a driver and he hangs up, a seven-mile walk back to the motel ahead of him.

Darrell Torok, three thousand miles across the country, sounds high or drunk. He's not so out of it he isn't making sense, but he's definitely mellow, even sympathetic to KC's plight.

"I'll pay you back Darrell. Every penny. I promise," KC pleads.

Darrell says it feels like old times again, when KC depended on him for handouts and gifts. Every pair of spikes, every batting helmet, every gallon of gasoline to drive KC to travel ball games, every airfare between Albany and Tampa/St. Pete, all of it funded by the generosity of Darrell Torok.

"Money's a little tight these days KC. I don't know if I can help you."

KC resists mentioning that Darrell was just boasting about his new home entertainment system and the fully loaded Silverado parked in front of the barn. He needs to be careful not to piss off him off as he doesn't have anything Darrell wants any more, no currency to bargain with. Others have replaced KC in Darrell's affections. Darrell's been black-balled from coaching in the American Legion league after one of his players told his parents he'd been partying in Darrell's hot tub. The outraged father wanted to press charges even though his son insisted nothing had happened. The new friends Darrell talks about aren't ball players; he meets these young men online, responding to ads with code words—*boi seeking older, looking to PNP, have parTy favors.*

"You know I lost the election for president of the Local. Because of the shit that kid's parents made over nothing. I have to be careful with my money now."

KC knows he's bullshitting. Darrell was the only child of a pair of Slovaks from the old country, cheap motherfuckers who never spent a dime so they could leave everything they earned from their hard work and sacrifice to their beloved son. He's got plenty of money for an HD television and a new pickup and frequent vacations to the Dominican Republic and Central America where he takes provocative pictures of naked boys even younger than KC had been when Darrell started filming him while he jacked off to porn.

"I understand," KC says, deflated, bursting into tears, sobbing into the telephone.

Darrell Torok can be an asshole sometimes, but he'd always been there for KC. It's not like everything was all bad with Darrell. And making the jerk-off movies wasn't all that terrible. Sometimes it was even fun. KC wouldn't have had anyone after his Pop-Pop got demented and went into the home if he hadn't met Darrell. He'd felt safer, more welcome, with Darrell than he did in the house where his mother lived with his asshole stepfather. There was that bad time between them, a couple of summers ago, and he and

Darrell didn't speak for more than a year. But Darrell didn't slam the door in his face, didn't mock his sadness, didn't even seem surprised that KC had returned, seeking sympathy and consolation and a place to crash when he returned to Albany for his Pop-Pop's funeral.

"Hey, hey, hey," Darrell says, slightly slurring his words. "Don't cry little buddy. I didn't say I wasn't going to help you. Fuck that piece of crap you've been driving. Come on back home and we'll get you a decent car. Or a truck. You always wanted to drive a truck."

Darrell's offer is grandiose, which means he's even higher than he sounds. But it's tempting. KC's car, a Honda Civic on a three-year lease, the only indulgence Coach Freeman allowed him from his signing bonus, is a lost cause and he'd never wanted to drive one of Red's fucking ugly Hyundais anyway. He's sure he can persuade Darrell into helping him score something with a little muscle, more style. It doesn't have to be new. He'll settle for a nice used pony car, a Camaro or Challenger. He'll pay Darrell back, every last penny, when Mr. Stapleton releases his money.

"I got a better idea," Darrell says, his voice pumped with enthusiasm. "Why don't I come out there? We'll find you something out there so you don't have to drive it back across the fucking country. You can meet me in Seattle."

Darrell says he could use a little time away. The Albany police have been out to the farm, asking questions. It's fucking crazy. They'd accused Darrell's new young friend of cooking crystal meth in the barn. They didn't find anything. Darrell wanted his lawyer to sue the force for coming onto his property, only to learn that it isn't trespass when the cops have a warrant.

"Yeah, I can do that," KC says reluctantly. He feels more defeated than ever. Maybe he should just call Coach Freeman and tell him he's taking the next bus to Sacramento.

"I'm gonna go online and buy a ticket. I'll get us a nice

room, a suite in one of the good hotels near the water. It'll be fun. Stop worrying, KC. I'll take care of everything."

KC, I know you're picking up your voice mails. Please call me back. I'm worried about you. We all are. There's nothing you've done the Lord won't forgive if you're willing to ask.

Coach Freeman has been flooding his mailbox with messages. KC knows he needs to respond. The Freemans have been good to him, treated him like family. The Coach hadn't wanted KC to return to Albany the summer after his first year of junior college. He'd tried to persuade him to stay in Tampa, clearly sensing something amiss with the domestic life of the family KC rarely spoke about, and, even then, only in short, evasive answers to direct questions. They took him into their home after that trouble with his stepfather, gave him the room of their son who had died at the age of seventeen. The Coach's wife says KC's a gift from God, a blessing to help ease the pain of losing their only child.

He owes everything he's thrown away to their kindness and support. It was Coach Freeman who had invited scouts from the Mets and Rangers organizations to watch the gifted star centerfielder on the junior college team he managed. He'd hired an agent to negotiate a very generous signing bonus that Mr. Stapleton invested after the Rangers selected KC as the 94th pick in the second round of the draft. When he pulled a muscle in his groin playing in the Texas Winter League, the Coach and his wife had insisted he recuperate at their new home in Sacramento where the Coach had accepted a position at a Division II college. KC hates being cruel, refusing the Coach's phone calls, ignoring his heartfelt pleas. The Freemans deserve better than the silent treatment.

PLEASE DO NOT WORRY. I AM OK. WILL CALL SOON, he texts.

He's ashamed at his cowardice, but he can't bear hearing the disappointment in Coach Freeman's voice. He wonders if it would be kinder to simply disappear from their lives, as if he had never existed.

GOD BLESS YOU, he adds, remembering that all conversations with the Coach end with a salutation to God. Shit, he thinks. He should have written *Praise the Lord* instead. That's what the Freemans say instead of goodbye.

He sits on the bed, forlorn, uncertain where tomorrow will take him. It's his last night at the Travel Lodge on Mr. Chandler's dime. He's not wasting eighty-nine dollars of his meager cash reserves to stay any longer. He'll buy a bus ticket and head to Seattle tomorrow even though Darrell won't be there for another day. He needs to get out of Spokane. He can find a Y or a hostel for a few bucks a night in Seattle until Darrell arrives. There's just one last piece of unfinished business.

"Please Rodriquez, don't hang up on me," he pleads when his former roommate answers the phone.

"I ain't," the baby-faced prodigy says. His voice sounds neutral, even a bit intrigued. "You know I'm gonna catch a lot of shit if anyone finds out I talked to you."

The fact he stays on the line is encouraging.

"I got to ask you a favor. It's real important. I'll pay you. I promise," KC says.

Rodriquez doesn't answer. KC can hear him chewing, something crunchy, probably those disgusting nacho-flavored chips the kid lives on when he's away from home and missing his mother's cooking. KC takes it as a good sign that Rodriquez is willing to hear him out.

"My records. You know. The really old ones. The ones my Pop-Pop left me."

He'd found them in the dormer when he went to clean out his grandfather's house. Heat had warped most of them, but eleven were undamaged, in perfect condition, including his three favorite Ricky Nelson albums. They've traveled with

KC back and forth across the country. Losing them would be losing the last connection to his Pop-Pop.

"I really got to get them. They weren't in the duffel bag they sent over."

"They're all here. I got your turntable too. You left it behind."

"You can have it. I don't care," KC says, hoping a magnanimous gesture will earn him sympathy.

"I don't want it. What am I gonna do with a fucking turntable? I don't have no records," he snorts, as if KC's offer is ridiculous. "Maybe my papi will want it. He's got some records he bought in Mexico. Mariachi shit," he says, reconsidering.

"Sure," KC says, hoping to encourage him to take up the offer.

"I'll bring you your records. I sprained my ankle running sprints and I'm rehabbing while the team's traveling to fucking Boise. I can come see you tomorrow."

"No," KC blurts. "Bring them tonight. Please. Tomorrow's too late. I'm leaving tomorrow."

"Where you goin'?"

"Seattle."

"I told my mama I would come home tonight," Rodriquez says. He sounds like a boy of his tender teenage years, whining about being inconvenienced. "So, what's in Seattle?"

KC hears him crumpling the empty chip bag in his hand.

"Someone I know."

"Someone from the Chiefs?"

KC doesn't want to play twenty questions, but can't risk losing his only chance of getting his records.

"No. Someone from Albany."

"Oh," Rodriquez says, quickly losing interest in KC's travel plans. "I guess I can bring them. I'll call my mama and tell her I'm staying in Spokane tonight. Where you want me to meet you?"

KC suggests a T.G.I. Friday's out near the interstate, an

easy walk from the motel. They agree to meet in thirty minutes.

"It's a good thing Tecchio didn't answer when you called," Rodriquez informs him. "He would have hung up on you."

Rodriquez saunters into the restaurant wearing what he calls his "best" shirt, a powder-blue pima cotton slim fit, nipped and flared at the waist, with tailored shirttails not meant to be worn tucked in. He's shaved, leaving only a wispy soul patch, and has gel in his hair.

"Holy shit, dude. You look like Freddie Krueger!"

"Thanks, man," KC says sarcastically.

"How come you don't have one of those metal splints like Tommy Garcia got when he busted his nose?" Rodriquez asks.

"They can't set it until the swelling goes down."

"How long is that?"

"I dunno," KC answers, trying to recall if Mr. Chandler told him it would be one week or two.

"It hurt?"

No, asshole, it feels great.

"Yeah," KC answers. "Not as much as it did at first."

The pain is less severe each day though his nose is still extremely sensitive to being touched. Rodriquez's short attention span seizes on the open Bible KC has been trying to read while waiting.

"How come you're so into all this religious stuff?" he asks, incredulous that anyone would take interest in a book without superheroes. The word of God fails to impress him. "I mean, like I believe in Jesus and all that, but I don't want to read about Him."

"Just put it down, okay?" KC asks.

"I'm Catholic. You Catholic?"

"No," KC says. His days at Augustinian Academy, a parochial high school for boys, are in the distant past. KC's a

Christian now, or at least that's what the Freemans expect him to be.

"I was an altar boy when I was a little kid. The fucking priest was a real weirdo," Rodriquez offers.

KC ignores him and flips through the stack of records Rodriquez has brought. All are accounted for. He drinks a Coke and plays with a greasy grilled cheese while Rodriquez makes short work of the Deluxe Platter—a double cheeseburger, fries, and an extra-thick milkshake.

"Dude, thanks for bringing me my albums," KC says, reaching for the check. But Rodriquez is quicker and insists on paying. He's always been generous, at least with KC. His four-and-a-half million dollar signing bonus was reported in *Baseball America*, even meriting a mention in *USA Today*. His teammates, struggling to live on a couple hundred bucks a week, resent an eighteen-year-old kid, months out of high school, driving an Escalade with a list price of seventy-five grand. They would have taken it out by hazing him but management forbids it. First round draft picks like Rodriquez, a five-tool prospect who can play both middle infield positions, are a rare and precious commodity. Physical intimidation is forbidden so they tormented and harassed him with sarcasm and cruel comments about his presumed virginity until KC stepped in and told them to cut the shit.

Rodriquez had gravitated toward KC since arriving in Spokane. He'd asked to change his locker so he could dress next to KC and, as always, special consideration was paid to keep him happy. He'd practically begged KC to move into the digs where he'd been set up with Tecchio and always sat beside him on the long bus rides to away games. Their teammates snickered they're queer for each other, but KC assured his young shadow they're just breaking balls. No one could ever imagine an actual fag being on the team. They're buds, that's all.

KC doesn't like seeing anyone getting bullied and picked

on, not even a teenage millionaire, a phenom who's a sure bet to be an All-Star in the majors by the time he's twenty-three. Rodriquez needed someone to look after him and protect him from the bitter jealousies of young men who will never make four-and-a-half million over the course of their lifetime. Anyone else on the Chiefs would have mocked Rodriquez without mercy if they'd come upon him locked in a bathroom stall, homesick and sobbing into a towel, the cocky and confident hot shot exposed as a scared kid who'd never been away from his mother for more than two days. KC, though, had acted as if he'd stumbled on nothing out of the ordinary, casually telling Rodriguez to blow his nose and wash his face. The new *Fast and Furious* was playing at the multiplex and then they'd go to Chipotle.

"Hey. What's your name?" Rodriquez asks, in no rush to call it a night.

"You know my name. KC."

"No. You're real name."

"Kevin."

"Mine's Domingo."

"I know that. Everyone knows that."

"You know what it means?"

"No."

"Sunday."

KC thinks it's stupid to name your kid after a day of the week. It must be some kind of Mexican thing.

"I guess I'll see you around," KC says, waiting for Rodriquez to leave so they won't have to walk to the parking lot together. He'd rather part ways without needing to explain why and how he'd lost his wheels. Rodriquez already knows enough about the humiliating circumstances of KC being cut from the team. He doesn't need to hear all the ugly, sordid details.

"I don't got to be nowhere. I told my mama I was staying at the apartment. Wanna do something?"

"Naw. Thanks. I got to get up early in the morning."

The waitress is clearly irritated by them lingering at her table, there being only so many opportunities to collect tips in an eight-hour shift.

"Can I get you boys anything else?" she asks, which KC correctly interprets as *get the hell out.*

"Where's your car?" Rodriquez asks, surveying the lot for KC's blue Civic.

"I walked," KC says, not offering an explanation.

"How far?"

"It's just down the road."

"Dude, you're gonna get killed walking on the side of the highway in the dark. Come on. I'll drive you."

"I'll be okay."

"Get in the fucking SUV, KC. I said I was gonna drive you."

KC reluctantly agrees and settles into the passenger seat. It's a clear night and the brightness of the full moon is undimmed by the hazy skylight that blankets Spokane. There's a pair of entwined rosaries, far gaudier than Mr. Chandler's simple wooden cross, dangling from the rearview mirror. The kid is either more religious than he'll admit or he's superstitious and they're some sort of lucky charm. Rodriquez, who's just been ragging KC for having his nose in a Bible, assumes he's about to be called out as a hypocrite when KC fingers the string of beads.

"I know. They're embarrassing. My mother made me hang them so the Virgin Mary will protect me. She gets wacko sometimes. She made the priest bless this car before I could drive it."

He cranks up the volume of the local hip-hop station, making conversation impossible. It's a short ride to the motel and KC thanks him again for bringing the records.

"So, where's your car?" Rodriquez asks.

"There it is," KC lies, pointing at a random silver Camry.

"What happened to your Civic? It was bomb, man. I loved that color. Why'd you ditch it?"

"Lease was up. I got a good deal on this one."

"Come on dude," Rodriquez says. "Let's take it out and see what it can do."

"It's kinda late. I got to get up early in the morning."

"It's fucking nine o'clock, KC. I'll fill your tank when we're done if you don't have money for gas."

The kid's persistent. He walks across the lot and circles the car, giving the Camry the once over.

"Come on, dude. Toss 'em over," he shouts, demanding KC throw him the keys to a stranger's car.

"Fuck it, Rodriquez. It ain't mine," KC confesses in exasperation. "The Civic got trashed."

"You in a wreck? That what happened to your face? Tecchio said you got busted up by a queer. I knew he was full of shit."

"Yeah, something like that," he mutters, a vague, ambiguous answer.

"So how you goin' to Seattle if you don't have a car?"

"Bus."

"Dude, that will take you like a whole fuckin' day."

"Yeah."

"I'm gonna drive you!"

"No."

"I fucking mean it. It'll be fun. You and me. The team ain't back until Saturday and fucking rehab is a joke. They're just making me go because the Rangers said I had to. My agent says I'm getting called up to high A next week anyway."

KC's stung by the announcement of Rodriquez's good fortune and the opportunities that lie ahead for him. KC's bonus was a pittance compared to Rodriquez's, but last week they'd both been valued prospects with promising futures. Coach Freeman was certain KC would be in AA next season. Now he's got nothing, not even a car, and no one's gonna step up to rescue him. Even the Freemans will turn their backs on him when he's forced to admit why he's been kicked off the team.

"Go get your shit, KC. You can come back home with me tonight and we'll get an early start."

"No, man. This place is cool. You don't need any trouble. What if Tecchio comes back and finds me?"

"Seven o'clock then," Rodriquez says, juiced for an adventure. "I'm gonna set my alarm."

"Sure," KC says, knowing Rodriquez never gets out of bed until noon and that he'll be long gone when the kid comes to pick him up, if he even remembers his offer in the morning.

KC's up at dawn, carefully packing his records in the duffel so they're well-cushioned with socks and tee shirts if the bag gets knocked around. He nearly jumps through his skin when he's startled by a fist banging on the door. Check-out time isn't until noon but that creepy Indian guy wants him gone and is going to send him on his way without offering him the free breakfast buffet of instant coffee and powdered donuts.

"Let's go man! The sun's up and I'm ready to hit the road."

Rodriquez is dressed like a trucker, or at least a teenage kid's idea of a trucker. His jeans are tight and his boots are scuffed. He's wearing a sleeveless work shirt over a white, ribbed guinea tee. His mesh CAT cap is too big for his head.

"You can just drop me off at the bus station, Rodriquez," KC says. "You must have a million things to do today."

"Hey, can I ask you a favor? Can you call me Domingo? Just for today. You want me to call you Kevin?"

"No. No," KC responds, sounding harsher than he'd intended. "My name is KC. No one calls me Kevin."

Except his Pop-Pop. Even his mother has called him KC since his Little League days.

"Throw your duffel in the back seat, KC," Rodriquez says as he climbs behind the wheel.

KC's surprised to find a packed bag already in the Escalade.

"Running away from home?"

"No. Why?" Rodriquez asks.

KC's only busting balls and thinks it odd that the kid seems so nervous. Rodriquez probably keeps a change of clothes in the SUV for whenever he can make a spontaneous trip to see his mama.

"Nothing. No reason," KC says.

"Hey, I brought you something to listen to, KC. I know you hate my music. So I borrowed some of Tecchio's discs. You like these dudes, don't you?" he asks as he slips *Vitalogy* into the disc player.

"Sure," KC says, not wanting to disappoint Rodriquez. And he does like Eddie Vedder. He actually loves him, but listening to Pearl Jam makes him sad. Sometimes if he hears "Nothing Man" when he's alone, it's hard not to cry. He and Charlie Beresford had driven to the Meadowlands to see the band play the summer they were hauling furniture. That was the first time they'd kissed and he's never allowed anyone else to kiss him since Charlie. He was stupid back then, believing they would always be close, that time and distance would never change their feelings for each other. His face still burns with shame whenever he thinks about how Charlie had treated him, how embarrassed he'd seemed when KC had shown up at his college after his stepfather threw him out of the house. He'd never wanted to see or hear from Charlie again and thought he'd covered his tracks if the jerk he'd once thought was his friend ever came looking for him. But anyone can find him now by typing *KC Conroy* into a search engine.

He never responded when Charlie tracked him down in Kingsport, Tennessee, during his Rookie League year. Charlie's frequent emails to the message board on the Spokane

Chiefs web page, asking KC to contact him, went unanswered. Sometimes he is tempted to write back to ask how Charlie's mom is doing, if her cancer is gone, and if his dad still pesters him about not having a girlfriend. Charlie always insisted he couldn't wait to get out of their house and be on his own, never appreciating how lucky he was to have a real mom who made lasagna and spaghetti and meatballs and a dad who worried when his son was out all night. Charlie didn't know anything about growing up in a house where he was an unwanted burden, an outsider, a mistake his mother regretted, an unwelcome intrusion on the life she'd made with the man who'd married her. KC's never had a family, not a real one, only his Pop-Pop. His stepfather had given him his name but never thought of him as a real Conroy like the sons and daughter who shared his blood.

"Hey, you hungry?" Rodriquez asks.

They haven't passed three exits on the interstate before he's insisting they hit a drive-through for sausage and egg sandwiches before the breakfast service is over. KC thinks the kid must have a tapeworm since he eats everything in sight and can't gain any weight. Rodriquez is trying to bulk up, put on twenty or thirty pounds of muscle. Tecchio says he knows someone who knows someone who knows how to score this shit that's guaranteed undetectable. Completely, totally undetectable. KC threatened to break that fucking Tecchio's neck if he tried to get Rodriquez mixed up with juicing. Two guys on the Chiefs roster have already been suspended this season, their already slim chances of making it to the Show now a lost cause. He hopes he's scared the kid straight by threatening to call Rodriquez's mama if he ever uses any supplement stronger than soy protein.

Rodriquez forces a loud, impressive belch as they take to the road again. He turns down the volume of the music as if he wants to say something, then reconsiders, and decides to call his mother. Someday he's gonna have to stop being a mama's boy, but KC knows it must feel good to know his entire family dotes on him. One of his older sisters lives in Spokane with her husband and is always bringing home-cooked meals to the apartment for her baby brother and his roommates. The tamales are the best KC's ever eaten.

The phone rings as soon as he says goodbye to his mama, but this time Rodriquez's face is stern and grim. He gives one word responses, *yes* and *no,* then abruptly cuts the conversation short.

"Look. We'll talk about it when I get back. I don't know. A couple of days. Okay. Yeah, me too. I'll call you later."

KC stares out the windshield, focusing on the highway ahead, not wanting to intrude on a private moment. But he can't ignore the obvious when Rodriquez starts pounding the dashboard with his fist. He spits out a torrent of Spanish that even a gringo like KC recognizes as curses, all a prelude to tears.

"What's the matter Domingo?" he asks.

"I'm fucked. Really, really fucked."

KC doubts a kid with the world at his feet is truly fucked. Every small speed bump in the road is blown out of proportion when you're eighteen. Someone with a charmed life like Rodriguez is immune to disaster. Only one thing could precipitate such an emotional reaction.

"Fuck it, Rodriquez. What did you do? What did you take? Where did you get it? From that fucking Tecchio?"

He hands the boy a clean handkerchief to wipe his face and allows him a few minutes to catch his breath.

"You flunk the test Domingo? They gonna suspend you?"

"No. No. It ain't nothing like that," he says, sucking up a nose full of snot and handing the soiled hankie to KC.

"Keep it dude," KC insists. "Who was that?"

"Maria."

KC's only met her a few times. Rodriquez rarely brings her to the apartment. KC's having a hard time recalling her face. He remembers she's shy, quiet, a surprisingly plain and heavy girlfriend for a teenage millionaire whose bank account and the promise of a life of fame and recognition could easily score him a smoking hot babe. Tecchio's woman, who can be a real cunt, mocks her behind Rodriquez's back. She calls her Mrs. Babar, the lady elephant. Everything about Maria is subject to criticism. Her frumpy clothes, her frizzy hair, the dimples in her chubby elbows.

"I was so fucking stupid. If I'd tried to use a rubber she would have accused me of cheating and that I was afraid of giving her VD or AIDS or somethin' because I was fucking around. And she said she couldn't get pregnant. She told me she was on the pill. And I fucking believed her."

No one knows about the pregnancy but the prospective parents and now KC. They need to decide their future without the moral supervision of parents and priests. Maria's a good girl, Rodriquez says. He insists he made her do it, that she wanted to wait until they were married or at least officially engaged.

"She says we'll go to the clinic if that's what I want. Fuck. Fuck. Fuck. Fuck. Fuck," he cries as the tears begin flowing again.

KC realizes Maria is cleverer than anyone had given her credit for. It's apparent now there was always something going on behind that blank, round face. She's known the father of the child in her womb since the third grade. He's too frightened his mama might learn of their grievous sin if they choose to end the pregnancy.

"Maybe she could put it up for adoption," KC suggests. "Don't you think that's the best thing to do?"

Rodriquez says he's cool with the idea but Maria's given him an ultimatum. Either she gets rid of it before anyone knows she's pregnant or he marries her. She won't settle for having her reputation tarnished as an unwed mother who gave her baby to strangers to raise, bringing shame upon her strict, religious parents.

"She's a Catholic. So am I. It's a sin. Murder. What should I do KC? You gotta tell me. I don't want no kid. I don't want to marry her but I don't want to go to hell."

It's a terrible thing to kill a baby. But KC knows it can be just as bad, maybe worse, to let it live. He still remembers the bitter, angry voice of his mother, drunk and stoned, shouting at her father while KC lay trembling and frightened in the bed he shared with his Pop-Pop in the next room. Yet another man, like the one before him and the one before that, had just told her it was over, that he couldn't raise someone else's kid. Her words are burned into KC's memory.

I hate him. He's ruined my life. I'll never have anything now. I should have gotten rid of him when I could. Why did I listen to you?

"Maybe you should have it," he says quietly.

"The baby?"

"No. The abortion."

KC knows that one day Rodriquez will look at the child he's tried to love, feeling only anger and resentment, and blame his innocent son or daughter for being locked in his cage.

"Even if it's a sin?"

"There's worse sins, Domingo. I'm sure of that."

A blessing from a twenty-year-old kid with no future is all Rodriquez needs to justify his decision. KC expects that Rodriquez and the would-be-mother of his child will never speak again after they leave the clinic. This time next year, he'll be racing through AA, waiting for the call up to AAA and hoping to receive an invitation to spring training. Maria, unencumbered by a bastard child, will have settled for a cop or fireman with a steady income and health insurance.

"KC, would it be okay if we go back to Spokane? I'll buy you a plane ticket to Seattle. I'm sorry, but I gotta go back, now, and tell her we're gonna do it."

KC insists he'll be okay. There's probably a bus station

in the town at the next exit. He's pretty good at using his thumb, too.

"You sure?"

"Yeah."

They drive in silence, listening to the Pearl Jam disc. KC starts to choke up when Eddie sings "Nothing Man," but he doesn't cry. Rodriquez asks again if KC's sure he wants to be stranded alone in the middle of nowhere. Being alone doesn't scare him. It's how he's lived his entire life. He tells Rodriquez to drop him off at the Union 76 station parking lot at the next exit.

"When am I going to see you again?" Rodriquez asks, lingering a few minutes before he departs.

"I dunno. Someday."

"You'll make it to the Show. I know you will."

KC shrugs and smiles. "Maybe. Just remember how accurate my arm is when you're trying to snag an extra bag," KC reminds him.

Rodriquez impulsively opens his wallet and insists KC take it all, almost five hundred dollars. He unzips KC's duffel and stuffs the cash in the bag when KC tries to refuse him.

"Wait a minute!" he says, running back to the Escalade, returning with a rosary that he presses into KC's palm.

"I know it's dumb. But maybe the Virgin Mary will bring you good luck too."

The hotel room is okay, if nothing like the luxury suite Darrell had promised to book in Seattle. But the shower was hot and the bed was comfortable enough after a night spent in the cramped bunk of the trucker who'd picked him up at the Hillstop Travel Plaza at the Moses Lake exit on Interstate 90. Darrell had gone out for Chinese take-out shortly after KC arrived. That was just before midnight and he hadn't returned when KC finally awoke at eleven in the morning.

KC's stomach is growling, but Darrell hasn't left a room key. He's stuck here until his host returns. He could prop open the door with his duffel bag while he searches for a vending machine. He'll settle for a Coke and a bag of chips at this point. But when he opens the door a seedy-looking character is letting himself into the room across the hall. He's going to need to tough it out until Darrell gets back.

Darrell's laptop is open on the desk. KC's got time to kill and decides to do a search for used Camaros for sale in the Seattle area. The screen is open to a response to Darrell's craigslist ad by a skinny, smooth young man with a long, thick cock. KC scrolls through his inbox. Thirty-six other possible "buddies" have sent messages overnight. Most of them comment on the photograph Darrell used in his ad, skeptical that it's real. KC clicks the Sent file and finds the attached picture of Darrell's erect penis, measured against a ruler, verifying a hefty ten-and-a-half inches. Darrell's nickname for it is the Slavic Saber. KC feels like a sneak or a spy and closes the laptop. He flops on the bed and plays with the apps on his phone while he waits. He's racking up a decent score on Slot-o-mania when a text message arrives.

YOUR AGENT IS HAVING TROUBLE WITH THE RANGERS. NEED TO SPEAK TO YOU. WE NEED TO CONVINCE THEM IT'S NOT TRUE.

Coach Freeman signs off, citing scripture.

JOHN 3:3

He doesn't need to consult his Bible to decode the message. He knows this New Testament passage by heart. An incoming call appears on his screen. The number is familiar; the area code is Tampa/St. Pete. The caller leaves a message when he doesn't answer.

Hi, KC. It's Callie. I hope you are all right and can call me back. Mr. Freeman called and asked if I've heard from you. He told me not to worry. That everything's okay. He wants me to call him if I speak to you. Caleb wants to say hello.

Hello, KC, a child's voice says.

We both miss you. Please call me as soon as you have a chance, she says before hanging up.

He feels sick and dirty hearing the sound of her voice. They'd met in the young singles group at New Covenant. Mr. Stapleton introduced them—a shy young professional athlete with excellent prospects and the widow of an Army reservist, pregnant and only two years out of high school when her husband was killed by sniper fire in Afghanistan. She says KC is proof that Jesus has heard her prayers. KC respects her and loves her fatherless child. The Freemans think KC will make a good husband for Callie and role model for Caleb. They say it's obvious he and Callie love each other, but KC knows better. He's nervous around her; her expectations make him uncomfortable. She's a nice girl, quiet, not the type who thinks she has to constantly be talking. But he keeps his distance, avoiding every opportunity to be alone with her, insisting they include Caleb in everything they do. She knows that girls with prettier faces and better bodies stalk boys who play ball. He swears there are no other women. He holds her hand because it's expected, kisses her goodnight chastely. He likes Callie, but he knows he can't really love her if the thought of sleeping with her fills him with dread. He'd hoped she would forget him when he left Florida to play in the Texas Winter League. But, encouraged by the Freemans, she's moving to Sacramento so they can be together when she finishes nursing school next semester.

There's a sudden commotion in the hallway. Darrell is cursing on the other side of the door, frustrated his key card isn't working. Darrell stumbles as KC opens the door and, tripping over his feet, falls on his ass. The guy from craigslist, more sinister-looking than his picture, follows him into the room, dragging a ragged backpack behind him.

"Okay, are one of you jokers gonna help me up?"

KC grabs an arm and pulls Darrell to his feet. He's surprised at how light Darrell is; his bones feel practically weightless. He'd noticed last night how gaunt Darrell has become. His skin is blotchy and his cheeks have sunk into his once-broad face. But the hoodie he was wearing camouflaged the drastic change in his weight. KC had thought it was strange he was wearing a New York Giants sweatshirt in the middle of summer, but Seattle is cool and damp, not hot and muggy like July back east. He grabs Darrell around the waist to steady him until he can balance himself. He's shocked to feel his ribs through the layers of padded cotton.

"What are you doing?" Darrell asks, embarrassed in front of his new friend. "I can manage on my own now."

KC doesn't smell alcohol on him. But the stench of his body odor is strong, nearly overwhelming, and his breath makes KC wince. His once-bright teeth are the color of dirty chalk. Darrell's lost the Yankees baseball cap he was wearing last night. His thick hair, which he'd always worn clipped close to his scalp, with clean, sharp lines around his ears and along his neck, is long and shaggy and slick with grease.

"Seamus, my friend KC doesn't need to treat me like a baby, does he?"

"Of course not," Seamus says, winking and smiling at KC as if they were in a conspiracy.

"So, did I lie to you?" Darrell asks.

"No, sir you most certainly did not," Seamus says, clearly seeing beyond the ripe purple and yellow contusions to appreciate KC's good looks.

Darrell squints and leans forward, staring at KC's face.

"What the fuck happened to you?" he asks, as if they hadn't had a brief, but coherent conversation about KC's bruises when KC arrived last night.

"KC is my best friend in the whole world," Darrell announces solemnly to his new acquaintance. "You tell us who did this to you, KC. Me and Seamus are gonna make 'em pay."

Darrell sits on the bed, then immediately jumps to his feet. He opens and closes the empty drawers of the bureau, then drops to his knees and searches for something under the bed. He's hyper, not making complete sense, his speech on fast-forward. Jacked. That's what KC would call him. Darrell stands and starts to swear, his mood brightening instantly when he sees a paper shopping bag on the floor in the corner. He retrieves a bottle of vodka.

"You said you had the good shit," Seamus says, feigning disappointment. "This crap costs ten bucks a bottle."

"KC can run out and get something else," Darrell says, pulling two twenties from his wallet. "You like Belvedere? KC, how 'bout going down to the liquor store and get us a nice bottle of Belvedere. Get two, chilled if they have it," he says, pulling more money from his billfold.

"I'm just yanking your chain," Seamus says. "This shit's fine. You gonna join us my friend? What's your name again? Casey?"

"KC. Just the initials."

"Nice," Seamus says. He's got an accent. KC thinks he must be from Ireland since he has an Irish name. But he doesn't look like any Irishman KC knows. He doesn't have flaming orange hair and ruddy cheeks like KC's late stepfather and his half-brothers and sister. Seamus's face is long and thin, with grizzly muttonchop sideburns that almost touch at the tip of his pointy chin. His hairline is receding, but what's left is thick and black, tied in a tight ponytail that falls between his shoulder blades. He's taller than KC, but half his weight. No one would ever call Seamus handsome, but his blue eyes burn like lasers, making him inexplicably sexy.

"Hey," Seamus says, smiling at KC.

"Hey."

KC is wearing the tee shirt he slept in and a pair of baggy boxer shorts, but Seamus's gaze makes him feel like he's buck naked in a room where everyone else is buttoned up and zipped.

"Fuck man, your friend is something else," Seamus laughs while Darrell is rummaging in the tiny bathroom, searching for plastic cups. "How old is he?"

"Forty, I think. Somewhere around there. He's old."

"He says you're gonna be a famous baseball player," Seamus says as he sits and begins unlacing his boots. They're military surplus, calf high, scuffed and worn. The socks he tosses on the floor are thick and nubby and smell like sweat and damp wool. His feet are disgusting. They're filthy, with long, yellow toenails. Seamus pulls his Henley shirt over his head and kicks off his jeans. There are stains in the armpits of his undershirt and the elastic waistband of his briefs is frayed. He opens his backpack and retrieves a small nylon bag, one of those cheap toiletry kits KC uses for toothpaste and shaving cream.

"Whoa! Starting the party without me?" Darrell bellows as he emerges from the bathroom with a single plastic glass, still in its sanitary wrap.

"Don't worry dude. You ain't gonna miss anything."

Darrell strips off his shirt, baring his chest. Even after feeling his ribs through his sweatshirt, KC is shocked at his appearance. He looks like one of those photographs of starving people in Haiti after a hurricane, except, of course, that he's white. KC's surprised by the fresh bruises on Darrell's back.

Seamus is holding a baggie of crystal and pulls a glass pipe from the toiletry bag.

"This shit cost me, buddy," Seamus reminds his new friend.

"I'm good for it," Darrell insists.

Seamus gives him the *I've heard that line before* look, making no move to fill the bowl of the pipe with a hit.

"Fuck," Darrell complains as he drags himself to his feet and retrieves his wallet. Seamus zips the payment into a pocket of his backpack.

"How come you still have your underwear on? I thought

this was supposed to be a party," Seamus asks KC. "Let me see it," he insists, urging KC to pull his dick through the fly of his boxers.

Seamus flicks his cigarette lighter and settles the flame under the bowl.

"This is a non-smoking room," KC reminds him, a remark both Darrell and Seamus find unbearably funny.

KC gets a queasy feeling in his stomach as the crystals melt and smoke begins to curl through the stem.

Darrell looks anxious as Seamus inhales. "Hey buddy, don't be greedy. I just paid for this shit."

Seamus passes the pipe to Darrell, who chokes on the chest full of fumes he pulls from the stem.

"Whoa, slow down, dude. You trying to have a fucking heart attack?" Seamus says as he offers the pipe to KC. "Wassup?" he laughs. "Your turn."

KC hesitates. He can't imagine putting anything as filthy as the pipe, black with soot, in his mouth.

"Come on, man. You wanna party don't you?"

"I gotta piss," KC says, suddenly feeling paranoid, certain that the smoke alarm is going to summon the cops to break down the door.

He hides in the bathroom, squatting on the toilet, gripping his phone in his hands. Fucking Darrell Torok isn't buying him a new car. He's blowing all his money on skanky hustlers and crystal, then he'll fly back to Albany if he isn't arrested first, leaving KC high and dry. KC should have stayed in Spokane and haggled with the Mexicans for a cheap set of shitty retreads. Now he's stuck here in Seattle, with eight hundred dollars to his name and no car. The only way out of this mess is to call Mr. Stapleton again and beg him to persuade Coach Freeman to send him cash. Just enough for a used car. Nothing fancy. He's twenty years old and no one, not even the Coach, should be able to stop him from spending his own money.

"Hey man, what you doing in there?" Seamus calls.

He panics, worried that this freak Seamus could be ransacking his duffel bag and the pockets of his jeans, not satisfied with the cash he's taken from Darrell. Darrell's too high to stop him; he won't even try. KC jumps to his feet and rushes into the bedroom and finds them both naked. Seamus is on his back, sprawled across the bed; the soles of his feet are black with dirt. Darrell's on his stomach, lying between Seamus's legs, lazily sucking the younger man's cock. Seamus pulls himself up onto his elbows, not understanding why KC is putting on his pants and tying his shoes.

"Come over here, buddy, and fuck me. You're gonna fuck my ass, aren't you?"

KC picks up his duffel, still unpacked, and smiles, explaining he'll be right back.

"I gotta do my laundry first. All my clothes are dirty," he explains, promising to bring back a bottle of Belvedere.

"We'll be here partying, buddy. As long as there's cash to spend," Seamus says, falling back in the mattress.

The keys to Darrell's rental and the parking garage ticket are lying on the bureau. KC slips them in his pocket and closes the door behind him.

It takes KC an hour to find the rental car in the garage. Either the cashier gives him shitty directions to Interstate 5 or he makes a wrong turn. He's stuck in traffic near the Space Needle, then drives in circles until he finally finds the entrance to the highway. He doesn't stop until he's miles across the Oregon border. He parks behind a Burger King to call Mr. Stapleton. He reaches into his pocket for his phone, finding only a few loose coins. A frantic search of his other pockets yields nothing but his wallet and a dirty handkerchief. His heart is pounding in his chest and he feels the blood pulsing behind his eardrums. He unzips his duffel bag and dumps the contents on the back seat of the car. He finds the charger, but nothing to charge. He opens every door of the car and drops to his knees, running his hands under the seats, praying that the precious phone is lying on the floor. He slumps onto the asphalt and squeezes his skull with his hands, trying to remember the last time he held it in his palm. The bathroom. His phone is on the bathroom floor of Darrell's hotel room where he dropped it when he thought he was being robbed.

"Fuckfuckfuckfuckfuckfuckfuck," he hisses, spitting the words through gritted teeth.

He rises to his feet and pounds the hood of the car with his fists. His whole life is fucked, he swears as he kicks the tires. He could turn the car around and go back to Seattle. He can saunter into the hotel room as if nothing had happened, that he hasn't been AWOL since morning. Darrell's probably still too high to realize his car keys are missing, but the rental company won't be forgiving if the car has already been reported stolen. You can't use a phone in jail and it's not worth the risk he'd be taking if he returned to retrieve it.

"Hey!"

A kid in a fast food uniform shouts at him, keeping his distance, not straying far from the safety of the back door of the building. KC can be scary when he's angry and the fry cook doesn't want to be tomorrow's headline, the victim of a lunatic with a knife or a gun.

"Hey, dude. You gotta go."

KC starts to argue with him. It's a free country. He can park here if he wants. *Go fuck yourself, asshole,* he shouts.

"This lot's for customers only," the kid says, retreating a few steps further.

"I don't want your fucking shit burgers," KC yells as he slams the car door and races the engine. "You're a fucking loser," he shouts out the window as he peels out of the parking lot, barely avoiding a collision with a car traveling north. *Asshole!* the driver shouts through an open window. KC floors the accelerator, intending to chase the motherfucker, coming to his senses when he sees a patrol car approaching in the opposite lane. He makes a sharp right into the lot of a

Dairy Queen and the cops continue on their way. He realizes
he hasn't eaten all day and needs something in his stomach.

He orders ten bucks worth of food, thinking he's fam-
ished. But he barely touches the crap on his tray, choking on
a few bites of a cheeseburger. He's finishing his Coke, about
to dump the rest of the greasy shit in the trash, when a boisterous group of boys, none older than twelve, storm the door
of the restaurant. Their grass and dirt-stained jerseys are wet
with sweat and they're wearing blue baseball socks and Adi-
das shower shoes, with black-and-white striped flaps. The
Beaverton Grizzlies are celebrating a hard-fought victory.
The coach, a good-natured middle-aged slob with a belly
that droops over the waistband of his sweat pants, makes a
futile effort to get them to form a manageable line. They ignore him and rush the counter like a litter of wild puppies,
shouting over each other, confusing the young girl at the register trying to take their orders.

KC recognizes each of the boys from his own Little
League days. There's the fat kid, with power in his thick
shoulders and arms, but too slow to reach first base safely
unless he sends the ball deep into the outfield. The nerd with
Coke-bottle glasses won't be put in the game unless it's a
blowout, win or lose. The runt of the litter, a motormouth
who is always talking trash, runs like a demon possessed and
is the leadoff hitter on the team. Most of the boys still have
the smooth, pink faces of childhood; a few have a faint
shadow of hair on their upper lips. Some are gawky, with
arms and legs too long for their bodies. The larger boys will
soon develop the hard, defined muscles of young men. And
one, lingering at the edge of the crowd, is clearly the leader,
the captain, a boy who is deferred to, quiet, almost solemn,
the player on the team who commands everyone's respect.
KC knows that boy well—the one he used to be.

At that age, KC still believed that one day he'd stop being
a lonely kid whose real name was Kevin Conroy, resented by

his mother, beaten and abused by his alcoholic stepfather. He would be the Mighty KC, admired and envied, rich, with his face and stats on a Topps trading card. After he'd signed with the Rangers, his mother, a widow now, bitterly regretted how she had treated him. She seeks him out, sending letters pleading with him to write her a check because the house is in foreclosure or the car's been repossessed. Mr. Freeman sends her a little money now and then. He calls it Christian charity and she always complains it isn't enough. But KC won't return her calls, refusing to speak to her, punishing her for not protecting him from a childhood of drunken insults and fists. But now he's not a ball player anymore. The Mighty KC is just the stupid name of someone he will never be. He's no one special. He can hear his mother mocking his failure, proving she'd been right all along when she said he'd turn out bad. He's the loser she'd always known he would be. And worse yet, he's a fag she can't trust around her boys.

If you believe, you will receive whatever you ask for in prayer. Matthew 21:22.

Coach Freeman believes the Lord never turns His back on anyone, but God doesn't answer everyone's prayers. He picks and chooses, deciding who is worthy of His attention. KC's not among the chosen ones. He'd prayed every day that God would change him, make him normal, unburdened by secrets and shame. But Jesus hadn't bothered to respond, knowing KC's faith was never strong. He's not the Christian the Freemans believe he's become. He's a liar, a dishonest fake who told them what they'd wanted to hear, desperately needing to be accepted. He's a homo who has sex with other guys, sometimes for money. And now he's a thief too, a fucking criminal who will be thrown into jail when he's caught driving a stolen vehicle. It's too late for anyone to save him. If he ever prays again, he won't ask God to waste any time on him. There are plenty of people more deserving of His help, like the quiet, confident captain of the Beaverton Grizzlies who seems uncomfortable, even a bit frightened, when he realizes he's being stared at by a young man with a black-and-blue face.

It's a constant battle with the gas pedal. KC typically has a heavy foot, causing the needle of the speedometer to flutter into dangerous zones. He's been fortunate so far, avoiding speed traps and traveling below the highway patrol's radar screen. His heartbeat races each time he sees a cop car in the rearview mirror. He tries his best to look unconcerned and nonchalant as they overtake him in the passing lane. He's playing a dangerous game, driving a vehicle that's sure to have been reported stolen by now. Sooner or later, he's going to get pulled over. He needs to ditch this fucking car in a bus station parking lot the first chance he gets.

He absentmindedly sticks his index finger up his nose to pick at a dry and jagged scab deep inside his right nostril. He gently scratches, distracted by the gaudy tour bus of a country music star traveling to his next gig. He feels something wet and slippery and is surprised to taste blood as he explores his upper lip with the tip of his tongue.

Breathe through your mouth, don't blow too hard into your hankie, and, whatever you do, don't stick your finger up there no matter how bad it itches.

He remembers Mr. Chandler's advice but the damage is done. Mr. Chandler stopped the bleeding by pinching his nose, but it's hard to steady the car with only one shaky hand on the steering wheel. His clumsy attempt only makes matters worse and now the blood is actually gushing from his nostril. The front of his shirt is turning bright red. An exit for Eugene, Oregon, is two miles ahead. A road sign on the exit ramp, a white capital H on a blue background, directs him to a hospital one and a half miles to the left.

The woman at the emergency room registration desk doesn't appear to be too alarmed, or even much interested, in a young man with a bloodied face holding a dirty handkerchief to his nose. The triage nurse, a burly middle-aged man with a thick tuft of blonde chest hair sprouting from the neck of his scrubs, is kinder.

"What did you do to yourself?" he asks.

KC is too embarrassed to admit he'd been picking his nose to a handsome dead ringer for the *Six Million Dollar Man* he used to watch on cable reruns.

"Couldn't resist sticking your finger up there when the scab got itchy, I bet. Looks like you've broken the clot. Now this is gonna hurt like hell," the nurse warns.

"I know."

"Go ahead and holler if you feel like it. No one's gonna care," he says as he pinches KC's nose. "What's your name?"

"Ricky."

The nurse smiles, but doesn't comment on the obvious boner rising in KC's pants.

"Okay, good-looking, that ought to hold you 'til the doc can see you. Tell you the truth, I'm more concerned about that mark on your cheek. Who bit you? Barnabas Collins?"

KC looks at him, mystified.

"You're too young for *Dark Shadows* and I'm too old to know the name of the *Twilight* vampires," he laughs. "Seriously, though, we need to take care of that. We need to clean it out and get you a shot. But it looks like it's gonna be awhile before they can see you. You tell that gal sitting at the desk to call me if you start bleeding again."

KC nods his head.

"And don't shake your head. Try to sit still," he says as turns his attention to a young mother holding a barefoot young boy who's stepped on a piece of glass.

KC is still sitting in the waiting room two hours later. It's been fifteen minutes since the last patient was called to be seen. He suspects the sound of multiple sirens outside means the arrival of far more urgent cases than a bloody nose. He reaches for his duffel bag—he keeps it close by his side now, in case of an emergency—and pulls out the envelope to count his remaining money. He's got less than seven hundred dollars left after paying for fast food and filling the tank and ransoming the rental from the expensive Seattle hotel parking lot. There's no reason to waste more of it paying a doctor now that he's stopped bleeding. He throws his duffel strap over his shoulder and walks out the door. A dazzling full moon, white as a bleached skull in the sands of the desert, hovers over the horizon, illuminating the poorly lit parking lot. Ahead, he sees a cop standing behind his car, calling in the license number of a possible missing vehicle. He turns and runs back inside, throwing the keys, evidence tying him to the car, into a trash can in the men's room.

He locks himself into a stall, resting his feet on his duffel. He doesn't wear a watch. He always relies on his cell phone for the time. What could be only minutes feels like hours. His butt and thighs feel heavy and numb. Other men come and go. They do their business, wash their hands (well, most of them) and leave. He realizes he can't hide forever. Eventually he has to emerge. He may as well risk it now he decides, summoning the courage to walk to the parking lot where a tow truck operator in greasy coveralls is hooking a chain to the axle of Darrell's rental. The cop makes a last phone call, confirming the recovery of the vehicle, and leaves.

KC's stranded in a strange city, watching his way out of town being hauled away, dangling from a boom. Motels are expensive and even the desk clerk in the worst rat holes would be reluctant to rent a room to a kid who walks in off the street with no car and whose face bears the aftermath of a recent fight. Besides, he has to conserve every dollar and try to never let his nut dip below two hundred bucks. He might not sleep in a bed again for a while. Who knows the next time he'll be able to shower? He'll have to piss and crap wherever he gets an opportunity, most likely outdoors on many occasions. He'd better be prepared so he returns to the men's room to empty the toilet paper dispensers, stuffing the rolls into his duffel. He can't steal liquid soap, but he grabs a stack of paper towels that could come in handy. He washes his face and hands, paying close attention to the bite on his cheek and carefully avoiding touching his nose. He splashes water on his hair and makes a crude attempt to style it with the palm of his hand. He needs to make one last pit stop at the vending machine in the waiting room before beginning the long walk to the interstate. He buys pretzels, Snickers bars and Oreos, two cans of Coke and a Mountain Dew, his dinner tonight and his breakfast in the morning. He might wait all night before some bored and lonely trucker takes pity on him and offers a ride.

"Hey handsome, what are you still doing here?"

He feels a hand on his shoulder. The triage nurse is standing behind him, a backpack slung across his shoulder.

"I'm just leaving," KC says sounding like a guilty kid caught stealing cookies.

"What did the doctor say?"

"I'm okay. He said I can go."

"It's Ricky, isn't it? Your name's Ricky?"

"Yeah, Ricky."

"What did they say about that bite? Someone did a half-ass job cleaning it. Did you get a tetanus shot?"

"Yeah."

"You telling me the truth or do I have to go back and look at your record?"

"It's the truth."

"You have a script for an antibiotic?"

"Yeah."

"You call anyone to come pick you up?"

"No," KC says, nervously. "I don't live around here."

"Where are you headed?"

"Sacramento," KC says, unable to think of any other answer. "My family is in Sacramento."

"Let me walk you to your car. I just clocked out."

"No, that's okay. I gotta get going."

The nurse is too broad, too tall, for KC to push past him.

"Ricky, I'm gonna ask you a question."

He knows the Six Million Dollar Man smells fear dripping from his sweat glands.

"You have a place to sleep tonight?"

"My car. I'm gonna sleep in my car."

"So, where's your car again?

"In the parking lot," he says, unnerved by the man's persistence. Maybe he's heard a stolen car's just been towed off the premises and he's suspicious. Maybe he's stalling, detaining KC until the cop can rush back to the hospital.

"So is mine. Let's walk out together."

"I gotta go to the bathroom first. You go ahead. Don't wait for me," KC insists.

"Ricky, why don't you tell me the truth? There's no car and you don't have a place to sleep tonight."

KC's eyes well up with tears. He's embarrassed by losing control and acting like a frightened baby. It pisses him off that he cries so easily lately, like a little boy or, even worse, a girl. He reaches for his dirty handkerchief but the nurse intercepts him before he can blow his nose.

"Whoa. Whoa. We don't want you to start bleeding again. Stop worrying Ricky," he says wrapping his arm around KC's shoulder and leading him back into the treatment area. "You're not gonna run on me, are you?" he asks. "Christine, keep an eye on our young friend here and call me if he tries to disappear," he says to a young nurse. "I'll be back in a minute. Just sit tight."

None of the staff—doctors, nurses, orderlies, young women carrying baskets of syringes and empty vials, all wearing the same blue scrubs—are particularly interested in the young man seated at the nurse's station, clutching a duffel in his arms. KC starts to relax, allowing himself to trust his new friend. He suspects the nurse is calling home, warning his wife or girlfriend or roommate, maybe a roommate, another guy, that he's bringing an unexpected guest home tonight.

Don't worry. It's just for one night. Make up the couch.
He looks like he could use something to eat. Why don't you
order a pizza?

The nurse might be Christian, following the example of
the Good Samaritan, but Christians always find some way to
work Jesus into the conversation and he never once mentioned God or the Lord. He could be a gay guy. He did call
KC handsome, not once, but twice. Maybe he'll let KC stay
a few days while he figures things out. He'll think it's a riot
when KC tells him he looks like the Six Million Dollar Man
and asks if he has bionic powers. Maybe there is no roommate or boyfriend and he'll invite KC to sleep in his bed.

"Ricky, this is Mrs. Sutcliffe," the nurse says when he returns with a tired-looking middle-aged woman. "She's gonna
help us find a place for you to stay."

Her ID badge says she's a social worker though KC doesn't
know exactly what a social worker does. She tries to appear
friendly, but acts like she's being imposed upon and wants to
move on to more urgent matters.

"How old are you Ricky?" she asks.

"Twenty."

"Well, the bruises make you look younger. I'd believe you
were an abused kid. Tonight you're seventeen. If anyone
asks you for your ID, say you don't have one. They won't
challenge you. Runaways don't carry a driver's license. I
made the phone call, Carl. They're expecting him."

KC's devastated by the news. His new friend has betrayed
him.

"I've got it under control, Carl," she says. "You don't
need to stick around. Ricky, you're going to the juvenile
shelter for the night. They'll hook you up with Social Services tomorrow. Wait until then to tell them you're not a
minor. Now be honest with me. Are you clean? They're
going to drug test you in the morning," she says briskly.

"I think you're jumping to conclusions. I'll stay with him

until the taxi arrives." Carl says as she signs off on the cab voucher.

KC's sure that Carl would offer him a place to stay if only he would ask. But he doesn't, fearful of hearing the word no.

"Hey, cheer up. They'll help you get back home if that's where you want to go," Carl says when they're alone.

"I've got my own money. I don't need their help. You don't have to wait. I'm not a baby," KC says.

"No, you're certainly not a baby, handsome," Carl says kindly as the cab arrives. "Promise me you're gonna take care of yourself."

He offers a farewell handshake, and KC throws his arms around his broad back, hugging him tightly.

"You come see me if your ever get back to Eugene so I know you're doing okay. You're a good boy, Ricky. I know it. You remind me of my son."

The ride to the shelter seems to take forever.

"Where are we?" KC asks the driver when they stop at a traffic light.

"Blair Boulevard. You don't want me to let you out in this neighborhood, believe me."

There's a bar on the corner with a rainbow flag draped above the entrance. The neon beer signs—Bud Lite, Coors— all prominently feature the universal symbol of pride, proof of the breweries' commitment to the beer-drinking gay community. The place is called Lucky's. Easy enough to remember. He could tell the driver to drop him here, but tonight an uncomfortable mattress and smelly blankets feels like a better option than standing around, waiting for some horny guy to offer him a place to sleep.

Either breakfast at the shelter is better than KC expected or he's so starved that he's grateful for a plate of powdered scrambled eggs and a piece of dry toast. The intake counselor says he's concerned about the bite on KC's cheek. He thinks it looks like it's getting infected, KC lies and says he had a tetanus shot at the hospital. He refuses to answer any more questions and insists that the duffel and money they'd confiscated for safekeeping last night be returned to him. The counselor warns him he can't return tonight if he refuses to pee in a cup. It's eight o'clock in the morning when he walks out the front door. He hopes the gloom is only lingering fog and not the promise of a wet, drizzly day. It seems like forever since he awoke in a Seattle hotel room yesterday morning. He feels like his head is clear for the first time since the Odyssey. There's something he owes the Freemans for all they have done for him. They deserve a response to the last text he'd received from the Coach before losing his phone.

YOUR AGENT IS HAVING TROUBLE WITH THE RANGERS. NEED TO SPEAK TO YOU. WE NEED TO CONVINCE THEM IT'S NOT TRUE.

He can't stay silent and allow Coach Freeman, a devout Christian man, to break the Ninth Commandment by bearing false witness for him. He'd opened his Bible this morning as he shoveled eggs off a paper plate and the words from John 8:32 almost leaped off the page, *And you will know the truth, and the truth will set you free.* He takes it as a sign that God wants him to confess.

He wanders the streets, in search of a pay phone to call Sacramento. There's no dial tone on the only one he's able to find, a rusty and dented box on the wall of a service station. "That thing don't work. Line's been dead for more than a year. I don't know why the fucking phone company don't come and take it away. Those fuckers would charge me a goddamn fine if I ripped it out myself," the attendant says. "I think there's a pay phone at Walgreen's. Why don't you try there?"

The walk gives him a few moments to think. Words always fail him whenever he has something important to say.

He mumbles, unable to finish his sentences, never able to express his meaning. The Augustinian priests who taught him in high school tried to build his confidence, assuring him he was smart and capable, despite his pitiful grades. But he's only comfortable on the ball field where no one ever expects him to speak. He dials the Freeman's number on the phone at the Walgreen's and an automated voice asks him to either swipe a credit card or deposit three dollars and seventy five cents in coins. He hangs up and asks the lady at the cash register to change a five-dollar bill. She can't open the register; he needs to make a purchase. He wanders up and down the aisles as if he's in a daze, not wanting to waste money on something he doesn't need. He chooses a protein bar and a bottle of Muscle Milk. Walking back to the register, he passes the stationary rack. Inspired, he invests in a tablet and a cheap ballpoint pen. He'll write down what he wants to say in a letter to the Coach.

The sun is burning off the damp morning haze. There's a small park on the corner dedicated to the Indian woman who traveled with Lewis and Clark. Her statute is caked with bird shit, the shrubbery is brown and dry, and the garbage cans overflow with trash. But there's a comfortable bench and the sun feels good on KC's bruised but healing face. Soon enough he'll recognize himself in the mirror, a familiar face with a different nose. He's drinks the Muscle Milk and saves the protein bar for later. He opens the tablet and begins to write.

The first draft is sloppy, with words and entire sentences slashed through with ink. He fills the pages of the tablet with scattered thoughts that are briefly considered and quickly discarded. It takes all morning and late into the afternoon until he's satisfied with what he has to say. But there was no point writing it down if the Coach can't read KC's chicken scratch. So he painstakingly makes a more legible copy, printing the words in big, block letters.

Coach. There are so many things I am sorry about that I don't know where to start. You and Mrs. Freeman are the only family I have ever known except for my Pop-Pop and I am deeply ashamed by how I have treated you. I am sure you didn't want to believe the terrible things you heard when I was kicked off the team. I wish I could tell you they are all lies and that none of it is true.

I have asked the Lord many times to change me. I prayed that I could be a man who would make you proud. You have told me that every prayer is answered, but I think you must be wrong and that Jesus will not listen to someone like me. I will keep praying, but not for myself anymore. I will pray that you and Mrs. Freeman will meet another young man you can treat like your son who will not return your kindness with lies and dishonesty.

Please tell Mr. Stapleton to let me have my signing bonus. Since I am not the good man you thought I was you should not worry about what will happen to my money. I know I will never play ball again and accept that as God's punishment for being the kind of person that I am. I will always keep the Bible you gave me and I hope it will make you happy to know that I will read it every day. Maybe someday I will change, but I don't think so. Thank you for believing in me and trusting me even though I didn't deserve it.

P.S. Please don't worry and don't be mad because I stopped returning your texts. I lost my cell phone. I know you won't want to talk to me after you read this. I promise I will never bother you again after I write to tell you where Mr. Stapleton can send my money.

It's everything he wants to say. He needs to find a post office, buy an envelope and a stamp, and drop the letter in the mail. He signs it *KC Conroy*, then changes his mind and scratches his signature out, adding one last line.

Kevin Conroy (that is my name from now on)

He asks an old woman feeding the pigeons if there's a post office nearby. She turns, startled, throwing a fistful of dry bread crumbs in his face, and threatens to cut off his cock off if he tries to touch her. There's a junkie pacing in front of the statue, waiting for his dealer, and a noisy gaggle of old drunks are arguing over a bottle in a paper bag. It will be evening soon and the thought of wandering these grimy streets after nightfall is unnerving. He's wasted a whole day on his letter and hasn't got a plan or even an idea about his next move. He stumbles upon a post office as they are about to lock up for the night. The clerk takes pity on him and opens the door. He purchases an envelope and a stamp and carefully writes the name of the Freeman's street address.

"You're pushing your luck kid." The clerk sighs when KC asks if she can look up the zip code. "Now, on your way," she says as she finishes addressing the envelope and tosses it in the bin.

"When will it get there?"

"Monday morning. Tuesday at the latest."

He thanks her for helping and steps outside to hail a passing cab.

"Where to, young man?" the driver asks, growing impatient.

He can't go back to that fucking shelter and the only person he knows in Eugene is Carl. He's sure Carl doesn't want him sleeping on the streets. Carl likes him. Why else did he keep calling him handsome? He didn't flinch or back away when KC hugged him. But he didn't hug KC back. He just stood there, not moving, waiting for KC to release him. And he has a son. So what? But what if he's wrong and Carl isn't a queer? He can't just show up at the hospital and ask him. He's got an idea. It's Friday night. People like to go out after a long week at work.

"The meter's running, buddy. It's your money."

"Blair Boulevard," he decides abruptly under pressure to make a decision.

He feels like he needs to tip the driver well and gives him a ten-dollar bill for a three-dollar fare. Another waste of precious money. He waits until the taxi pulls away before walking into Lucky's. He hopes he does indeed get lucky tonight and Carl walks through the front door before closing time. Eugene is a creepy place, at least the parts he's seen. There's a cheap Best Western down the block, advertising rooms for fifty-nine bucks a night, but he can't spend the money.

The sign above the bar announces dollar well drinks during Happy Hour. The dancers start at nine o'clock. The place is nearly deserted despite the promise of cheap liquor. An old man is slumped on a stool at the end of the bar, his head resting on his hands. The bartender eyes KC suspiciously, asking for ID. The cop in Spokane took his fake license and his Florida license will only confirm he hasn't reached the legal age for drinking.

"Can I have a Coke?" he asks.

The duffel bag makes her wary and his bruises scream troublemaker.

"What's in the bag?" she asks before she agrees to serve him.

"Just my clothes."

"Let me see. I don't want no one bringing guns into my bar."

He's getting used to the routine by now.

"Is there a pay phone in here?" he asks, thinking he could call the hospital to make sure Carl's working tonight while she inspects his records and dirty clothes.

"Not for years. Why don't you have a cell?"

"I forgot it in Seattle."

"I'll let you use the bar phone if it's an emergency. For a local call only. Or collect."

"Thanks, I'm okay," he says. "My friend told me to wait for him here until he comes to pick me up."

"Who's your friend?"

"Carl. He works at the hospital."

"Carl Fisher?"

"Yeah, Carl Fisher," KC says, instantly brightening. It pays to follow your gut. He's absolutely sure this Carl Fisher must be his Carl, the Six Million Dollar Man.

"Where's Dennis? Is he staying in Portland tonight?" she asks.

"I don't know," KC says, unnerved by the mention of this unknown Dennis.

"Fucking Carl's like a dog in heat. If I were Dennis I would have cut off his dick years ago," she says. "You make sure that son of a bitch buys you breakfast in the morning."

Customers are starting to wander into the bar and the bartender quickly loses interest in the infidelities of her regulars.

"Nancy! Nancy! We need the fucking keys to the basement!" a young man shouts, trying to get her attention. "Fucking bitch expects us to undress here at the bar," he says to KC, expecting commiseration.

"I need you to bring up three cases of PBR right now," she shouts. "And stock the bar with vodka and tequila. You don't go on for another hour. Find something for those two assholes to do other than getting high. They're gonna be two sorry faggots if they're too fucked up to work tonight."

"What the fuck happened to your face?" the kid asks KC, ignoring her commands.

"I got into a fight," KC says.

"What's the other guy look like?"

KC just shrugs, not wanting to be the butt of a joke about

a blonde-wigged man in a dress and high heels kicking his ass.

"I never seen you around here before," the kid says. "What's your name?"

KC stops to think. Is he Ricky or KC? Neither. He's Kevin now.

"Kevin. Kevin Conroy."

He realizes he'll need to explain giving a fake name at the hospital to Carl when he arrives at the bar tonight.

"I'm Coleman Nguyen. You can call me Cole. That's my real name but everyone thinks I made it up because I don't want to use my real name working here. Like I give a fuck. They're the ones paying to touch my dick."

KC finds it strange that anyone would pay good money to grope this Cole. He's not good-looking, at least not to KC. His face is too broad and his nose is flat. He must look better undressed than he does in his street clothes. But KC supposes a guy might find Cole attractive if he's into Asian dudes.

"What are you doing in Eugene, Fucking, Oregon, Kevin?"

"I came up to see a friend"

"Who? I know every fag in Eugene, Fucking, Oregon."

"Carl Fisher."

Cole rolls his eyes and slaps KC on the back. "Ask him if he still has the crabs before you take your pants off."

Nancy is charging down the bar, on the warpath.

"All right! All right! Don't get your panties in a twist. I'm going! Christ," Cole says, turning back to KC. "I saw you sitting at the bar and was afraid Nancy had hired some new guy to compete for the few lousy dollars we make in this dump. But even she ain't stupid enough to pay a guy who looks like Freddy Krueger. Unless you have a really big dick. You have a really big dick?"

"Pay for another Coke or stop taking up space at my bar," Nancy says as she takes KC's empty glass.

"I got him covered," Cole insists, throwing two twenties

on the bar. "Let me know when he's gone through that and I'll give you more. Give him a beer. I know him. His name's Kevin Conroy. He's twenty-three."

"Well, aren't you fucking Lady Bountiful tonight?" she sneers as she pulls KC a draft.

Cole flips her the finger when she turns her back.

"Thanks. You didn't have to do that. I have my own money," KC says.

"I'll take it out in trade later," Cole informs him, winking playfully. "I'm a whole lot more fun than that ancient Carl Fisher and I won't give you an STD." He laughs as he heads for the basement to haul up the beer.

There are hours until last call and he's got nothing to do but drink while he waits for Carl to stroll through the door. He quickly grows bored staring into a pint glass. If he had his cell phone he could look up Carl on Facebook now that he knows his last name. There's probably pictures of him and Dennis doing couple things, like decorating their Christmas tree or playing with their dog. He'd send Carl a message, telling him he's waiting for him at Lucky's. He's soaking up beer like a sponge, getting drunk as a fucking skunk on an empty stomach. He should stop after he finishes this last one, or at least slow down. He doesn't want to make a bad impression when Carl Fisher walks through the door. The bar is starting to get crowded. Cole and his buddies are going to make some cash tonight after all.

The music changes from Toby Keith and Tim McGraw to pounding dance tracks with shrill female singers. KC doesn't recognize Cole at first. The body he'd thought was merely skinny is lean and sinewy, with well-defined muscles and a round ass. He's heavily inked, with Chinese characters along his calves and down his forearms and Celtic circles on each of his biceps, tattoos KC's seen on a hundred gay guys. But the design on his back is arresting, a finely rendered Pyramid Eye of the All-Knowing God. He's stripped down to a jock strap and athletic socks. There are a few appreciative catcalls as he scampers up on the bar.

"Keep drinking, stud, as long as you can get it up tonight," he teases KC before turning his attention to the slobbering drunk offering a ten-dollar bill to get a peek at the works.

Cole and his buddies are conserving their energy, barely working up a sweat. It's a long shift until closing time. They spot each other through the night, one of them having a smoke or snorting a little energy booster while the other two strut on the bar. They know how to work the crowd. Bending at the waist and spreading their ass cheeks is a favorite. Making eye contact will persuade a reluctant tipper to open his wallet. The bar is packed by midnight. So many ones and fives are flapping from the waistband of Cole's jock it looks like he's wearing a hula skirt.

"Well, you've been waiting all night for your boyfriend to arrive. Aren't you going to go say hello to him?" Nancy asks as she serves KC yet another draft.

He spins on the stool, losing his balance, almost toppling to the floor. How many beers has he drunk? Six? Seven? Enough to be shit-faced. He stands and steadies himself on the bar, searching for Carl's handsome face, unable to find him in the crowd. He's disappeared, probably taking a piss. He'll be right back; last call isn't for another hour.

"Carl!" Nancy screams, her piercing voice easily carrying over the loud music. "Your new boyfriend is nervous about seeing you! Come over here and give him a big kiss," she snarls, her voice dripping with sarcasm.

"What the fuck are you talking about you crazy bitch?" the man approaching the bar shouts. His smile is unfriendly, vaguely sinister. His beard is peppered with gray whiskers and he has a mouthful of jackass teeth. He's shirtless under his leather vest and is wearing studded wrist and armbands. His blue eyes are washed-out, faded, and his hair is cropped close to his lumpy skull.

"I don't know why she's being so shy, Carl," Nancy says, mocking KC. "This little queen's a fickle one. Maybe she's already found someone else. Two hours ago she was in love with you."

KC flinches when Carl Fisher places his hand on his shoulder. He believes Cole now. He can easily imagine crabs nesting in this guy's pubic hairs and deadly viruses floating in his bloodstream.

"Nancy says you been asking after me. You seen my profile on Leather Daddies?"

KC's vaguely aware of his guardian angel hovering overhead. Cole peers down from his perch on the bar and announces he's already staked his claim on KC for tonight,

"Bad choice, good-looking. That little Chinese pecker ain't gonna get any bigger when it's hard," Carl Fisher sneers.

"Fuck you, Leatherface," Cole spits as he dances away.

It's probably just all the beer KC's had, but Carl Fisher seems ominous, evil. Cole's right: the man looks like the mutant from *The Texas Chainsaw Massacre*. KC steps away from the bar, beyond Carl Fisher's grasp, and trips over his duffel bag on the floor by the stool. He tries to steady himself, grabbing at the bar to keep from falling, sweeping every drink in arm's length to the floor.

"Someone get this fucking mess out of here before he tears down the place!" Nancy commands and Cole hops off the bar to help KC to his feet.

"I think it's time to put you someplace safe until I can get out of here," he says as he leads KC to the storage area in the basement the dancers use as a makeshift dressing room. KC's aware of the curious stares and the cruel remarks as he's maneuvered through the crowd. He wishes he were invisible and could slip away without being noticed.

"Dude, try not to break any more glassware while I'm working. Just stay put for another hour and then we'll vamoose and go someplace to have some fun."

* * *

KC's mouth is as dry as a sand dune. His lips are cracked and his tongue is sore and swollen. He must have bitten it while he slept. Last night is a blur: the ugly man in the leather vest, sleeping on a bed of beer cases, being shaken awake and walked to a car, watching a video, passing out. His head is throbbing and he's nauseous. The undershirt he slept in smells vaguely like puke. His pants and socks are on the floor. His wallet's in his pocket and he quickly thumbs through the bills, relieved his money hasn't been stolen. His belly rumbles when he stoops to pull on his boots. He doesn't know where he is, but he wants to get out, now. There's only one problem. His duffel bag is missing.

He throws a blanket on the mattress, having been taught never to leave an unmade bed, and goes searching for his bag. The house is a small place, a ranch with cramped rooms and narrow halls. A flat screen television and an oversize sectional sofa dominate the living room; dirty glasses and empty bottles and an elaborate bong are on the coffee table. KC vaguely recalls taking a hit and chugging a beer as a pair of Asian twinks fucked on video. Across the hall is a larger bedroom than the one where KC awoke. There's a hospital bed and a twin bed pushed against opposite walls. The window is shut and the shade is drawn. The air is stale and smells of old people, like the nursing home room where KC's Pop-Pop died, a sour odor that reminds KC of boiled milk. He hears loud, staccato voices in the back of the house, speaking a language he doesn't understand.

"Hey," Cole says as KC enters the kitchen. "I was just gonna come in and wake you. You slept until dinner time."

Cole's looking dapper, wearing slacks with a sharp crease and a pressed dress shirt, modestly buttoned at the neck. He's sitting at the table between an old man and woman. The old man's right arm is a stump without an elbow. He points at KC with the tip of his chopstick and unleashes a furious torrent of words. KC doesn't need a translator to understand he's demanding an explanation why a strange white man is standing in his kitchen. Cole's answer must satisfy him since he drops his head over his bowl and resumes slurping noodles into his mouth. His bald scalp bears the fiery scars of napalm burns from the long ago war; the thick, ruined skin is the texture of wax dripping from a burning candle.

Cole is holding a sippy cup under the woman's chin, encouraging her to finish her smoothie. Her twisted body seems tiny in the large wheelchair. Her legs are shriveled and her withered feet are no larger than a child's. She seems agitated by KC's presence, shaking her head and refusing the straw.

"Strangers make her nervous," Cole explains. "Ba, this is Kevin. He's not going to hurt you," he says in English. "Say something to her. She needs to get used to the sound of your voice."

"I can't. I don't speak Chinese," KC says.

"Neither does she. She's Vietnamese." He laughs and KC thanks her for letting her spend the night in her house.

She stares at KC, unblinking, as Cole translates for her.

"Call her Ba. She'll like that. She doesn't really talk since the last stroke. But I can understand her. I know what she wants when she's making noises."

The staff at the nursing home swore KC was the only one who could interpret the meaning of his Pop-Pop's grunts and snorts. It still hurts to be reminded his grandfather died alone in that place with no one at his bedside.

"Where did you put my bag? Is it still in your car?" he asks, anxious to collect his records and clothes and be on his way.

Cole looks puzzled.

"What bag?"

"My duffel bag. The red one with the Spokane Chiefs logo. I had it with me at the bar."

"I don't know. It must still be there. We can pick it up tonight."

KC can't wait until tonight. He wants to be on the road as soon as he decides which direction to take. Definitely not south to Sacramento. And he'll never head back east, back to Albany, giving his mother the satisfaction of knowing she was right about him all along. He's just come from the north, and west is out of the question since he can't swim across the Pacific. He's been on the move since being cut from the team, racing from one place to another as if he had somewhere to go. He can't run forever. All things in motion eventually come to a stop.

Texas.

His gut tells him to head to Texas. He liked it there while he was playing winter ball. But everyone he knew in the state has scattered across the country, chasing their dreams of making the Show. There won't be anyone to offer him a place to crash for a few days, just long enough to get back on his feet. He'll need to find a way to earn money until the Coach releases his signing bonus. But he never finished his junior college degree and has no skills except hitting and throwing a ball. He's not qualified for a real job. All he can do is look for day work, like the Mexicans who stand on the streets in the early hours of the morning seeking cash wages for manual labor.

"There's leftover takeout you can microwave," Cole offers. "And there's more noodle soup in the refrigerator if you want a bowl. You need to eat to keep up your strength or you're gonna collapse after an hour."

Cole isn't in any hurry to send him on his way. He hasn't invited him to stay, but he hasn't asked him to leave either. He even seems to think he and KC are going to the bar tonight.

"We start work at eight. Saturday's the busiest night. You're gonna be dead on your ass by last call. We can get a six-pack and watch *The Notebook* when we get home. Love me some Ryan Gosling!"

Cole laughs at KC's confused reaction.

"You backing out on me?" I knew you were bullshitting last night when you said you wanted to dance. Too much weed and too much beer. I knew you wouldn't have the balls to do it! But just give me a little time. I'm gonna get you up there dancing on the bar flashing those buns of steel soon enough."

KC's beginning to recall the wee hours of the morning, but it's an incomplete jigsaw. Bits and pieces of the puzzle are still missing. He remembers music. Loud music. Stripping down to his underwear and dancing in the tiny living room. Auditioning for an appreciative audience of one. Tripping over his feet and falling on his ass. Cole rolling on the living room floor, laughing hysterically. A hit on the bong. Another bottle of Coors. Another hit on the bong. Cole slipping a disc into the DVD player. He remembers sitting spread-eagled, staring slack-jawed, too stunned to react as Cole fast-forwarded to a scene featuring a lean, sinewy Asian, with well-defined muscles and a round ass, heavily inked with Chinese characters along his calves and down his forearms, Celtic circles on each of his biceps, and a finely rendered Pyramid Eye etched on his back. An actor named "Cole Lee" was energetically fucking a smaller Asian boy in high definition television before enthusiastically giving up his own sweet ass to a brute who was a dead ringer for Vin Diesel.

"You want to wash your clothes, Kevin? They don't smell so good. There's a robe on the hook on the bedroom door. Fuck. Where is my fucking sister? She was supposed to be home an hour ago. Just keep your eye on these two 'til she gets here, okay? They won't give you any trouble. I can't be late for five o'clock Mass. I'm doing the readings."

He'd never expected to stay in Eugene for more than two or three days. He's been here nearly three weeks now. Cole and his sister have come to depend on him. He says room and board is all he needs for taking care of their grandparents, but they insist on paying him cash, two hundred a week at first, increasing it to three hundred when he talked about going south to Texas. Ba has grown attached to him—Cole calls it a crush—and fusses whenever anyone other than KC tries to feed her. Cole's amazed at KC's patience with her, how he can sit with her for hours, holding her hand, speaking to her in a low soothing voice, just like he did with Pop-Pop whenever he visited the nursing home. *Ong,* which Cole says means grandfather, and KC have become good buddies. They play endless games of checkers and dominoes and cards with the television volume cranked loud so the old man doesn't miss anything on the Vietnamese cable channel.

He and Cole share the same bed as chastely as brothers. Cole swears they got so horny watching his video that they sucked each other's dicks the night they met, but KC doesn't remember it and the suggestion of anything sexual has never come up again. Cole says it would only fuck things up. KC's the best thing that's happened to him in a long time. His cunty sister isn't much help with their grandparents. She's in the Nguyen family business and works the same odd hours as her brother. A headliner at the city's swankiest gentleman's club, she's a legend in every frat house on the campus of the University of Oregon. Since KC's arrival, Cole's finally got the freedom to book his "appearances" without needing to coordinate schedules with her.

KC is never in need of cash. Nancy's not such a terror once you get to know her. She was almost maternal when she handed him his duffel bag, lecturing him that he needs to be more responsible, that he's damn lucky she happened to catch that hopped-up meth head trying to walk out the door with it slung over his shoulder. And she was the one who insisted on driving him to the urgent care clinic and paying for a tetanus shot and an antibiotic for the infected bite on his cheek. She's slipping him a few bucks under the table, putting his broad back and strong shoulders to use hauling heavy cases of liquor and beer up from the basement. He's cheaper labor than a contractor. He knows how to use a hammer and a screwdriver and there are a million little jobs in the bar to keep him busy.

It's odd, strangely liberating, having no future ahead of him, no goals, no destination. It's not entirely unpleasant being stuck in a holding pattern. He's told Cole about the money being held captive in Florida. Cole thinks he should open an account at a local bank and tell this Mr. Freeman to make a wire transfer. He knows a lawyer who will sue the old man's ass if he won't give KC his money. But KC refuses Cole's offer to threaten the only friend who ever tried to help him. He promises he'll write the Coach when Cole gets back from California. He's leaving for Los Angeles next weekend for two, almost three, weeks. He's shooting in L.A. and San Francisco. He's developed a loyal following on the Internet and demand for his services is peaking. The casting agent for Squirt Studios says Cole's a sure bet for an AVA nomination for best Asian bottom. He's not blowing his fees up his nose like most of the models. He wants to be an entrepreneur. He'll have saved enough to produce his first video by the new year. He already has a name for his studio. Snake Eyes Productions. He thinks it would be a good investment for KC when he's got his hands on his money.

"And I ain't just doing Asian shit either. I'm gonna have a brand. Like Falcon and Catalina. Lots of twinks getting rammed by straight dudes. I'm always looking for talent," he teases KC, making him blush.

KC alludes to his own unhappy experience before Darrell Torok's camera. Cole's intrigued, pressing him for details.

"Dude, that guy is a perv. You should have called the cops."

Cole says he'll be able to concentrate on business in California knowing Ba and Ong are in good hands. He's leased a new Audi for the road trip and is leaving the Explorer so KC can drive his grandparents around. KC's settled in, a part of the household, with no good reason to leave. Lately he's been thinking he might stay in Eugene, Oregon. It's nicer than Albany, not as hot and sticky as Florida. He's got friends here, unlike Texas where he doesn't know a soul anymore. People seem to like him. No one treats him special, but no one thinks he's a freak either. For the first time in his life, he isn't keeping any secrets. He doesn't have to lie about where he goes, what he does, who he does it with. No one cares that he likes to suck cock and no one judges him because he sometimes takes it up the ass. He almost feels normal here. He's never felt normal before. Maybe he can even coach Little League if he's still here in the spring.

There'll be plenty of time to think about his future while Cole is gone. Today there's a party to throw. It's Ong's birthday and even Cole's sister is joining the celebration. KC's job is to pick up the cake at Safeway, a special order with extra frosting and plenty of buttercream flowers. It's a beautiful evening, a full moon and clear skies, perfect for a barbecue. Strings of colorful Christmas lights illuminate the yard and the guy Cole's sister swears is not her boyfriend (Cole says he deals prescription narcotics supplied by a connection in Canada) has come through with boxes of sparklers and firecrackers. He's promising an impressive backyard fireworks display after they cut the cake. They light the citronellas candles to chase away the mosquitos and gather at a picnic table set with festive plates and cups from the party store. Ong is pleased with his paper hat, but Ba struggles and grunts when KC tries to put one on her head. Cole says she's jealous of all the attention her husband's enjoying on his special day. He confides she was a real bitch before the stroke, constantly belittling his put-upon grandfather. He says Ong's a happier man now that his wife is unable to speak.

"How old is he?" KC asks, needing to know how many candles to put on the cake. He'd bought three boxes to be sure there were enough. The fucking cake is going to be a fire hazard.

"No one knows," Cole says nonchalantly. "Not even Ba."

Ong's age is a mystery to everyone. He met Cole's grandmother while they were in an encampment waiting to be evacuated. All of their documents had been destroyed; their personal histories are casualties of the war. Cole's father might have heard stories of the family's past when he was a child, but he was murdered during an armed robbery of the convenience store he'd bought with money earned and saved waxing and buffing the floors of the local hospitals and schools. But whatever his age, Ong's a spry old rooster, enjoying his liberation from the blistering tongue of his wife.

Cole's sister has prepared a feast to observe the occasion, a shock to KC who's never even seen her make a pot of coffee. There's sticky rice and steamed buns. KC, who had never heard of lemongrass and fish paste a month ago, is stuffing his face with spicy grilled sausages.

"So, how do you like your first taste of dog?" Cole asks, doubling over in laughter when KC, a look of horror in his eyes, spits a mouthful of half-chewed meat on the grass.

"I'm kidding, bro," Cole confesses, wiping the tears from his eyes. "It's pork. Just like Jimmy Dean."

But there's no mistaking the final course set before the birthday boy.

"Be careful you don't burn yourself Ong. I just took them off the grill," Cole warns his grandfather who's salivating over the delicacy that's been brought to the table.

"You gonna try one?" Cole asks KC who's too appalled to answer, unable to believe anyone would willingly put a charred chicken head, skewered and roasted, in their mouth.

"It's easy," Cole swears as he demonstrates the proper to crack the tiny skull and suck the brains from the head. "Make up your mind before Ong eats them all."

Cole, his sister, and the man who she says isn't her boyfriend laugh at KC's squeamishness, insisting KC will never be a real Nguyen until he eats a chicken head. KC impulsively cracks one open and swallows the contents too quickly to actually taste it, a small price to pay to be accepted into a family.

Cole says God doesn't care who or what he is. After all, who made him this way? All that matters is that you don't hurt anyone else, he explains. He and his sister are good Catholics. They attend Mass every week, taking communion, and there are holy pictures of the Virgin Mary and the Sacred Heart throughout the house. KC doesn't know much about being Catholic. He was baptized but never went to Mass as a kid and only attended Augustinian because they gave him a full scholarship to play baseball. He doubts he'll be going to any more churches or listening to any pastors and their sermons like he did when he lived with the Freemans. But he still reads the Bible Coach gave him every night, finding solace in the words he sometimes struggles to understand. He's started keeping a list of his favorite verses and is committing them to memory.

Matthew 5:16.

Luke 7:47

John 8:12

And always, he returns to his favorite passage and the words that prove Jesus doesn't hate him, that Our Lord and Savior has a place in His heart for everyone.

After David finished talking with Saul, Jonathan became one in spirit with David, and he loved him as himself. 1 Samuel 18:1.

"Fuck! Fuck! Fuck!"

He closes his Bible when he hears Cole screaming into his cell in the next room, ripping someone a new asshole in both English and Vietnamese. KC doesn't envy anyone who'll be working for the owner of Snake Eyes Productions. Cole's temper could sandblast an entire salvage yard.

"Kevin, you gotta help me out tonight. You got to. It's no big deal, I swear. That fucking Thanh is fucking high as a

kite and I promised a duo. It's nothing really. Just some old
dude's birthday party. Some really old dude. He's, like,
sixty-five. He's paying us two-fifty each just to dance in our
jocks. You don't have to do anything else. I promise. If anyone asks if you want to go off to a bedroom and do a private
dance, just say no."

He took money from that old rich guy in Spokane. What's
the big deal? He doesn't have to get naked and no one's
gonna expect him to blow a load at the end of the show. He
can't really say no. KC can shake his bare ass in a bunch of
guys' faces to help out Cole who's done so much for him.
Just this once, he swears.

"You want to get high first?" Cole asks as he parks the
car in the driveway of a three-story house in a tree-lined
neighborhood near the university campus. It's an impressive
residence, solid brick, with a real front porch with a green
canvas awning, shaded by two massive pines. Men, most of
them balding or silver-haired, wander in and out of the
house. They're well dressed, in khakis and bright pastel polo
shirts, and carry drinks and bottles of beer.

"Nah, I think I'm okay," KC says tentatively, already regretting agreeing to do this favor for Cole.

"Well, I do," Cole says, firing up a joint.

KC wonders if it was really such a short time ago that he
would have been worried about second hand smoke causing
a positive drug screen on the frequent random samples that
are the scourge of the minor leagues.

"Don't worry. They're all really nice. And they're all fucking harmless. This is the easiest money you'll ever make."

The birthday boy, according to Cole, is a big shot at the
university. Cole's been told he's actually famous and gets
paid a lot of money to lecture around the world. Cole thinks
he's some expert in Greek or Roman, one of those ancient
languages nobody speaks. He's also morbidly obese, three-
fifty at least. Cole warns KC not to laugh when he's introduced to the host. He'll be wearing a silk kimono and gold

slippers and has a big pumpkin head that makes him look
like Jabba the Hut.

"But he's really, really cool. The Professor's a real gentleman. So don't get all grossed out if he asks to touch your
dick. Don't piss him off. It takes me a whole weekend at that
fucking bar to earn what I'm making tonight."

Even Cole's vivid description doesn't prepare KC for his
first sighting of their host. The Professor drifts among his
guests like a parade float, utterly placid, able to move while
appearing to remain perfectly still. His arms are folded across
his rotund belly and his hands are hidden in the sleeves of his
kimono.

"Lovely," he announces when Cole introduces him to KC.
"A wise choice. Many of my guests have a distinct appetite
for these All-American boys. Now don't be jealous Master
Coleman. You know my preference for exotic and delicate
things," he says, causing KC to breathe a sigh of relief,
knowing he won't be asked to offer his pecker to the Professor tonight.

They'd been invited to arrive after ten, just in time for the
champagne toast and the cutting of the cake. The Professor
graciously offers both young men a slice and a flute. Cole
whispers to KC to accept the champagne, but decline the
cake. Eating carries the risk of a pooching stomach and the
flatter the belly, the fatter the tip. Cole quickly gives KC
the run down. Once the music starts, everyone will gather
in the living room. The two of them are being paid to be
showmen. There's an art to dancing. Timing is everything.

"Just follow my lead. Milk it for tips. Don't rush to strip
down to your jock, but don't take so long they start to get
restless. We have to dance for a half hour. After that you
don't have to do anything else unless you want to. Use the
blue bedroom if you want to make some extra cash."

KC doesn't feel particularly sexy as he begins to sway to
the music. The soundtrack is almost as old as the guests.
Cole expertly pantomimes every groan, every moan, of

"Love to Love You Baby." KC mimics his mentor as best as he can; he's never really learned to dance. But he's an athlete so he's coordinated enough that he doesn't move like a spastic monkey. No one seems interested in his dance steps anyways. They're admiring his pecs, his biceps, his tight abdomen, and his perfectly shaped ass. They practically throw bills—five, tens, even twenties—when he reluctantly obliges the request that he spread his cheeks and show off his pink hole. He's exhausted after ten minutes and the idea of keeping this up for the entire bargained-for performance seems impossible. But more and more bills are flapping from the waistband of his jock strap. Cole lied to him though. This *isn't* the easiest money he's ever earned.

The show is over by eleven and some of the guests have left. KC senses that those who remain are anticipating an after-party, something less button-down and proper (all things being relative) than the official celebration that preceded. Cole has disappeared. Most likely he's entertaining the birthday boy in the red bedroom, soliciting a significant withdrawal from the Professor's wallet. KC's standing alone, nursing a beer, aware that he's the topic of several whispered conversations in the room. He's been allowed to put on his jeans, but is expected to remain shirtless until it's time to leave. He smiles awkwardly as a man shyly approaches.

"I wanted to tell you that you are very beautiful," his admirer admits, his eyes falling on KC's chest rather than his face.

"Thank you," KC says, feeling stupid and vain for acknowledging the compliment.

"Would you like to come upstairs with me?" the man asks.

"No. No thanks," he says nervously. Kevin Conroy will never take money to have sex with men again. He'll let them stuff dollar bills in his jock, but nothing more.

He's rude to the next man who approaches him, helping

himself to another beer and putting on his shirt despite the expectation that he keep the goods on display until he leaves. A pair of unattractive bald men with sloppy guts are kissing and groping each other on the sofa, attracting an audience who are stroking the bulges in their pants. KC's rejected admirer is on his knees, working on a silver daddy who's removed his shirt and is tweaking his own nipples.

"Let's get the fuck out of here before they push aside the furniture and start fucking on the Oriental carpets," Cole says, sneaking up behind him, giggling as they make their escape unnoticed.

Cole's in high spirits as they speed across town, ignoring stop signs and barely touching the brakes at traffic lights. It's been a more profitable night than expected. Between his fee and tips and a generous donation of an additional two hundred dollars to ram a ten-inch dildo up the Professor's ass, he's eight hundred dollars richer than he was at the beginning of the evening. He's curious about how much KC was able to earn. Cole assures him his four-hundred-sixty-dollar haul counting tips is a good showing for a novice.

"But with that fucking body you should be making more. Don't worry. You'll get the hang of it."

Cole cranks up the volume of the car radio. They're playing his favorite, Brad Paisley, on the Country Hot 100.

"You know what?" he says, stricken by inspiration. "We're gonna get you a white cowboy hat like Brad wears. That's a good look for you. I even got a name for you. *Brock Paisley.* Like maybe you're his hot gay brother or cousin."

"I don't think I want to do that again," KC says, refusing to commit.

"Of course you do, dude. Just think of all the fucking money you'll be making."

Further discussion is put on hold. Cole's got an incoming call he has to take.

"Hey, man. How's it coming? When can I see it? Excellent! I'm gonna pick up a bottle of Jack and come on over. See you in about twenty minutes."

Cole is too anxious to wait until he returns from California to see what Omar, his trusted tattoo artist, has designed for his lower back.

"I'll ask him to do something for you too. My gift to you for looking after Ba and Ong while I'm gone."

The idea of allowing someone to scar his skin with ink and needles frightens KC. Not the pain, though he's always been squeamish about shots. It's something more compelling that bothers him. It's a sin, forbidden, if he remembers his Leviticus correctly. *Do not cut your body for the dead or put tattoo marks on yourselves. I am the LORD.* Just like Leviticus forbids him from lying with another man.

The studio is brightly lit, modern, a respectable place of business in an ordinary shopping center, nestled between a craft supply shop and a vitamin store. It's as sterile and antiseptic as a doctor's office, hardly the dingy, filthy back room he'd imagined. He expected Omar to be a squinting Popeye, an outlaw biker, with shaky hands, not the well-spoken, clean-shaven, and modestly dressed man who could pass for a schoolteacher if not for the erotic and colorful tableaux of mythical creatures—naked sea nymphs and sirens—inked into the skin of his arms. He and Cole greet each other with an elaborate ritual of palm slapping and arm grappling, culminating in an affectionate embrace.

"This is my buddy Kevin," Cole says, introducing KC.

KC feels more naked than when he was wearing nothing but a jock strap. But Omar's intense gaze isn't sexual. He looks at KC and sees an unblemished canvas, a bare wall crying out for a mural.

"Okay, my man. Don't keep me waiting any longer," Cole pleads. "The suspense is killing me."

Cole is awestruck by the intricate stencils presented for his approval. Two crouching dragons, mirror images standing face-to-face, encrusted with bejeweled scales, breathing fire, will make a noble pedestal for the Pyramid Eye.

"It's fucking beautiful," he whispers. "You are a fucking genius. I wish I didn't have to go to California so we could get started tonight."

He cracks open the seal on the bottle of Jack and proposes a toast. He and KC knock back three shots in a row while Omar barely sips from the rim of his glass.

"I want you to design something real special for my buddy Kevin. He's a fucking virgin and he's gonna get his cherry busted by the master."

The whiskey and the late hour weaken KC's resolve. After all, Josh Hamilton's a Christian who's famously and proudly inked. He's a walking billboard for his faith. Jesus would never disapprove of that.

Omar has dozens of sample books. He recommends that KC study them closely, take his time, and not make any rash and impulsive decisions.

"Think about it, use these ideas for inspiration. While Cole's in California, reflect on what is most important in your life and how you want to express those ideas on your body," Omar advises.

KC insists that Omar provide him with a consent form. He knows exactly what he wants and where he wants it. Nothing can deter him. If Omar won't do it, he'll go to one of those sleazy tattoo parlors on Highway 99 where the only question they'll ask is if he has the cash.

Omar capitulates, encouraged by Cole. It's a simple enough task and KC's chosen to have it stenciled at the base of his neck, easily hidden by a shirt collar if he regrets it in the morning. KC snorts another shot of Jack, bracing himself for the pain. He removes his shirt and offers his back. For some strange reason he feels like crying as the needles pierce his skin. It's an act of courage, irrevocable, irreversible. He's branding himself an outlaw, a pariah to some, hopefully an inspiration to others.

"All done my friend," the artist announces.

Cole takes a picture with his cell phone for KC's final approval before Omar covers the wound with a bandage. It's perfect. A short and simple statement rendered in beautiful calligraphy, a solemn declaration: *1 Samuel 18:1*

Omar says he'll have a real shot of Jack now and Cole pours another round to celebrate the milestone. KC, without any forethought and only a fleeting moment of regret afterwards, reaches for Cole's phone and texts the photograph to a number with a Sacramento, California area code.

The worst thing about Cole being gone is there's no one but KC to bathe and dress Ba. He'd pleaded with Cole's sister to relieve him of the job, but she'd laughed, promising him the old lady's cunt lips don't have teeth and can't bite. At first, he tried averting his eyes from her shriveled titties and was too squeamish to wash her pussy and her ass. But familiarity and necessity are a sure cure for modesty and he barely blushes now whenever a small turd floats up in her bath water. Ong expects his breakfast and his dinner on time and at least one game of checkers or a hand of cards with his nightly glass of Four Roses at bedtime. KC drops him off each morning at the community center to spend the day throwing dice and smoking cigarettes with other survivors of the black days of the war. He picks up a few extra bucks bar backing for Nancy when Cole's sister isn't working. Usually he's in bed by ten, his Bible open beside him, falling asleep while the Mariners lose yet again on the nightly broadcast.

He still has the deep tan of long days in the bright sun, but now he spends far too many afternoons indoors, tending to Ba and watching cable reruns and DVDs during her frequent naps. Nancy warns him to take advantage of the heat and the bright skies. The coming months will be wet and dreary. So, one afternoon, he buckles Ba into Cole's Explorer and tosses her folded wheelchair in the back. He drives out into the country, stopping in a small farm town when they come upon a sandlot. He straps Ba into her chair and they find a cool spot under a tree, close to the batting cage. The local boys are engaged in fierce competition, playing a pickup game as intensely as if it were the bottom of the ninth inning of the seventh game of the World Series with the score tied at two all. One of the bolder kids approaches him to settle an argument and he offers to call balls and strikes behind the plate.

The rival teams are only interested in tussling in the dirt and claiming victory for the day. But a few of the boys linger after the game, taking him up on his offer to teach them a few fundamentals. He shows them how to shift their weight to their back legs before swinging for the fences and demonstrates the proper grip for throwing the ball, "thumb to thigh, fingers to the sky." No one has ever taught them that touching the inside corner of the bag is the shortest route around the bases. He picks up a bat, launches a few bombs deep into the outfield and critiques their fielding, patiently explaining how to get in front of the ball while on the run. He could stay for hours but Ba is getting restless, struggling with the restraints on her wheelchair. The kids plead with him to return tomorrow. Not tomorrow, but maybe he'll come back later in the week. No promises, but he'll try his best.

Driving home, he realizes he misses being a ball player and the game that had been his entire life. He's never told anyone in Eugene he was once a promising prospect, not even Cole, who thinks the money in the Florida account was left him by his Pop-Pop. He doesn't want to answer any questions, doesn't want to have to explain his fall from grace. What's done is done and he can't go back and change the past. It's best to keep looking forward, as hopeless as the future may seem. He's seen the ads for trade schools, promising him high-paying jobs as an auto mechanic or an electrician. But the work that really interests him is becoming a medical assistant and then maybe one day going to nursing

school. He doesn't care anymore that stupid people will assume he's queer for doing a woman's job. He'd like taking
care of sick people more than trying to repair an engine. He
prays every night for God to show him what to do with his
life, the right path to take. But when he falls asleep, he
dreams he's the Mighty KC again, tying the laces of a pair of
cleats and sprinting onto the field.

He's tired tonight, but has to deal with Ba's unexpected
attack of incontinence. She's agitated, making it difficult to
undress and bathe her. He's upset when he discovers a rash
on her bum. Cole will be back in two days and he'll think
KC's neglected her. He dusts her with baby powder and
sings to her. "Hello, Mary Lou" always cheers her up. He finally gets her into bed, then pours Ong his tumbler of Four
Roses. He's throwing Ba's soiled sweat pants in the washer
when the front door bell rings. It's probably someone looking for Cole's sister. Last night a police officer showed up,
pressing his card into KC's hand and asking him to tell her to
get in touch when she comes home. He decides to ignore the
bell, wait for whoever it is to go away, but the visitor is persistent and has a heavy thumb. He's just gotten Ba settled
and the racket is sure to wake her up.

The sun is setting, casting long shadows on the porch,
and the visitor's face is partially obscured by the screen door.
But KC's startled by his resemblance to a man he assumed
he would never see again. It's impossible. It has to be someone else. There's no way Coach Freeman could have found
him.

"Can I come in, KC?"

He looks much older than he had only a few months ago
when he dropped KC at the airport for his flight to Spokane.
He's lost weight. It shows in his face; his skin seems to sag
from his cheeks. His eyes are puffy and ringed with dark circles.

"Praise the Lord!" the Coach says as he gathers KC in his

arms. He's not ashamed of sobbing and clings to KC as if KC is something precious he'd lost and despaired of ever finding again. KC's too stunned to speak at first, over-whelmed by the unexpected reunion.

"I'm sorry. I'm sorry. I'm sorry," KC repeats over and over again after finding his voice, trying to console his old friend, apologizing for each of the many transgressions he's committed. For running away. For not returning the Coach's calls. For lying. For not being the man the Coach believed him to be.

Ong is standing in the hall, holding his tumbler of whiskey in his hand, jabbering in Vietnamese. The words are incom-prehensible, but the tone and volume of his voice make it clear this stranger isn't welcome in his house.

"Hello, I'm John Freeman," the Coach says, composing himself and extending a hand which he awkwardly pulls back he realizes he's reaching for a shortened stump.

"He doesn't know English, Coach. Just smile at him and he'll understand you're my friend."

KC remembers his manners and invites the Coach into the kitchen. He fears the Coach will assume the worst, that he's taken up a life of drugs and drinking, when he sees the open bottle of Four Roses on the table.

"How about pouring me a shot of that, KC," the Coach says. He swallows the whiskey and sighs heavily, closing his eyes and taking a moment to steady himself.

"I forgot how much it burns. It's the Lord's way of re-minding us of Corinthians," he says, smiling. "Can we talk somewhere, KC? In private?"

Ong has lost interest in their unexpected visitor anyway so KC sits him in front of the living room television and turns on the Cartoon Network. Animated hijinks and prat-falls need no translation. Coach Freeman insists they pray together when KC joins him at the kitchen table. He takes KC by the hands and asks him to close his eyes. He thanks

the Lord for answering his prayers, for reuniting him with
KC, for watching over KC while he was lost, and for keeping him safe until he was found.

"Well, it's not as bad as I thought it could be," the Coach
says after *Amen.* He touches KC's chin and inspects the
damage to KC's face. It's obvious his nose has had an unfortunate encounter with a blunt object.

"I can see the bones have started to heal. They're going to
have to break it again to set it straight. We can deal with it in
the offseason. I heard you were bitten on the face, too."

"It's okay now. I got a tetanus shot and took an antibiotic."

"KC, you need to be honest with me," the Coach says.

KC's prepared to tell the truth, knowing the consequences
of admitting he will never be the person the Freemans want
him to be, that he can't marry Callie and be a good father to
her child, that he hadn't just wandered into Club Odyssey by
chance, that he'd been there before, many times. That he is
gay.

"Will you pass a drug test?"

KC squirms in his seat. He only toked once, that night he
met Cole, but grass lingers in the bloodstream. And he's inhaled plenty of Cole's second hand smoke that could show
up on a screen.

"We'll have one done as soon as we get home. A test run.
Jerry can stall the Rangers a while longer. They're sending
you to Hickory as soon as you're released from rehab. The
Lord is looking out for you, KC. You're getting another
chance."

"But I don't need to go to rehab! I only did it once since I
left Spokane. Just a couple hits off a bong. I swear to you,
Coach! I swear on Jesus's name!"

"I believe you, KC. But Jerry needed a reason to explain
why you're AWOL. He's told the assistant G.M. there was an
intervention that night in Spokane and that you're in an in-
patient rehab program. You're clean now and committed to

your recovery. I'll be traveling with you as your life coach. The college season's over and I'm taking a leave."

KC's confused by the Coach's willingness to participate in the deception. He'd come clean in his letter so that the Coach would never have to lie on his behalf. The Commandments forbid you to bear false witness *against* your neighbor. But maybe it's not a sin to lie to help someone. Coach Freeman would know better than him.

"You're a lucky boy, KC. Jerry represents the Ranger's ace and they're desperate to sign him when he hits free agency at the end of the season. Management wants to keep Jerry happy and is willing to believe his version of the story about your leaving the Chiefs rather than vicious rumors started by Bill Keller. There was no police report filed. It's Jerry's word against that vindictive man."

There's no need to acknowledge the obvious. They both know KC would never be welcome in any clubhouse if the truth about his expulsion from the Chiefs were known. It's an unfair world where it's better to be an addict than a homo.

"Do you want me to lie, Coach?" he asks, needing confirmation of what he's being asked to do.

"The Lord wants you to play ball, KC. That's why he blessed you with your gifts. *Commit to the Lord whatever you do, and He will establish your plans.* You remember your Proverbs, don't you?"

"No," he admits, an honest answer. "Why are you doing this for me? I didn't think you would ever speak to me again."

The Coach pours himself another shot of whiskey and tosses it back in a single belt.

"Take this bottle away, KC. I still have to drive back to the motel tonight. We're flying back to Sacramento day after tomorrow. I know you promised your friend you'd look after his grandparents while he was gone. I told him I wouldn't take you home until he was back."

The Coach says he thinks Cole is a very impressive

young man. His faith must be truly strong to enable him to care for his aging family members while pursuing his commitment to his missionary work.

"I thank the Lord you met a good Christian fellow to help you through this crisis. He's very protective of you. I called the morning I got the photograph. I didn't need to see your face to know it was you. At first, he denied knowing anything about it. I had to work hard to earn his trust. It took him a week before he admitted he knew someone named Kevin and several more days before he would say his friend's last name is Conroy. He only agreed to tell me where to find you two days ago. He promised he wouldn't tell you I was coming and give you an opportunity to run away."

The Cole Nguyen who stands so high in the Coach's admiration is finishing up a mission visit to the Navajo reservation in Arizona with his church group, gathering fresh souls for the Lord. The Freemans have promised to make a substantial donation to his ministry.

"We're going to have to do something about that tattoo, KC. You might as well be branded with the scarlet letter. We can have it removed. I suppose the Lord can overlook a few scars on the back of your neck."

KC's not really sure what a scarlet letter is. All he remembers is that it was a book he was supposed to read in high school. But he understands why Coach Freeman is worried. There are plenty of Christians in the game familiar with the story of David and Jonathan. Going back to his old life means living in fear again, knowing that, at any moment, he could be exposed and everything he wants, his dreams of being the Mighty KC, will be snatched away from him a second time. How does Coach Freeman know that's what God wants for him?

Commit to the Lord whatever you do and He will establish your plans.

Things aren't so bad here in Eugene. Maybe *this* is God's

plan, that he live his life as Kevin Conroy, unburdened by secrets, looking after people who can't care for themselves.

"I can't think right now," he says, pulling away from the table. He walks out the front door and sits on the stairs of the front porch, staring intently into the starry sky as if he expected God to appear in the heavens to explain what is right and what is wrong and reveal what it is He wants KC to do.

"Can I sit with you, KC? I haven't been tipsy in years," Coach Freeman smiles, holding another tumbler of whiskey in his hand. "You're going to have to call me a cab." He laughs.

"It's true. What they told you. What they're saying. What I wrote in my letter. I know you don't want to believe it, but it is," KC says.

"So, what's there to do around here tomorrow, KC?" the Coach asks cheerfully, changing the subject. "Are the Emeralds at home or are they on the road?"

"I don't know."

He doesn't know the Northwest League schedule anymore. He'd never dream of going to a game. He's even taken detours and side streets to avoid driving by the ballpark where the Eugene Emeralds play.

"And it would be too weird," he confesses.

The Emeralds are a league rival of the Spokane Chiefs. It would be awkward, watching young men he once played against, even from the safe distance of the bleacher seats.

"KC, you're going to have to face these boys again somewhere along the road. I want you to stand proud and look them in the eye. *Watch out that you do not lose what we have worked for, but that you may be rewarded fully.*"

"You shouldn't have come looking for me. You know what I am," KC says angrily, frustrated by the Coach's refusal to acknowledge the truth that will never change. "Why won't you say it?"

Coach Freeman clears his throat and speaks softly, taking the young man's hand in his own.

"I'm an imperfect man, KC. Just like you. Just like every one of God's children. I've made mistakes in my life and the Lord has given me the opportunity to set things right."

"What kind of mistakes?" KC asks.

"There were days when we didn't think we could make it. Days when Miriam couldn't bring herself to get out of bed. Days when we didn't think even our faith would help pull us through. I never knew, never saw it coming, KC. I thank the Lord it was me, not Miriam, who found him hanging from a beam in the basement. I don't know why he did it. God may forgive me, but I can never forgive myself for being so blind.

"He never told me he was unhappy. I thought I knew him and I didn't. There's nothing so terrible that life's not worth living anymore. He could have told me anything, KC. Anything. I was his father, KC, and I loved him and nothing could have ever changed that. But he didn't know that. He was my boy and he thought he couldn't come to me. He was my son and he didn't know there was nothing he could ever do, anyone he could be, that could make me turn away from him."

The Coach pauses to take a long sip of his whiskey. They sit quietly, listening to the comforting sounds of an ordinary summer evening. Cartoon voices squabble on the television in the living room. A hunting dog paces in its pen, barking for its dinner. Boys challenge each other to keep playing until it's too dark to see the ball. Snatches of loud music, rap and classic rock and power country, blare from the open windows of cars driving down the street.

"Promise you'll never be afraid to come to me. With anything. Anything. Promise me, KC. Will you promise me?"

"Yes, sir."

They sit quietly until the Coach finally breaks the silence.

"So you want to go see the Emeralds tomorrow?"

"I have to watch Ba and Ong."

"We'll take them with us. I bet they'd like that. Trust me. Everything is going to be okay, KC," the Coach promises, putting his arm around his shoulder and giving him an affectionate squeeze. "You believe me, don't you?"

It's odd, smelling whiskey on Coach Freeman's breath. KC carefully considers his words before answering.

"Yes. Yes, I do."

LONESOME
TOWN

NOTE

The author and Ricky Nelson share the
same birthday, May 8th.

After David finished talking with Saul, Jonathan became one in spirit with David, and he loved him as himself.

—1 Samuel 18:1

The last guest of the morning, the Legend himself, the greatest power forward in the local franchise's history, isn't scheduled until the top of the hour. None of the callers in the queue has anything of interest to add to the current topic at hand, at least nothing that can be said over the airwaves. The first commandment in broadcasting is to never, ever, allow dead air, and tormenting young Charlie Beresford for laughs is Sal Corelli's latest favorite fallback.

"Put that Ivy League education to good use, Boo-Boo."

Everyone who toils from 6 to 10 A.M., five days a week, on *Corelli and Crew,* 820 on the AM dial, simulcast in stereo at 1340 FM, is saddled with a stupid nickname, the more ridiculous the better. Everyone. Even a lowly in-studio researcher like Charlie, the youngest and least experienced member of the staff and the only one who doesn't know a fucking thing about sports except for the few bits of baseball knowledge he'd picked up during those couple of months he'd followed KC Conroy around like a lovesick puppy.

"Good God, Sal. Stop torturing the poor kid," the sole

female member of the Crew clucks. Her face looks like it's been smacked flat with a cast-iron skillet, but her deep, husky voice reminds Sal's audience, mostly men in the late forties through sixty-five demographic, of Kathleen Turner in her Jessica Rabbit days. Deirdre (aka Double D, which Sal swears is a reference to her initials, her last name being DiNardo, and not to her impressive cup size) is the voice of reason, the bemused and halfhearted scold, den mother to a pack of middle-aged men with adolescent ids, the only adult in the room. Sal's given Boo-Boo some crazy research assignments the past few months, but Double D thinks this latest request is over the top.

The banter during the eight o'clock segment had meandered from bitching about the overpaid whiners who play for the local MLB franchise to the latest rumors swirling around NHL players who will become free agents after the interminable play-off season to Sal's tirade about the rabbits and squirrels who treat the vegetable garden he lovingly tends at his weekend country home as their personal buffet. A fan who works as an exterminator had called in to share a trade secret that fox piss, available in both spray and pellet form, is the most effective rodent deterrent on the market. Corelli and Crew pounced on this unexpected opportunity to titillate their 5.8 AQH audience share with bawdy and off-color speculation about the best way to get savage animals to pee in a cup.

"Ah, well, Sal, technically rabbits are lagomorphs, not rodents," Charlie says, setting the record straight.

"Huh? What? Lagowhats?" Sal sputters, playing the bombastic blowhard for comic effect.

"Lagomorphs."

"Wow. That's my boy! That's some pretty impressive stuff! Did you get that, Double D?" Sal asks with mock seriousness. "I told you the kid is smarter than he looks. We're counting on you, Boo-Boo. Okay, folks, Big Pink's having a meltdown.

We have to take a break. Don't go away. We'll be right back from the beautiful Borgata here in Atlantic City."

The executive producer, called Big Pink because he chugs two bottles of Pepto-Bismol every morning, starts frantically barking at the sound engineer the second the mikes are off. The girl who screens the callers is quaking from a blistering dressing-down for putting through a fan who'd been banned from the show. These live remote broadcasts are a fucking son of a bitch, a technical nightmare. Something always goes wrong, and the crackerjack studio team of Killer Joe, Gizmo, the Annihilator, and Jo-Jo, the Dog Faced Boy—ninety-six years of radio experience among them—race the clock to smooth out any glitches.

"Hustle, motherfuckers! Thirty seconds to airtime!" Big Pink shouts. "You get the answer for Sal yet, kid? We're going live."

Charlie's mundane explanation that the fox piss used in vermin repellents is collected from the drainage systems of animal pens on wild game farms is a big disappointment to the potty-mouthed Corelli and Crew. Fortunately the Legend is on the line, ready to announce his prognostications for the upcoming NBA finals. The highly opinionated Hall of Famer is on fire this morning. Nothing and no one escapes his disdain and derision. The incompetence of Sixers ownership. The complete mismanagement by the team president and his bootlicking coaching staff. The frustrating diffidence of the first-round draft pick point guard. The fans love arguing with him. As always, the discourse never rises above the lowest common denominator, all scurrilous insults and ill-informed opinions. It's a smooth ride to the ten o'clock sign-off, with Charlie being called upon only once in the segment to confirm the average number of technical fouls per quarter committed by this year's squad. He removes his headphones at 10:01 and, standing to stretch his legs, finds himself facing an obviously irritated Big Pink.

"You're going into the studio when you get back to Philly, aren't you?" the producer asks Charlie before turning his attention to the more urgent matter of Sal's displeasure with the sound mix of this morning's show.

Charlie had been planning on soaking up a few rays at the Borgata pool and playing a few hands of blackjack before driving home. Billy's doing his summer internship at Sullivan & Cromwell in New York and the only thing waiting for him at the apartment is a microwave package of Hot Pockets in the freezer and a bony stray cat he'd argued against adopting. But he recognizes it's not a question, but a directive. Charlie makes a mental note to not be a fuck face to the lowest slug on the food chain when he becomes executive producer of a hit radio show.

"I will if you need me to," he responds, doing his best impersonation of a lapdog eager to serve his lord and master.

"I'm not sure what I need yet. I have to talk to Sal about tomorrow's show. I got the Phillies beat reporter for the *Inquirer* booked for the eight o'clock hour and the GM might be calling in. The Eagles' new defensive coordinator will be here for the nine-o'clock segment. I might want you to run a few queries and prepare some stat screens this afternoon."

Charlie's tempted to ask Big Pink if he's aware that modern cellular communications can track him down and summon him to the studio at a moment's notice if he's actually going to be needed. But an open writer's position is about to be posted, and Charlie needs the producer's support for a promotion.

"Aye-aye, sir," he says, sounding as chipper as possible and muttering obscenities under his breath as he slinks away, defeated by a superior force.

New Jersey is one motherfucking ugly place. It's a mystery why they call it the Garden State. Where are all the goddamn gardens? Most of the state smells like an EPA hazardous waste site. The toxic industrial emissions of the refineries and chemical plants. The sulfurous rot of the coastal barrier marshes. Headache-inducing gasoline fumes from nine million registered vehicles clogging its toll roads. It's more like a sneak preview of the Apocalypse than a botanical paradise. "Goddamnit," he mutters as he wrestles with his uncooperative Levi's, trying to retrieve the phone ringing in his pocket while speeding west fifteen miles over the posted limit on the Atlantic City Expressway.

"Oh shit," he mumbles, seeing the number of the incoming call. There's no escaping. He may as well pick up and face his punishment. The longer he waits, the worse it will be.

"I know, I know. I'm so sorry. We'll do it tonight. I promise. Anytime she wants."

"It never ceases to amaze me how well that phone of yours works when you want something, Charlie, but it always seems to be out of range whenever someone needs to reach *you.*"

The glittering towers of the Atlantic City skyline can indeed play ping-pong with cellular reception, but each and every one of his kid sister Madeline's texts had come through loud and clear last night. One every ten minutes. Like clockwork. For almost two hours, until she finally signed off with a tirade of obscenities that would shock even their typically unfazed mother. The kid had every right to be pissed. She hadn't *asked* for his assistance. He'd volunteered to Skype with the tightly wound little perfectionist after she'd fretted over her inability to master an acoustic "Blackbird." He'd tried to persuade her to select a less difficult choice from the Lennon-McCartney catalogue, "You've Got to Hide Your Love Away" maybe, but, hardheaded as usual, Madeline had been adamant.

"Ma, I'm a grown man. I can't just drop everything to teach my little sister the correct fingering for a damn Beatles song. I have an important job now, with a lot of responsibilities."

"I thought you told me they paid you to look up sports statistics on a laptop."

He'd ordered his third beer in the hotel bar with a few guys from the crew when the first text from his sister had arrived. His guitar was in his apartment in Philadelphia because he'd forgotten his promise as soon as he'd made it. Now his mother is acting as if he'd broken a solemn oath. If Madeline really needed help, she could have found a hundred video lessons on YouTube by typing in the word *blackbird*.

"Charlie, you're going to be twenty-three years old this fall. It's time to pull your head out of your ass and start acting like a responsible adult."

Sometimes Charlie tries to imagine some of his mother's colorful sayings rolling off the tongue of Clair Huxtable. She can be a real pain when crossed. He'd thought she would lighten up when she embraced the practice of yoga after recovering from cancer. But meditation and mala beads and breathing exercises haven't transformed her into a benign and smiling Earth Mother who leaves a trail of lotus blossoms in her path.

"Okay, Ma. I admit it. I fucked up. I'm sorry. Tell Madeline I'm sorry. Are you smoking?" he asks, incredulous, hearing a suspicious-sounding inhalation on the end of the line.

"Don't be ridiculous. Of course not," she insists, as if the idea were utterly preposterous, even though it's perfectly obvious she's exhaling a chest full of tar and nicotine. "Sorry's not good enough anymore, Charlie."

"Okay. I understand. Why are you trying to make me feel like crap? What do you want me to do?"

"Try being a little more considerate. That would be a good place to start."

"It's been a really hard day, Ma. You know what I had to do this morning? Research fox piss! This job really sucks sometimes."

"Stop complaining. You'd think you'd just finished the

Twelve Labors of Hercules the way you're carrying on. Everything's always come too easy for you. Not everything is always going to go your way."

"I gotta go, Ma."

"Your father is really looking forward to coming down there next month. You promised he could sit in the studio. Don't disappoint him!"

"It's already taken care of."

Well, it may as well be. Sal's not going to give him a hard time since he's practically forcing Charlie to be his college-bound son's summer play date.

"You know I know when you're lying. Why do you even still try?"

"I'll take care of it. I promise. Now I really got to go. I love you," he says, picking up the call-waiting.

"Hey, honey," the voice on the line purrs when he answers. Billy's lovey-dovey tone puts Charlie on high alert. There's only one reason he's calling at noon on a Thursday afternoon.

"Sorry, baby. I miss you so much. But if I don't have this fucking memo on the hiring partner's desk by eight o'clock Monday morning, I can kiss any chance of getting an offer good-bye."

Bullshit. Charlie's tempted to ask Billy if he'll be pulling an all-nighter at the Fire Island Pines law library, but decides to let it pass.

"I bought the airline tickets to Vancouver this morning," Billy says, extending a peace offering. "Start counting down the days until August when we'll be breathing the sweet pine-scented air of the Pacific Northwest."

Ten days of enforced solitude trekking in the wilderness of British Columbia could help repair the cracks and fissures of their strained relationship. Not that Charlie's intending to put much effort in attempting to salvage it. They'll be going their separate ways when Billy graduates from Penn Law in the spring. Charlie's made it clear he can't be persuaded to put his own ambitions on hold to follow a boyfriend first to Washington, where Billy's accepted a clerkship on the D.C. Circuit Court of Appeals, and eventually to Manhattan, when Billy becomes an associate at the venerable Wall Street law firm. They'll play the long-distance relationship charade for a few months until it peters out, that is if they're able to make it as a couple until next May. It's become impossible to ignore they're a mismatched pair, with barely any interests in common, and the sex has become perfunctory and infrequent.

"You're not saying anything. You're pissed off. I know it."

"Why don't I come up Friday afternoon and spend the weekend?"

Charlie has no intention of going to New York. He'd paid a premium for tickets to see the British band Temple at the Troc, and he loathes the idea of spending Saturday night dancing shirtless in a dark gay dance club surrounded by deluded middle-aged men inappropriately attired in wifebeaters and skinny jeans. But he wants to leave Billy twisting in the wind over the unexpected monkey wrench Charlie has just thrown into his weekend escapades.

"Sure, sure. That would be great," Billy says, choking on his words. "I won't be able to spend much time with you, and the guy I'm sharing the sublet with invited his girlfriend to come down from Boston. There's only one bathroom, and I know how you freak out about germs."

"Hey, man, I'm driving into a dead zone. I'll call you back later."

The sadist in Charlie is going to make the little bastard suffer a few hours of anxiety before calling him back to announce he's decided to stay in Philadelphia this weekend after all. He considers making a pit stop at the travel plaza as a precaution in the event of a bottleneck on the Walt Whitman Bridge. He's consumed a *venti* Starbucks, two Red Bulls, and a sixteen-ounce Diet Coke this morning. Pissing his pants one hundred feet above the Delaware River wouldn't be cool. His stomach is queasy, and something more ominous than a fart is stirring in his bowels. He makes a vow to throw those fucking greasy Hot Pockets in the trash and swear off Mickey D's and Church's Chicken in favor of a healthy diet. But the brief moment of urgency passes and the next exit sign says PENNSAUKEN, TWO MILES. He has to make a quick decision. He swears he's not giving in to temptation this afternoon even as he steers the car toward the off-ramp.

A landscaping road crew, saddled to a small convoy of tractors, is working on the barrier knoll, their brown faces protected from the midday sun by wide-brimmed floppy hats. He turns off the AC and opens the window, enjoying the sweet smell of freshly cut grass. The sky is a brilliant pale blue, and the fluffy white clouds float aimlessly with no threat of rain. It's a beautiful day for a blow job at the ABS on State Road 30, one mile off the last exit before the bridge.

Charlie counts eight vehicles in the gravel lot, mostly pickups and delivery trucks parked behind the tall fence that assures discretion for the customers of Adult Discount Videos (no clever names like Aphrodite's Den for this barebones operation). It's a lunchtime crowd, mostly blue-collar married guys looking for a quick, anonymous pump and dump. Charlie's instantly aroused by the prospect of musky armpits, scratchy stubble, and filthy baseball caps. The cashier working the register is irritated at being distracted from the latest issue of *Iron Man* when Charlie approaches.

"You gotta pay a five-dollar minimum for tokens," he mumbles. "Well, you want 'em or not?" the kid asks, finally looking up from his comic.

The boy's face is punctured with piercings. He's got loops in his eyebrows, his nostrils, and, creepiest of all to Charlie, his upper lip. He's smeared kohl over his eyelids, and his fingernails are painted black. His T-shirt is worn, a souvenir from a tour by a band Charlie's never heard of. The kid's a goth and is, without a doubt, the owner of the rust bucket plastered with anarchist/vegan/death metal band bumper stickers that's parked out back. The front room, crowded with racks of used DVDs and sex toy display cases, reeks of the strong onion of his Subway veggie patty lunch. Ordinarily Charlie would spend a few minutes nonchalantly flipping through the video packages, seemingly disinterested in what's going on in the back room. But today he's impatient and pushes aside the dirty curtain drawn across the entrance to the peep show arcade. He stands in a corner, his back against the wall, waiting for his pupils to adjust to the dim lighting so he can wander the maze of booths without stumbling over his feet.

He'd expected a parade of horny plumbers and deliverymen; maybe a hot suburban dad who'd wandered in from his sales route. But the aisles are deserted, no sound of shoe leather slapping the cement floor, no glowing orange tips of lit cigarettes. Charlie's arrived too late for the party. Everyone's already paired off and barricaded themselves in the narrow booths to finish their business. He hears the metallic *clink* of tokens being fed into the meters and female voices on the sound tracks begging to be fucked harder, faster. The hidden men behind the latched doors grunt and announce they're about to cum. An enormous black dude with a shaved head emerges from one of the booths. He tosses a crumpled tissue on the floor and pushes past Charlie, his semen still dripping from the chin of the fat little bald man on his knees in the cramped cubicle.

Charlie feels a hand lightly brushing against his ass. He doesn't resist as the man slips his fingers between his legs and tickles his taint. The stranger leads Charlie to a vacant booth and kicks the door shut behind them. The guy's good-looking enough, and his calloused hands and ropy neck muscles are proof he's obviously well-acquainted with physical labor. The man pulls Charlie's T-shirt over his head, a prelude to groping and the awkward fumbling with buttons and buckles and zippers until their pants are around their ankles. At least he doesn't refuse to kiss. His breath tastes like peppermint lozenges and cigarettes. They grind their hips together and the selfish bastard disappears without saying good-bye as soon as he shoots his load, leaving the door to the booth open and Charlie standing exposed, nearly naked, a stranger's cum splattered on his thigh.

A young man, his face half-hidden behind the wide bill of a baseball cap, is standing in the aisle, staring at him. There's something vaguely familiar about his mouth and chin, the way he tilts his head, something recognizable even in the poor lighting and despite the hat he's wearing like a mask. Before Charlie can speak, the man spins on his heel, clearly unnerved, and dashes toward the exit, nearly tearing the curtain from the rod. Charlie chases him through the front room and into the parking lot.

"Hey! Hey! It's Charlie Beresford! Hey!" he shouts, feeling like an idiot as he pounds on the window of the guy's truck.

The man reluctantly opens the window and stares him down. Charlie hasn't lost his mind. He's not hallucinating. How the fuck did the Mighty KC Conroy find this shitty little ABS in nowhere New Jersey? What's he doing here? Well, it's obvious what he's *doing,* but why *here?* The last time they met, KC's hair was buzzed to the scalp, but it's grown back into the same mop of unruly curls he'd had in high school. The small scar from a home plate collision with the tip of a cleat is exactly as Charlie remembers. But he's different, menacing, seething with a nervous energy that could spontaneously ignite.

"What do you want?" KC snarls, his tone hostile, the glint in his still-piercing black eyes threatening.

"Hey, man, how's it going?" Charlie asks, unable to steady

his trembling voice, nervously acting as if they're having a casual conversation while he's hanging white-knuckled on the door handle.

"Get off my truck if you don't want to be dragged across the parking lot," KC warns as he rolls up the window.

Charlie can't believe KC really intends to hurt him, assuming that stubborn persistence will force KC to speak. But KC pushes the accelerator to the floor, spraying gravel like a blast from a tommy gun. The truck loses traction on the pebbly surface, spinning in tight circles, and centrifugal force sends Charlie flying across the lot where he makes a hard landing on his back. He hears the *crunch* of KC's boots on the gravel and opens his eyes to see KC staring down at his face.

"I could have killed you! What's wrong with you? Are you crazy?" KC shouts. Charlie plays possum, taking some small satisfaction in the abrupt change in KC's attitude now that he's worried that his rash and thoughtless aggression has inflicted serious and permanent damage to someone who was once his friend. "Don't move! I'm calling nine-one-one."

Charlie slowly rises and settles into a sitting position. His muscles are already beginning to ache. He's going to be stiff and sore tomorrow, but nothing's broken, no injuries more serious than a few bruises and cuts.

"I'm okay," he insists, taking the hand KC offers to help him to his feet.

There's an awkward moment when they would be standing nose to nose if Charlie were a few inches taller. KC steps back, keeping a safe distance between them. Charlie had long ago given up all hope of ever finding KC. After he'd learned KC had been signed in the MLB draft, he'd followed his progress from the Rookie League to winter ball in Texas and finally to a Short Season Class A team in Washington State. Charlie had tried in vain to reach him on the Spokane Chiefs' Web site message board. After several weeks he finally received a terse one-line response that KC Conroy was no longer on the roster. He finally called the Chiefs' front office, telling the wary receptionist he was KC's brother and it was extremely important that he contact his family. She denied having any knowledge of KC's whereabouts and, annoyed by Charlie's skeptical persistence, told him to hire a private detective if it was so important they find him.

"How come you never answered any of my messages?" he wants to know now that KC is standing an arm's length away. "Are you pissed at me?" he asks disingenuously. Anyone who had been treated the way Charlie welcomed KC the weekend he'd appeared at Dartmouth would be pissed at him. He can't even remember now exactly why KC's presence had made him so uncomfortable. He's perfectly normal-looking with two eyes and a well-proportioned nose. His diction is unremarkable though he still has the unfortunate habit of dropping the letter *h,* saying *wit* rather than *with.* Why had Charlie been so embarrassed by him, so worried about the impression he would make on a few pretentious assholes whose faces he barely recalls and whose names he can't remember?

"Look . . ." KC, clearly uncomfortable, starts to respond but, after confirming Charlie Beresford is in one piece, turns and walks away instead, not needing or wanting to explain himself. But Charlie reaches out and grabs him by the wrist.

"Wait, please," he pleads.

They stare at each other, avoiding any further reference to a broken friendship and damaged feelings.

"Where's your shirt?" KC finally asks.

Charlie just now realizes he's bare-chested, having forgotten his T-shirt when he chased KC into the lot. God only knows the disgusting uses the patrons of Adult Discount Videos have put it to in the past five minutes. It was just a cheap station giveaway anyway. There are boxes of them in a closet back at the studio if he wants another one.

"Uh, you know, it's in there . . ." Charlie mumbles, embarrassed about having been caught *in flagrante* by KC. They gaze at their shoes as a burly customer emerges from the bookstore and walks to his van.

"I got a shirt in my truck I can give you," KC offers. "It's clean," he promises when he returns carrying an official jersey of the Camden Lampreys. "Look, man. Take care of yourself," KC mumbles, anxious to break away.

"You playing for them this season?" Charlie asks, stalling for time.

"Yeah," KC mumbles. There's no reason for him to lie since a quick search of the team's Web site would confirm he's on the roster.

"I work at a radio station in Philly. We just did a live remote from the Borgata," Charlie sputters, hoping to pique KC's curiosity and stall his abrupt departure.

"I know where you work, Boo-Boo."

"Christ, it's so fucking lame," he says, acting as if the nickname's a burden and that he isn't secretly pleased KC's aware of his small local notoriety. "*Beres*-ford. Bears. Yogi and Boo-Boo. Get it?"

"Yeah, Charlie, I get it. I know I only went to junior college, but I'm not as stupid as you think," he says as he climbs behind the wheel of his truck.

Charlie's face flushes, blood rushing to his cheeks.

"Hey, wait one minute," he says, flustered.

He runs to his car to retrieve a pen that hasn't gone dry and writes his number on a greasy McDonald's napkin.

"It's my cell. Call and I'll save you in my contacts. I can meet you to return your jersey."

"Keep it," KC says. "I don't need it back" are his last words as he drives off.

At least he didn't crumple the napkin and toss it to the ground. But Charlie remembers KC is always carefully polite and would wait until he's long out of sight before throwing it out the window.

* * *

Billy's very presence is irritating. He'd arrived Friday on the 5:45 and by seven o'clock Charlie wanted to put him on the next train back to New York and resume obsessing over KC Conroy without the unwanted distraction. It's been nine days since their awkward reunion. Eight days and twenty hours to be precise, and it's getting harder to resist the temptation to call the Lampreys' front office.

"You bitched and complained because I haven't been home in three weeks, and now that I'm here you act like I'm carrying the plague."

Charlie rolls over on his side, turning his back on Billy, trying to ignore the obvious erection poking at the crack of his ass. *How am I supposed to react? Am I expected to put on a porn star performance because Billy has deigned to give me a mercy fuck?*

"Put a rubber on it," he says, mumbling into his pillow. "When's the last time you were tested?"

The question has the desired effect. Billy throws back the sheet and jumps to his feet, furiously indignant.

"You fucking prick. I'm leaving for Manhattan right after the meeting."

The editorial staff of the *Law Review* is convening at noon. Billy, of course, denies it's the only reason for tearing himself away from New York for two nights, but Charlie knows that, but for Billy's academic obligations, he'd be spending the weekend as a houseguest of some investment banker in the Hamptons. Despite the supposed long hours and the fevered competition of a summer associate program at one of the nation's most prestigious firms, Billy has found time to develop a defined pair of pecs he proudly exhibits at every opportunity that arises to shed his shirt.

"You need to leave a check for your share of the rent," Charlie shouts when Billy slams the bathroom door to put an exclamation point on his angry reaction. It's force of habit and not an act of thoughtfulness that drags him out of bed to grind the beans for Billy's morning coffee.

"Who the fuck is this?" Billy asks as he studies the new screen saver Charlie's chosen for his laptop. "My competition?" he asks snidely as he skims through Charlie's viewing history.

"It's Ricky Nelson, asshole," Charlie says. "Stop messing with my shit."

"He looks like a douche."

What the fuck was Charlie thinking when he let Billy Riddle talk him into moving to Philadelphia? Their paths had never crossed in New Hampshire until six weeks before Billy's graduation. They were in different classes, Charlie being only a junior, and they shared only one friend, the lesbian who'd insisted on introducing them. At first, Charlie avoided any physical contact, pretending to be naïve and distracted whenever Billy suggested they get together alone, maybe somewhere more private than a coffee shop or bar. It wasn't as if Charlie was playing hard to get. He'd earned his reputation as the biggest whore in Hanover, becoming a legend for his smooth seduction of "questioning" confused young men and his ability to dump them without bitterness and hurt feelings when they began to express a desire to be something more than friends with benefits. The women in his hipster clique teased him, claiming he could turn a good-looking hirsute straight slacker gay in under three hours.

Billy Riddle, a pale redhead whose eyebrows faded into his forehead and who only needed to shave once or twice a week, wasn't his physical type. Worse yet, he was obsessed with politics and cable news and had been involved in student organizing for every left-to-mid-center Democratic candidate on the New Hampshire ballot during his undergraduate years. Billy had even run and lost his own close election for student body president. The first time they'd had sex—if rubbing their peckers together while fully clothed could be called sex—Charlie had picked up his iPod while Billy was having

a post-coital slash and was appalled to find he'd just performed frottage with a man whose taste in music ran to Barbra Fucking Streisand and the Original Cast Recordings of
Rent and *Wicked*.

But Billy was something that none of Charlie's other
boyfriends or casual bedmates had been since Larry Coleman
back in high school. Persistent. Billy had freely admitted he
had practically no experience with men, having not come out
until the Christmas break of his senior undergraduate year.
He'd decided they were in love the first time Charlie actually
fucked him, pledging eternal fealty before Charlie pulled
out of his surprisingly receptive asshole. Billy had e-mailed
or called from Pennsylvania every twenty-four hours while
Charlie finished his last two semesters. Lacking any prospects
for gainful employment after graduation, he'd agreed to follow Billy to Philadelphia, a better option than moving back in
with his parents. One year later, everything about Billy—his
habits, his voice, his sudden embrace of promiscuity and desire to be a top—irritates the hell out of Charlie.

"He was a musician. A fucking good one. I don't think
you would have heard of him since he didn't sing Broadway
show tunes."

"Whatever," Billy says, spinning in his chair to confront
him. "By the way, what is that lunatic you work for making
you dress up as these days?"

Billy will never let Charlie live down that Sal had insisted Boo-Boo wear a diaper (over his jeans, of course)
and a dunce cap after Charlie, predictably, got the lowest
score in the station's March Madness bracket office pool.

"What are you talking about?"

"That stupid baseball jersey hanging in the closet. What
are you? Thirteen years old?"

"Fuck you."

"No. Fuck *you,*" Billy says, without any particular anger
or venom. "Should I pack my bag or do you want to stop
fighting so we can try to enjoy the rest of the weekend?"

Just because he doesn't love, or even like, Billy very much, it doesn't mean he hates him. He understands that Billy's torn between the security and stability of a relationship and the need to sow a few wild oats before male-pattern baldness makes him look ten years older than his actual age. And it isn't in Charlie's interest to upset the status quo. His parents aren't moneybags like Billy's and those of most of his friends from college whose families send generous checks to subsidize their privileged lifestyles. School loan payments consume most of Charlie's paycheck, and he's going deeper into debt living on the pittance the station pays him. He can't afford the rent on this apartment alone and doesn't have the deposit to move to a cheaper place of his own. He's willing to let the current situation run the course, at least until Billy's law school graduation.

"Put the bag down and go to your meeting. You want sushi or Thai tonight?"

"You sure?"

"Of course."

Billy may be running wild in New York, but at home, all he needs to be happy and content are spicy Asian take-out, *SNL* reruns, and Bassetts Chocolate Swirl ice cream. Charlie supposes it's better than the alternative of spending Saturday night alone with a six-pack brooding over letting KC Conroy slip through his hands. Enough time has passed to confirm what he had expected as he stood in the gravel lot and watched KC drive away. And even if Charlie's gut instinct is wrong and KC hadn't tossed Charlie's number out the window, hell will freeze over before he would use it to call.

It had been nearly a year since Charlie picked up his guitar, and his calluses have long faded. He'd made the mistake of using his bruised and tender fingers to excuse his temporary inability to type a query fast enough to satisfy Big Pink. His careless blunder has inspired Corelli and Crew to speculate on the cause of his injuries with the smarmiest innuendo the censorship police will allow to be broadcast over the airwaves. He's acting like a man of mystery, confiding only in Deirdre that he's been relearning the entire Ricky Nelson songbook and, after a few false starts, had quickly picked out the chord progressions of all of his greatest hits. But he didn't admit even to Double D that he's re-creating the tribute to KC's idol he'd recorded just before leaving for college. He knows he's wasting his time. Even if he's able to get a flash drive of his melancholy covers of Ricky Nelson's signature songs into KC's hands (which he figures would be easy enough, access to the front offices of the local franchises being a perk of working at the market's highest-rated sports radio network), why does he think KC would be curious enough to listen? And what would he think of Charlie if he did? Anyone in their right mind would question the sanity of a grown man still so obsessed with his first love that he had devoted time and effort to record a silly musical love letter a pair of adolescents would be embarrassed to pass between themselves.

"Hey, Charlie. Tomorrow. The kid's really looking forward to it. You made quite an impression, my young friend," Sal says after the show.

He'd completely forgotten until Sal reminded him. His mind has been elsewhere these past two weeks, preoccupied with thoughts of KC Conroy, dwelling on the many possible reasons why he had never called.

"Yeah. Of course, Sal. Just tell me where and when."

"I'll ask him to meet us after the show. You guys can take it from there."

Sal makes a very good living playing the bombastic know-it-all for laughs. Rumor has it the station agreed to a most-favored-nation clause in his contract guaranteeing him the highest salary in the local market when a Fox affiliate tried to lure him to New York. He goes to great length to protect his image as a loudmouth and blowhard whose favorite term of endearment is moron. But off the air, his keen intelligence and savvy instincts—and, yes, sentimental heart—are immediately apparent. He's loyal to a fault and fiercely protective of the cast and crew who work so hard to make him shine. Every member of the staff would walk the plank for him, which is why Charlie never hesitated before agreeing to meet and spend quality time this summer with Sal's seventeen-year-old son. Something unfortunate has recently happened between young Eric and his closest friend, but he refuses to talk to Sal and his mother about it. He's turned moody and sullen and is prone to depression. He's unwilling to open up and won't confide in his parents. All of the advice books they've studied say he should be allowed to come out to them on his own terms and in his own time, that it's his decision, not his father and mother's, to make. Sal and his wife are convinced that Charlie, who must have negotiated the same difficulties and experienced the same insecurities, is the perfect role model to help their son grow more confident and become more comfortable in his own skin.

"Just remember one thing, Boo-Boo. If he comes home with some god-awful tattoo, I'm gonna break your neck."

Not everyone can appreciate the artistic merit of the carefully drawn portrait of the Dancing Ganesha rendered in a shockingly bright palette of colored ink across Charlie's back. He'd ruminated for nearly a year before choosing a personal statement that was deeply spiritual and also the essence of cool. Skull and crossbones and bloody, dripping hearts were too old school, a cliché more suited to military veterans of Southeast Asia and the Middle East. The face of Jesus wearing the crown of thorns would have been too creepy, and a fanged demon fleeing the bowels of the earth would have been too weird. He'd almost committed to a mystical theme of runic inscriptions and primitive Native

American petroglyph symbols before deciding to pay tribute to the Hindu god. Even his mother approves.

"Come on, Charlie. Let me see it. Puh-leez!" Eric pleads.

Young Eric is considerably less shy about expressing himself when out of the presence of his overprotective parents. If this boisterous, almost-annoying firecracker is suffering from depression, his energy level must be off the charts when he's content and happy.

"I promised your father I wouldn't do anything to encourage you. I need my job, and your old man will fire me if I show you my ink," Charlie warns.

"I just want to see it. It doesn't mean I want one. I'll probably hate it."

The five-year age difference between seventeen and twenty-two is momentous, but they had quickly bonded over their shared interest in comics. Young Eric, however, is a walking encyclopedia of Marvel comics trivia, meaning he's an Avengers fan who thinks Charlie's lionized Justice League of America is lame, leading to a friendly argument comparing the cumulative superpowers of the elite teams of the rival comic presses. The kid also has a healthy interest in the local music scene. He sure as hell isn't the innocent babe in the woods his parents believe him to be. But Charlie's pretty sure that the kid's sexual experience is limited to passionate groping with his former boyfriend and maybe a few rushed hand jobs and clumsy blow jobs with other high school kids with similar longings.

"Your old man wants you home by six tonight," Charlie says at the end of a long afternoon spent perusing the shelves of Atomic Comics.

"I thought I could come over to your house and blow you."

Charlie acts like Eric's only joking, but he suspects the lascivious twinkle in the kid's eye means the offer is serious and he's eager for Charlie to take him up on it.

"Cut the bullshit."

"At least show me your stupid tattoo."

The kid's certainly tenacious.

"You swear you're not going to tell your father?"

"I don't tell him anything."

"I better be able to trust you," Charlie warns him as he reluctantly unbuttons his shirt.

hi

Charlie doesn't recognize the area code of the incoming text. A quick search on the computer indicates the message is coming from Sacramento, California.

its kc

Charlie's palms are sweating and his hands are shaking. He doesn't know why he hesitates before responding. He's been consumed with angst since that fateful day in Pennsauken. This is what he'd wanted, but was sure would never happen.

u there charlie?

yes, he finally answers.

its kc

i know

where r u

home u?

n jersey

Charlie's stumped, uncertain how to respond, settling on the noncommittal.

cool

Thirty seconds pass, then a minute, then, three, five, without KC making further contact. KC hasn't changed. He's always and forever elusive, just beyond reach. Charlie finally sends a message, *call me,* that he's sure KC will ignore.

The phone immediately vibrates in his hand.

"Hello?"

He forces his voice to drop an octave or two, trying to control the nervous quiver in his greeting.

"Hi."

KC's tentativeness boosts Charlie's confidence.

"I'm glad you called, KC," he says, trying to sound casual and only mildly pleased.

He hears the loud voices of young men, shouting to be heard over the noise of the passing traffic.

"I gotta go," KC says.

"Hey, wait."

Someone, likely a teammate or coach, is calling out to KC, *"Let's go, dude, the bus is going to leave."*

"You wanna meet me tomorrow?" Charlie asks, emboldened, seizing an opportunity unlikely to occur again.

"Yeah."

"I'll call you," Charlie promises before hanging up.

His happiness about the unexpected reunion is short-lived, though. Why the fuck did he agree to take Sal's kid to the all-ages Punk-O-Rama tomorrow, a commitment it would be professional suicide to break?

Senior citizens (meaning anyone over the legal drinking age) are slapped with a green Day-Glo wristband at the door. Charlie is ancient at twenty-two. He feels conspicuous having outgrown adolescent skin problems. Maybe he'd have fit in better if he'd streaked his hair with hot pink or baby blue dye. The crowd observes the strict dress code for these events despite the stifling heat and poor ventilation. They're in full punk regalia, vintage 1977, clad in black leather jackets, motorcycle boots, and enough chains to weigh down Luca Brasi. It's as much a costume party as a concert with kids competing for the prize of most outrageous appearance. Eric's style is slightly offbeat. He favors a military look of camouflage pants and a snap-brim patrol hat. His snug army-issue T-shirt flatters his surprisingly well-defined pectorals, and the dreadlocks he's begun growing for his arrival at Hampshire College are a funky, sexy look.

Eric's lingering at the merchandise tables, studying the wide selection of hemp products. An argument between a vegan vendor and a kid in tight leather pants is escalating to a full-out brawl. A girl with a shaved head and more piercings than a pincushion fronts the band on stage. Her voice is shredded from screaming over the earsplitting feedback. The only lyrics Charlie can make out are *"fuck"* and *"cunt."* But it all sounds sweet to his ears. He's tired of faking enthusiasm for electronic trance and progressive house and the metronomic beats of the masters of the turntable. He misses the pounding chords of adolescent aggression.

He flashes his wristband to enter the bar and orders a large plastic cup of watered-down beer. Security may be tight for underage drinking, but no one is policing the blatant violations of the posted NO SMOKING signs. The haze of reefer smoke is thick enough to make Charlie's eyes water, and he's tempted to fire up the weed clip in his back pocket. He pushes through the boisterous imbibers, seeking a good vantage point to observe his young charge from the restricted over-twenty-one-only area. The little fucker's slipped off in the few minutes Charlie left him unsupervised. He ought to go find the brat before he gets himself into trouble, but the phone in his pocket is vibrating. The return call he's been awaiting has finally arrived. But the noise in the club is deafening and it's impossible to hear KC's voice.

"Text me!" Charlie screams into the phone.

It's impossible to know if KC can hear him or if he's even still on the line. Something intelligible must have gotten through since a message appears on the screen.

where r u
explain it to you later
we still on?
yes
what time?

Charlie realizes he'd failed to establish with Eric beforehand he's got other obligations and can't hang the entire night.

Whenever, he types.

u eat?

no

11 ok? game is in extra innings.

11 ok

might be 12 will call u

It's half past nine. Where is that fucking little pissant? The break between acts seems like an eternity. The pace of the show is so ragged the headliners aren't likely to take the stage before midnight. The next band on the bill finally finishes its sound check and rips into a psycho-billy set, playing at breakneck speed. Charlie, for whom the gold standard of the genre will always be the Cramps, is impressed by the dexterity of the speed freak playing lead guitar. A few kids are pogoing in the center of the room. He's been in enough mosh pits to know when the body slamming is about to begin. Sal will have Charlie's head on a platter if his precious baby breaks an arm or suffers a concussion. He's panicking now, desperate to find the little shit.

"Hey! Hey, Charlie! Over here!"

Eric's stripped off his shirt and is eager to show off the amateurish and sloppy image of a dragon spiraling around his long neck. Charlie hopes Sal doesn't go into cardiac arrest before someone has the chance to explain that henna fades without a trace in less than two weeks.

Charlie figures KC chose Chinatown for the late hours and cheap menus. He didn't object. In fact, he's jonesing for greasy egg rolls and soggy fried rice after all the beer he drank at the show. Eric had been surprisingly agreeable when Charlie announced they had to leave before the headliner. He'd hinted at a certain nefarious appointment he needed to keep tonight as Charlie put him in a cab. Charlie didn't believe him, but even if it's true, his responsibility ended when he saw him safely into a taxi.

"Hey, Boo-Boo! Over here!"

KC's standing on the opposite street corner, towering over a pair of humpbacked old Chinese ladies waiting to cross.

"This way!" KC shouts, waving Charlie toward him.

Charlie steps off the curb without looking and is nearly clipped by a taxi trying to beat the light. Fortunately the only injury is to his pride. Karma's a fucking bitch. So far KC's caught him bare-assed in a dirty bookstore, sent him sprawling spread-eagled on his back in a gravel lot, and now witnessed his brains almost being splattered on the street. How many times is he going to have to embarrass himself, stripped of any last shred of dignity, before he's paid back his debt for humiliating KC at Dartmouth all those years ago?

"Hey, you okay, Charlie? For a minute there I thought you were roadkill."

Charlie's not sure how to greet him. Shake his hand? Offer one of those backslapping rituals performed by athletes and fraternity brothers? He takes his cue from KC and doesn't attempt to initiate even the most innocent physical contact.

"You like Vietnamese?" KC asks.

Charlie's willing to go along with anything KC suggests.

"Good. Vietnam House okay with you?"

The restaurant isn't white table linen elegant, but it's a cut or two above the run-of-the-mill dim sum palaces. KC and the waitstaff seem to know each other. He greets them in Vietnamese and drops a few words of their native vocabulary into the conversation. A variety of appetizers are brought to the table. Spring rolls and dumplings; grilled sausages and squid. Charlie orders a Bud Lite and doesn't ask why KC isn't drinking anything stronger than Diet Coke. It must have something to do with the small wooden cross dangling from the leather cord KC wears around his neck, a suspicion KC confirms when he reaches across the table and clasps Charlie's hands to offer thanks for the food on the table. He asks if Charlie would like to say anything, but Charlie only knows the Catholic grace, "Bless us, O Lord," and he'd feel foolish reciting impersonal words he'd learned as a child. All he can manage is a simple *amen*.

This KC—the one who knows a little Vietnamese and eats exotic food, the one who feels obligated to express his gratitude to God for a plate of spring rolls, and then asks Charlie to tell his parents he keeps them in his prayers—is a stranger. The young man sitting across the table only resembles the boy he remembers. He's one of the Pod People from *Invasion of the Body Snatchers,* a walking, talking facsimile of the guy he once knew.

"You know, I saw one of your stepbrothers last spring. He and my sister, Madeline, go to the same high school."

Charlie is taunting him, mentioning the hated stepfamily to get a reaction from this smiling alien.

"Peter. Scouts from the NHL are already watching him. He's going to enter the draft after he graduates."

KC had once refused to come home for his stepfather's funeral. Now he's speaking with almost paternal pride about one of his despised stepbrothers.

"I think Madeline's going to be a dyke," Charlie announces. It's a blatant lie, meant to shock, to wipe that bland smile from KC's face. He orders a second beer, assuming KC doesn't approve though he's said nothing that could be interpreted as judgmental and condescending. The waitress brings another round of drinks, and KC asks if Charlie knows what he wants off the menu.

"I'm not really hungry," he says, wishing KC would ask for the check so they could go their separate ways. This was a bad idea. He could never be friends with this born-again KC, and Charlie's intentions of jumping his bones tonight now seem ridiculous in retrospect.

KC orders soup that he offers to share when a huge, steaming bowl is brought to the table. Charlie winces at the taste of the broth.

"Lemongrass," KC explains. "It takes getting used to."

"Where did you learn so much about the Vietnamese?" Charlie asks.

"I lived in Oregon a few years ago."

He doesn't offer any more information, apparently assuming that residing in the Pacific Northwest is sufficient explanation for his familiarity with Southeast Asian language and cuisine.

"Can I ask you something, KC?"

"Sure."

"Do you ever see Darrell Torok?"

"Darrell passed last year," KC says matter-of-factly, as if Charlie had just asked him the time of day.

"Jesus!"

Charlie immediately regrets taking the name of KC's lord in vain.

"They arrested him in the Dominican Republic. He was paying little boys to do things to him. You know. Things."

KC's emotionless account of the death of Darrell Torok is more disturbing than the sordid story of the man's demise.

"They extradited him to Miami. He died before his trial. They found him naked on the prison shower floor, lying in his own blood. Someone had slit his throat from ear to ear."

KC lowers his eyes and returns to his noodles.

"You know," he says after a brief pause, "they said he had AIDS when he died."

"Are you okay? I mean . . ."

"Yeah, I'm okay. I prayed a lot before I got tested and the Lord stood by me."

"It must have felt good knowing he got what he deserved."

KC frowns and shakes his head.

"It's not my place to judge him, Charlie."

He wants to shout that no one has more right to judge that fucking prick than KC Conroy. The man across the table has become a robot.

"Look, KC. I'm really glad you called, but I left my friend back at a show," Charlie lies, needing an excuse to bring this ill-advised reunion to a swift conclusion.

"It's okay, Charlie. I know you have things you have to do."

His voice is steady and pleasant, but the resigned expression on his face is unsettling. Charlie finally sees the KC he knows, the kid no one can disappoint because his expectations are so low. He understands that KC sees he *hasn't* changed. Charlie's the same selfish asshole who pushed him away that frigid weekend five years ago, someone so callow he never even considered the damage he'd done to a friend whose greatest fear was rejection.

"Can I still get something to eat?" Charlie asks abruptly. "All of a sudden I'm starving."

KC assures him the place serves until three in the morning. He calls to the waitress and orders for Charlie in Vietnamese. Charlie wonders if he and the girl are conspiring to feed him scraps and organ meat or, even worse, one of the deformed, hideous fish swimming in the huge tank near the kitchen.

"Dude, I wish you could see your face." KC laughs when Charlie's meal is brought to the table. "It's just pho. Flank steak and noodles. No lemongrass. A little cilantro."

Charlie orders another beer, his fourth, getting buzzed while KC is sober on Diet Coke. He's drunk, not stumble drunk, but soused enough to summon the courage to pepper KC with questions—about his family, his career, Oregon. Anything and everything but the one question he really wants to ask. Why the fuck was KC, who wears a cross around his neck and prays for Charlie's parents, prowling the aisles of a dirty bookstore on a summer afternoon?

He realizes they're sitting alone in the dining room and his loud voice is carrying through the empty restaurant. The kitchen staff is out on the sidewalk, smoking. The waitress is sitting alone a corner, resting her head on the table. She stirs and stretches, yawning, and walks to the kitchen.

"I guess we should go. They want to go home."

"Don't sweat it, Charlie. The bars close in twenty minutes and this place will be packed again."

"You come here a lot?"

"Sometimes," KC answers, a straightforward answer that sounds cryptic to Charlie's ears.

KC insists on paying. Charlie leaves two tens on the table, adding to the already generous tip. A raucous crowd—Asian workingmen who've been drinking in cheap beer parlors, club kids, a few young couples not wanting the evening to end, a large party of thirtysomethings who've come from a bachelor party at a gentlemen's club—is gathering on the sidewalk. A line forms at the entrance to Vietnam House. A whole new party is just beginning on the streets of Chinatown. Every seat of every table of every neon-lit Cantonese greasy spoon is taken.

"You going to meet your friend at the club?"

"Naw. I'm goin' home," Charlie says.

"You need a ride? My truck is two blocks away."

A cab ride to West Philadelphia will set Charlie back fifteen bucks, maybe more. The buses run once an hour after midnight. And he senses KC is going to disappear from his life again after they say good night. The possibility of spending a few more minutes together makes Charlie strangely happy.

"You can give me a ride," Charlie says magnanimously. "Got any Ricky Nelson music in your truck?"

KC's broad grin is a small crack in the veneer of his impassive face.

"I can't believe you remember!"

Charlie's too drunk to care about the attention he's attracting with his loud, off-key rendition of "Hello Mary Lou." He pauses, resisting, when KC helps him into the truck. He wants to kiss him—really kiss him, tongue and all—and knows that he can't.

"Well?" KC asks after buckling his seat belt.

"Well, what? A well's a hole in the ground, KC."

"Well, where am I dropping you off?" KC laughs.

Charlie tells him to take Walnut and then a left on Forty-sixth Street. He reaches for the radio dial, but KC's reflexes are quick and he grabs Charlie's hand.

"What? What's wrong?"

"Nothing's wrong. I just don't want to listen to the radio."

Charlie suspects it's tuned to one of the many fire-and-brimstone gospel stations on the AM band.

"How about a little Ricky Nelson, then?"

"You settle for Pearl Jam?" KC asks.

"Yeah, sure."

It's the first reference KC's made all night, an oblique one to be sure, to the summer before Charlie left for Dartmouth. Charlie knows he's drunk when "Nothingman" brings tears to his eyes.

"Hey, look," he says as they turn onto his street. "There's a parking space. There are never any parking spaces. We're in luck!"

"Which house?"

"That one," Charlie says, pointing at a shabby Stick-East-lake converted long ago to spacious if relatively Spartan apartments for graduate students. KC stops the truck in front of the building and shifts into Park, leaving the engine running.

"You okay from here? You got your keys and everything, right?"

"Come in, come in," Charlie pleads, tugging the sleeve of KC's shirt. "There's a parking space. That means you should come in."

"I ought to get going. I got to be at the ballpark by ten."

"Please come in." He's practically begging, refusing to release KC's arm. "You only have to stay a minute."

KC finally concedes, deciding he should use the bathroom as it's a long drive back to Jersey.

"I got a toilet. A nice one," Charlie insists. He realizes even in his inebriated state how ridiculous he sounds.

"Just as long as it flushes," KC laughs as he skillfully backs the large truck into the small space.

Charlie can't remember the last time he cleaned the bathroom. There's probably dried piss and pubic hairs on the rim of the bowl.

"Man, am I going to regret this in the morning," KC says as they cross the street.

"Regret what?"

Charlie's expectations are rising. Once they're inside, KC's going to set aside all this Christian shit for one night. They're gonna pick up where they left off five years ago. He'll make sure KC doesn't regret anything in the morning. In fact, he's gonna want to do it again.

"Staying out this late. Pray for a rainout, Charlie."

KC has to steady Charlie when he trips climbing the staircase to his third-floor apartment. Charlie's disappointed when his hands don't linger, releasing him as soon as he's steady on his feet.

"Here, let me do that," KC offers when the key stubbornly refuses to be inserted into the lock.

The front room looks respectable enough. Charlie had cleared any empty take-out containers from the coffee table and the floor by the sofa. He'd thrown out the garbage and emptied the litter box so at least the kitchen doesn't stink. (Billy had just assumed Charlie would look after that fucking cat while he was in New York this summer.) That's as far as he got before he'd needed to pick up Eric. The bed's unmade, as it always is when Billy's away, the rumpled sheets buried under piles of unfolded laundry and dirty clothes.

And of course there's the fucking bathroom, a hazardous waste site.

"I got soda," he says, searching the refrigerator for something to offer his guest. "Diet Pepsi, okay? How about orange juice? Milk?" he asks, wincing as he sniffs the carton.

"Don't worry, man. I'm okay. I'm just going to use the head and hit the road."

"Water. I got water," Charlie says, insisting KC accept a bottle of Poland Spring.

"Thanks. I'll drink it on the way back. So, where's the bathroom?"

Charlie slumps onto the beat-up cushions of the sofa, waiting for KC to finish taking a piss. Across the room, propped against a bookshelf, is his guitar. His fingertips have developed a layer of calluses. Charlie's perched on the arm of the couch, a study in nonchalance, strumming the chords of "Lonesome Town" when KC emerges from the bathroom. Alcohol has improved the skills of many a guitar man and stringing together an open G, C, and D isn't exactly challenging. He's not inebriated enough to consider serenading KC with a love song, but the beer has loosened his inhibitions enough for him to make a confession.

"That summer. After you went back to Florida. I learned every Ricky Nelson song and recorded them on a disc I was going to send you."

KC stares at his feet, looking uncomfortable, like he's waiting for the first possible opportunity to bolt.

"I tried to make another one. After I saw you a couple of weeks ago."

He sits perfectly still, barely breathing, knowing KC, like a startled rabbit, will take flight at his slightest movement.

"Well, nice to see you, Charlie," KC finally says after a long, silent pause.

"Same," Charlie says, rooted to the arm of the sofa as KC turns and leaves, closing the door behind him.

The tension snapped, Charlie feels as if he's collapsing in on himself, stricken by an overpowering sense of loss. Someone is knocking on his door, and he braces himself for a confrontation with an asshole neighbor complaining that Charlie's quiet guitar has roused him from a peaceful sleep. *Fuck you,* he shouts, launching a preemptive strike, his roiling emotions finding a deserving target, the blistering tirade abruptly silenced when he finds himself standing face-to-face with KC as he opens the door.

Apparently being a devout believer doesn't confer any special status with God the Almighty as KC's prayers for a drenching morning rainfall have gone unanswered. The bright sunlight pouring through the open window rouses Charlie, who crashes into something that feels like despair when he finds himself alone in his bed, twisted in the tousled sheets. The limp sticky rubber clinging to the ball of his foot is proof that it hadn't been only a drunken fantasy.

"Hi," KC says shyly. He's standing in the doorway dressed in the clothes he wore last night. "I waited 'til you woke up before leaving so I could say good-bye."

"I'll make coffee," Charlie insists, scrambling out of bed. He grabs a pair of boxers off the floor and roots through the closest pile of clothes for a clean T-shirt. "Or we can go get coffee," he says, searching for his sneakers. He's never quite gotten the hang of using that stupid pour-over Chemex Billy bought when he'd decided that anything brewed in a Krups machine tastes bitter and acidic. "You hungry? You want to get breakfast? You want eggs?"

Charlie barely recognizes this pathetic pussy boy who's practically begging KC to stay.

"I got to be at the park before ten, Charlie. It's a day game. First pitch is at one."

"That's four hours away!"

"We got to be there three hours early for BP and stretching. I'll get fined if I'm late. This ain't American Legion ball, Charlie," he says. "You don't just show up, put on your cleats, and take the field."

Charlie's not sure how they part. Do they hug? Should he give KC a kiss good-bye? Does he ask if he'll see KC again or simply suggest a day and time to meet?

"Look, Charlie," KC mumbles, staring at his feet. "I like you and everything. I wanted to see you again, but—"

"Hey, no worries," Charlie interrupts, sparing KC an awkward moment. "I have a boyfriend. I should have told you last night, but, you know . . ."

"Where is he?" KC asks, visibly apprehensive, as if an enraged cuckold were about to break down the door and put a gun to his head.

"He's working in New York this summer."

"I gotta go," KC says, anxious to be on his way. "I'm gonna be late."

"Can I call you?" Charlie blurts out as KC turns toward the door.

"We're on the road a lot. I don't get much free time."

"Call *me* when you do, okay?"

"Sure, Charlie," he says, obviously willing to say anything to bring this uncomfortable good-bye to an end.

Charlie stands in the doorway, listening to KC's footsteps as he descends the staircase. If he were a betting man, he wouldn't take the odds on ever hearing from KC again. And there's nothing he can do about it but crawl back into bed, pull the sheet over his head, and bury his face in a pillow so that anyone who might wander into the empty apartment won't hear him crying.

An incoming text from a Sacramento number arrives just before seven later that evening.

hi

hi

how r u
good
what r u doing
nothing got to get up early
He has to be in the studio by five in the morning. He'd
barely slept last night and he should be in bed, lights out, before nine, nine thirty at the latest.

ok
He knows KC most likely struggled for hours, doubting
the sincerity of Charlie's request, debating whether he
should risk the sting of rejection or retreat to the security of
loneliness.

u want to come over? Charlie types.

yes
It's a forty-five-minute drive, enough time for Charlie to
stash his clothes in drawers and closets, not bothering to sort
the laundered from the dirty, and change the sheets on his
unmade bed. He can even manage a quick, if not thorough,
scouring of the toilet and the tub. Somewhere in the drawer
where he and Billy toss random odds and ends is a set of
spare keys so he doesn't have to rouse KC from a sound
sleep when the alarm clock rings hours before daylight.

Billy's in a beneficent mood. He's bought Charlie, who
usually travels to New York on the ten-dollar discount bus, a
round-trip ticket on the high-speed express train to Penn Station. Tonight's reception isn't a formal event, and Charlie
needn't wear a tie, but Billy pleads that he bring a pressed,
collared shirt and clean khakis and elicits a promise Charlie
won't do something stupid and juvenile like wearing red
Converse high-tops instead of leather shoes. He's unusually
solicitous when Charlie arrives at the sublet and doesn't
even criticize him for being thirty minutes late. He doesn't
argue when Charlie announces he has to leave early tomorrow morning, claiming the station's sponsoring a weekend

charity event for Habitat for Humanity and Charlie's expected to contribute his nonexistent carpentry skills to putting a roof over the heads of a poor, deserving family. The truth is the Camden Lampreys are home after a weeklong road trip to Long Island and Bridgeport and KC has comped him for Saturday night's fireworks promotion. And it's only a half lie. He *is* doing his bit for charity Sunday afternoon by volunteering at the Lampreys' baseball clinic for the inner-city kids of Camden. He'd even persuaded the station to donate three boxes of promotional T-shirts to distribute to every kid participating in the event.

The usually self-possessed Billy is anxious this evening. It's not the heat and humidity that's causing perspiration to form on his brow. They'd stood on the curb less than a minute before hailing an air-conditioned cab.

"I'm not going to embarrass you by sticking green beans up my nose and standing on my head." Charlie sneers.

"What are you talking about?" Billy asks, clearly puzzled by Charlie's attitude.

"You seem to be regretting forcing me to come to this fucking thing."

"This fucking thing" is a cocktail reception and buffet supper on a river cruise sailing from Chelsea Piers at seven and returning at midnight.

"Jesus Christ, Charlie. Not everything is about you," Billy says as he pays the fare.

Billy's not the Sphinx he believes himself to be, at least not to Charlie. It's obvious Billy fears this long evening on the Hudson is going to be uncomfortable and awkward.

"Who keeps sending you all those fucking texts?" Billy asks, irritated by Charlie's inability to resist responding to every message.

"It's work."

"Yeah. Those assholes are texting you on a Friday night after being locked up in a studio with you the entire week. You expect me to believe that?"

"It's Sal's kid, if you really need to know. Eric."

"Isn't he in high school? You just discovered your inner pedophile?"

"Fuck you. He graduated in May."

"What? Are you supposed to be some fucking role model? What do you do? Take him on field trips to the comic book store?"

Billy's hit an exposed nerve without knowing it. Charlie's on the verge of admitting it's KC who is sending the messages, of rubbing his face in the revelation that Charlie's been fucking someone else in their bed while Billy's been cavorting in Gotham. But they're boarding the ship and any confrontation will have to wait now until landing.

The excesses of the new Gilded Age are on full display, intended not to impress, but to intimidate. All of it—the extravagant floral tributes, the fine wines and aged whiskeys, the carving and sauté stations, the dessert tables, the corps of undocumented aliens bearing sterling-silver trays of finger foods—is an unsubtle message reminding their summer guests of the absolute power these potentates wield over their futures. Charlie and a porcelain-skinned young Englishwoman, both insignificant others, seek refuge in each other's company, making small talk and acknowledging an unspoken pact to support each other through the long evening ahead. Their respective partners occasionally seek them out for the obligatory introduction to a member of the hiring committee, some of whom take an uncomfortable interest in the lovely young Brit.

"I think I'm being pimped out to that repulsive land tortoise staring at my chest," she observes, mocking her spouse's obsequiousness. She's clearly married beneath her station; her voice carries the plummy tones of the peerage.

Across the room, Billy is engaged in deep conversation with a strikingly handsome Indian. His head's slightly cocked, his lips hovering too close to the young man's earlobe. One hand is resting on his friend's shoulder, suggesting a familiar intimacy, and he gesticulates with the other to emphasize his point. Billy's eyes scan the room as he speaks, alert to the danger of being observed in a compromising situation. He sees he's attracted Charlie's attention and flashes an insincere smile. He says something to the Indian and, together, they approach, like hunters stalking their quarry.

"So, this is the famous Charlie," the stranger says, offering his hand.

"Charlie, I want you to meet Ashim. He's at Yale and is going to be clerking on the D.C. Circuit next year, too."

"A real pleasure, Charlie."

Charlie senses a slight hint of condescension in his Oxbridge inflections. This fucking boat is a United Nations of posh upper-class accents. Charlie disliked this Ashim from across the room, and proximity isn't improving his initial impression. Now he understands why Billy's been so nervous about this outing. Billy wasn't being honest earlier. His skittishness has *everything* to do with Charlie, who has no intention of making the situation easier for either of them. He makes it difficult, impossible actually, for this exotic, high-cheeked, black-eyed creature to engage him in friendly conversation. He correctly reads his conjugal replacement's meaningful glance at Billy: *I warned you this wasn't a good idea.*

"Billy says you're quite conversant in the ethnography of my little corner of the world," Ashim says pleasantly, making a last attempt at civility.

"He hates the Ganesha tattoo on my back. He thinks it's offensive—'cultural imperialism,' I believe were his words—because I'm not a Hindu."

"I'm Anglican." Ashim shrugs. "My grandfather is a bishop of the Church back in India."

"I didn't know that!" Billy exclaims.

"I'm sure I told you!"

Charlie recognizes the giddiness of a couple falling in love as they discover countless fascinating things about each other. All Charlie wants is for this evening to be over, but the only way to escape this floating prison is by swimming to shore. The summer associates grow more lubricated as the night drags on. Most of them will need half the day tomorrow to recover from a serious hangover, and more than one will spend the remainder of the weekend twisted in knots with worry over the imagined consequences of their drunken antics on the dance floor. Billy disappears for the final hour of the cruise, and Charlie's fully aware that Ashim is nowhere to be seen during that time. He expects Billy finds it titillating to play kissy-kissy and gropey-gropey in some dark, hidden corner knowing his boyfriend is waiting patiently for him to return. There's no proverbial lipstick on his collar, but he's got a happy spring in his step when he rejoins Charlie as the ship approaches the dock.

"Did you have a good time, Charlie?" he asks as they disembark.

"I behaved well, didn't I?" Charlie asks with mock seriousness as they enter a cab. "I was the perfect spouse. Knew my place, smiled, and limited my conversation to *very nice to meet you.*"

"An Oscar-worthy performance." Billy laughs, taking his hand in a demonstration of affection. He thinks he's skillfully negotiated a difficult evening and is stunned when Charlie tells the driver to drop him at Penn Station. Charlie jumps to the curb and disappears into the underground station without a single word of explanation, ignoring the persistent calls from Billy's phone.

He slumps dejectedly in one of the uncomfortable seats in the waiting room. The 12:20 has left the station and the next train to Philadelphia boards at 5:10 in the morning. He sends a text to KC and receives an immediate response commiserating with the prospect of spending nearly five hours sitting on a hard plastic seat while an unsavory crew of homeless schizophrenics prowls in the shadows. Charlie's battery is low so he signs off, typing *i love u,* already regretting it as he hits the SEND button. He turns off the phone and shoves it in his pocket, sparing himself the anguish of waiting for the response that will never arrive. He's been awake since before daybreak and quickly dozes off, sleeping soundly until a hand gently jostling his shoulder rouses him. It's KC, urging him to *"wake up, sleepyhead"* as his truck's parked in a tow zone and the security guard threatened to have it hauled away if he's not back in ten minutes sharp.

"How come you have Dumbo tattooed on your back?"

They slept past noon and neither one of them wants to be the first to crawl out of bed. Charlie flops on his belly to allow KC a closer inspection of the elephant god. He's ticklish and squirms happily as KC traces the outline of the image with his fingernail.

"What's so funny?" KC asks.

Charlie knows KC is sensitive about being laughed at, mocked.

"You," he says, turning and grasping KC by the shoulders, making certain he knows he's not being ridiculed. "Because you're right. It looks like a Disney cartoon. His name is Ganesha, and he's a Hindu god, the remover of obstacles."

KC furrows his brow in disapproval.

"I didn't know you were religious, Charlie," KC says, clearly uncomfortable over the prospect of facing a pagan deity every time Charlie rolls onto his stomach.

"I'm not. It's just a good-luck symbol. That's all."

"Are you Christian?"

"You mean, am I still Catholic?"

"No. Christian."

"What's the difference?"

He's being disingenuous, feigning ignorance to elicit an explanation for the citation to a Bible quote tattooed below

KC's neck. He'd looked up 1 Samuel 18:1 online as neither he nor Billy kept a Bible on their bookshelves, not expecting to find a reference to the love between David and Jonathan.

"Well, to be Christian you have to be born again."

"Are you born again?" Charlie asks, sensing KC wants to be asked.

"I don't know."

"Do you go to church?"

"Sometimes. When I'm home."

"In Albany?"

"No. California."

"You live in California?" Charlie asks, confirming what he'd surmised from the Sacramento area code.

"In the off-season."

Charlie picks up KC's hand and places it on his chest.

"Alone?"

"With the coach and Mrs. Freeman. They're Christians. They're good people, Charlie. They really are."

"I'm sure they are," Charlie says unconvincingly.

"You wouldn't hate them just because they're Christian, would you?"

Some wire has come loose in KC's personality. He's never sought or needed Charlie's approval before. What difference does it make how Charlie feels about a pair of Holy Rollers? He's never going to meet them.

"What does this Coach Freeholder think of that tattoo on your neck?"

"Freeman. His name is Freeman. He wants me to have it removed. He said he would pay to have it done."

"It figures."

"No, you got it all wrong, Charlie. He wants me to be able to play ball, and he doesn't want trouble. That's the only reason. I swear."

"So, why don't you?"

"Because I know God loves me. He loves you, too, Charlie. He doesn't care what we are."

Charlie props himself on an elbow and stares at KC's face. He wonders if KC's a little soft in the head. Most people Charlie knows don't believe in God, and the ones who do never talk about Him. This is all some crazy shit. Why is he doing this, letting himself get involved with KC again?

"What?" KC asks. "What are you staring at?"

Charlie, rarely at a loss for words, doesn't have an answer.

"Do you want me to leave?"

This time Charlie doesn't hesitate.

"No fucking way," he says, rolling on top of him.

KC's beliefs are his own and it isn't Charlie's place to judge him. All this Jesus shit seems to make him happy, and KC Conroy has had very few reasons to be happy in his short life. It could be worse. KC could be a vegetarian. Just as long as he doesn't ask Charlie to go to church with him. That's where he draws the line.

Charlie's tried asking KC about the intervening years since the long-ago summer they'd spent hauling furniture, but KC's evasive, a man of a mystery, forcing Charlie to resort to a bit of amateur sleuthing. Double D is his secret weapon in the subterfuge. She's curious about his sudden interest in the Camden Lampreys. It's the Independent League, the black hole of professional baseball, a team of washed-up major-leaguers, former prospects who fizzled out like Roman candles and marginally talented kids who'd never even been signed by a major league affiliate, still chasing the dream of making the Show for five hundred fifty bucks a month.

"What's your friend's name again, Boo-Boo?"

"KC Conroy. His real name is Kevin, but no one ever calls him that."

The Camden Lampreys never get press in the big city across the river, and the publicity director—who's probably also the clubhouse manager, the ticket agent, and the guy who collects the five-buck parking fee—will do cartwheels when he gets a call from the co-host of *Corelli and Crew* inquiring about a player on his roster.

"Christ, that was too easy," Deirdre laughs when an anxious Charlie arrives fifteen minutes earlier than usual the next day. "Your friend's certainly gonna turn some heads in the front office over there. They're not accustomed to media interest in anyone wearing their uniform."

She'd learned KC had been a highly rated prospect out of junior college, drafted ninety-fourth overall in the third round by the Rangers and signed with a considerable bonus. His stats in Rookie League were more than impressive, batting .326 with an OBP of .432. He went west to play winter ball in the Texas League and tore a ligament. He was playing Short Season Level A ball in Spokane when the story gets a little murky. He fell off the radar halfway through the season. Rumor was, he'd become addicted to the painkillers he'd taken after his injury and spent a few months in rehab. The Rangers still thought highly of him, and he tore up Single A the next season, in the top ten for average hits, runs, and RBIs. He was runner-up for Most Valuable Player in the League. He was promoted to AA the next season, and his stats for the first two months were impressive. He was a sure thing to make the All-Star team, and there was talk he was going to be called up to AAA in late July. But nine weeks into the season, he was in a head-on collision with a drunken driver.

"He's lucky to be alive. Escaped with three cracked vertebrae and a broken leg. God must have been looking out for him. I'm sure the Rangers sent him flowers, but they cut him anyway, what with him being in a back brace for months and his prognosis unpredictable. At least that was the public story. They knew his history with prescription painkillers in Spokane and wouldn't risk a relapse. His agent negotiated a contract with the Lampreys, finding him a temporary landing spot until another organization gives him a chance. The publicity director says the agent's a barracuda, one of those bland Christians who 'praise the Lord' while they're sticking it to you in the back."

Even Charlie—who's never played a day of sports in his life—has sensed that the men gathered in the Lampreys' clubhouse seem more like a random selection of players than an actual team. They're polite in the way strangers might treat each other. A few of them have struck up casual friendships, needing a drinking buddy to hang with at the local TGI Fridays or Applebee's. But the anxiety level is high, and the "smell of fear" isn't just a figure of speech in the locker room. These are men who've reached the end of the line, clinging to a slim chance at advancing in professional baseball. No one is interested in developing a camaraderie, an *esprit de corps,* when very few of those on the lineup card on Opening Day will still be with the club on the last day of the season.

The first time KC brought Charlie to the clubhouse, he'd worn his press pass on a lanyard around his neck, providing an excuse for his presence. But no one, not the skeletal security staff, not even the distracted manager, took the slightest interest in KC's friend, assuming he was some local bud KC had recruited as his one-man entourage. By the midsummer, KC's acolyte is taken for granted. KC's official residence is still with his host family, members of the New Jersey outpost of the Freemans' megachurch. But the two of them have been inseparable since the night KC rescued Charlie from Penn Station. Their schedules dovetail beautifully. Charlie's workday ends in the early afternoon just as KC is preparing to leave for the ballpark. They head out to a diner or McDonald's. (KC's teammates resent outsiders grazing on the measly spread provided by the owners.) They fill the long, deadly dull hours between drills and the first pitch playing *Call of Duty* whenever KC can claim first dibs on the Play-

Station. They exist in a world of their own in the cramped space of the clubhouse, oblivious to the noisy antics of restless ballplayers in various states of undress.

Charlie rarely watches any actual games, preferring to lie on his back on the beat-up Naugahyde clubhouse sofa reading or, more likely, fucking around with the gay cruising apps on his phone to see how many homos are within 670 feet. Which is what he's doing when he stumbles across a photograph that seizes his attention. The little thumbnail portrait is blurry, but there's no mistaking the identity of the person describing himself as a total bottom cum slut into Military, Jock, Geek, Muscle Daddy and seeking Friendship, Relationship, Dates, Chat, Random Play/NSA. He dials Eric, who picks up on the third ring, clearly excited to be hearing from Charlie.

"Spartacus? Really, Eric? Spartacus? Are you fucking kidding me?"

Eric thinks his Grindr profile ID is awesome and doesn't understand why Charlie disapproves.

"What the fuck are you doing?"

"Nothing. Watching the Kardashians."

"No. I mean why the fuck are you announcing to the world you take it up the ass?"

"I'm just looking. I never meet anyone."

Charlie's got the distinct sense he's being lied to.

"Your old man will have a stroke if he finds out about this."

He hears the roar of the cheering capacity crowd of six thousand–plus fans. He looks up and sees a Lamprey limping in from the dugout, leaning heavily on the shoulder of a trainer, and loses interest as soon as he confirms it isn't KC.

"Look, I can't talk now. I'll call you after the radio show tomorrow."

"Not until afternoon."

Of course. Eric never rises before one in the afternoon. He no sooner hangs up than his phone begins ringing. He's only spoken with Billy a few times since the night of the cruise nearly three weeks ago. He refused to respond to his numerous messages for ten days and only relented when Billy texted he was going to be on the next train to Philly if he didn't hear back in an hour. They've had one long conversation and several cordial but brief exchanges. The relationship is over, and they both agree they'll continue to live as roommates until the lease expires next May. There's another editorial board meeting on campus this Saturday and sleeping arrangements must be negotiated. Billy, who paid for the mattress and box spring they once slept on together, clearly expects to arrive and find Charlie residing in the smaller bedroom sparsely decorated with a card table, two folding chairs, and an ancient laptop.

"Don't sweat it, Charlie. You have no idea some of the places I've slept."

None of the bedding stores will deliver until Monday. It was KC's idea to drive to Target to buy an air mattress. He says he sleeps in too many crummy motels when the team is on the road and an inflatable bed on the bare floor is preferable to another night at a Comfort Inn or Motel 6. They're halfway home when they turn around and go back to the store. They don't have any pillows, and Billy's unlikely to offer to share.

Billy's arrived by the time they get back. Charlie's chest can't help swelling with pride as he sees the appreciative once-over KC gets when they enter the living room. KC always looks best after physical exertion. The sweat circles under his armpits are a definite turn-on, and Billy actually rises to get a closer look as KC's T-shirt creeps up his back when he bends to lift the air mattress box.

"Hi. I'm Billy Riddle," he says, flashing a smile that cost more than Charlie's parents paid for his first car.

"KC Conroy."

"You work with Charlie at the radio station?" Billy asks, acting almost coquettish as KC shakes his hand.

"No. Naw," KC mumbles, looking at Charlie for cues on how to respond.

Charlie wonders if Ashim or whatever his fucking name is knows his loving boyfriend well enough to suspect that, less than three hours out of New York, Billy's prowling for fresh meat.

"You from Philly?"

"California now. Originally from Albany."

"How do you know Charlie?"

"We're friends from high school," Charlie says abruptly.

Billy knows nothing about KC as Charlie had erased him from his romantic history when he and Billy were sharing tales of past crushes, both requited and unrequited, and sexual encounters. Billy looks skeptical. He clearly knows there's no way this specimen, obviously a high school BMOC, would have ever taken notice of the fruity geek Charlie claimed to be in his teenage years.

"Actually, KC's parents lived next door," he adds, a more plausible explanation of Charlie's enduring friendship with a boy who sat atop the adolescent pecking order. "Look, KC's got to get to work, so he doesn't really have time to talk."

He closes the door of his new bedroom on Billy's face. KC goes to work inflating the mattress and flops on his back to give it a test run.

"We didn't get any sheets," he suddenly remembers.

"I think the asshole can spare a sheet," Charlie says, not knowing if the Jersey suburban Walmart will be open after the game.

Billy, feeling generous, offers two sheets in exchange for an answer to his question.

"Are you fucking him?" he asks, withholding the bed-clothes until Charlie admits it.

"So what if I am?"

"It serious?" Billy asks, doing the inquisitive Groucho Marx thing with his eyebrows, trying to look sly and suggestive.

Jesus H. Christ! Charlie thinks. *The bastard's always full of surprises. He's actually trying to determine if a three-way tonight is a possibility.*

"Don't you have to call New York or something? I expect that new boyfriend of yours is clutching his phone in his fist, waiting to hear from you."

Billy shrugs, clearly unconcerned about causing any angst ninety miles to the north.

"What are you doing tonight, Charlie? You want to go to the Thai place we like?"

The presence of competition as desirable as KC Conroy has reignited Billy's interest in his now-former boyfriend. Charlie knows his M.O. If Billy can't get KC, either alone or as a part of a package, he'll do his best to fuck up things between them by seducing Charlie.

"I told you. KC's got to go to work."

"So?"

"I go with him."

"What are you two? Joined at the hip?" Billy sneers.

"Sometimes."

Billy actually winces at the comeback.

"And sometimes we sixty-nine. And sometimes he sits on my face. What else about him would you like to know?"

Billy spends a surprising amount of time in the apartment the entire weekend though the weather is splendid—rare hot, sunny days with no humidity. KC's presence clearly irritates him. He's unfailingly polite to him, even solicitous. It's Charlie who bears the brunt of his foul mood. Billy doesn't do jealousy well. He bitches about everything, some of it valid, like the pitiful state of the housekeeping; much of it ridiculous, like picking an argument over how Charlie sorts the mail. Charlie can almost feel him seething in the next room when he and KC are behind closed doors.

Saturday's uncomfortable, but they manage to survive without any major blowups. Billy's already left for the *Law Review* office when KC and Charlie wake up Sunday morning, and Charlie assumes he's seen the last of him for a few weeks at least. He's surprised to find him waiting when he returns alone from the ballpark, the team having boarded a bus for a road trip to York and Somerset after the day game.

"Your fucking bobblehead doll is a fucking thief."

Charlie has an immediate flashback to five years ago when he cowered as some smug Dartmouth bitch referred to KC in the same dismissive manner. That was then and this is now, and he reacts differently this time, literally shaking with anger, straining to contain his rage.

"What?"

"You heard me. He's a fucking thief."

"What are you talking about?"

"My American Express card. It's missing. I had to call to deactivate it. Now I'm going to call the police."

Billy never sees it coming. Charlie pounces and smashes him against the wall, slamming his fist like a jackhammer into Billy's guts.

"Fuck! Fuck! Fuck!" is all Billy can manage. He's spewing snot and spit and blood and throws his hands up to protect his face, not even trying to defend himself.

"Go ahead, motherfucker," Charlie gasps, winded. "Call the fucking police. And tomorrow I'll be making a visit to the dean of students. What do you think will happen when he finds out you plagiarized your fucking *Law Review* Note?"

They separate and Charlie even helps Billy to his feet. He brings him an ice compress for his aching face. He's going to have a beaut of a shiner in the morning. Billy clears his throat and makes a self-mocking comment about all the

Rocky-run-in jokes he'll suffer when he gets back to New
York. He says he has a crushing headache and is going to
delay leaving until morning. Will Charlie wake him before
he goes to work? Billy pauses at the door of his bedroom and
stares plaintively at the young man he'd once passionately
loved.

"You're not going to say anything about the Note to anyone, are you, Charlie?"

Charlie feels no pleasure holding the executioner's sword
over Billy's neck. It's an unwanted burden, this knowledge
he wished he didn't have.

"That depends on you, Billy," he says, not unkindly.

Billy's phone is ringing and he stares down at the screen.

"Hello?" he says, his voice tentative.

He looks up at Charlie, locking eyes with him.

"Thank you very much. My friend will pick it up tomorrow. Charlie Beresford. B-E-R-E-S-F-O-R-D."

He hangs up and straightens his back, his body language
a portrait of regret and submission.

"That was the Thai place. I left the card there after lunch.
They have my cell number from all the take-out we order."

"Call them back and tell them to cut it up. You cancelled
it. It's no good now. Never mind. I'll get it and shred it myself."

Charlie should be ecstatic that KC's been vindicated and
his accuser humiliated. But instead he feels guilty and ashamed
for considering for a fleeting moment the possibility that
Billy was right and KC had run off with his card.

The days are slowly getting shorter, another summer—
and another season—inching to its inevitable end. Only someone who knows KC as well as Charlie, certainly no one
affiliated with the Lampreys, can sense the occasional rip-
ples of anxiety troubling the confident and self-possessed
young ballplayer. Self-doubt and fatalism torment him while

he sleeps. He stirs when the alarm rings before dawn, the iri-
descent face of the electric clock the only light in the room,
and reaches for some part of Charlie—an arm, a shoulder—
to cling to, seeking comfort in the warmth of his body. On
this bright, sunny Sunday morning, Charlie is wakened by
the sound of gagging and finds KC naked and on his knees,
heaving the contents of his stomach into the toilet.

"I'm okay. I'm alright," KC insists as he pulls himself to
his feet.

"Are you sick? Do you want me to go to Walgreens and
get you something?"

"It's not that," KC mumbles, gargling mouthwash. "I
need to get to the park early."

Charlie assumes KC's been enlisted for another stupid
meet and greet with Lampreys fans whose kids want to exchange a few words with a real live professional ballplayer
after batting practice.

"The guy from the Reds is going to be there again today,
Charlie. Coach Freeman called last night to say he's praying
for me. He says I should relax, not try to impress him, just
play my game, and I'll be golden."

He fears he's drifting further and further from ever reaching the majors. The season for AA and AAA division clubs,
real minor league teams affiliated with MLB franchises,
ends in August. KC's still young and talented enough to at-
tract interest and a possible contract, and a few scouts looking for prospects to fill farm club roster spots vacated by
promotion or injury have come to see him play a few innings
this summer. But this afternoon will be the first time one has
returned. The Reds organization is sending a man up from
Maryland to cast his critical eye on whether KC's skills and
abilities are a match for the hole in their Carolina AA club's
outfield.

"Why didn't you tell me?" Charlie asks, not for the first
time wondering if he is nothing more than an afterthought in
KC's life.

" 'Cause it's probably nothing and I knew you'd be upset."

It's the closest they've come to acknowledging their comfort with each other and the dependence that's grown between them over the past few weeks, that something that feels like expectations now exist and parting will be difficult for both.

Most of the fans have abandoned the field box seats before the bottom of the third. Only the most foolhardy, Charlie among them, stubbornly refuses to surrender to the 103-degree heat. He's light-headed and queasy and the ultraviolet rays burn through his sunscreen, searing the flesh on the back of his neck. KC, patrolling the outfield, must be suffering, fully exposed to the blistering sun. But he seems undaunted, as if immune to the cruelties of nature, sprinting to the dugout at the end of each inning, light on his feet and barely winded. His three-run homer and five RBIs with at least one more chance at bat, have given the Lampreys the lead over their rivals from Long Island. He performs a miracle catch in the top of the eighth when he leaps to snag what looks to be a bases-clearing double that would even the score and crashes face-first into the outfield wall. There's an audible gasp and a moment of unbearable tension until he picks himself off the field and, earning a standing ovation, raises his arm to show the skeptical second-base umpire the ball in his glove.

Charlie, being naïve about such things, expects to find the scout handing KC pen and paper when he enters the clubhouse. KC, wearing only a jock, is sitting on a stool, mopping his wet curls with a towel.

"You were a fucking superstar today," Charlie says excitedly. "Did the guy from the Reds make you an offer?"

KC, conscious that his teammates are aware this afternoon was an important audition, shakes his head and, in almost a whisper, asks Charlie to lower his voice.

"It don't work that way. I'll hear from my agent and

Coach Freeman in a few days. I'm gonna be hurtin' tomorrow," he says, inspecting the bruises that have already begun to color.

"Well, you were fucking awesome," Charlie says, softly this time.

"I was okay," he says.

Others may accuse KC of false modesty, but Charlie knows he's sincere.

KC stands, a sign of respect, when one of the older players on the team, showered and wearing street clothes, approaches.

"You are very special today, KC. This is very good. I am very happy for you," he says in fluent but heavily accented English.

"Thank you, sir. It's a privilege to take the field with you every day."

Charlie sees the effect a few appreciative words have on the man. His athletic skills are rapidly deteriorating, and his frustration at the plate is painful to watch. KC says the talk is his teammate is actually forty-five, Latin American birth certificates being notoriously unreliable, but he'll be back next season. The Lampreys will offer him another contract because he'd been a member of the National League team across the river the year they won it all and will always be a draw. The Hall of Fame will never come calling and he never even made an All-Star team, but he was an everyday MLB position player for eleven years, never suffering a serious injury, his name penciled into the line-up card at least 130 games a season. The road back down is simply the path to the majors in reverse. The Phillies didn't try to resign him when his contract expired, and the only interest he drew as a free agent was a one-year deal with Baltimore. No one picked him up the following season until Cleveland unexpectedly needed a veteran second baseman in late June. He wasn't put on the post-season roster when the Indians made the play-offs that year, a deep humiliation for a proud former World

Champion. He knows his playing days are dwindling, but the game is his life and he won't let go until it's pried from his hands.

"Mr. Ramos, you know my friend Charlie. We're going to Chinatown tonight. Why don't you come with us?"

"No, no," the older man says, declining the invitation. "I call my wife and go to bed. Very hot today. Very hot."

"Next time?"

"Yes. Next time, KC."

"Man, I fucking stink," KC says, sniffing under his arms.

His words startle Charlie, as KC rarely swears like he did when they were kids. But he's right. Yes, he does. He smells like a goat, all musty and damp, and Charlie wishes they were alone in the clubhouse so he could climb aboard and bury his face in his armpit.

Charlie knows something is wrong as soon as he enters the studio. There's no banter, no sarcastic put-downs, no random bitching and moaning about the penuriousness of the owners. The technical crew is polite, even solicitous. Double D is biting her lower lip, a sure sign she's anxious and upset.

"Okay, people," the producer says, rallying the troops. "We go live in ten minutes. You're going to have to improvise if Kelsey isn't here yet."

Garrett Kelsey, who reports on the current status of the Eagles during the afternoon drive time show, is the go-to pinch hitter when one of the station's star broadcasters is ill or on vacation. Something is seriously wrong if he's been called in to cover for Sal.

"You've gotten friendly with Sal's kid this summer, haven't you, Boo-Boo?" Deirdre asks.

Charlie tenses, sensing that something has happened to Eric.

"Don't worry. He's being discharged this morning, and Sal and his wife are taking him home. He has a broken rib and a hairline fracture under his eye. It could have been a lot worse. They could have had to wire his jaw. The cops found him wandering in a daze in that park down by the river."

Deirdre leans forward to confide some piece of information not to be shared with the other members of the staff.

"He wasn't wearing a shirt, and his pants were soaked with blood. And he was barefoot. What in the hell was that kid doing roaming around some deserted park in his bare feet at one o'clock in the morning?"

Double D is neither naïve nor unworldly and is clearly fishing for prurient details. He doesn't doubt her concern for the boy and his parents is sincere, but it's human nature to be curious about all of the salacious particulars.

"I don't know, Deirdre. I can speculate, but I really don't know."

He'd never suspected Eric to be a night crawler. He'd assumed the kid's erotic adventures mostly were limited to his cell phone, nothing more than unconsummated seductions conducted from the safety of his bedroom.

The show must go on, and the somber mood has lifted by airtime. After all, Eric isn't dead and the producer just got a call from Sal who will be back in the saddle tomorrow morning. The day seems to drag and, after Charlie's finally released, he boards a bus and goes directly to Sal's town house. Sal's wife greets him at the door and invites him into the kitchen, offering him soda or iced tea. She says Sal is asleep and she'll ask Eric if he's up for visitors.

"Go on up," she says after a quick consultation with her son. "Second floor, back bedroom."

Eric's bedroom is fully outfitted with the latest, most expensive video and audio technology. The room is twice as large as the one Charlie's parents share, complete with a European walk-in shower. Eric's cheerful affect is at complete odds with his physical injuries. He's as excited as a Labrador puppy, eager to share the tale of surviving his first walk on the wild side.

"He told me to give him my shoes. No fucking way! They were Diesels! My dad paid three hundred dollars for those shoes! So he took them."

"He like your shirt, too?" Charlie asks sarcastically.

"Shut the door. I don't want my mom to hear this," he whispers.

"Your wish is my command."

"I was giving him a blow job. He said we were gonna get naked so I took off my shirt."

"How did you even know about this place?"

"Duh. Where do you think?" he asks as if he can't believe Charlie is unfamiliar with Squirt, the notorious Web site guide to public places where horny men prowl for anonymous sex. "Hey, help me out of bed."

Eric's bathrobe is loosely tied, and Charlie gets a bird's-eye view of his surprisingly impressive penis before averting his eyes. The rumors about the length and girth of Sal's manhood are obviously true, and he's blessed his sole male heir with the Priapus gene.

Charlie flips through the stack of comics on the nightstand, trying to ignore the sound of Eric's piss striking the water in the toilet bowl. What's with this kid and X-men? He's given up trying to teach him to appreciate classic icons like the Man of Steel and the Caped Crusader.

"Charlie! Charlie! Come here!" Eric shouts from the bathroom.

"What? What do you want?" Charlie asks warily.

The kid's been pumped full of painkillers, so his already poor judgment is further impaired by narcotics. What's he planning to do next? Wave his fat Italian sausage in his father's employee's face? *"Unbelievable,"* he mutters as Eric curses, stumbling as he rises from the toilet and taking a hard fall on the thick glass wall of the European shower. Eric's on his ass on the floor, spread-eagled, his junk on full display, but it's not the family jewels he wants Charlie to admire.

"So, what do you think?" he asks, proudly displaying the fresh Spider-Man tattoo on his left calf.

"What did your old man say when he saw that?"

"Not much. He told me to pick a better artist if I do it again. And to find another family if I ever come home with a piercing."

The craftsmanship is poor, the work of a hack. Charlie knows just the man to salvage this crude etching and transform it into a thing of beauty.

"Go take a nap. Don't take any more of those fucking pills. I'll be back tomorrow."

The repair job is more extensive, and consequentially more expensive, than Charlie'd anticipated and, of course, Eric is short on cash. But at least Spidey now looks like Spidey instead of a Paleolithic cave drawing.

"Can I finish this if you're not going to eat it?" Eric asks as they sit in a dimly lit booth at his favorite sushi restaurant.

Charlie orders another draft beer. A boy from Albany, he's never developed an appreciation for eel and sea urchin. He still can't wrap his head around KC's story about eating chicken heads while living with his Vietnamese surrogate family in Oregon.

"Are you okay, Charlie?"

"Sure. Of course," he insists.

He must be more distracted than he'd realized. *It's all in my head,* he tells himself. He's overreacting, jumping to conclusions. It's been three days since he and KC have spoken. He's tried to convince himself it's a long road trip and it's hard for KC to get away and find a few minutes to call. There's probably a good reason KC hasn't returned any of his messages. He's trusted Charlie with his most valued possessions, his grandfather's vinyl records. He wouldn't just disappear and leave them behind.

"You're acting kind of weird tonight."

"Just finish up. I've got to get to bed."

Maybe KC doesn't care about the records anymore. He's probably received some divine revelation from the Bible and has taken flight. It's the easy way out, the coward's way, disappearing without a good-bye. Or maybe the whole summer has been one big setup and KC's avenging Charlie's rejection years ago. He nearly jumps out of his skin when his shrill ring tone shrieks. It's just his mother calling, and he hits the IGNORE button.

"You wanna go to the Trocadero tonight, Charlie? It's death metal night."

"I have to work in the morning. I should be in bed already."

"Can we at least get water ice?"

He agrees, knowing he's not going to be able to sleep anyway. He'll lie in the dark, his cell phone on the pillow where KC used to lay his head, willing it to ring. And when it doesn't, he'll get out of bed and sit with the lights off, reliving the last few hours he and KC spent together, parsing every word, every silence, trying to divine the reason he drove KC away this time. He'd stood holding KC's duffel bag as the team boarded the bus so KC could take the call he'd been waiting for. He can cite verbatim KC's side of the conversation as he paced the length of the asphalt parking lot. *"What did he say?" "How soon?" "Why?" "Why not?" "When will he talk to them?"*

The bench coach called out to KC to get his sorry ass on the bus or they would leave without him. Charlie couldn't have said anything to offend him since they didn't exchange a single word, not even a good-bye. He didn't touch KC when he handed him his travel bag, avoiding any embarrassing gesture that could have been seen by a teammate staring out of the bus window. KC just turned and trotted back to the bus. The driver closed the door and they were on their way.

Charlie stood and watched until the bus disappeared, stricken by a chilling premonition that KC wasn't coming back.

Coming home to an empty apartment after seeing Eric safely to his door, he kicks his shoes across the room and walks to the closet. He brushes his teeth and swallows one of the Ambien Deirdre gave him this morning after he'd confided he hadn't been able to sleep. He undresses and crawls into bed, clutching the Lampreys jersey KC gave him that fateful afternoon earlier this summer to his chest. The pill works its magic. Misery and loneliness begin to fade as he tumbles down the rabbit hole. His sleep is deep, untroubled, and he doesn't hear the alarm hours later.

"Hey, hey, you got to get up."

KC, shirtless, his curls falling over his eyes, groggy as if he'd just awakened, is sitting up in bed, gently, but firmly, trying to arouse him.

"What's the matter, Charlie? I tried to wake you but you were dead to the world when I got back last night. Did I scare you?" he asks, assuming a bad dream is the reason Charlie clasps his arms around KC's shoulders and crushes him as if he were a drowning man and KC was his life raft.

The bus had already traveled 120 miles before KC discovered he'd left his phone on the counter at Denny's. The manager of the restaurant promised to overnight it to the Lampreys' business office, leaving KC incommunicado for three days.

"I couldn't call you," KC explains. "I didn't remember your number. I always use speed-dial."

Anyway, he's back and there's a long home stand ahead, no traveling for over a week. Eric's been badgering Charlie to go out all week and Charlie, succumbing, invites him to join them in Chinatown after Saturday's game. Charlie had promised to knock the little snot into the middle of next

week if he acts obnoxious around his friend, but it's obvious
from the outset Eric's enamored with KC. Not that he gives
a shit about his accomplishments on the baseball diamond.
The son of the host of the market's highest-rated sports talk
program has no interest in athletics. But KC's imposing
physical presence impresses him. Charlie feels a mild twinge
of jealousy witnessing Eric's too-obvious infatuation. Eric
doesn't hold it against KC that he seems to know nothing
about punk and metal or that his knowledge of comics is
limited to Hollywood superhero blockbusters. Being a real
athlete who sleeps with other boys is more than sufficient to
elevate KC to mythic status in Eric's eyes. KC's being a good
sport, tolerating Eric's unrelenting interrogation, though he's
clearly distracted. His agent had called this afternoon to tell
him the scout wouldn't be attending tomorrow's game. Charlie relaxes when KC lightly sets his foot atop Charlie's and
squeezes his knee under the table.

"Come on, Charlie! Let me come back to your place.
Pl-eeee-ze!" Eric whines. "I got Blue Diesel."

KC visibly winces at the mention of any chemical that
could cause a positive drug screen.

"Jesus Christ, Eric!" Charlie hisses, failing to catch his
unfortunate slip of the tongue. His lapses into profanity are
less and less frequent. He knows KC is uncomfortable when
he takes the name of the Lord in vain. "Get in the truck.
We're driving you home. Where you wander off to when we
leave is on you. And I'll snitch to Sal if you dare to fire up
your weed in our faces."

Eric jumps into the truck before Charlie, assuring himself
the middle position in a tight squeeze. Sal's kid or not, Charlie's gonna kick the shit out of him if he sees one of his
hands resting on KC's thigh. But Eric is well-behaved—by
Eric standards.

"You wanna meet my dad, KC? Maybe you can be on his
show! He'll do it if I ask him!"

Charlie won't embarrass KC by setting the record straight. The odds are less than nil that *Corelli and Crew* would ever consider booking a player from the Lampreys.

"Thanks, Eric, but I'm not much of a talker," KC says, declining gracefully.

"Okay. Let me know if you change your mind," Eric says, impulsively giving KC a seemingly innocent good-bye kiss on the cheek.

KC, who usually sleeps soundly, is restless that night. Charlie assumes it's disappointment over the scout not returning. As always, KC's larger body spoons into Charlie's smaller one. His ass is twitching, pressing against Charlie's crotch. One sweaty bout tonight obviously hadn't satisfied him, and the second is even more vigorous than the first, climaxing with Charlie on his back, his wrists pinned to his mattress, and KC riding his cock so hard Charlie's pelvis starts to ache.

"Charlie?" he asks when he rolls on his back. They're both breathing heavily, waiting for their heart rates to return to normal.

"What?"

"I have to ask you something."

Charlie assumes the future is on KC's mind, too. Billy will be returning at the end of the month from his British Columbia trek—a solo expedition, as it happens, Ashim, who'd never had any intention of ending his six-year relationship with a wealthy Congressional chief of staff for a summer distraction, having declined his offer of Charlie's airline ticket. The idea of the three of them living under the same roof, even if only until the end of the Lampreys' season in September, is untenable, but the thought of banishing KC to his Christian hosts in Jersey is unbearable.

And what happens *after* the season? There's nothing keeping Charlie in Philadelphia; he'd only moved here on Billy's insistence. He's prepared to rebut any argument over quitting his job to follow KC. He's been thinking about applying to graduate school for an advanced degree in communications, and he needs to earn more money for tuition than the station can pay, even if it means waiting tables or tending bar. He'll go anywhere KC wants, anywhere but fucking Sacramento where those fucking self-righteous Christians will try to control KC again.

KC flips on his side and, giving Charlie a gentle kiss, absentmindedly strokes Charlie's chest.

"Charlie, do you think he was serious? You know. Eric. About his father booking me on his show."

The look on his mother's face could freeze the balls of a brass monkey. The message is coming through loud and clear. *Don't even think about saying anything.* At least his father isn't the only middle-aged man in the stands dressed like an aging Pony Leaguer in his Camden Lampreys official team jersey. But "Chumley," the official mascot plush doll he'd purchased in the merchandise shop, is over the top and so are the team rally towels he'd bought for each of them. His dad lets Charlie's sarcastic remarks roll off his back, acting as if he's in on the joke, but his mother fails to see the humor in taunting his passive father with caustic words. He's being given fair warning she's not going to allow Charlie to spoil a special occasion—box seats behind home plate, comped by KC—with smart-ass criticisms of his father's overenthusiasm.

Charlie, chastened, even waves his rally towel when the Lampreys take the lead on KC's sacrifice fly in the bottom of the seventh. KC's a showman, always able to rise to the occasion. Charlie has no doubt that KC's theatrics are inspired by the presence of his almost-worshipful father. He'd been surprised, no, make that shocked, by KC's excited response when he told him about the dreaded weekend visit. And the much-anticipated highlight of the trip, sitting in the studio at a broadcast of *Corelli and Crew*, became little more than an afterthought when Charlie's dad learned of the almost-too-improbable-to-believe reunion of his son and the Mighty KC.

Charlie's mother, always the more restrained of his parents, seemed genuinely sincere when she greeted KC with a hug. She'd refused to hear his protests and his attempts to decline her invitations to dinner and breakfast because he didn't want to intrude on their family time alone. Tonight, walking his parents back to the hotel, Charlie actually feels a twinge of jealousy when his mother, strolling with KC a few steps ahead of him and his father, takes her companion by the arm, listening with intense concentration, nodding her head, either acknowledging or agreeing with whatever he is so enthusiastically confiding in her.

"What the hell were you and my mother talking about?" Charlie asks as KC drifts off to sleep.

"Just stuff. I told her about the Freemans and how they've been good to me. I told her they think I'm a good Christian and that I'm trying but I don't think I ever will be. She told me she thinks of me often and was really happy to see me."

The weekend is a pleasant success, and come Sunday morning, Charlie and his parents have an early brunch before they drive back to Albany, the first time they've been alone as KC had to report to the park for a day game. His mother is unusually quiet, barely eating and playing with the tea bag in her cup. Charlie knows she's waiting for his father to excuse himself for a bathroom break to seize the opportunity to confront him.

"Charlie, that boy has been through enough for two lives. Do you understand me? Can you even imagine how it feels to have nobody? He's attached to you. You encouraged him and now he's attached to you. You're not seventeen anymore. You can't just walk away when you're tired of him."

* * *

Manny Ramos sits ramrod-straight in his chair, visibly nervous as the tech adjusts his headphones. The man of the hour—or at least the 7:45 segment—has dressed formally for the occasion. He's the only guest in Charlie's short tenure who has worn a suit for a crack-of-dawn appearance. The sleeves of his French-cuffed shirt are cut long, and the diamonds in his cuff links sparkle under the studio lights. But nothing can distract from the majestic World Championship ring on his finger. KC is standing outside the broadcast booth to support his teammate. Sal, returning from a bathroom break, greets the older ballplayer as a long-lost friend. Mr. Ramos cracks a broad grin, showcasing his bleached teeth. Charlie realizes it's the first time he's seen the man smile.

Sal, as always, immediately puts his guest at ease, introducing him on-air as he would visiting royalty. They start off light, laughing about the clubhouse antics of the championship team, revered in a lunch-bucket, blue-collar town like Philly as a collection of scruffy miscreants. The interview smoothly flows into Manny's recollection of each of the six games of the Series, highlighting, of course, Ramos's double in the bottom of the ninth driving in the winning run in Game 2. Charlie had spent hours preparing detailed research—career stats, the value and length of his contracts, notable plays on the field, anything quotable—for Sal and the Crew to consult. The interview goes so well and the call-in queue is so long, Sal asks his guest to stay for a second segment and most likely would have invited him for a third if a national correspondent from the network hadn't been scheduled. Charlie is convinced Mr. Ramos is standing two inches taller as he makes his round of farewells.

"I'm going to walk Mr. Ramos to his car, then go home for a few more hours' sleep, Charlie," KC says before shyly approaching Sal and the producer to present them each with a box of expensive cigars to show his appreciation for their generosity in agreeing to book his teammate for the interview they had originally offered to him.

"Eric was right about you. You are an impressive and thoughtful young man," Sal tells KC. "I'm looking forward to watching you play in the majors soon. And what are you up to now, sport?" he asks his son, who for reasons unknown to Charlie, has managed to crawl out of bed before noon for this special occasion.

"KC's gonna drop me off at the bookstore in University City. I've already got reading assignments, and classes don't start for three weeks."

It must seem reasonable to KC that a school as challenging as Duke would begin making academic demands on its incoming freshman class during their last days of freedom. Charlie's suspicious, though. Why doesn't the little shit just download the books onto his iPad? Tomorrow's program is heavily booked, and Charlie's facing the challenge of preparing research files of player statistics and biographical backgrounds for each of the guests. He texts KC at noon, telling him not to wait before leaving for the ballpark.

"Hello?" he shouts when he unlocks the apartment door at the end of a grueling day at work. He hadn't expected to hear voices engaged in conversation in the kitchen.

"In here," KC calls.

Charlie recognizes the strained pitch of KC's voice when he's nervous. It certainly looks innocent enough. Eric, fully dressed, is leaning against the sink, holding a can of Pepsi. KC's perched on the opposite counter with a bottle of Gatorade in his hand.

"Did you get my text?" Charlie asks casually, as if he hasn't stumbled into an awkward situation.

"Yeah. I decided to wait for you so we can drive over together."

KC peers into the mouth of the bottle, avoiding Charlie's eyes.

"Well, I guess I ought to get going," Eric says, looking unbearably smug and self-satisfied, like he's just successfully pulled off a scam.

Charlie takes note that KC's shirt is not the one he'd worn this morning and that he's barefoot.

"You wanna go see Creepoid play tomorrow night, Charlie?" Eric asks nonchalantly as he opens the front door.

"Aren't you forgetting something? Your books? I don't see them. Did you leave them in KC's truck?" Charlie asks coolly, rattling the fucking little twat at last.

"What?"

"Your books. You came all the way out here to buy them."

"Ah, they didn't have what I needed," he says, thinking quickly as he scampers down the staircase.

KC hasn't lifted his eyes from his power drink. Even more taciturn than usual, he waits for Charlie to speak.

"You got your stuff, KC? I'm gonna change my shirt and shoes and I'll be ready to leave."

He knows it's difficult for a Christian to lie and doesn't want to put KC through the ordeal of confessing. Besides, he can't be 100 percent certain, and he really doesn't want to know. There's one thing he's sure of, though. That goddamn little fucker can find some other asshole to go with him to see Creepoid and any other fucking band that comes to town before he leaves for school.

The call had come as a complete surprise. He'd completely forgotten posting his résumé on the Internet one exhausted evening when he'd honestly believed he couldn't possibly continue to drag himself out of bed hours before the sun rose. It's only a Skype interview, but wearing a collarless shirt would be disrespectful though a suit would come across as too formal. He settles on a basic white button-down and tie. He's surprisingly nervous about this audition for a job he isn't interested in. He can feel the sweat dripping from his armpits when the fickle wireless connection threatens to leave him staring at a blank screen.

The first few minutes are spent swapping memories of Dartmouth with his prospective new boss, both being proud alumni. Then it's time to get down to brass tacks, specifically Charlie's barely minimal qualifications and the vice president of original programming for the Golf Channel's unexpected interest in his résumé.

"Mr. Weitzman, I have to admit I've never even held a golf club in my hand. I don't think I'm the person you are looking for."

"What did you know about football before you started at the station?"

"Nothing."

"Basketball?"

"Only that I got a concussion in junior high school when I hit my head on the hardwood floor after being run down by a six-four physical aberration called Stretch."

"Baseball?"

"That I know something about."

"You play?"

"No, I'm gay," he blurts out, putting his cards on the table early. He hadn't come out to Sal and the producer of *Corelli and Crew* until after he'd been offered the position.

"Can I ask you what the hell that has to do with base-ball?"

"Well, my boyfriend's a ballplayer."

"He any good? He interested in playing in our network softball league?"

"Uh, probably not. He was a third round draft pick."

"Who is he? What's his name? No, never mind. I don't need to know. But I can assure you the Golf Channel and our parent network have a strict non-discrimination policy. I'm on the diversity and inclusion committee myself. And despite the misconceptions you probably have, Atlanta is a very progressive city with an active LGBT community. I haven't seen a single Klansman patrolling the streets the entire three years I've been here. Of course, I can't vouch for what goes on outside the city limits."

Mr. Weitzman is more interested in the skills Charlie's acquired and his natural aptitude than his love life. *Describe a typical working day. How do you approach an assignment you've never been asked to do before? How do you respond to extreme deadlines? What would you say to a colleague if you saw her making a mistake? What's the best way to handle a temperamental on-air personality? The producer tells you to do one thing and then the anchor insists you do the exact opposite. Who do you have to keep happy?*

"Look, Charlie, don't be impressed by the big shot job title. Assistant director of original programming. I made them remove the words 'to the' between 'assistant' and 'director' because only graduates of secretarial schools were applying. It's an entry-level job. Most of the time you'll feel like a well-paid gofer. But if you're not too proud to be at everyone's beck and call, you'll learn a thing or two about television broadcasting. I'd like your permission to speak with your producer and the host of the radio show."

Maybe the threat of losing him might induce the miserly station into giving him a raise.

"Sure. Can I ask you a question, Mr. Weitzman?"

"Dave."

"Dave."

"Sure."

"There must be hundreds of applicants who are more qualified for this job. Most of them probably love playing golf. Why did you call me?"

"Well, there's the Dartmouth connection, of course, so I know you're smart. And I saw you're a guitarist in the per-

sonal interest information. Not many young men of your age
ever describe Classic Rockabilly as a 'passion.' You still play?"
    "I just started again recently. I'm finally growing some
decent callus."
    "I'm a musician myself. I play in a little covers band. We
do two or three weekend bar gigs a month. You ever play in a
band?"
    "I played only solo acoustic in high school. I was too shy.
Well, that's not exactly the truth. No one wanted a sissy in
their garage band. But I played in two bands at Dartmouth.
Sophomore through senior years. The first was a kind of
lousy Wilco knockoff. You know. The son of a hedge-fund
manager singing about being down-and-out with nothing
but lint in his pocket. The second was a lot better. Very good,
actually. Sort of progressive dream rock."
    "We play a lot of Carl Perkins. You know 'Matchbox'?
None of us can do it justice."
    "Sure. I know it."
    "Who's your favorite artist from that era?"
    "Ricky Nelson," he says without hesitation.
    "Ah," Dave says, humming a few bars of "Lonesome
Town." "Look, Charlie. You can expect to hear from me after
the weekend."

    The Monday morning call from Atlanta was timed at
9:05, though Charlie didn't see the message until after the
broadcast. Dave Weitzman wants to fly him to Georgia Saturday morning. Charlie's going to accompany the crew covering the final round of a PGA tournament in Savannah on
Sunday. Dave says a tent revival preacher couldn't have praised
Charlie more than Sal and the producer of *Corelli and Crew*.
He assures Charlie it's just a formality before he receives a
formal offer. He's already told the recruiters to secure Charlie temporary housing.

"You're not going to sue me for harassment if I force you to play in my band, are you?" He laughs.

He makes the decision on the spot. The important one. Not about taking the job. That's a no-brainer. He barricades himself in a bathroom at the end of a long, rarely used hallway. The first person he tells is the one who will be proudest of the choice he's made. His mother sounds more harried than usual when she answers the phone, but her voice softens with both affection and pride when he says he's going to ask KC to come to Atlanta with him.

Sal is already calling him Mr. Big Shot and jokingly reminds Charlie to remember his handsome pug and Roman profile when he's programming director at ESPN. Deirdre's planning the blowout celebration at the Saloon, the preferred steak house of the professional athletes of Philadelphia. The only one who hasn't offered premature congratulations is KC, and that's only because he's yet to be told. It's Thursday, forty-eight hours before Charlie's flight, and a rare day off for KC.

"So, when are you going to let me in on the secret, Charlie?" KC asks, wary and nervous about Charlie's undisclosed surprise.

"I'm moving to Atlanta," he blurts out.

Charlie sees KC's hands are shaking as he puts down the bowl of ice cream he's holding.

"When?"

"In a few weeks. I have to fly to Georgia on Saturday. They want me to spend time with members of the staff. Sal already knows and I'll give my formal notice when I get my offer letter on Monday."

KC's chest heaves and he slumps, withdrawing to some secret hideaway deep inside himself, resigned. He picks at his cuticles, not knowing how to respond, stricken by this unexpected news.

"I'm happy for you, Charlie. I really am. I might make it to Atlanta someday. You never know."

"No. No," Charlie says, reaching for KC's hand. "No, no, no. You don't understand. Let me finish."

KC looks perplexed.

"I want you to come with me. I'm asking you. Please."

"I can't leave, Charlie. The season's not over until September. I've got a contract."

"I know. I mean after the season. Come live with me in Atlanta."

KC looks as if he's been shot by a stun gun, meaning he's never, not once, considered living, actually living, with Charlie or any other man. *Living,* meaning something more than staying over every night, all the possessions he needs to get by packed in a single duffel bag. Charlie means *living,* as in having your mail delivered to the same address, the same residence recorded on both of your driver's licenses. It would be a big step in becoming the man he's struggled to accept being. Charlie doesn't hesitate to raise the one edict KC can't ignore.

"Maybe that's why God sent you to that place the afternoon we found each other again. Maybe this is what He wants for you."

KC, who's neither devious nor manipulative, would never suspect Charlie of exploiting his faith to get what he wants. A life with Charlie may indeed be the path the Lord intends for him. A true believer cannot reject the will of God.

"What would I do in Atlanta, Charlie?"

"Whatever you would do in California in the off-season. Rest. Work out. Train. Prepare your body and mind for next season."

Money won't be an issue. Charlie's among the very few in whom KC has confided that he has substantial assets in a trust controlled by a tightfisted business agent who marches to the orders of the Christian Svengali in Sacramento. And if

they want to be assholes and punish KC with a pittance of an
allowance for not returning to California, the salary offered
by the Golf Channel is a substantial raise that will keep them
comfortably housed and fed. Somehow, he'll find the funds
to hire a professional trainer to work with KC through the
winter.

"I got to answer this, Charlie," KC apologizes when his
phone rings. "It's Coach Freeman. I don't know how to tell
him. What should I say?"

Charlie feels the adrenaline rush of victory surging through
his body. He puts aside any lingering doubts about the wisdom
of his decision, about how long they can sustain this before the
difference in their interests, their intellectual curiosity, becomes an issue. And what happens when lust and physical
desire begin to diminish? Will it be enough that KC is thoughtful and kind and faithful, the occasional dalliance with the
likes of Eric Corelli notwithstanding? Yes. It's more than
enough. He's certain. If what he and KC feel for each other
isn't love, then what is?

"He's definitely going to be there? You're sure, Coach? I
know. I know. I will. I promise. I love you, too. Praise the
Lord!"

Charlie's unsettled by the unexpected turn of the conversation. The subject of Atlanta was never raised. Nothing was
said about KC's intentions. But KC is glowing. It's obvious
that Georgia and Charlie are the farthest thing from his mind.

"The Reds are sending another scout to Sunday's game.
They've been talking with my agent. They want to confirm
the reports they've received. They were going to offer a two-
and-a-half-week contract to the end of the AA schedule, but
my agent held out for a commitment for next season. They
need me. If the scout likes what he sees, Coach Freeman
says the Reds will buy out my contract with the Lampreys
and I'll officially be a Carolina Mudcat by noon on Monday."

Carolina? Charlie wonders. *North or South?* KC will be one state away from Atlanta, two at most. For two-and-a-half weeks. Then what? Any further decisions about the future must be deferred, but at least KC's not being shipped across the country.

KC sounds groggy, heavily medicated, his voice drifting into long silences. A woman, identifying herself as a nurse, takes the phone from him. She's non-committal and unwilling to answer Charlie's questions, even when Charlie lies, claiming to be KC's brother, his closest next-of-kin.

"I'm sorry. I'm not authorized to share any information. He insisted I call you and put him on the line. He's in no shape to talk tonight. Call back in the morning."

She takes pity on Charlie and shares that KC's had an injury. It's certainly not life-threatening and they expect a full recovery. She can't say what it is. There are laws that protect a patient's privacy, but she can assure Charlie he has no reason to worry. He should get some sleep. Everything will be fine. But he's still awake at five thirty, searching online for the earliest flight to Philadelphia. He hears his phone ringing while he's in the shower. He trips, his wet feet slipping on the tile floor, and smacks his wrist on the bathroom vanity as he runs to answer.

"Did I wake you?"

KC still doesn't sound like himself, but it's an improvement over last night.

"There's an eight fifty-five flight on Delta. I'll come straight to the hospital."

"No. No. No. Don't do that. They're discharging me soon. It's no big deal."

A torn meniscus and mild concussion sound like a big deal to Charlie. KC admits he was eager to impress yesterday afternoon and used poor judgment, colliding with the catcher in an attempt to knock the ball from his glove while sliding into home plate. He says it's a radial tear in something called the white zone of his knee. The surgery is arthroscopic. He'll be fine, good as new, after rehab. They were more worried about the concussion. They say he was unconscious for almost five minutes. He's had a CT scan. They kept him in observation overnight, waking him every few hours to ask him his name.

"So much for the Reds," he says, trying to sound upbeat despite the catch in his voice. "Charlie, I think God must hate me. Coach Freeman says He's testing my faith, but I don't believe him anymore. . . ." he says, his voice trailing off.

He insists there's no need for Charlie to take an earlier flight. He'll sleep all day anyway. His next words are the ones Charlie dreads.

"I'll be good. Coach Freeman will be with me. He took the red-eye and will be here before they send me home."

The rest of the day feels like an out-of-body experience. By the time Dave calls for the car to take him to the airport, Charlie knows he's blown any chance of working at the Golf Channel. Yesterday's tournament final had been a rainout, leaving the crew with idle hours to fill until the official announcement of the postponement of the final round. The camaraderie, the banter, the friendly put-downs, the passionate arguments about GM versus Ford, *The Godfather* versus *Goodfellas,* had made him feel like he was back in the studio with Corelli and Crew. He'd been comfortable enough to relax and have a second beer at dinner with Dave and another executive and realized he really wanted this job, badly, as he had undressed for bed.

Then came the call from KC and this morning's news that the Christian missionary has made a stealth attack on Philadelphia. He must have appeared robotic, vacant, as Dave introduced him around the office. He wouldn't be surprised if they suspected he was on drugs. So Dave's parting words come as a total shock.

"The formal offer will be in your e-mail when you get home. I hope you're as excited about working with us as we are to have you."

Charlie had thought it odd KC had turned his phone off when he tried calling from Stapleton International. Now he's worried when his calls still fall directly into voice mail when he lands in Philly. He's apprehensive as he opens the door to his apartment. No one answers when he calls KC's name. The only sign of life is Billy's mangy cat as it jumps from the arm of the couch.

The clue something is amiss is the perfectly made bed, the sheets pulled taut and secured by perfect military corners. Someone has done laundry and the folded clothes, *Charlie's* clothes, are neatly stacked. Not a sock or pair of boxer briefs belongs to KC. KC's duffel bag and vinyl records are missing. Charlie kicks any object in the way of his feet and throws everything in reach against the walls. He doesn't care if his neighbors hear him screaming and cursing when he opens the closet door and the Camden Lampreys jersey KC gave him in the parking lot of the adult bookstore is missing.

KC doesn't need to ask why Charlie is upset and angry when he finally returns his calls. He knows the reason. He tells Charlie to take a cab to the airport Marriott; he'll spot him the fare, both coming and going, when he arrives. The man who greets him at the hotel isn't what Charlie had expected. He'd always thought Coach Freeman must be imposing, severe, like Daniel Day-Lewis as Lincoln. But he's just an ordinary guy in Dockers and a sports shirt, still trim and in good shape well into middle age.

"You must be Charlie. I'm John Freeman. It's good to finally meet you."

"Thank you, sir."

"It's John. No formalities here. I feel as if I already know you."

"Hey! Hey! I thought you came to see *me!*"

KC's propped against a bank of pillows, his right leg wrapped in a soft cast from his groin to his ankle. There's a pair of crutches within easy reach and an open Bible on his nightstand. He's watching *South Park.* The Son of God is making a guest appearance, hosting "Jesus 'n' Pals." Much to Charlie's amazement, both KC and Mr. Freeman think the cartoon is hilarious. Charlie spots KC's packed duffel and vinyl records on the floor at the foot of the bed.

"Well, I suppose you boys have a lot to talk about," Mr. Freeman says cheerfully as the credits roll and KC reaches for the remote. "I'm very glad I got to meet you, Charlie. I hope you'll come visit us soon. You're always welcome."

His handshake is firm and the invitation is sincere.

"Don't keep him up too late, Charlie. He's got a long flight tomorrow," he says as he closes the door.

Charlie almost wishes Mr. Freeman hadn't left them alone. It's awkward. Neither wants to be the first to acknowledge the obvious, that Charlie's been summoned to say goodbye.

"Coach Freeman went to your apartment to get my things this afternoon. I gave him my key. It's over there, on the dresser."

Charlie pockets the key and starts to say something, then hesitates, and stands there silently.

"I told you he's a good guy, Charlie. I knew you'd like him."

"I don't like him, you asshole. He took the Lampreys jersey you gave me."

KC struggles to pull himself up on his elbows and asks Charlie to bring the duffel to the bed. The jersey is carefully folded, the first thing he finds when he opens the bag.

"He probably thought it was mine, Charlie," KC says, offering him the shirt.

Charlie refuses to take it from his hand.

"Keep it, KC. What am I going to do with it?"

He hadn't intended to sound cruel and wounding. He only meant KC could take it back if it held some special meaning for him. But his words clearly sting and KC turns his face to the wall so Charlie can't see him crying.

"I don't want you to go," Charlie says quietly, sitting on the bed, staring at the drawn curtains.

He feels KC's hand groping for his. He picks it up and squeezes his fingers.

"I'm going to have the surgery in LA. Some big expert on knees at UCLA. I gotta start rehab right away if I'm going to be ready for spring."

"You can do it in Atlanta," Charlie says.

They both know the idea's unfeasible. KC is going to need the undivided attention of his mentor to support him, to encourage him when he falls into despair, to urge him to work through the pain and push him to the fastest recovery possible. Charlie lies down beside him and they both gaze at the ceiling.

"Coach Freeman is going to buy us both Xbox Live. We can still play *Call of Duty* whenever we want. I'll still kick your ass."

Charlie rolls on his side, facing KC, and drapes his arm across his chest.

"You're gonna stay here with me tonight, aren't you, Charlie? We can't do anything but sleep. But please don't go home."

*   *   *

Charlie's still a member of Corelli and Crew for the next few weeks and he picks up the phone on one ring when the hotel operator calls at 3:30. KC doesn't stir; the painkillers have left him dead to the world. Charlie dresses quickly and stands beside the bed, wondering if he'll ever wake up beside KC again. He ought to rouse him. KC will be upset in the morning when he finds Charlie is gone. But saying good-bye would feel too final and mean that everything between them has ended. He picks up the folded jersey and quietly closes the hotel door behind him.

The only vehicles on the interstate at this hour are tractor-trailers traveling at dangerous speeds. Charlie arrives home with time to spare before he needs to shower. He strips to his boxers and puts on the Lampreys jersey, flopping on the sofa to challenge himself to a solo round of *Call of Duty.* He knows he can't stay in this place any longer and that he will never sleep in the bed he shared with KC again. He doesn't want to be here when Billy returns. He opens his e-mail and reads the official offer letter. He hits the REPLY button, asking if Dave's band could use a lead guitarist who plays a nasty "Matchbox."

His mother is going to panic when the phone rings at five o'clock in the morning. But he needs to talk to her, now— even waiting an hour seems unbearable. She clears her throat and says his name with a wary uneasiness he's not used to hearing in her voice. There's a long silence before he's able to speak.

"KC tore his knee up. They're taking him back to California. He's going with that coach."

His mother has always been his steady ship on turbulent waters, offering safe passage until he can safely go ashore.

"Why don't you come home for a few days before you leave for Atlanta? You should at least start your new job with clean and pressed clothes."

"Okay," he says, doing a poor job at sounding stoic and unemotional.

"Are you going to be all right now?"

"Yes. I think so. Yes."

"Charlie?"

"Yes."

"If it's meant to happen, it's going to happen."

EPILOGUE

Teenage Idol

(Seventeen Years Later)

*Then he threw his arms around his brother Benjamin
and wept, and Benjamin embraced him, weeping.
And he kissed all his brothers and wept over them.
Afterward his brothers talked with him.*

—Genesis 45:14–15

"Please. When it's my time, just throw my naked body into a cardboard box and tell them to fire up the oven."

"God, Charlie. Stop being so melodramatic."

Madeline, brisk and efficient as always, her mother's daughter, isn't interested in morbid ramblings about mortality. In fact, she isn't interested in anything but the steady stream of phone calls from her office.

"Shit, I promised I would be there when she delivers. I know. I know. She's an entitled little princess. I'm sure if my mother knew her baby was due today, she would have postponed dying," she says sarcastically.

Madeline has permanent bags under her eyes and is perilously thin. Her demanding medical practice and the constant travel between Mamaroneck and Albany, three, lately four times a week, have taken their toll. Charlie and his father had deferred all end-of-life decisions to her. An obstetrician was certainly more qualified to make medical judgments than a retired business agent for a union local and the president of content development and original programming of a cable comedy network. She'd nagged their mother for years about her stubborn refusal to stop smoking, but was completely nonjudgmental, never blaming or pointing fingers, after the cancer diagnosis was made. They'd continued to bicker and argue and complain about the other behind her back, but the gradual, gruesome process of dying had strengthened the bond between them. Charlie's father had complained that the two of them had shut him out, rendering him useless with nothing to do but watch from the sidelines. Charlie, for his part, had made the occasional trip from the city to Albany.

Charlie, the neglectful son, is burdened by guilt. Not that anyone has accused him of abandoning his mother. He'd taken her on a two-week cruise to Alaska, a lifetime dream of hers, before she became too fragile and weak to travel. He'd sent her books, mysteries and thrillers, and agreed to read *Gone with the Wind,* her favorite book, with her, calling several times a week to discuss their progress. His mother, not for the first time, had thrown him a curveball with her declaration that she'd never before understood that Melanie's infatuation with Scarlett was a romantic one. Theirs was the true love story of the saga. It had taken a while to wrap his head around the concept of Melanie and Scarlett as dykes, but the more he thought about it, the more sense it made.

"I'm worried about Daddy," Madeline confides. "How is he going to live in this house alone?"

Always willing to allow his wife to be the dominant personality in their long and, all things considered, happy marriage, he'd become so dependent she had laid out his clothes in the morning and dispensed his blood pressure medication as if he couldn't be trusted to count the correct number of pills.

"One of us is going to have to keep an eye on him. It's going to be hard for him to walk into the room and see her in her casket. Are you even listening to me, Charlie?"

"Of course."

"What did I just say?"

"About the old man. Breaking down when he sees her."

The hour arrives for the three of them to leave for the funeral home. Madeline's husband will join them for the public viewing. (They've decided as responsible parents that their four-year-old son is too young to be exposed to these barbaric burial rituals.) Charlie and Madeline are surprised by their father's stoicism. He takes the seat closest to the casket. It's a little weird and creepy when he starts a one-sided conversation with his wife. They hover at the back of the room to allow him some privacy.

"What do you think he's saying to her?" Madeline asks.

It would have been less odd if he'd been stricken by grief, making declarations of eternal love, but he's simply chattering nonstop, his affect no different than if he were reading back the items of the grocery list to her.

"Do you think he's losing it?" Charlie asks.

"Probably not, but don't let him out of your sight."

Everyone warns Charlie he won't feel it, really feel it, until after the funeral, when life has resumed its everyday rhythms. He'll read or hear something he knows she'd find interesting, something he wants to share with her, and realize she's gone, really gone, that he'll never speak to her again. But tonight he only feels relief that the exhausting bedside vigil at the hospice is over. The doors have opened and the first visitors are arriving. Madeline's husband, a handsome radiation oncologist, touches Charlie's shoulder and asks how he's doing.

The room fills quickly. His mother had died young, in her sixties, and most of her friends and acquaintances are alive and able to attend her viewing. The old man surprises his children with his calm demeanor, graciously greeting the guests. Charlie's proud of his mother's ability to relate to such a diverse group of people. Members of her cancer survivors group of years ago and those from the more recent living-with-cancer gatherings. Women from the yoga classes she attended and later taught until she was no longer physically able. The members of her book club arrive *en masse*. Some of the mourners are obviously disciples of Shiva or Buddha. They're mingling with the rosary society from her parish. Charlie is grateful for their genuine expressions of sympathy, but after forty minutes, his responses are beginning to sound canned, lacking emotion, at least to his own ears. The phone vibrating in his pocket is a welcome opportunity to slip away for a few minutes.

"I am soooooo sorry, Charlie. There was a lot of drama about whether my understudy had fully recovered from the flu and could perform tonight. Then the idiot cabbie insisted on taking Madison Avenue to the station. The next train is at eight forty-eight. I'll be on it. I swear."

"Don't worry about it, Troy. There's really no need for you to be here. It's just a small thing. My dad. My sister and her husband. Please. I'll talk to you tomorrow."

"When are you coming back?"

Troy's not missing Charlie and pining for a reunion. He needs to know how long he has before he has to kick his latest paramour out of the apartment and change the sheets on their bed.

"The day after tomorrow. In the morning, most likely."

"I miss you," Troy says with all the sincerity of an actor reading lines.

"Uh-huh," Charlie responds, ending the call.

Their relationship has been on life support for almost two years. He'd expected Troy to announce it was over when he was cast in a jukebox musical with a score of early sixties Brill Building hits. He was amazed Troy hadn't moved out when he was a surprise Tony nominee for Leading Actor in a Musical. Now it's apparent Troy's just riding it out until he leaves for California (temporarily, he claims, though Charlie knows better) at the end of his one-year contract on July 31st. It makes perfect sense. Why should he need to find a new place to crash before embarking for LA, where his agent has snagged him auditions for pilot season, mostly for the cocky sidekick role in cookie-cutter tongue-in-cheek cop or lawyer or doctor buddy shows? (Troy had reached the age of thirty-eight before he accepted he's not handsome enough to be cast as a network television leading man.) Charlie's been expecting this call tonight. It would be completely out of character for Troy to sacrifice two days to mourn the matriarch of a family he'll never see again after leaving New York.

The crush of bodies in the viewing room has grown denser. It's pushing eight o'clock, peak visiting hours. Madeline is likely cursing him for abandoning her and their father to deal with expressions of sympathy and short testimonials to their mother's good life.

"Excuse me, excuse me," he apologizes as he snakes his way toward the casket, where a tall man with a shaved head is speaking with his sister. She seems genuinely touched by his presence and gives him a big hug before greeting the next person in line. Charlie takes his place beside her just as the bald man turns to walk away. Madeline reaches and grabs the man's wrist.

"Oh wait!" she says. "Here he is! He'll be so happy to see you!"

Charlie's too stunned to speak.

"Don't you remember me, Charlie?" the bald man teases him.

Even with a whistle-clean scalp shorn of its once thick black curls, Charlie would know KC Conroy. No one else has those same pitch-black eyes or the smile that manages to seem modest and shy, yet bracingly confident. And, of course, there's the small scar on his chin.

"Of course I do. How did you get here?"

"I live here."

"In Albany?"

"Yeah. In Albany."

Charlie's causing a logjam at the casket and has to resume his official duties.

"Can you stay? Just a few minutes? So we can talk?"

"Sure."

"He's the last person I ever expected to see in Albany again," Madeline says quietly in her brother's ear. "I saw his idiot stepbrother a few months ago at Taco Bell when Mommy had a craving for a burrito. He was working there. I would have thought he would have ODed by the time he was twenty-one."

Charlie's too distracted to make much of an effort to appear sincere when expressing his appreciation for the condolences extended to the family of the deceased. The official viewing hours are mercifully drawing to a close, but a significant number of people are lingering for the benediction by the family's parish priest.

"Go ahead. I know you hate this," Madeline says as the priest bustles through the door wearing a New York Giants jersey and waiving a missal.

Charlie wanders from room to room, growing despondent when it becomes obvious KC has left.

"Hey."

He's startled by a tap on his shoulder and turns to face KC. His emotions gather momentum quickly until he's sobbing like a heartbroken child, behavior unworthy of a grown man.

"I'm sorry. I'm sorry," he apologizes, backing away, trying to get his feelings under control. "You must think I'm an idiot."

"Your mom just died, Charlie. Why would I think you're an idiot?"

Charlie breaks down again, and KC doesn't cringe or back away. He embraces Charlie and encourages him to let it all out, speaking with a soft, reassuring voice.

"What are you doing tomorrow morning?" Charlie asks after crying himself dry.

"Working. Why?"
"Can you get the morning off?"
"I work for myself."
"Will you be a pallbearer?"
"Of course. I really liked your mom. It would be an honor."

The funeral lunch is well attended, but Charlie's disappointed when KC says he can only stay a minute.
"When do you go back, Charlie?"
"Tomorrow morning."
KC nods his head. Charlie knows he's reluctant to be the one to ask.
"Let's get together tonight, KC. You name the place. Anywhere you want to go."
"It's Kevin, Charlie. Kevin Nelson. That's my name now. I'll pick you up at seven. Are you still fifteen minutes late for everything?"

Charlie insists he would have loved Vietnamese, but KC says you have to drive all the way to Putnam County for decent pho. But there's a surplus of pricey steak houses where lobbyists ply legislators with expensive wines and aged beef.
"I hope this is okay. I picked it because it's close to your dad's place. That must be nice, Charlie, knowing the house you grew up in will always be there."
"Yeah, but I don't know for how much longer. Madeline's already ordering brochures for retirement communities. I keep telling her the old man's not going to be happy living somewhere he has to wear a tie to the dining room."
Away from the disapproving eyes of Troy and his New York friends with ethical and cardiac reasons for swearing off animal flesh, Charlie orders a bone-in rib eye.
"I don't get a chance to eat meat very often," he explains

sheepishly, embarrassed by his carnivorous yearnings when KC orders grilled tuna.

"Go for it." KC laughs.

Charlie asks the waiter what beers are on tap.

"Make that two," KC says when Charlie orders an IPA.

"You don't drink, KC," Charlie remarks.

"People change."

KC's words remind Charlie that he isn't to call him KC anymore. His name is Kevin.

"I'm sorry, Kevin."

"Don't worry. Most people still call me KC. It doesn't bother me."

"Why did you do it? Change your name?" Charlie asks despite knowing the reason.

"You remember my pop-pop? You came to the nursing home with me once. His name was Nelson. Arthur Nelson. It was no big deal. I just went to the courthouse with my lawyer and filed some papers."

"What did your mother think?"

"Who knows?" KC shrugs.

"She didn't say anything?"

"I haven't seen her in nine years. She could be dead."

"I'm sorry. What about her kids?"

"Marty, he was the middle boy. He got shot in a drug deal. He was still a kid. I came back to Albany to get Peter into rehab. He could have played in the NHL but he fell in with the wrong crowd. He's got a nice wife and a little boy now. I put Dana through Syracuse and she's getting her master's."

"You did all that? Why?"

KC looks puzzled by Charlie's question.

"They didn't have anyone, Charlie. I know how that feels."

Charlie wants to ask if KC has someone now. A wife, a partner, someone he sees on a regular basis? A girlfriend? A boyfriend? Maybe a kid? Who does he sleep with, that is, if he sleeps with anyone at all? He'd noticed at the funeral home KC doesn't wear a ring.

"What about you? What have you been doing?" KC asks. Charlie's uncharacteristically modest about his success.

"It seems I have a previously unsuspected talent for knowing what adolescent boys—and their fathers—think is funny. Poop jokes. Tit jokes. Sexual humiliation. Ridiculously dangerous pratfalls and stunts."

KC is a huge fan of one of the more profane-animated series Charlie green-lighted, surprising for a Christian.

"I really don't eat like this, Kevin. Believe me," Charlie says shamefully, fearing he's coming off as a glutton. The meat and beer and buttery mashed potatoes are settling in his stomach.

"You can still call me KC. Don't worry. And why are you apologizing? You don't have to explain yourself to me."

Yes. He does. He should. At least the second time he and KC parted ways was less abrupt and certainly gentler than the first. The truth was, that during his one trip to Sacramento, he'd finally accepted their worlds, their lives, were too different to be able to sustain anything than brief, passionate interludes. The Freemans were kind and generous. They insisted on paying Charlie's airline ticket and picked up every check during his weeklong stay. They'd been genuinely happy to see KC so excited about seeing his special friend again. But when Charlie questioned why he and KC were staying at a modest motel, KC explained they would have had to sleep in different bedrooms in the Coach's house. The Freemans didn't judge him, but they would never let *that* go on under their roof.

Charlie and KC grew resigned to accepting that living on opposite shores of the country wasn't working. They would see where they were when KC's life had settled. They'd sworn to always be friends, to have each other's back. But gradually, the texts and calls and long-distance rounds of *Call of Duty* sputtered, becoming less and less frequent, until they fell out of touch. Charlie would occasionally visit the *Baseball America* webpage searching for any mention of KC. He was a career minor leaguer who peaked three years after his stint with the Lampreys as a September call-up for the Baltimore Orioles. He'd made it to the Show, even if it was only seventeen games. But his life had mostly been an endless cycle of reassignments and options and trades, with frequents stints on the disabled list with a variety of injuries. The last Charlie had heard KC was at Arizona State, getting a degree in something or other, exercise physiology if he remembers. That was more than ten years ago.

"You know, my mother always liked you. You should have looked her up when you moved back here."

"Albany's not that big, Charlie. Your mom knew I was here. I owe her a lot. I would have made a lot of mistakes with Peter if she hadn't been there to talk to."

Charlie's stunned by his casual revelation.

"Why didn't she tell me? She never mentioned you!"

"I asked her not to."

Charlie's first reaction is shock and anger at his mother for honoring his request. He feels betrayed by her allegiance to KC, for harboring a secret from her own flesh and blood.

"Why? Why would you ask her to do that?"

"I just did. She never asked why."

She wouldn't have needed to. Twice burned, forever shy. Not that Charlie was entirely to blame, though, truth be told, KC had been the more reluctant of the two to let go. They have a friendly argument over who will pick up the check. The bill's expensive and Charlie has no idea of the state of KC's finances these days. He assumes four years of tuition at Syracuse must have been a strain on KC's resources. But KC insists on paying the tab.

"You need to go home?" KC asks as they stand in the parking lot.

"No. Why?"

"Come on. Get in the truck. I want to show you something."

Either KC's deeply in debt or he's making a more-than-comfortable living as evidenced by the luxury Ford F-150 he drives.

"Okay, I'm gonna ask you," Charlie says he buckles his seat belt. "You married?"

"No."

"Girlfriend?"

"No." KC laughs. "I haven't changed *that* much."

"Boyfriend?"

"Did. Don't. You?"

"For about another month. How the hell do you meet people up here?"

"I don't," KC says emphatically as he backs out of the parking space.

Cloaked in the darkness of night, Albany looks almost appealing. The State Capitol Building is still impressively majestic, and the floodlit Empire State Plaza has a dignified, ghostly mien.

"Where are we going?"

"You'll see."

Charlie doesn't understand why they pull into the parking lot of a Taco Bell (OPEN UNTIL TWO EVERY NIGHT) when he's so stuffed he needs to let his belt out a notch. But he follows KC inside, thinking they could probably both use the bathroom.

The brightly lit interior of a quiet fast-food franchise seems as eerie as the deserted capitol. But there's a line of cars outside and the drive-through is doing a brisk business. A stocky man with thick orange hair is busy in the kitchen supervising a crew of tired teenagers. He looks up and, wiping his hands on a cloth, comes out front to greet them. His name tag says PETE CONROY, MANAGER, and his white short-sleeved dress shirt is splattered with food stains.

"Wassup, Kevin?" he says cheerfully. "Frigging busy for a Wednesday night."

"Just wanted to show the place to my buddy. You remember Charlie Beresford, Peter? Charlie, this is my brother, Pete."

Charlie takes note the fellow is introduced as KC's brother, not stepbrother.

"I went to school with your sister, Madeline. She was one of the smart kids," Pete says jovially, pumping Charlie's arm. "She wouldn't remember me."

"Oh, I'm sure she does," Charlie responds truthfully, refraining from repeating her recent comments.

"Okay, buddy. Gotta roll. Place looks good," KC remarks, nodding approvingly at the spotless interior.

"Uh, are you like the regional manager or something?" Charlie asks.

"I own the place. And two more and a KFC. I'm closing on a second chicken franchise next week. That's why I can barely stand the smell of meat anymore. Coach Freeman's guy did well investing my sign-on. His son still manages my money."

"Holy shit! You're rich!"

"Gettin' there," KC says modestly.

"Where is the coach?"

"He passed. I moved Mrs. Freeman back East when she couldn't live on her own anymore. She's in a dementia unit in Albany now. A nicer one than my pop-pop's. Come on."

They drive beyond the hazy night light of strip malls and neon.

"You wanna hear some music?" KC asks.

"Ricky. Ricky Nelson."

"You serious?"

"Yes. I'm serious."

KC parks the truck in the lot of a familiar ballpark. The Ryan Allied Van Lines ads on the scoreboard are long gone, replaced by the logos of Taco Bell and KFC.

"I put in new bleachers last year. I was tired of listening to complaints about splinters in the ass. You tired?"

"No. No," Charlie says, as awed by KC's small empire as a kid entering the Magic Kingdom the first time.

They drive for what seems miles in a still rural area. Charlie doesn't need to be told the destination.

"Why are we going there?" Charlie asks, slightly unnerved.

"I live there, Charlie. Darrell left me everything. I tore down the house and built a new one."

But it's not the surprisingly tasteful large mock Tudor built on the footprint of Darrell Torok's home KC's eager for Charlie to see. He seems almost giddily excited as he leads Charlie behind the still-standing ancient barn, cautioning him to watch his step.

"Labs. I breed them as a hobby," KC says proudly as he opens the kennel gate. "I love them all like they're my own kids. It breaks my heart when I have to sell them."

The protective mother, alert in her sleep, opens her eyes and bares her teeth, a warning to anything that might threaten her whelps. KC softly calls her name, Lacey, and she lays her head on her paws, comforted by his soothing voice. She doesn't stir when he gently picks up one of her pups.

"Charlie, meet Charlie. Here, hold him."

The anxious puppy squirms in Charlie's hands.

"I name one male in every litter Charlie," KC says. "I wanted you to meet this little guy before you leave. Hey. It's getting late," he says, suddenly seeming embarrassed by what he must assume Charlie thinks is a sentimental, mawkish gesture. "I've got an early meeting tomorrow morning, and I want to stop at the nursing home before I go."

Charlie believes his disappointment at not being invited into the house isn't obvious, but KC is intuitive.

"The place is a wreck. The cleaning lady comes tomorrow," KC says as he climbs behind the wheel of the truck.

Charlie is sinking into a tar pit of remorse, feeling crushed by the weight of lost opportunities. His mother's dead. His father's lost and alone. Troy is leaving and Charlie will be forty come fall and new companions will be harder and harder to come by. And now this strange encounter with the boy he once thought he loved. No, this boy he *had* loved. The first, and sometimes he thinks only, boy he ever loved. All of this longing and regret, it has a name. Homesickness. Not for a place. Certainly not for Albany. But for a time in his life that has slipped through his fingers. He's young. Forty isn't old. There's a long future ahead, but he also feels the heavy presence of the past he's left behind.

"Don't worry about your dad, Charlie," KC says. "I'll keep an eye on him. I can stop by every few days. Take him to dinner. He still like baseball? I'll find something he can do for my Legion team."

"I appreciate the gesture, but you don't need to do anything for him, for me. You don't owe me anything."

KC clears his throat and keeps his eyes focused on the road ahead.

"You saved my life, Charlie. I owe you everything,"

Charlie's speechless, wondering, not for the first time, if KC is a bit touched, not right in the head.

"You remember when we were hauling furniture, the first time I asked you to stay overnight? I was afraid to be alone. I kept a loaded shotgun under my bed all summer. But every time I picked it up, I thought about seeing you again and I would put it away," he says, his voice as matter-of-fact as if he were reading from a transcript.

He parks the truck on the street in front of Charlie's father's house and Charlie lingers a moment before walking away. He doesn't want their parting to be awkward, but he can't unscramble his thoughts to find the right words to say good-bye.

"I'm not a Christian anymore, if you want to know. I don't think I ever was. But the Freemans were good to me, treated me like a son, and it made them happy to think I believed," KC finally says, breaking the silence. "Catch you later, Charlie," he says, smiling. "Albany's just a two-and-a-half-hour drive from the city. You want to have dinner again when you come back? Call me sometime."

Charlie stands in the lot watching the taillights fade in the night. Has it really been more than twenty years since the Mighty KC, the teenage idol, seemingly perfect, had made a scrawny, awkward adolescent feel special by taking an interest in him? He remembers the words his mother once said to him when he was in the depths of despair.

If it's meant to happen, it's going to happen.

Maybe he should wait a day or two before making the call. Charlie doesn't want to seem desperate. Or lonely. Or both. *Kevin, Kevin, Kevin, Kevin.* He says it aloud, repeating it as a mantra. Soon enough it will start to come naturally and the name KC will belong to another life, another time. KC answers on the first ring, as if he'd been expecting the call.

"Hey, Kevin. I don't think I should leave the old man alone this weekend. I'll take him to a ball game. I gotta admit, though. I never really learned to like baseball. You up for it?"

S. Gagliano & Son has been a barber shop fixture in South Philly for decades. Frankie and Michael Gagliano's Italian immigrant father—Luigi to his customers, Papa to his sons—presides over the store, enlisting his children as soon as they're big enough to wield a broom. On their mother's deathbed, eight-year-old Frankie swears that he and his little brother will always take care of each other, a vow he endeavors to keep through their father's violent outbursts and the string of wives who try to take their mother's place.

After their father's death, Frankie takes over the shop, transforming it to fit in with the gentrifying neighborhood. Michael becomes a successful prosecutor with a rising political career, still close to his big brother despite the differences between them. Then comes an unthinkable, impulsive act that will force Michael to choose between risking his comfortable life and keeping a sacred oath— made before he knew how powerful a promise can be.

The Boys from Eighth and Carpenter is a stunning evocation of working-class Italian-American life— a story of brotherhood, loyalty, and the contradictory, unpredictable nature of family love.

Please turn the page for an exciting sneak peek of Tom Mendicino's newest novel, *The Boys from Eighth and Carpenter* now available wherever print and e-books are sold!

For my sister, Pamela, who did everything I couldn't.

There were two brothers called Both and
Either; perceiving Either was a good,
understanding, busy fellow, and Both a silly fellow
good for little, King Philip said,

"Either is both, and Both is neither."

—Sayings of Kings and Commanders, attributed
to Plutarch

. . . and remember, a boy who won't be good
might just as well be made of wood.

—The Blue Fairy

PROLOGUE

giuramento di sangue

April 14, 2008

*Promise me you'll always take care of each other.
Frankie, you make sure you tell your brother I
asked you both to do that when he's old enough
to understand.*

Frankie (morning through the late afternoon)

He's going to the Hair Show just as he'd planned. Frankie
Gagliano, proprietor of Gagliano Cuts and Color, Family
Owned Since 1928, always goes to the Hair Show. People
would notice his absence. But now that he's sitting in the
parking lot, he's wavering, questioning the wisdom of his
decision and lacking the stamina to engage in the usual banter about how quickly time seems to fly and that it's hard to
believe it's been a year since the last Hair Show. And, of
course, he no sooner picks up his badge when he finds himself face-to-face with Beppe Lopato, his nemesis back at
South Philadelphia Beauty Academy, who's wearing a pair
of snug, crotch-grabbing jeans and looking like he subsists
on steroids and nutritional supplements. Beppe strikes a
pose, giving Frankie a dramatic once-over. Frankie feels the
perspiration dripping from his armpits, fearing guilt is written
all over his face. Even a Neanderthal like Beppe Lopato can
see it.

"I hope the other guy looks worse."

The swelling has subsided and the bruises are fading,
more yellow than purple and green. The cut on Frankie's lip

hasn't completely healed. He'd considered covering the damage with make-up, a little foundation, something subtle of course. But in the end he decided to show himself to the world and resort to the tale of an errant taxi running a red light if anyone asked.

"It's very butch. I like it!"

Frankie doubts his sincerity. Beppe, one of those unfortunate Sicilians who resembles the Missing Link in a Time-Life series on the History of Man, has always been envious of Frankie's blue eyes and fine features. He'd mocked Frankie in beauty school, calling him Fabian after the baby-faced erstwhile teen idol from South Philadelphia.

"Are you doing Paul Mitchell? I'm headed over to the booth. Walk with me, Frankie, and let's catch up," he says, obviously curious about who's been using Frankie as a punching bag.

An internationally renowned expert on color application is lecturing in ten minutes and Beppe wants to get a good seat. Frankie begs off, saying he's signed up for the extensions demonstration at the Matrix exhibit. They part ways, air-kissing, swearing to have lunch or cocktails soon, a promise made and broken every year. Frankie wanders from booth to booth over two acres of concrete floor, from Healing Haircare to Naturceuticals to Satin Smooth Full Body Waxing. His mind is distracted. Nothing registers. He needs to sit for a few minutes, and the *Be a Color Artist, Not a Color Chartist* presentation is as good a place as any.

It's still 1983 here at the Valley Forge Convention Center Hair Show and Michael Jackson has never gone out of fashion. Over the years, Frankie's seen thousands of stylists choreograph their presentations to "Beat It" and "Rock with You." The kid on stage is shimmying and shaking to "Wanna Be Startin' Somethin'," brandishing a pair of shears and a can of hairspray like he's headed for a high noon showdown. The boy wasn't even born when *Thriller* topped the charts and wouldn't recognize the King of Pop in a picture taken when he still had his own nose. It's exhausting watching him multitask up there, demonstrating a revolutionary new color system while auditioning for *Dancing with the Stars*. Frankie's seen enough and trudges back onto the exhibit floor.

He's restless, living on caffeine. He's barely slept since he flushed the Ambien down the toilet, a terrible mistake. Those pills were his opportunity to take the easy way out. It was a rash decision he deeply regrets, leaving him to choose one of the more grisly, and likely more painful, alternatives, any of which is still less terrifying than the possibility of being confined behind bars for the rest of his life, spending the next two or three decades as a caged animal.

An army of bitter and burnt-out old stylists flocks to him, sensing fresh prey. They harangue him with brochures and order forms and discount coupons for the products they're hawking. He'd had the good sense to hide the color-coded ID badge identifying him as a PROPRIETOR in his pocket, but they're still circling him like vultures descending on fresh carrion, their instincts sensing he's a salon owner with a shop to stock and inventory to replenish.

"Francis Rocco Gagliano. You get more gorgeous every year. And that black eye is *sooo* sexy!"

He's staring into a blank slate of chemically-induced preternatural youthfulness. He loves her cut though, a no-nonsense *Klute*-era Jane Fonda shag that looks shockingly hip and contemporary.

"It's me, Estelle Prince!"

"Oh my God. What's the matter with me?" he apologizes, though she's been remodeled beyond recognition. "You look incredible."

She assumes he means it as a compliment. Parts of her face, the moving ones, seem to be made of putty. She seems perpetually startled, a talking wax doll who's been zapped by a stun gun. She babbles on, much ado about nothing, and he shakes his head in agreement though his mind is elsewhere and he doesn't hear a word she says. He knows now it was a mistake coming here. They'll all agree in hindsight he was acting strange at the Hair Show. Most people will say they didn't know he had it in him. A few will claim the news came as no surprise. *He wouldn't look me in the eye now that I think about it. It's a damn shame, but what can you expect if you get mixed up with those kinds of people?* But he foolishly agrees to join Estelle for a glass of wine after the *Beyond Basic Foiling* presentation. They embrace, promising to meet in forty-five minutes. He waits until she disappears into the crowd and turns towards the exit, attempting a quick getaway, and nearly collides with the young woman who steps in front of him, blocking his way.

"You cannot say no. I'm going to make you an offer you can't refuse."

She's the very model of scientific efficiency, dressed in a crisp, white lab coat, cradling a clipboard in the crook of her elbow. She's wearing *I-mean-business* eyeglasses, the tortoise frames suggesting the serious dignity of a wise owl; her hair is pulled back in a ponytail with a few tendrils liberated to flatter the strong cheekbones of her lovely face.

"You get a fifty dollar honorarium and a sample selection of our top-of-the-line hair products. And you'll leave the show today a new man with a brand new look. Satisfaction guaranteed."

He's about to politely decline her generous offer when she introduces him to the stylist, licensed as both a barber *and* a cosmetologist, an expert, she assures him, in both professions. Vince is his name and his Clubman Classic aftershave, crisp, antiseptic, is vintage 1967, the year Frankie's Papa put his seven-year-old son to work sweeping clippings from the barbershop floor and emptying ashtrays heaped with smoldering cigarette butts. His younger brother Michael had resented being conscripted into Papa's labor force as soon as he was tall enough to push a broom, but Frankie never minded. He would linger in the shop after his chores were done, too young yet to understand why he was drawn to the longshoremen and refinery workers who sat flipping through ancient issues of *Sports Illustrated* and *Car and Driver*, crossing and uncrossing their legs with casual grace as they waited their turn in the barber chair. Their loud, deep voices would rumble through the shop as they argued about sports and politics. They called him Little Pitcher, a reminder that certain language wasn't meant to be overheard by Big Ears, and teased him about his long eyelashes and wavy blonde hair, saying it was a shame Frankie hadn't been born a girl, all those good looks going to waste on a boy. Forty years later, he's still aroused by the memory of their unfiltered Pall Malls, the Chock Full o'Nuts on their breath, and the Brylcreem they used to landscape their hair.

"You game, my friend?" Vince asks. "Feeling brave today?"

He's neither short nor tall, broad through the shoulders and barrel-chested. He's thick around the waist, not quite pot-bellied, certainly not sloppy but carrying a few extra pounds; his loose Hawaiian shirt, a relatively sedate design of bright green palm leafs on a navy background, is a generous fit. His forearms are sturdy, built for heavier labor than barbering, and dusted with a fine spray of sun-bleached hair. The visible tattoos are Navy port-of-call vintage, clearly not the handiwork of a punk rock skin art boutique. He's wearing Levi 505s, full cut, and Sketchers, probably with inserts for extra support. He's a man who's clearly comfortable in his own skin. His blunt, still handsome face is branded with a raised flaming red scar from his right ear lobe to the corner of his mouth, a warning he's a man with a past: mysterious, dark, dangerous, the survivor of a bar fight or a prison term in the Big House or a tour of duty in the first Gulf War.

For all his foreboding appearance, Vince is a friendly enough guy, approachable. He tells Frankie he has fifteen years' experience cutting hair and owns a small shop in Johnstown, Pennsylvania, where he makes a good living doing volume in ten dollar haircuts. He recently moved in with a "special lady" he met in his motorcycle club and he's paying to put her through beauty school. He suggests a much shorter cut for Frankie, to give him a more masculine look. He'll try a fade on his neck and up the sides, something that won't need any upkeep or grooming. He'd like to bring a little color back, nothing terribly dramatic. He suggests they try a Number Two solution for a natural looking blend.

"Get ready to rock and roll!" Vince says as he leads Frankie to the chair.

His gruff but soothing voice preaches the gospel of men's styling as a life raft in tough economic times to a rapt audience gathered for the demonstration on his willing guinea pig. *Do the math: more potential bookings per week, none longer than twenty minutes and most of them in and out in ten, more visits per year, every two weeks for most men, none less frequent than monthly. Pay close attention now,* he cautions, demonstrating the most effective way to use a number one guard on his clippers while eulogizing the dying art of scissors-over-comb. He promises his skeptical audience the product he's about to demonstrate will break the final barrier of a guy's reluctance to color his hair. *It's a simple shampoo, leave it in five minutes, a quick wash and they're out the door. The construction workers or long-distance haulers who come into my shop wouldn't be caught dead under the dryer.*

Frankie surrenders to the strong hands massaging his scalp. Vince lowers the chair to rinse his hair with warm water and briskly dries it with a barber towel.

"So there you have it. A fresh new look in nineteen minutes."

The audience approves of the results, nodding and throwing a thumb's up.

"So whaddaya think?" Vince asks, spinning the styling chair so Frankie can face himself in the mirror.

He's showing more skin than he expected, especially in

the close-cropped area above his ears. He likes the cut; it's a clean look, almost military. And the color is soft and natural, even to his critical professional eye.

"Happy?" Vince asks.

"Very."

"Thank you, brother. Don't forget to pick up your free sample bag," he says as he shakes his hand and quickly dismisses him, turning to introduce himself to his next challenge, a faux-skateboarder/ bike messenger with spiky extensions who's about to be transformed into G.I. Joe. Frankie tosses the bag into the nearest trashcan as he walks to the exit. What difference does it make if his earthly remains look ten, maybe fifteen, years younger than his forty-eight years? No one's ever going to see them. It's not as if he's going to leave a pretty corpse suitable for display in an open casket.

There are ways to do it that would be less traumatic for his brother Michael than needing to identify whatever gruesome pieces are left on the railroad tracks. An overdose would have been calm and peaceful, but his internist won't refill the Ambien and the Ativan. She suspects he's abusing since she called in a month's worth just last week. Swallowing a bottle of an over-the-counter drug wouldn't be lethal and he could end up in the ED having his stomach pumped. He doesn't own a gun and his hands would shake too badly to attempt slitting his wrists. Drowning would be painless but those few moments before he lost consciousness would feel like an eternity, enough time to regret what he's powerless to reverse as his lungs filled with water. Same problem with jumping off a building: He doesn't want his life passing before his eyes as he falls twenty stories. He'd considered hanging himself until he realized he would strangle to death, gasping for breath, if the rope didn't break his neck.

He's considered all the alternatives and the swiftest, most efficient way to do this is to step into the path of an approaching train. He'll leave the car in the wasteland of cargo terminals and storage units surrounding the airport and walk to the railroad tracks with his iPod set at maximum volume, Stevie's magical voice singing "Rhiannon" and "Gold Dust Woman" the last sounds he wants to hear as he leaves this earth. In a few hours he'll know whether there's a heaven waiting to welcome him or a hell to which he'll be condemned for taking his own life or if it's all just a black nothing. He's collected all of the official documents Michael will need to put his affairs in order – his will, the deed to the building, the insurance policies, the numbers of his various bank accounts. They'll find his wallet with all his I.D. on the driver's seat of the abandoned car. This morning he locked the doors of the home he's lived in his entire life for the very last time. He didn't leave a note. His reason will be obvious. Not immediately, but soon enough.

"Frankie! Frankie! Did you forget our date?"

Estelle Prince, laden with shopping bags full of brochures and samples, is chasing him, teetering on her skyscraper stiletto heels.

"Should we take one car or two?" she wheezes.

It's likely the most exercise she's had in years and it's left her short of breath. Thankfully, she doesn't object when he suggests they drive separately. He considers losing her in traffic, but fortifying his resolve with a liberal dosage of alcohol isn't a bad idea. Estelle insists the local outpost of a national chain of 'authentic Italian bistros' has a decent wine list. A lone salesman is nursing a bottle of beer at the bar and two well-heeled blue-haired old ladies are lingering in their booth. The hostess seats the latest arrivals, offering menus which Estelle refuses, saying they're just having a drink.

"We have a nice selection of wines by the glass," the young lady offers.

"We need more than a glass. You don't have anywhere you have to be, do you Frankie? Let's share a bottle."

Red or white? Something fruity or a vintage that's clean

and crisp? Frankie shrugs and says he'll be happy with whatever Estelle chooses.

"Chardonnay," she predictably instructs the server. "The one from the Central Coast. Not one of those ridiculously expensive bottles from Sonoma."

"Bring us the Cakebread Cellars. My treat, Estelle."

His last glass of wine should be a good one.

Estelle's not about to argue with his generosity. Frankie waves away the cork and tells the server to pour. He's sure it's fine.

"What are we celebrating?" Estelle asks, proposing a toast.

"Nothing. Nothing at all."

"We have to celebrate something! Let's toast your new look then. Oh sweetie, the color takes ten years off your age. I hope you're ready for all the young men who are going to be running after you!"

She's far too self-absorbed to question Frankie's insistence on quickly changing the topic to her favorite subject—herself. All he's called upon to do is occasionally nod his head in agreement to encourage her to keep the one-sided conversation going. He settles back and lets his mind wander, allowing her to vent about her philandering soon-to-be-ex-husband and the crushing legal fees she's paying her attorneys to punish him in the divorce settlement.

"We'll have another bottle," he tells the server as she approaches the table.

"Are you planning to get me drunk so you can take advantage of me?" Estelle teases.

He laughs mirthlessly and swallows a mouthful of wine. When the time comes to settle the bill, he'll be as ready as he's ever going to be. He wishes he could remember the name of the song and the singer who sang it, but all he can recall is the line about finding courage in the bottle. Estelle says she's getting light-headed and places her hand over her glass when he offers a refill. *More for me,* he thinks. The alcohol doesn't exactly transform fear into courage like the song promised, but it's loosening his grip on any remaining doubts about stepping onto the railroad tracks. He needs to finish the job before the effects of the wine wear off and cowardice and misgivings weaken his resolve.

"Are you sure you're okay to drive?" Estelle asks as they walk to their cars.

He brushes off her concerns. He's not stumbling or slurring his words, but he's clearly under the influence, which, of course, is exactly where he needs to be.

"Don't worry. I'll stop for a coffee at the Wawa before I get on the expressway. I promise."

It's a few minutes past five according to the digital clock on his dashboard. The evening rush hour is building to full force and traffic is at a near standstill. At least he doesn't have to worry about drifting between lanes at sixty-five miles an hour. He squints and peers over the steering wheel, not trusting his ability to accurately gauge the distance between his front bumper and the brake lights of the car ahead. He's confused by the jumble of directional signs overhead. South to West Chester. The Pennsylvania Turnpike to Harrisburg and points west. East to Center City Philadelphia and the Philadelphia International Airport. That's the direction he needs to travel. Distracted and anxious, he nearly misses the access road to the interstate and makes a sharp right. In his confusion, he's misread the road signs and doesn't realize he's trying to enter the expressway on the one-way exit ramp until he hears the siren and sees the flashing blue dome light in his rearview mirror.

Michael (evening and into the night)

"You know, I could just put you out in Norristown and let them press charges if that's what you want."

News travels fast and bad news flies at the speed of sound. The Upper Merion township police contacted the young on-call prosecutor of the Office of the District Attorney for Montgomery County who then called her supervisor for guidance after Frankie disclosed his brother Michael was Chief Deputy District Attorney in the neighboring county. After a brief phone conversation between Michael and his peer, the officer in charge told his partner to tear up the report he'd begun to write and released Frankie from custody. Michael made arrangements to pick up Frankie's car in the morning. He assumed Frankie was too embarrassed to face his sister-in-law and nephew Danny (a nine-year-old asks a *lot* of questions) when he refused the offer to spend the night in their guest room in Wayne. He'd pleaded with Michael to drop him at the nearest station so he could take a train back to the city. He'd only agreed under protest to allow Michael to drive him home and has been sullen and hostile the entire ride.

"So I take it you're not talking to me. Fine. I won't ask again what happened to your face. I like your haircut. But the color. It looks good, but I never thought you were the type," Michael comments as they sit in stalled traffic on the expressway.

He reaches for the radio and slaps his brother's hand when Frankie tries to stop him.

"I just wanna hear the traffic report. Then I'll turn it off. I promise."

He sits behind the wheel of the car, staring at a seemingly endless ribbon of red taillights. The headlines of the day are the same as yesterday and the day before that. Natural disasters. Military skirmishes in distant lands with unpronounceable names. Domestic tragedies. Children killed in crossfire between street gangs. Hillary. Obama. The Dow Jones. The five-day weather forecast for the Delaware Valley and, finally, the traffic report.

Somewhere in that mash-up of the important and the inconsequential, all stories read in a comforting monotone, he's startled to hear a sound bite of his own voice. Was it only this morning he'd spoken to the press on behalf of the District Attorney, announcing the decision ". . . . *not to seek a retrial of the first degree murder charge of Tommy Corcoran whose capital conviction on that count was recently overturned by a federal court. Corcoran continues to serve a life sentence without parole on the remaining charges. Now on to traffic and transit. Eastbound traffic is experiencing forty to fifty minute delays from 202 to the Vine Street underpass due to an overturned tractor trailer."*

What began as a trying day is ending on a bad note. Michael's unhappy about being forced to suffer this endurance test on the expressway. It would have been perfectly reasonable, not to mention convenient, for Frankie to spend the night with his brother's family. And it's out of character for him to disappoint his nephew and godson. Danny's been begging for a new pair of Puma sneakers and Michael had proposed the three of them drive out to Foot Locker after dinner. There's only one explanation for Frankie's anxiety about rushing back to the city. He's worried that goddamn little Mexican illegal is pouting in front of the television, feeling neglected and abandoned. It astounds Michael that his brother trusts the kid with the key to his house and thinks nothing about leaving him there alone.

"We could sit here for hours," Michael grouses. "Call him and tell him you'll be back as soon as you can."

"He isn't there."

"Where is he?"

"He's gone."

"I hope you told him not to come back. That little shit. I knew this was going to happen. How long did he smack you around before you gave him what he wanted? How much money did he squeeze out of you before saying *adios?*"

He immediately regrets his angry, aggressive tone. He'd intended to give Frankie time to recover from the shock of being arrested before interrogating him about this fresh set of bruises and split lip. He feels as if he's kicking a wounded puppy.

"It doesn't matter. He's gone. He's gone and he won't be coming back," Frankie says wearily.

"You're an easy mark, Frankie. He'll be back when he needs a quick cash infusion or a roof over his head. And if he shows up again, I'll call the authorities myself. I mean it, Frankie," Michael swears as traffic begins to move, a crawl to be sure for the next mile or two, then slowly gathering steam as they pass the accident site.

Michael and his wife need to start throwing age-appropriate gentlemen with steady incomes at Frankie until one finally sticks. Looking back, he should have appreciated the ten years of relative peace and quiet when Frankie was involved with that pompous alcoholic high school teacher. He should have been less critical, more welcoming of the harmless old fool. Sometimes he thinks Frankie believes he's never really accepted his lifestyle. But Michael stopped resenting his brother's sexuality years ago, though he still isn't going to be marching in any parades to celebrate it. It's Frankie's poor choices and naïveté that make Michael uncomfortable. He wouldn't take the odds against Frankie running into his own Tommy Corcoran some day and ending up like the ill-fated Carmine Torino. His worst fear is that this Mariano is just a test drive for a more lethal liaison yet to come.

"I don't know how you do this every day," he complains, growing more frustrated by the minute.

He's circling his brother's neighborhood, searching for that elusive place to park within walking distance of Eighth and Carpenter and the house where they grew up. Years of suburban living have dulled his parallel parking skills, but he manages to squeeze the car into a tight space, much to the horn-blaring frustration of the driver trying to pass him on the narrow street. He hasn't eaten yet, having gotten the call

THE BOYS FROM EIGHTH AND CARPENTER 309

from his colleague in the Montgomery County office before dinner, and insists they stop for a slice. Standing at the register, he hears his stomach rumble and he orders an entire pie, large, half sausage for him, half mushroom for his brother. "What are you doing?" Frankie frets as the girl at the cash register counts out Michael's change. "I thought we'd go back to the house and share it. Do you have any cold beer? I'd settle for a Bud Lite. For me. You've had enough booze for one day." "You don't need to come back with me. I just want to go to bed," Frankie insists. He seems a bit too despondent to Michael for the circumstances. Things are looking up now that the fucking little Mexican has jumped ship. Frankie should be jumping for joy to be rid of him. And Michael's assured him no D.U.I. charges will be filed. No report will be made. The arrest never happened. There won't be any points on his license or need to attend a mandatory alcohol counseling class. No one will ever mention it again. He wonders if Frankie's on some medication that's causing him to act strange. He realizes he has to piss too badly to wait until they're back at his brother's house. Frankie's gone when he emerges from the men's room. Something feels out of kilter, ominous even, and he wonders if it's safe for Frankie to be alone. He grows antsy during the interminable wait before the counter girl announces his order is ready. He opens the box and practically swallows two slices whole as he walks back to the house. He tries slipping his key into the locked door of the private entrance in the alley on Carpenter Street, but the blade resists sliding into the keyway. The shop key doesn't open the Eighth Street entrance either. Frankie must have changed the locks after the kid took off and forgotten he hasn't given Michael the new keys. He sets the pizza box on the sidewalk and dials his brother's number on his cell, but Frankie doesn't answer. So he stands in the middle of Eighth Street and shouts his name. The lights are burning on the upper floors so he knows Frankie's in there.

He's surprised some neighbor trying to sleep isn't shouting profanities through a bedroom window. A strange, cold fist grips his heart. He tries calling Frankie's cell one last time, then calmly, purposefully, walks around the side of the building and kicks in the back door. He runs up the stairs, taking two and three steps at time, until he reaches the master bedroom suite on the highest floor where he finds his brother slumped on the toilet, cradling his head in his hands. The ceramic lid of the toilet bowl is lying on the floor in two pieces. He assumes Frankie must have stumbled and broken it trying to break his fall. He looks so pitiful and helpless sitting there, needing comfort and reassurance and all Michael has offered is an unpleasant harangue and criticism.

Frankie barely resists as Michael walks him to his bed. He doesn't protest when his younger brother unbuttons his shirt, unzips his pants and takes off his shoes. He's lying in bed, his eyes wide open, when Michael turns off the light and urges him to try to sleep. He calls his wife with the good news the parasite is gone. The bad news though is Frankie's acting odd and Michael doesn't want to leave him alone overnight. *I love you too. Talk to you in the morning.* He hopes there's beer in the fridge and he'll finish off that pizza if some street dog hasn't run of with it. But first he needs to secure the back door. The tools and nails are in the basement, likely untouched since the last time he did a minor repair.

Everything down here is just as he remembers. The damp moisture of the earthen floor. The metal storage shelves, odd pieces of furniture and broken lamps, the wide, deep freezer chest, an ancient Frigidaire model, antediluvian, but still serviceable. His eyes are slow to adjust to the harsh light of the bare ceiling bulb and he slips in a puddle underfoot, noticing an odd smell, fetid but not overpowering, the distinct scent of meat beginning to rot. There are two trash bags on the floor, not full but securely tied. He opens one and finds chicken breasts and cuts of beef soaking in water and blood. The freezer must be broken, despite its gently purring motor.

"What the fuck are you doing down there, Mikey?" Frankie shouts from the top of the stairs, his voice shrill and twisted in his throat as he races down the steps, sweating and gasping for breath.

"You need to replace this goddamn freezer."

"There's nothing wrong with the freezer," Frankie insists, grabbing the trash bag from his brother's hand. "Go upstairs and I'll clean up this mess."

"Let's put this shit back before it stinks up the entire fucking house," Michael says, opening the lid before Frankie can stop him. A blast of artic air slaps his face and he blinks and jumps back, confused, staring at Frankie in disbelief, not trusting his eyes, needing a moment to gather his wits before confirming that, yes, Frankie's little Mexican is lying in the freezer, shrouded in frost, his twisted and contorted remains a snug and cozy fit.

BOOK ONE

parenti serpenti

1920-2007

Papa and his wives 1920-2001

"Please, Boo. Please!"

"Tonight. Just for one night. You're getting too old for this," Frankie said, finally relenting and lifting the covers so Michael could slip into his bed. Michael's thoughts were racing too quickly for his older brother to keep pace. He'd been spinning in circles since the service and funeral lunch for the stepmother he'd become deeply attached to. He should have been exhausted, but he was too agitated for sleep and began peppering Frankie with questions.

"How come Papa talks funny?"

He was never Dad, certainly not Daddy. A father who allowed his brats to call him Pa or Pop wasn't worthy of his children's respect. He was Papa, as the man who had sired him had been. His children's few words of Italian were awkward, barely recognizable to a man who had never heard, let alone spoken, English until he was nearly nine years old. His boys understood enough of the dialect of Calabria to get the gist of his outbursts whenever he relapsed into the language of his childhood, but always responded in their own native tongue. Michael, always the more willful and bolder of his two sons, would grow up to be a resentful teenager who referred to his father in the hated American vernacular as his *old man,* drawing empty threats of banishment with no possibility of ever returning. Michael was defiant, unbowed. He complained that none of his friends had to live in a dark apartment above a barbershop, with holy pictures on the walls and plaster saints on every table. Michael would live with Sal Pinto if Papa didn't want him around. And once he was gone he would never come back.

Michael's grandfather would have thrown Papa into the streets if he'd ever dared to challenge his unquestioned authority. This country had made his son weak, a man who allowed his children to run wild and treat him with contempt. His naturalization papers, granted after his service in the war, had made him a citizen, but Luigi Rocco Gagliano only finally, truly, became an American the day Michael turned his back on him and walked away, suffering no consequences for calling his father an embarrassment, a stupid old wop who should go back to Italy if he hated the *medigan'* so much.

"Why is Papa so mean?"

"You're a lucky boy Luigi. You're going to live in America."

Even at the age of eight, he knew his mother was frightened and wary of leaving the only home they'd ever known. She'd been a white widow for so many years she'd began to think of herself as a maiden. She was only a girl when she married her husband, a man who'd come back to Calabria to take a bride after emigrating at seventeen. He'd returned to his life in America less than a month after the birth of his son. His letters were short, to the point, hardly filled with the romantic declarations a young girl yearned to read. But the money he earned put meat on the table and paid to repair the roof when the rain leaked through the seams. She received frequent gifts of bolts of expensive cloth and small luxury items like lavender sachets and combs and hair clips made of ivory and tortoiseshell. Luigi was likely the first boy in Italy, certainly Calabria, to own a bright red Liberty Coaster wagon, elevating his status among his cousins who vied for the privilege of pulling him through the streets of the town.

Then, finally, instructions arrived with the name and address of a man who had booked their passage on the Konig Albert departing from Naples. She tried consoling her son who cried bitter tears as they sat in the cavernous terminal waiting to board the ship.

"We'll come back soon to see Nonno and Nonna," she promised, assuming the separation from his doting grandparents was the cause of his despair.

A man wearing a uniform and a whistle around his neck was calling names from the front of the room.

". . . . . Gagliano, Santamaria; Gagliano, Luigi Rocco . . . . ."

He pulled away when his mother tried to take his hand. He wasn't a baby. He could walk by himself. He knew she needed the reassurance of his touch and wanted to punish her, refusing to forgive her for promising the wagon to his cousin Aldo when they left for America.

Nonno had tried to console him, promising him that, in America, he would have two or three wagons and live in a palace like the Savoy kings. His father was a rich man now, a person of stature and influence, a citizen of the United States with money to grease the palms of the right people in America and Italy to spare his son from a life under the boot heel of *Il Diavolo*, Nonno's name for the godless *Il Duce*. But the old man's words failed to comfort and, late in the evening of his last night in the village, Luigi climbed a steep hill, dragging the wagon behind him. He'd stood at the edge of the cliff, tears running down his cheeks as he threw his beloved

Liberty Coaster from the rocky precipice and watched it disappear into the leafy ceiling of the trees far below.

"Why does Papa hit you?"

The stranger who met Luigi and his mother at the port when they arrived in America was a terrible disappointment to a boy expecting to be greeted by a hero. Salvatore Rocco Gagliano was barely taller than his wife and looked much older than the man in the wedding photo his mother kept on a table beside her bed. The first meeting was awkward, formal, without kisses or an embrace. They boarded a train in a town called Newark and travelled to a city named Philadelphia, arriving after midnight at an enormous building with a barbershop at the street level. S. Gagliano, Barber, Est. 1928, was painted on the window glass. Luigi awoke early his first morning in America, eager to claim the Liberty Coaster wagons his nonno had promised awaited him. His mother fed him a simple breakfast of bread and cheese, telling him to eat quickly as he was needed downstairs.

"Do as he says Luigi. He's your father."

The barber had decided his son was old enough to be put to work and ordered him to wash the shop windows with water and vinegar. Perfection was expected. Being an eight-year-old boy was no excuse for streaks on the plate glass. His efforts were rewarded with a blow that knocked him to the sidewalk. He knew his life had changed, his position in the world diminished, when his mother rebuffed his tearful attempts to seek consolation and sympathy, deferring to her husband in the discipline of his son.

"Are all of Papa's wives in heaven? Does Polly's mother know who we are? What are we supposed to call her when we die and go to heaven too?"

*   *   *

Luigi returned to Italy to take up arms against his own blood, fighting in the Battle of Anzio. He returned with an honorable discharge and enrolled in barber school. He assumed his place beside his father in the shop, renamed S. Gagliano & Son, Since 1928, their chairs only a few feet apart. Ten hours a day, six days a week, he suffered endless criticism about squandering his money and his time drinking alcohol with his worthless friend Sal Pinto. What had his father done to be cursed with a *minchione* who chose to keep company with *donnaccias*, unsuitable to be a wife and mother?

The deal was brokered before Luigi met the woman who would become his first wife. The Gaglianos had known the Avilla family for generations. Pasquale Avilla's two daughters, the loveliest girls in the neighborhood, fair-haired and blue-eyed, had survived near fatal infections of streptococcus, developing rheumatic fevers that had kept Teresa, the oldest, bedridden for seven months, and her sister Sofia, ten years younger, for nearly a year. Doctor and hospital bills had left the family deeply in debt, making the offer of money for the hand of Avilla's eldest daughter impossible to reject.

"She is a very pious girl," Luigi's father advised him on his wedding day in 1949. "Don't tear her apart the first night with that big, fat cock you're so proud of."

She'd bled for two days after their wedding night. But she seemed to take to the act quickly, even enthusiastically, until he struck her, calling her a *puttana,* when she made the mistake of touching his prick. Their first child was born within a year, a girl named Paulina Rosa, as useless to Luigi as her mother would become after two miscarriages and years of marriage without giving him a son.

Desperate, she risked damnation of her immortal soul by consulting the local shaman, seeking talismans to protect her from the evil eye that had cursed her womb. The baby was a boy, carried to term, perfectly formed, eight-and-half pounds.

He was delivered stillborn, never drawing a single breath. Luigi would have dragged his wife from her bed and beaten her if the priest and Sal Pinto hadn't been there to restrain him. He accused her of being a witch and a whore. God had taken his son to punish him for marrying a woman who practiced the black art of forbidden sorcery. He said she was cursed for bargaining with the devil. He refused to sleep in her bed again, barely exchanging words with her until she died, literally from a broken heart, its valves corrupted by childhood disease.

"Do all of Papa's wives live in the same house in heaven?"

Luigi waited the obligatory year of mourning, then, in 1959, married Sofia, as lovely as her sister and with the same quiet, resigned disposition. Eleven months later, she delivered the long-awaited heir and, after five years, provided Luigi with another son. The second pregnancy had been difficult to achieve and the delivery of a ten-pound baby was fraught with risks. She never fully recovered from the Caesarian and congestive heart failure made Luigi a widower a second time when his youngest son was three years old.

"Who will be my mother when I die and go to heaven?"

Sal Pinto's wife had a friend named Eileen Costello who had been on the New York stage; her husband had died leaving her with no money. Dire circumstances had forced her to take a job giving dancing lessons at Palumbo's. No one could conceive of Luigi choosing a *medigan'*, Irish no less, a woman unafraid to speak her mind, to be his wife and mother to his boys. She'd had a mysterious past, actresses being women of questionable reputation, and had already put one husband into the ground. The women of the neighborhood, loyal to the memories of the sainted Avilla sisters, gossiped that she'd put a spell on Luigi, blinding him to the plain and unremarkable face she painted with makeup. Their envious husbands, though, lusted after Luigi's *figa* and the carnal pleasures to be had between her long legs.

Miss Eileen, as Papa insisted his sons call her, restored calm and a sense of order to the house at Eighth and Carpenter. Luigi's new wife had an uncanny gift for calming gathering storms and had mastered the art of gentle, but firm, persuasion, prompting her husband to take pause and reconsider before raising his hand to his children. Still, his older son clearly resented her presence, though he was always polite and respectful. She refused to allow her husband to pressure the boy into accepting her. She lavishly praised his mother's beauty and gentle nature, which she said was obvious even by her pictures, trying, without success, to relieve Frankie's aching heart.

Michael, though, adored her, embracing her from the outset. No other woman had ever gently cleaned and bandaged his frequent cuts and bruises or praised his smallest achievement and fussed and clucked over his appearance. Miss Eileen provided a lap where he could rest his head while they sat on the sofa, laughing at the antics of George and Weezy on *The Jeffersons*. His own mother existed only as an image in the framed photograph beside their bed, a benign specter whose presence hovered over their lives like a guardian angel or Mary, the Blessed Mother. Miss Eileen was flesh-and-blood. She smelled of Estee Lauder Private Collection, Virginia Slims and cinnamon sticky buns. She loved him fiercely, as if he was her own child, and he sought comfort in her arms whenever he was tired or sick.

"Lou, bring the car around," she'd insisted one cold, rainy night. "His fever is a hundred and five."

Michael, always large for his age, was almost too heavy to carry two flights of stairs to the sidewalk where her husband was waiting. She held him in her lap and stroked his head, calming and reassuring him. Her clothes were damp with his sweat when they arrived at the emergency room. The nurse had to pry Michael from her neck to lay him in bed. Frankie and his father could hear his terrified voice behind a pulled curtain, repeating her name, as they sat, banished to a hallway, useless, unneeded, out of the way.

"Mama! Don't go! Mama!"

"I'm here baby," she assured him as she held his hand. "I'm right here. I'm not going anywhere.

"Is Papa allowed to get married again?"

No one expected Luigi to take another wife. Eileen Costello's death seemed to have broken him. His sons would hear him sitting alone in the darkened living room, having one-sided conversations with her about the events of the day. His hair had turned white; his face was gaunt and haunted, his back more stooped. His quick temper returned, unrestrained by any calming influence, and he began swinging his belt again out of anger and frustration at the slightest provocation.

His sons said nothing when he brought a woman home one Sunday evening and announced the banns of marriage would be published in the next week's parish bulletin. Frannie Merlino, recently widowed, was a constant complainer, happy only when Luigi conceded to her demands that he spend money on a Mediterranean color television console and a pale blue Ford Fairlane with the title in her name. Knowing he'd spoiled *that dance hall girl* (an insult she never dared utter in his presence) with annual vacations, she insisted her husband take her on expensive trips; cruises in the Caribbean and a fifth anniversary excursion to Europe. Luigi even agreed to spend one week each July sweltering in a vacation trailer in Virginia left to her by her first husband. She tried to win Michael's affection, but he would never grow attached to another of his father's wives after losing Miss Eileen. She was cold and arrogant towards Frankie, treating him as something vile and disgusting, stalking him like a starving cat, waiting for any opportunity to expose him as a disgusting degenerate who should be cast from their home. She was a patient woman, knowing the day would come when she would hold the evidence in her hand.

Papa was waiting for Frankie as he let himself in the back door. He assumed his father was angry because it was long past midnight. Frankie and his friend Jack Centafore had gone to see Barbra Streisand in *A Star is Born,* both agreeing once wasn't enough, and had stayed to watch it from beginning to end a second time. But when he saw Frannie Merlino standing behind her husband, clutching the torn pages from a magazine in her hand, he knew he was being confronted with something far more serious than breaking his curfew.

"I found this under your mattress," she hissed, gleeful in her triumph. "Do you think we don't know what you're doing with this in your bedroom," she said, tearing a photograph of a bare-chested Robby Benson into shreds as if it were the vilest pornography.

Papa seethed with rage, his face flush with blood. He held his clenched fists at his side, having been warned by the priest of the consequences if he ever left marks on his sons again. Michael, awakened by the shouting, wearing only his underwear, stood on the staircase, ready to attack if his father dared to raise a hand against his brother.

"*Finocchio.* Queer. Thank God your mother is dead or this would kill her."

Frannie Merlino, too self-absorbed to gauge her husband's fleeting moods and shifting loyalties, gloated over her victory, seizing an opportunity to continue the humiliation.

"At least you can be grateful one of your boys is growing up to be a man and not an embarrassing faggot."

Papa's voice was even, but cold and chilling. Frannie Merlino's face blanched at her husband's reproach.

"This is my house. You live under my roof. If you cannot respect my children, pack your suitcase and leave."

As fate would have it, Luigi's most miserable marriage

was the longest, lasting fifteen years until she made him a widower a fourth time. Obsessed with clean teeth and fresh breath, Frannie Merlino Gagliano had been too engrossed in searching her pocketbook for a Chicklet to see the Number 57 bus jump the curb. Neither father nor sons mourned her passing and rarely spoke her name after the day she was buried.

"Do Papa's wives sleep in the same bed in heaven?"

Helen Constanza. Luigi's last wife, was happiest working in the kitchen, standing at the stove from morning until night. She treated his sons with deference, insisting on feeding them whenever they walked through the door, regardless of the hour of the day or night. Michael, then a hard-working assistant prosecutor residing less than a mile away in an apartment he shared with the young nurse he intended to marry, returned infrequently and then only to see his brother, a grown man who, though a successful stylist, still lived under his father's roof. It was the great mystery of the family at Eighth and Carpenter that Michael, who had only occasionally suffered from the barber's temper and moods, despised the man while Frankie, the brother their father had treated so harshly, had remained the loyal son.

Both boys were genuinely fond of Helen Constanza, Frankie in particular. Frankie invited her to nights at the Forrest Theater and dinners with his friends, the ugly priest and the fat school teacher he affectionately referred to as his "husband" except, of course, in the presence of Papa. Luigi began to become confused and forgetful, sometimes referring to his wife as Eileen and insisting she wear the green dress he admired so much. He would scoff, becoming angry when she reminded him that Eileen Costello had passed many years ago and would accuse her of thinking him an idiot. Of course he knew who was dead and who was living flesh and blood. Helen's daughter in California insisted on moving her out west after she suffered a mild stroke, fearing that Papa, then in the obvious early stages of Alzheimer's, was unable to care for her. Luigi refused to consider a request from Helen's children that he agree to an annulment and they remained married until a fatal aneurysm did them part. He'd raged at his son the lawyer, calling him useless, when Michael refused to sue the Constanza family for cremating their mother, whose remains Luigi insisted were his legal property as the widower, and scattering her ashes at a marina in San Diego.

"Is Papa going to be nice to us in heaven?"

All but his most loyal customers gradually began drifting away. Even Sal Pinto feared his shaking hands and dreaded his lapses into irrational rants about the Polish Pope being a plant by the Kremlin. Frankie argued, but finally conceded, when Michael insisted their father surrender his driver's license. But he was adamant he would never condemn him to a nursing facility where Michael argued he could be cared for and protected from himself. Frankie kept him at home as long as he could, up until the day Michael received a phone call from a colleague in the Philly DA's office, saying he was having a hard time persuading an irate family from pursuing a private complaint against their father.

"I know I told you about it," Frankie insisted when his brother confronted him. "You must have forgotten it, Mikey."

"No," Michael assured him. "I'm goddamn certain I would remember hearing my father had been arrested in a school zone, sitting in a parked car with his limp pecker in his hand."

"Not arrested," Frankie corrected him. "He was picked up," meaning he'd been rescued and escorted safely home by the Ottaviano boy on the force, who was kind enough to wrap an Eagles commemorative fleece blanket around his waist to preserve his modesty.

"Paul Ottaviano," Frankie explained. "The one who looked like Elvis. He had an older brother Bobby. Their parents had that luncheonette at 15th and Dickinson. *You're a very lucky man Papa*, I told him. *You'd be sitting in the lock-up if some stranger had picked you up, some Irish cop or a moulinyan.* They would have hauled his flabby, pale ass to the round-house, called him a *vecchio schifoso* and charged him with indecent exposure."

"Did Paul Ottaviano accuse him of that?"

"He just said he found him holding his sausage with his pants and boxers on the passenger seat, neatly folded, and his shoes and socks on the floor. He didn't accuse Papa of anything. He said Papa must be confused. I thanked him and told him how much I appreciated him looking out for the old man. After he left, I asked Papa why he was driving around South Philly bare-assed. He stood there with his big fat shlong resting against his thigh and told me I was crazy. He said I was his curse, a *zia*, and that only an ungrateful *finocchio* would make up such hateful lies about his own father."

Luigi lost his ability to speak even the most basic English after being admitted to a dementia unit. Frankie was secretly relieved to be rid of the responsibility of caring for him, no longer torn between the demands of his father and those of Charlie Haldermann, his school teacher "husband." He dedicated three evenings a week and Sunday afternoons to sitting with Luigi. Michael, at his brother's insistence, came to the nursing home on his father's birthday and Christmas and an occasional weekend when he couldn't bear Frankie's nagging any longer. His sons were puzzled by their father's frequent crying jags. Frankie could make out a few of his words, but they amounted to nonsense, something about a red wagon. Michael shrugged, not terribly interested, and said whatever memories tortured him would forever remain a mystery. Maybe they'd been fooling themselves and Papa had known all along about the secret they and Miss Eileen had conspired to keep from him that long ago Christmas

Day. Luigi faded slowly, his limbs withering with atrophy, refusing even small bites of food. He died two days short of his eighty-first birthday. His funeral Mass was 10:00 A.M. on Tuesday, the eleventh of September 2001.

Only his sons and the pallbearers accompanied the body to the cemetery. The other mourners had raced directly to The Speakeasy where the staff brought television sets into the private dining room Frankie had reserved for the funeral lunch. Luigi was an afterthought at his own wake, the guests too preoccupied by the unimaginable images of horror ninety miles to the north to mourn him. The booze flowed and everyone lingered long after the meal, eyes riveted to the screens.

It felt like an eternity before Frankie was able to collapse on the sofa with a vodka tonic, his first drink of the day. He remembered Helen Constanza had had a son who worked at the Trade Center and offered a quick prayer he wasn't among the many lying in the rubble. He reached for the remote, having seen enough death and tragedy for one day. He heard Jack Centafore's heavy footsteps on the back staircase, returning with Indian take-out despite Frankie's protest he had no appetite. The vodka went to his head quickly and he decided he shouldn't have a second, knowing his embarrassing tendency to get sad and sentimental when under the influence. But he didn't argue when Jack poured him a refill, even stronger than the first.

"Can I ask you something?" Frankie ventured, emboldened by the liquor.

Jack nodded his head without looking away from Peter Jennings reporting live from the smoking rubble.

"Were the terrorists good men?" he asked.

Jack looked at him as if he were crazy.

"What do you think? I can't believe you would even ask."

"Do you think they're burning in hell?"

"That's a better fate than they deserve."

"Was my father a good man?"

Jack carefully chewed his food, cogitating, trying to compose a diplomatic answer.

"That's not for us to judge, Frankie. The only opinion that counts is God's," he said, contradicting his own knee-jerk condemnation of the men who had brought down the tallest buildings in New York.

"What would you say if I told you I didn't believe in heaven or hell? That when you die, you die, and there's nothing more to it."

This time Jack was quick to respond.

"I'd say you're exhausted, you're grieving your father's death, and you're starting to get a little tipsy."

It was pointless to argue and Jack was right. He was a little drunk.

"You know what I've never understood?" Jack asked, finally asking a question that had perplexed him for years. "Why did your little brother hate your father so much? If anyone had a reason to despise the old man it was you."

"It's my fault. I'm to blame. Even when he was a little boy he thought he had to protect me. He would cling to Papa's leg, crying when Papa would hit me with the strap, begging him to stop. When he was six, Mikey threw a can of tomatoes at his head for slapping my face. God only knows what Papa would have done if it weren't for Miss Eileen. Mikey hated Papa because of me."